Edward Topol worked as a journalist and screenwriter in the USSR before moving to New York where he now lives and writes. His previous bestsellers include RED SQUARE (with Fridrikh Neznansky), SUBMARINE U-137 and DEADLY GAMES (with Fridrikh Neznansky).

EDWARD TOPOL

Red Gas

A Novel

Translated by Alan Myers

Futura

A *Futura* Book

Copyright © Edward Topol, Ltd 1985
Copyright © this translation Macdonald & Co
(Publishers) Ltd 1986

First published in Great Britain in 1986
by Macdonald & Co (Publishers) Ltd.
London & Sydney

This Futura edition published in 1987

ISBN 0 7088 3060 9

Reproduced, printed and bound in Great Britain by
Hazell Watson & Viney Limited,
Member of the BPCC Group,
Aylesbury, Bucks

Futura Publications
A Division of
Macdonald & Co (Publishers) Ltd
Greater London House
Hampstead Road
London NW1 7QX
A BPCC plc Company

I dedicate this book to Sarah Dvorkina, my mother, whose grave lies in the USSR, and Sarah Adèle Topol — my daughter, who was born while I was writing the final pages of the manuscript.

Acknowledgement

The author would like to thank Lev Roitman and Isaac L—s for their assistance in collecting material for this book.

He would also like to take this opportunity to express his profound gratitude to Jennifer Bradshaw and Naim Attallah, his first English editor and publisher respectively for their invaluable assistance at the time of his first literary efforts in the West.

Author's note

In my former — Soviet — life I travelled so often to the Far North of the USSR on journalistic assignments that the living prototypes of this novel — and even the taste of bilberries with sugar, that rare dish you only get in Soviet restaurants above the Arctic Circle — live on in my dreams — dammit! as clearly as ever . . .

I reckon therefore that I dreamt all the events and characters in the novel, and that any coincidences with actual reality up to and including the construction of the Siberian-Western Europe gas pipe line are simply part of a nightmare.

And the triple-edged arrow with the signal for revolt has flown over our land, and all must go to the battle: both valiant warrior and common man . . .

from a Nenets ballad

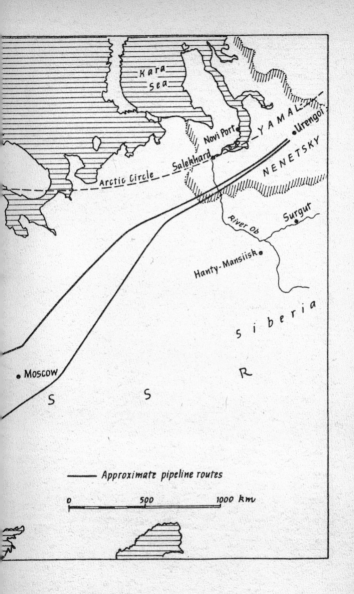

Kara
Sea

Novi Port

Arctic Circle · · Salekhard

YAMAL

Urengoi

NENETSKY

River Ob

Surgut

Hanty-Mansiisk

Siberia

Moscow

S   S   R

——— Approximate pipeline routes

0   500   1000 km

Part One
Three Corpses Beyond the Arctic Circle

Extract from radio message:

To: Militia Lieutenant Anna Kovina, investigator, Urengoi CID:

Near Yaku-Tur shift settlement the naked corpse of Vitali Voropayev, leader of the seismographic expedition, has been discovered by Nenets fishermen. The body bears marks of sadistic violence: ears and sexual organ have been cut off and severed sex organ thrust into victim's mouth. At the same time, near the river jetty in Salekhard, fishermen have found the body of the chief consultant physician at Salekhard District Hospital, Oleg Hotko, mutilated in similar fashion ... The location of the crimes coincides with the probable route of escaped prisoners from Camp No. RS-549.

Extract from a government telegram:

To: First Secretary Yamal-Nenets District Committe CPSU

SERIES OF MURDERS COMMITTED BY ESCAPERS FROM CAMP NO. RS-549 THREATENS SECURITY OF OFFICIAL OPENING CEREMONY OF SIBERIA-WESTERN EUROPE GAS PIPELINE.
TAKE IMMEDIATE MEASURES ...

▌ *Chapter One*

They escaped from the camp on the night of 6 December 1983, while the usual blizzard was raging across the polar tundra. Nobody ever did discover the exact time of the escape. Most likely, they intended to clear the camp compound by midnight so as to put more distance between them and the camp itself by morning. In any event it happened on that night, when cosmic darkness shrouded the Yamal peninsula in the Soviet Arctic. A force-nine gale whipped-up whirlwinds of powdered snow above the eternally frostbound tundra. Even on the ground there was no withstanding the biting storm, never mind up on the watchtowers; sheepskin jackets were no use, the wind chilled right through to the skin, took the breath away, slashed the eyeballs. The searchlights were unable to penetrate half a yard into the blizzard. It was on such a night that three convicts noiselessly quitted their hut.

Getting out of a hut full of three hundred prisoners snoring on rough wooden bunks is not difficult: the camp guards don't keep watch on every individual hut, they stay on the towers along the wire fence. Besides it often happens that prisoners leave their huts in the middle of the night to sprint over to the latrine, a nasty little nesting-box of planks raised above the permafrost on four timber posts.

In fine — that is calm — weather the soldiers on the towers can easily see who nips out of which hut and runs where he should and who decides to do his business there and then on the path trodden in the snow. For the fun of it, the soldiers blind the transgressors with their tower searchlights. In the morning, the erring con could draw a spell in the cooler from the head of camp administration — even in a camp above the Arctic Circle, rules of hygiene have to be observed!

But in a blizzard no searchlight can penetrate the dancing snow. Three convicts left their hut and skirted the latrine. Thirty yards away stood the camp fence edged with coils of barbed wire. The wire carried a powerful electric charge, and the slightest touch meant death. Yet the cons had no intention of touching the wire; instead, they moved away from the fence and towards the high-voltage metal pylon which towered over the camp compound.

This cable, one of dozens laid across the Yamal tundra in the last few years, supplied energy to a whole group of gas bore-holes.

Helping each other up, the cons climbed the pylon. Needless to say, the storm could have plucked off the daredevils at any second, and no one would even have heard their last cries for the howling of the wind. Yet they climbed to the top of the pylon towering over the middle of the camp. In the pitch darkness, beneath the searing wind, they crawled out onto an arm of the pylon, a hundred and twenty feet up, and lobbed some X-shaped wooden spools with metal clamps through the centre straight onto the thick high-tension cables. Clinging onto the clamps, they rolled — literally rolled — away, through the air and out of the camp — over the fence with its barbed wire, six feet from the watchtower!

They were missed in the morning, if morning was the word for the same polar night, black and blinded by the unceasing blizzard. They were missed from the count at six-thirty a.m. during work allocation, while the camp guard was busy handing over the cons one by one to the outside escorts.

Of course, the alarm was raised and the whole of camp security turned out. But there was no special panic: the head of camp security, an Ossetian named Orudjev, was renowned for the fact that in his twelve years' service in guard units not one runaway con had escaped him or returned to the camp alive. Just the opposite, in fact: Orudjev, a dashing broad-chested major with his hand-picked squad of crack troops, felt a surge of euphoria. In the first place, hunting down escapers was an excellent way of enlivening the monotony of service life. Secondly, for every runaway brought back to camp alive or dead the successful hunters got ten days' home leave. And so it

16

was that an entire company of excited soldiers and NCOs with tracker dogs sped off at once in pursuit of the fugitives.

Despite the blizzard, the Alsatians were pretty quick at finding the spools discarded by the absconders close to the next pylon beyond the camp compound; the manner in which the cons had contrived their escape was now clear. Yet beyond the spools, the dogs found nothing: the wind had obliterated any tracks and swept the tundra snow-crust clean of their scent.

After five hours of battling against the elements, becoming more brutal by the hour, the dogs had cut their paws to pieces on the rough ice; they were dropping or, as policemen say, 'They'd croaked.' Major Orudjev had cracked his voice and exhausted his ample supply of Russian and Ossetian obscenities. Three soldiers had frostbite in their feet; nine others, in their cheeks and other poorly-protected spots.

Shortly thereafter, two identical radio messages arrived in Urengoi, centre of the most extensive gasfields in the world and dispatch point for the Siberia–Western Europe gas pipeline. One was to the local KGB, the second to us at Urengoi CID:

> On the night of 6 December three prisoners, criminals Zaloyev and Shimansky and political Tolmachov, broke out of Camp No. RS-549. Blizzards have obliterated tracks of fugitives. Essential to involve search helicopters and reinforce patrols on Salekhard railway.
>
> Camp Commandant RS-549, Shviryov
> Head of camp security, Orudjev

Chapter Two

There could be no question of using search helicopters on the seventh or eighth of December, though: the storm increased in ferocity to force sixteen and the temperature dropped to forty below.

The deputy head of the Urengoi KGB directorate, Major Gromov, rolled up in his Sno-Cat to pay the CID a visit. In view of the official opening of the Siberia–Western Europe gas pipeline in ten days' time, we investigators — like all employees in Urengoi — were engaged in a blitz on our post: painting floors and whitewashing walls. Gromov, a flamboyant man of forty with shrewd hazel eyes, strode purposefully along the corridor on the old newspapers we had put down. Without a word to anyone, he walked straight into the office of our chief, Major Zotov. Needless to say, he hadn't bothered to knock the snow off his calf-leather boots and left wet footmarks on the floor.

A visit from the KGB was nothing unusual: Zotov was an old Arctic hand, one of the most experienced police detectives in Siberia. Naturally, we rank-and-file investigators heard nothing of what passed between Gromov and Zotov in the office; we carried on whitewashing, slapping the distemper over the old dirty-brown walls until Gromov emerged ten minutes later. He looked reassured and was obviously no longer in a hurry.

'Greetings to the heroes of the paintbrush!' He bestowed an intent masculine stare on me and Katya, our typist.

'Hello there, Anechka.' He spoke with a familiarity I had given him no pretext for in the four years I had worked in Urengoi. On the whole, relations between us in the militia and the KGB are pretty complicated: there is a certain amount of rivalry. They think they're the elite, the *crème de la crème* of

18

national security; their pay and allowances are way above ours. But we know who does the basic, everyday dirty work all right, looking after law and order in the country. Especially in Siberia, in the Yamal tundra, where the government has mobilized more than a million workmen over the last few years: welders, fitters, drivers and convicts to develop the gasfields and construct the Siberia–Western Europe gas pipeline. Along with these, naturally, came drifters and profiteers, prostitutes and suchlike criminal elements pouring in from all over the country — every one of them after a quick Arctic rouble. Drunken brawls and knife-fights in restaurants and working men's hostels, crimes of passion, dance hall punch-ups with fatal consequences, poaching in the taiga, gang rapes liquor-induced or otherwise; add to that list narcotics, prostitution, unreported syphilis, speculation in furs and fruit — and you have the criminal dung heap we have to rake over day after day. Needless to say, the lily-white hands of the KGB keep well away.

But it was probably the fact I was wearing paint-splashed dungarees instead of my usual militia lieutenant's tunic that made Gromov feel he could call me Anechka and run his male sizing-up glance over my figure. I've no idea what scale Major Gromov uses in awarding points to women, but it looked as if I scored pretty highly, spattered dungarees and all. He came up to me and spoke:

'I've had good reports of your work. After the pipeline opens, we're having a New Year conference for KGB high-flyers. Why not come along? I'll send you an invitation.'

Of course, everybody in the corridor froze into silence, watching how easily a KGB major could pick up CID investigator Anna Kovina. As for myself, I believe I blushed — a thing I hardly ever do.

'Thanks,' I said. 'I'm on duty over at the fitters' settlement at New Year. There'll be a few knife-fights, I expect, and other assorted entertainments. Why not come over here? Don't bother about an invitation.'

Our people turned away, smiling. Someone couldn't hold back a belly laugh, while Katya fluttered her overpainted lashes in alarm.

Gromov, however, rose to the occasion. He guffawed loudest of all, as his intelligent hazel eyes flashed recklessly.

'You're on! I'll be over!' said he, giving me a mock salute and even clicking the heels of his calf-leather boots. 'Permission to leave?'

'At ease. Off you go,' I smiled. The son of a bitch had wrung a smile out of me all the same!

Later on during the lunch hour, when all the investigators assembled in the common room and piled the sandwiches they'd brought from home onto the table, and Katya had placed an enormous potbellied teapot on top of the samovar, the conversation turned to the escaped cons.

As we listened to the howling storm outside and watched the streetlamps shaking as icy powdered snow lashed against the windows, somebody joked:

'Actually, this is what the runaways are banking on: the blizzard will cover their tracks and no helicopters can take off in this. And while we're sat here swilling tea they're crossing the tundra to Salekhard, jumping a moving train and away to "the mainland", Russia.'

'I'll bet you those two criminals only took the political, Tolmachov, with them as a "piglet",' said somebody else. In plain language, this meant that the two criminal runaways had taken the third with them in case they got lost in the tundra — and ran out of food . . .

'They made just one slip,' announced old Zotov, briskly rubbing his left knee with a mixture of Tiger balm and pure methylated spirits. This knee of Zotov's always ached during a blizzard; for this reason, whenever the weather was bad he wore special fur trousers with a zip down the side instead of a seam. Whatever the company, he would unzip his trousers practically to the hip, take out a bottle of his special rub and without the slightest embarrassment set about treating his knee.

'Those cons had no weather forecast, or my knee neither. I mean, if the weather was all right they could get across the hundred and forty kilometres of tundra from the camp to the railway; they wouldn't even need a piglet. They might get past the militia detachments on the railway. But they went on the run in eighteen degrees of frost and a force-nine gale, not knowing that today it would get up to force sixteen and forty below! Towards night it'll be knocking on for all of fifty. I can tell by my knee — that's better than any barometer. If I were them I'd go back to the camp before it was too late.'

We realized as well as Zotov did what the worsening of the storm meant for the escapers. Under local conditions, every point of wind was equivalent to two degrees of frost. So if a wind factor of thirty-two were added to forty degrees of frost — well, no normal person could stand seventy below out on the open tundra. At all events, if it gets to fifty below all working operations on the tundra are suspended, except for the drilling, of course. Even the Nentsi, the indigenous population of Arctic Yamal, halt their dog- and reindeer-teams and lie down in the snow if they run into a storm like this one. They huddle the reindeer or dogs around them for warmth and call on the spirits of the tundra and on Num, God of the Universe, to send a snowdrift swiftly over them.

But the escapers had no dogs, no reindeer and no warm clothing. Above all, they couldn't wait out the storm under a snowdrift. Very likely that's what Zotov had told Gromov, to send the latter away reassured.

'They would go trudging on through the blizzard, of course. As a rule, people tend to overestimate their strength, especially at the start — especially runaway cons,' old man Zotov told us. 'It's all right; as soon as the snow lifts the helicopters are bound to spot their bodies, it's not the first time. Spoil the report, though — bastards!' he concluded, meaning that three frozen corpses in the taiga wouldn't look good on our report showing a sharp decrease in crime on the eve of the great event: the official opening of the Trans-Siberian gas pipeline.

On the seventeenth of December, a government delegation from Moscow headed by practically everybody up to Andropov himself was due to fly in, together with a hundred or more guests of honour and foreign pressmen. That's why a frantic rush was in progress across the whole territory — Salekhard, Surgut, Tarko-Sale, Nadym and Medvezhe; gas reserves there were somewhat fewer than in Urengoi but could still be counted in billions of cubic metres. It was all hands on deck, a whirlwind of building activity, and the centre of it all, our town of Urengoi, was being decked out like a bride: old buildings such as our police post were festooned with colourful posters, slogans and exhortations, while fresh wooden planking was being placed over the potholes in the roads. A new hotel, the Polar, rose up in the centre of town. At the town party HQ, a government rostrum was getting its finishing touches and the Moscow architect in charge of all these operations had the brainstorm of deluging the town not just with electric and neon lighting but roman candles as well! The idea was that just at the moment an 'ordinary' working man, Boris Dunik, celebrated pipe welder and hero of socialist labour, and Lenin laureate Rasim Salakhov, the geologist who discovered Siberian oil and Arctic gas, stood up on the rostrum together as a symbol of the harmony of labour and science and yanked open the valve sending Yamal gas from the Urengoi compressor station through to France, Germany and other European countries, gigantic fireworks would suddenly light up all the taiga conifers around the town!

Before the celebrations, naturally, we removed all the labour camps and — as in Moscow before the Olympics — got rid of just about all the drunks, drifters, prostitutes, people with criminal records and similar undesirable elements from Urengoi and the other Yamal gas installations that the government delegation and foreign journalists were due to visit. The town was so quiet that the local sobering-up station was temporarily converted into a public bath-house, and we CID folk had it so easy we even found time to whitewash our establishment.

The escape of the three cons spoilt our quarterly report for the Yamal peninsula, yet no one could have dreamt that their break-out would prove fateful for the entire Trans-Siberian pipeline.

Chapter Three

On the morning of the ninth of December, the storm died down. It had blocked the Urengoi streets, so that boys were launching their sledges from second floor windows. The entire population had turned out with wooden shovels to scrape the snow from the porches and clear the roads and pavements.

I sank in the snow up to the knees — even to the waist — on my way to work. I was living in a hostel for young single specialists that was only seven blocks away from our directorate, yet it took me over half an hour to cover the first five. I could reach out and touch the tops of the streetlamps. Somebody had taken the opportunity to decorate them with old children's dolls — the same little boys, probably.

However, the town centre — the square in front of party HQ and a few neighbouring blocks of flats — had already been cleared by mechanical diggers. Near our militia directorate there were only 'fifteen-day men' at work. These were men who had got fifteen days for petty hooliganism or breaches of public order while drunk. They were brandishing shovels in dilatory fashion, clearing the path to the directorate; they were in no hurry.

But I was. I was duty investigator today, and already twelve minutes late for work. I had barely got in, out of breath, kicked the snow from my boots and placed my fur jacket on its hanger, when Katya said:

'Hurry up! Zotov's waiting for you.'

I adjusted my tunic and tapped on the door; now for a bit of a telling-off for being late.

'Comrade Major! Investigator Kovina, may I come in?' I said as cheerfully as I could, to disarm the old man with a brisk tone and smart appearance.

'Well now, Kovina,' said Zotov. 'You're always yelling I never give you anything "exciting", just routine jobs. Well, here's something "exciting" all right. You're flying to Camp RS-549 and taking statements from the guard and the cons in the runaways' hut.'

'When did I ever yell, comrade Major?' I said, annoyed. 'I'm not a fishwife, yelling — '

'All right, all right — ' Zotov waved it away.

'No, wait a minute! Of course I get annoyed if you don't trust me to round up poachers in the taiga just because I'm a woman — or to help in stake-outs to pull in real criminals. You keep me on the "everyday" stuff: rows in working men's doss-houses, nabbing junkies and anti-Soviets — your Solzhenit-syns, Avtorkhanovs and Zinovievs. Those Leningrad students I caught reading Solzhenitsyn even called me the "Urengoi Alsatian" — '

'There you go getting wound up again!' sighed Zotov. 'The Alsatian's a pedigree breed, you should be pleased.'

'But I have never yelled and never complained,' I inter-rupted; I really did find it exasperating. 'Five years I've been ploughing through all this muck, the preliminary work. Even Major Gromov's heard of my successes. Anyway, it's not fair: as soon as any hot job comes up you turn the investigation over to men, not to me.'

'Well, I am giving you a hot job: you're going to Camp RS-549.'

'What sort of a hot job is that?' I sneered. 'Looking for frozen corpses!'

'I'm not sending you to look for frozen corpses,' said Zotov. 'The helicopter boys will find them without your help. Your job is to ferret about inside the camp; maybe the runaways had accomplices. While you're at it get three or four sacks of sturgeon from Shviryov and Orudjev, they'll load it into the helicopter for the return flight. They swap the Nenets fisher-men liquor for it. They won't be stingy about it — they're hardly in any position to be, are they? I'll get them on the radio.'

I smiled sarcastically. So that's why Zotov had chosen me for this assignment! I was the only single person in our directorate. That meant that out of all the sturgeon loaded onto my helicopter in RS-549, Zotov would give me one or two fish and all the rest would go to just him. If he sent one of the married operatives, he'd have to give up a whole sackful: for the wife and kids. That the staff of RS-549 would load as much fish as I ordered was not in doubt. They'd had a group escape, and it was up to us in the CID to apportion responsibility for this 'extraordinary occurrence'.

Still, I was glad of the assignment. Drawing up a 'report on infringement of regulations for security of prisoners' was hardly interesting work, God knows — yet it was better than whitening walls for the arrival of Moscow bigwigs, or poking about in students' suitcases. You never knew what you'd find there — Indian contraceptives with 'whiskers' ('have you tried them, comrade investigator? — fabulously exciting!') hashish, opium, marijuana (' have you ever smoked it, comrade investigator? — in bed, it's just ecstasy!') or the routine Western detective novel with an anti-Soviet slant ('have you read it, comrade investigator? — one ought to know what our enemies write about us, after all!').

To cut a long story short, at noon on December the ninth, when the road to Urengoi Airport had been cleared, the driver, Sergeant Krylov or 'Uncle Kolya' as we called him, took me there in the duty Volga. The helicopter boys had already excavated their MI–8s from the snow. I boarded one, and off we flew north-west towards Camp RS-549. An enormous, lustrous moon lit up the tundra. In the forty-degree chill the entire helicopter fuselage was covered with hoar frost while it stood on the ground; only the vibration of flight shook free the icy carapace to expose the bright red body of the MI–8, the livery of polar aviation.

Immediately beyond Urengoi, the majestic panorama of the gasfields lay spread out below us: hundreds of drilling derricks, the enormous, almost extraterrestial complex of the main compressor station — a complete plant for the purification, cooling and condensation of gas — and we had built it in the teeth of the American embargo on rotor and electronic know-how. Around the station, gigantic spherical gasholders glowed silver; the intertwining threads of dozens of gas pipelines, substations, fuel depots, temporary pipe-dumps, the vast agglomeration of modern technology out on the tundra, now churned up by tracked vehicles. At various points flickered the lights of electro- and gas-welding, earth movers and bulldozers swarmed, management Volgas scurried hither and thither among Gaz trucks and heavy-duty carriers on caterpillar tracks. The storm had held up construction for three days, but the pipeline still had to open on the seventeenth come hell or high water. The top men in Moscow loathe having to wait: once they'd said Europe would get Siberian gas by the New Year, so they would!

'Shit, it's beautiful! Just like Mars!' shouted the pilot to me flying the chopper high to take in the panorama — which was truly Martian — in one sweep.

▌Chapter Four

After fifteen to twenty kilometres, the pipeline filaments began
to snake away in all directions across the tundra. The tundra
itself grew whiter; the further we flew, the paler and more lifeless it became. Now and then, at the edge of this bare snow-
filled dish, there appeared the contours of some oil-workers'
settlement, or else a drilling derrick, the choom[1] of a Nenets
encampment, the frosted thread of a pipeline, or Nenets
reindeer-sledges racing across the tundra.

But the last traces of civilization soon vanished: we were
flying north-west deep into untamed wilderness. Only now,
from the air, could the absolute madness of the escapers'
decision — to cross on foot this inhumanly dead landscape, this
endless savage conglomeration of ice-hummocks and snow
stretching to the horizon in every direction — be fully compre-
hended. Even in my rucksack, the bottle of vodka I had
grabbed before starting had separated out into about two
hundred millilitres of pure spirit and a matt lump of ordinary
ice: in other words, the temperature here was below minus
forty. How would it be for a man down there in such a temperature — in a blizzard, too — wearing a threadbare state-issue
convict's quilted jacket and tarpaulin shoes? Of course they'd
frozen: it stood to reason.

About two hours further on, the frozen white field of the Ob
estuary came into view and, twenty kilometres or so beyond
that, Camp RS-549: grey rectangles of camp barrack huts
sloppily repaired and strung round with barbed wire. Like the
rest of the camps on the Yamal peninsula, RS-549 had moved
on a month before so as to be further away from the itinerary

---

[1] choom: dwelling made of reindeer hide, like a wigwam.

of the guests of honour and foreign visitors at the official pipeline ceremony. No one was going to build a new camp, needless to say; they just patched up a thirty-year-old Stalin one. From the south, through the camp and on to the north-west, marched the notorious electric pylons. Two kilometres from the camp, the work zone could be seen: on the banks of a frozen tundra stream the cons were using crowbars to make holes in the permafrost, which rang under the blows like metal. From above, the dark figures in their camp jackets looked like a flock of sheep scattered over the tundra, surrounded by the campfires of shepherds and their dogs — the guards. At first glance this might seem idiotic: why force people to cripple themselves hacking at the permafrost in temperatures of forty below? The clanging crowbar leaps back off the ice, frozen chips smack you in the face — even in calm, still weather a man gets worn out working like that in half an hour. But there's method in the madness. The holes they make in the permafrost lay bare the top stratum of the tundra; after the cons come the explosives men, who lay their charges in the holes and open up beneath the ice a layer of sand and gravel — valuable construction materials. Naturally, the howls about us using convict labour on the pipeline are a pack of Western lies. Who would let a con get near a gas pipeline, or trust one to weld a pipe? But ancillary operations, like digging out sand and gravel, clearing forests, building moorings, laying roadways across the swamps — that's hard labour the cons can do.

The helicopter passed over the work area and approached the deserted camp.

At the noise of the helicopter, soldiers and the head of camp security, Major Orudjev piled out of the guardroom. The helicopter put down alongside, let me disembark and then headed off south-west to hunt for the bodies of the fugitives. There, south-west of here, in Salekhard the railway begins, so they could only have gone in that direction.

I got on with the routine: personal details of the escapers, questioning the guards who had been on duty on the night of the break. In his office Major Orudjev got out of the safe three thick grey files bound with tape — the fugitives' personal files. I opened the files and for a few minutes examined the standard

28

prison photographs of the runaways. A tartar, Timur Zaloyev, a recidivist with three terms for 217 house breakings — a gloomy face with high cheek bones and narrow eyes; Gleb Shimansky, icon forger and dealer in Russian antiques — forty, tall, with a well-groomed face but a stubborn chin; Boris Tolmachov, a twenty year old dissident with a snub-nose and fair eyes — a mere boy. I noted down the addresses of their relatives so as to send official notification — if they wanted, they could come for the bodies when these were discovered that day or the next. Then came the interrogation of the camp security staff. The chief thing I wanted to get clear was where the wooden spools had come from that had helped the escapers to whizz over the fence on the electricity cables. The spools Orudjev also got from the safe. They were clearly handmade and shaped like the letter X. Through the holes in the centre, bent steel brackets had been inserted rather like the handles on the Metro. Maybe somebody had brought these things into the zone, or sent them in a parcel?

'What do you mean, "brought", "sent?"?' Major Orudjev was indignant. 'D'you think we don't check parcels? They made those rollers themselves, in the zone. We've got a mechanical workshop here in the camp. We repair Friendship electrical saws here, and other tools as well. This one, Boris Tolmachov, was a turner in the shop. He was the one who made the rollers.'

I walked over to the workshop. It was a rickety, unheated temporary structure built of planks; the tundra wind blew in through the chinks in the walls; the lathes stood directly on boards placed on the frozen ground; sundry pieces of metal, wooden billets and machine components lay scattered about the floor — in contravention of the regulations, incidentally. From these wooden battens Tolmachov had made the rollers for his escape, and his own destruction. The thing that really stood out was that right over Tolmachov's own lathe hung the standard camp slogan 'TO FREEDOM — WITH A CLEAR CONSCIENCE!'

From the workshop Major Orudjev led me through the compound to the officers' mess to have lunch. He had been walking behind me like a shadow, supposedly in the line of duty but really because my fur trousers increased my backside to a size his Ossetian temperament found hard to bear. As we were passing the fateful high-voltage electricity pylon he gave the pole a hearty kick and said bitterly:

'It's all Hudya Benokan's fault — Nenets bastard!'

I shot an astonished glance at the major. Hudya Benokan was a CID operative in Salekhard. He was the only Nenets investigator in the whole territory — how could he be blamed for three convicts escaping from this camp?

■ Chapter Five

I knew Hudya Benokan. I had been a fifth-year law student at Moscow University when a legend began circulating that some simple Nenets reindeerherd from the shores of the Arctic Ocean had rolled up to join our faculty. And he had got there by his own efforts too! Neither exempt on ground of nationality nor part of the Yamal-Nenets area quota, he had got there not, of course, through influence — where would an Arctic Nenets get that? — but through open competition! Of course, he wasn't actually pulled by reindeer, he was wearing a *malitsa*[1] instead of an overcoat. 'Another suicide,' I remember thinking at the time. In the four years I'd been at the university there had been nine cases of suicide among students from the Arctic territories, Chukchi, Evenki, Nentsi and Khanti. Young Eskimos just can't handle the stress of a big city, and take their own lives, odd as it may seem, always in the same way: by throwing themselves out of the windows of the skyscraper hostels on Lenin Hills. 'One more suicide,' I thought when I heard of this wild 'prodigy' coming to the university — and, needless to say, forgot about him. A few days later, though, in the students' canteen I noticed a boy with high cheekbones and narrow eyes — Japanese or Korean, perhaps — staring fixedly at me. (Half the university consists of foreigners, yet there are no western students in our faculty — why the hell should they study Soviet law when they have quite different systems of

---

[1] *Malitsa*: The Nenets' outer garment, an amply cut knee-length smock-shirt put on over the head. It is stitched from reindeer skin, with the fur side outside. Mittens are sewn onto the sleeves. Sometimes the *malitsa* is decorated with patterns made from the skins of reindeer.

31

their own?) Anyway, this boy wasn't a Japanese or a Korean; he was Hudya Benokan, the 'prodigy from Yamal'. Pretty soon the whole of my group, then the entire year, got to know that he had fallen heavily for me. He would hang about in the canteen just when our year had their lunch break or if there happened to be a break between lectures. As a rule he sat in the farthest corner, and drank tea — five, six, ten glasses — sweating in his new, baggy Soviet suit and waiting till I appeared. Well, in the fifth year I was twenty-two and, without being over-modest, I was all right: a blue-eyed blonde with a plait down to the waist and a figure like Anouk Aimée's — a classy bit of goods, as they say. Anyway, I couldn't walk down the street without a Fiat or Volga homing in alongside and the driver, some film-maker or photographer, thirty or forty maybe, inviting me to go with him to Cinema House to a restricted screening of a Western film.

Still, when you're doing your law finals there's no time for love affairs or even a brief flirtation. I couldn't have cared less that some Eskimo Nenets had worked out our group's time-table and hung about waiting for me, sweating out his tea and gazing at me gulping down my cabbage soup or a cutlet that tasted like mattress. Very soon he shifted his observation post from the canteen to the library; that really annoyed me. I couldn't possibly swot up Soviet law or summarize *Fundamentals of Criminal Legislation* with this Nenets staring at me from the next desk with his narrow grey eyes — well, could you have done?

It's true I only had to look back and he dropped his eyes to his book straight away, but that was only for as long as I was looking at him; after that, he was staring again. In the end, I couldn't stand it. I got up and went over to him. Of course, he stopped looking at me and pretended he was reading Lenin, volume thirty-three, *Dual Subordination and Legality*. I came right up to him and said, 'Listen! What's the matter?' The whole library turned in our direction: everyone was looking at me — except him. That Nenets sat with his eyes glued on Lenin, as if he were deaf. Only his short neck turned purple above the collar of his Moscow-tailored suit. At that I grabbed Lenin volume thirty-three from under his eyes, slammed it down on his desk and repeated: 'Well, how long do you intend to stare at me?'

The amazing thing was, he didn't bat an eyelid at this; he didn't budge or even look up at me. I stood over him like a fool, expecting an answer, while he just sat stock-still looking at the table. I turned on my heel and left the library.

Next day he wasn't in the canteen or the reading room. The day after that was the same — and the next. Then somebody told me he hadn't been seen at lectures for four days, or in the hostel; the dean had reported his disappearance to the police. To tell the truth, I was terrified and decided that this Nenets had committed suicide as well for all I knew. For two days I walked about in a daze. Then the police came across Hudya in the woods beyond Izmailovo Park: he was sleeping on the ground under a pine tree, wrapped in his *malitsa*.

When a man sleeps out in the woods for six days because of you — even if he is a Nenets — you can't just ignore it and go on as if nothing had happened. Especially when you've got friends and so on. Nobody said anything to me, of course, but they all looked at me as if I was a surgeon who'd taken out a patient's stomach when he had appendicitis. Anyway, when the police brought Hudya back to the hostel I braced myself and set out for the men's zone. It's an odd thing that Moscow's most prominent landmark, the 24-storey skyscraper of the university students' hostel on Lenin Hills, with the *à la Russe* towers Stalin drew onto the original plan with his own hand and the spire with the star — that hostel is divided up inside into zones and blocks, just like a camp. I went past the porter by the lift, went up to the fourth floor of Zone G, the law faculty, and headed along the corridor to Block 404. The blocks are living units with two separate rooms and two bunkbeds in each, with shared toilet and shower. As I neared number 404, which Hudya Benokan shared with some other Siberian national, I was expecting to see a gaunt, emaciated unkempt individual whom it was my duty to release from love's thrall in case he should up and throw himself out of the window the following day. Of course I had no intention of starting a love affair with him, though I did have the idea of inviting him to the Saturday concert at our students' club.

Hudya opened the door for me. He was neither unkempt nor emaciated. He wasn't wearing his *malitsa* or any other article of Nenets national dress: he had on a T-shirt and navy blue sports slacks. His narrow grey eyes looked at me calmly, without anxiety.

'Hi!' I said, somewhat at a loss. 'Can I come in?'

He let me enter his room. It was clean, unlike the usual men's quarters with their mess and photos of nude girls on the walls. Two bunks along the wall, a cupboard, a book case with legal books, a desk and table lamp: a totally Spartan scene. A pile of books lay on the table, an open volume of *Fundamentals of Crime Classification* and a summary. Next to it a glass of strong tea, half-empty.

'Some idiot said you slept on the floor,' said I, just to break the ice. 'I read somewhere that it's good for you. There was a famous ballerina who slept on the floor.'

'Yes, I used to do that,' he spoke in a low, even voice. 'I don't now, however. I make myself sleep in a bed.'

'You make yourself?'

'Yes, we don't have beds in our tents, I'm not used to them. I'm training myself now, however.'

'I see — ' I didn't know how to carry on the conversation. 'Listen, I've got my old notes on that *Fundamentals*. Would you like them?'

'Thank you, however,' he said. 'But I have to read it all through myself and make notes.'

'Why do you say "however" all the time?'

He smiled for the first time.

'It's a habit. Everybody talks like that in the north.'

'Ah. Listen, I've got some tickets for the variety concert at our club this Saturday. Do you want to come?'

He looked me straight in the eyes and I suddenly understood that it was a case of 'the rabbit and the boa constrictor.' His eyes held alarm, terror. But the very next second he spoke, still in that even tone.

'You must excuse me, however. I can't go to the concert. I'm behind in all my subjects and there are a seminar and exams coming up.'

'Really?' I was surprised. I hadn't expected a refusal at all.

34

This Nenets — refused me!

'Well,' I came out with, with no idea of what to do next. 'Well, as you like . . . I'll be off, then.'

I'd never been in such an idiotic and humiliating position in my life. He hadn't even invited me to sit down! I tried to get a bit of my own back as I was going out.

'And what were you doing in the woods?'

'I was curing myself,' he replied coolly.

'What of?'

'Moscow and — and of you, however.'

I understood what he meant, but smiled.

'I'm not infectious, am I?'

'No. But you — ' He faltered, then looked me directly in the eyes.

'I came to Moscow to learn to be a criminal investigator, not to fall in love, however.'

'Quite right. It's pointless anyway,' I said vengefully. 'Well, how did it go? Are you cured of me?'

He kept his eyes on mine. It was the fixed, protracted stare of a man who had resolved to endure any torture in silence.

I turned and went off down the corridor, deliberately swinging my hips a little and flinging my plait over my shoulder as a crowning gesture.

He stood that as well. He sat it out for days on end in the library, but no longer on my account: if I came in he would get up and move to another room. The winter sessionals were a month later and I saw his name among the Lenin grant winners — he'd got As in everything. I don't know if the professors made any allowances for his Nenets origins, but some well-wisher related to me how Hudya grafted away even when his brain was too tired to take in all that dull stuff the first-years have to learn; he beat his head against the wall, insisting:

'No! I will force you to work, however!'

When he'd done his exams he went off into the woods again and slept out in the snow for five days in his *malitsa* — getting rid of his tension. A year later, when the work allocations had been posted up in the university and 'Tyumen Province' stood against my name, a formal reconciliation took place with

Hudya. He came up to me in the canteen and said:

'Hello. I found out you were going to work in our Tyumen Province. I'm very glad. It's just your sort of place. This'll come in handy, however!' He held out two books: *Russian-Nenets Dictionary* and *Nenets Fairy-Tales and Legends*.

'Thank you,' I said. 'Maybe now you'll accept my old notes.' He smiled and shook his head.

'I have to learn everything myself, however.'

Four years had passed since then. Five months ago, in Urengoi, I had discovered that Hudya Benokan had returned to Yamal — to Salekhard — with Moscow University's 'red' diploma of outstanding merit — and a two-year-old daughter. It's only a stone's throw from Salekhard, capital of Yamal, to Urengoi — about five hundred kilometres — but in those five months not once had I seen Hudya. He had become an investigator at the Salekhard CID as I was at Urengoi: police gossip, always faster than the telephone, reported that Hudya's daughter was by a pretty little Nenets girl who had got to Moscow University through her dad's influence. He was head of the Department of Nenets and Khanti Affairs with the Tyumen regional party committee. Hudya had married her when he was in his third year, but the girl had turned out to be a bit free and easy, as the saying goes. She quickly went from hand to hand or, to be more precise, from the studio and bed of one Moscow artist keen on foreign exotica to the next. A year later she left the university and her husband with a two-month-old child on his hands, and went off with the latest artist to a Black Sea resort; then the scent grew cold even for her own father. How Hudya had brought up his little girl in the university and lived and studied on his seventy rouble-a-month Lenin grant, God only knows; but somehow or other he had turned up in Salekhard this summer and at once got a job as an investigator at the Salekhard directorate. And now for some reason the head of camp security at RS-549, Major Orudjev, considered Hudya to be the man responsible for the convicts' escape.

▌Chapter Six

I stared in amazement at Major Orudjev, even asked:

'Hudya? How?'

'Very simple!' said Orudjev. 'He was here about three weeks ago. The cons were still repairing their huts, we'd just arrived here from Nadym. And this Hudya flew over from Salekhard to interrogate one of the cons on some old business. So here he stands, and in front of the cons blurts out to the camp commandant: "Who was the prick who chose this as a camp site, if the power lines go right through it? You could get clear of the compound along the cables from this pylon," he says. "They say the swan waits for spring and a con waits for freedom!" And cackled his head off, the bastard! The cons heard him — and took the hint!'

I smiled.

'That's not nice, comrade Major. Don't try and shift the blame. You've permitted an escape, and now it turns out the CID even warned you about it. It looks as though you're going to need more than sturgeon to keep clear of us!'

Orudjev stared at me with his prominent dark eyes: he now realized he shouldn't have mentioned Benokan and was wondering if I was pulling his leg or if I really did want more from him than sturgeon. This unaccustomed mental exertion caused the film of male lust to fade from his dark eyes, and they really became beautiful, in their frame of bushy black brows lightly powdered with the hoar frost settling from his breath on the fur of his hat, on his moustaches, his eyelashes.

'All right!' I took pity on him. 'No bloody point hanging about in the cold, my nose is ready to drop off — '

When speaking to army or police officers I try to adopt a rough tone straight away to cool down any overheated thoughts they might have about me belonging to the opposite sex. But not always, of course — and Orudjev was closer to the exception than the rule. A few minutes later, in the officers' mess, while a prisoner-cook served us salmon soup and sturgeon *shashlik*, Orudjev brought from his quarters one bottle of Armenian brandy and another of Tsimlyansky pink champagne (to drink cognac with pink champagne is considered the height of chic in the Arctic). Once more the transparent velvet of lust swam in his beautiful eyes and the powerful shoulders played under his uniform, while his chest swelled out so much that the brass buttons on his uniform seemed about to fly off at any moment. Quite a hunk, I thought to myself; a champion goer at the bedtime fences. He had already poured the cognac into cut-glass tumblers, mixed fifty-fifty with pink champagne.

'To the runaways, Anna Borisovna! May the Arctic tundra feel like eiderdown to them! Otherwise you would never have flown over to us ...'

I drained my glass in one pleasurable gulp. I'd got really frozen on the flight, in that repair shop and round the camp. Right down to the bones, as the saying goes ...

What happened afterwards? Explanation means justification, and I don't need to do either. I'm single and my own woman. If I fancy a guy, it is my choice and my right; I don't have to account to anyone. Orudjev and I drank up the rest of the brandy and champagne, and then, instead of waiting for the cons to finish digging up the tundra and continuing my work, I allowed Orudjev to talk me into staying the night in camp.

'What's the hurry, then, Anna Borisovna?' said he, grinning slyly into his moustache. 'They'll bring the cons back around six. By the time they're counted, then supper and whatnot it'll be eight. Interrogating cons after eight is forbidden in the regulations. Better to rest up after your journey, get your sleep out. We've got a grand room by the guardhouse. And in the morning I'll exempt all the runaways' hut-mates from work; you can question them all day if you like. What say?'

Needless to say, I knew perfectly well what a night in camp parked next to the guardroom would mean. Every camp has one: once a year every con has the right to a visit from a close

38

relative, who is put up for three days in a room like this. If it's the con's wife, he has the right to spend the night with her.

Naturally there are no locks, and right next door you have a whole camp full of male prisoners, but I could sleep soundly — who would stick his nose into a guardhouse crammed with soldiers and guard dogs, clanking metal doors and bars on the windows? Of course, any fool knows that for head of camp security Major Orudjev no such obstacles existed. That evening — if polar nights can be said to have evenings — he sent the duty con to light the Dutch stove. Then, outside the window, came the tramp of the column of cons returning from work. They were kept waiting at the camp gates for nearly an hour; the outside guards, the escort, handed the prisoners over to the in-camp guards. The latter took over the column in ranks of six men, counting as they went: 'First rank, forward! The rest, stand fast! Second rank, forward! The rest, stand fast! Third ...' Even the guard dogs were whimpering from cold and impatience. At last all the cons were allowed into the compound, the camp gates were clanged shut and the centrepin was slammed home. The steel doors of the guardhouse stopped clattering; the dogs ceased their barking and whining, and only a lone polar wolf, either from cold or misery, carried on howling somewhere far out on the tundra, the camp was settling down for the night.

I lay in bed, dozing off slowly and wondering when on earth friend Orudjev would appear. My legs began stretching out of their own accord as desire grew, and my nipples hardened, making my breasts ache. This stopped me getting to sleep, and in any case I don't like being woken up in the middle of the night, even for sex. (Why interrupt one pleasure with another?) Finally, at nine, when the guard had been dismissed, Major Orudjev opened my unlocked door without knocking. He didn't fail my expectations, either. He carried me from the narrow camp bunk to a mattress on the floor so that the creak of bedsprings wouldn't be audible in the guardroom — that mattress could tell a tale or two! But I was his equal in our joint labours. Well, hell, when you take off your tunic and holster, everything kept in check under your rough officer's uniform during the day suddenly bursts out of you with such frantic energy you don't need Indian contraceptives with exciting whiskers — or hashish or imported marijuana for that matter! All you need is a man who can stand the assault for hours on end and not weaken. And Orudjev was just that hammer — I'd not been mistaken about that.

An hour before camp reveille, that is at five a.m., Orudjev left, having lifted me, with difficulty this time, back onto the bunk along with the mattress. Through sleep I heard him promise to leave the cons I needed for questioning on camp duty so that I could sleep as long as I liked; no one would come and wake me. And I did sleep through reveille, the clang of the camp gates, the dogs barking, the tramp of lines of cons leaving for work on the tundra. Half a day passed in sleep; to me it seemed like a minute. At all events, when Orudjev came into my room again, perched on the edge of my bunk and yelled insistently, 'Anya! Anya, wake up!' I had the greatest difficulty dragging myself into wakefulness — hadn't he had enough? I saw his face bending over me, and said: 'No! Go away!'

'Wake up! Read this!' He held out a radio message form. I opened my sticky eyelids and stared at the words:

To Militia Lieutenant Anna Kovina, investigator Urengoi CID: Thirty kilometres from the camp where you are now, near Yaku-Tur shift settlement the naked corpse of Vitali Voropayev, leader of the seismographic expedition, has been discovered by Nenets fishermen. The body bears marks of sadistic violence: ears and sexual organs have been cut off and severed sex organ thrust into victim's mouth. At the same time near the river jetty in Salekhard fishermen have found the body of the chief consultant physician at Salekhard District Hospital, Oleg Hotko, mutilated in similar fashion. Clothing of murdered men has been stolen. The location of the crimes coincides with the probable route of escaped prisoners from Camp RS-549 through Yaku-Tur towards Salekhard railway. Since storms have again disrupted air transportation, it is impossible to send an investigator and forensic medical expert to Yaku-Tur from Urengoi. Leave for Yaku-Tur immediately by Sno-Cat to examine the corpse and collect evidence.

Zotov.

I gradually came to as the message proceeded. This was it, the big one! By some miracle the cons had survived the tundra and, what's more, committed two murders — *so far* only two, but what murders! And nobody from Urengoi CID — none of the men, including Zotov — could get to Yaku-Tur because of this new blizzard. But I, Anna Kovina, the 'domestic', 'the spare wheel', I would be there in an hour — the first one!

I scanned the message again swiftly; at the words 'severed sex organ thrust into victim's mouth', I woke up completely. Needless to say, old man Zotov had no time for literary niceties. I understood him; I understood even more than the message stated. If the railway was screened off by patrols and the cons were unable to slip away to 'the mainland', they would either lie low in Salekhard or move around it on the tundra. How could members of the government and foreign visitors be received here if three murderers were loose in the territory? That was why Zotov was chasing me over to Yaku-Tur 'urgently . . . by Sno-Cat'.

Suddenly another idea occurred to me: what if the cons had split up? Suppose only one or two had got as far as Salekhard, and somebody was still in Yaku-Tur or close by?

I leaped out of bed and peered through the window.

Outside there was no moon, no stars, no silvery-blue tundra sheen. The usual blizzard covered everything. Powdery snow flailed the window; the barbed wire of the camp fence was creaking, and through it could be heard the nervous barking of dogs and the crunch of snow beneath the feet of lines of convicts. I glanced at Orudjev, amazed.

'I can't have slept all day to the end of the shift? The clock only says eleven —'

'Fifty below, work suspended,' he explained.

So they were bringing in the cons from the tundra; to them the storm meant relaxation and rest, while to me it meant my first chance of a real hot job, an actual crime, a chance to prove that the 'Urengoi Alsatian' was good for more than sniff-

41

ing out anti-Soviet trash. Terrific! I wouldn't miss this chance! Like Jews, women investigators — all female specialists, in fact — working in so-called male professions have to demonstrate that in practice they are not only as good as but actually better than men at coping with the job. Only then are they forced to recognize us as more or less equal.

Woollen stockings, men's underpants, sweater, tunic, fur flying suit, leather belt, holster, pistol, felt boots, sheepskin jacket, fur hat with earmuffs — as I hastily got dressed I did some thinking: the fugitives needed clothing, papers and money. That's why they had stripped and robbed their victims. But there were three of them, and so far only two corpses. That meant someone else might be lying out on the tundra pretty soon. Unless, of course, they had made use of their 'piglet' on the journey . . .

'Well, what are you gawping at me for?' I said to Orudjev. 'Get the Sno-Cat ready!'

'It's ready and waiting,' he nodded towards the window. 'I'm going as well. There could be a trail for the dogs to follow.'

I had no time to wonder if this was just an excuse to go with me in the hope of another night of passion or if he really was itching to get hold of the runaways. In any case, I felt, he could think as well as I could, and in a hectic affair like hunting down escapers there couldn't have been a better partner. And, after all, if fortune were to smile on us — well, we could celebrate with another hot night . . .

I stuck the three slim folders containing the escapers' personal details into my rucksack and followed Orudjev at a run. The blizzard burned my face like a razor and cut off my breath. The Sno-Cat, engines roaring, stood only two steps from the guardhouse, and I vaulted over the caterpillar track in blasé fashion (it wasn't the first time, was it?) and into the cabin. Apart from the driver, there were four gallant sergeants. All four displayed their highly polished 'merit guard' badges under their sheepskin jackets, casually unbuttoned. They made no effort to hide dreamy smiles as they contemplated ten days' leave in the event of their taking even one escaper, the while stroking the full-grown Alsatians at their knee.

42

▌Chapter Seven

Needless to say, I wasn't the only one thinking at that time of the link between the official opening of the gas pipeline and the escaped cons. A few hours later, someone a little higher up than me sounded the alarm. This is the full text of the telegram with which I began this narrative:

URGENT TELEGRAM

Government

Salekhard, to First Secretary Yamal — Nenets District
Committee CPSU, Comrade Pyotr Tusyada
Copies to:
Head of directorate Yamal — Nenets KGB, Major V. Shatunov
Head of directorate Yamal — Nenets militia, Colonel N. Sini
Military commander Salekhard garrison, Soviet Army, Colonel
   S. Buryatko

SERIES OF MURDERS COMMITTED BY ESCAPERS
FROM CAMP NO. RS-549, THREATENS SECURITY OF
OFFICIAL OPENING OF SIBERIA–WESTERN EUROPE
GAS PIPELINE.

TAKE IMMEDIATE MEASURES TO APPREHEND OR
ELIMINATE. MAXIMUM TIME LIMIT FOR EXECUTION
OF THIS PARTY INSTRUCTION: 24 HOURS. EVERY
EXTRA HOUR MURDERERS REMAIN AT LIBERTY
WILL BE YOUR PERSONAL PARTY RESPONSIBILITY.
First Secretary Tyumen Province Committee CPSU,
Member of Central Committee CPSU,
V. Bogomyatov

Tyumen, 10 December 1983, 18.30 hours.

Chapter Eight

While our Sno-Cat ground along the ice of a frozen river, battering its way into the snowstorm and night, Orudjev, the four sergeants and I were all busy wondering: why such a savage and barbaric method of murder? All right, they were killed for their clothing, money and papers; that was understandable. But why cut off their ears and the rest while they were about it? The first explanation that occurred to me was revenge. But why should the escapers revenge themselves on this Voropayev or Hotko, people they'd never seen in their lives? That left sadism — clinical maniacal sadism. But the twenty-year-old dissident Boris Tolmachov was doing time, according to his personal file, for 'reading and distributing Solzhenitsyn's books among Moscow University students'. And Gleb Shimansky, the icon-faker, had graduated from the Moscow Art Institute in 1965 as a specialist easel-painter; he had been represented in Moscow and at international exhibitions. Neither of them seemed likely sadistic murderers.

'That Tartar!' Orudjev confidently asserted. 'The Tartar, that bastard Zaloyev, I know their little ways! Never mind! If I get him, I swear by my father, I'll cut his off! No, I won't lay a finger on him — he'll do it himself, he'll cut the lot off himself, I swear by my mother's grave!'

'It's not his style, though,' I said. 'Two hundred and seventeen burglaries, never used a weapon once. We were taught at the institute that criminals never change their trademark. Robbing a shop in Yaku-Tur is more his style — '

'What for?' grinned one of the sergeants. 'Rice and stew. What they need is papers, identity cards — '

'But people don't get their ears and members cut off for that —'

44

'At the institute! Trademark!' said one of the sergeants, bobbing up as we went over a hummock. 'We've got an architect in the camp. He was going off on a job, so he fitted his wife's vagina with a lock — a real iron lock. Of course she turned up her toes after three days — blood poisoning. Did you learn that at the institute? And he was an engineer with higher education, an architect. The tundra does things to people too. This Tolmachov, maybe he accepted the thieves' code[1] and now he wants to be a *pakhan*[2], to prove himself. Or Shimansky.'

'Bollocks!' jeered Orudjev contemptuously. 'I'll bet a case of cognac on it: it's the Tartar, Zaloyev! Blood of Genghis Khan, shit . . . it's their trademark. If we could just get to Salekhard — he's there, near Salekhard, skulking around. How could they get to Salekhard in a blizzard like that, fucking hell!'

'*Kekliki, Kekliki*, comrade Major! Shall I stop?' shouted the driver.

Sure enough, in front of the machine, blinded by the headlights, white clumps of Arctic partridges — known locally as *Kekliki* — could be seen pressing themselves into the ground. When danger threatens, the stupid birds freeze where they are, trying to make their white plumage blend in with the whiteness of the tundra. Even close to, from a couple of metres, they look just like lumps of snow. In fine weather, when there are no blizzards, all the drivers in the north, whatever the trip, come home with a sackful of Kekliki: they kill them with sticks, even caps, and the sharpest pick them up off the road with their bare hands. There's nothing tastier in the whole world than these game birds. But for now . . .

'Drive on! Drive on!' ordered Orudjev savagely. The driver stepped on the gas.

---

[1] Thieves' code: Idiosyncratic code of morals among professional thieves.
[2] *Pakhan*: leader of gang of thieves.

▮ Chapter Nine

The flickering lights of the wagon-town of Yaku-Tur swam up
out of the blizzard, unexpectedly close at hand. In each of the
wagons, positioned in long rows above the ice-bound river, a
light was burning. On the edge of the settlement the siren of an
electricity substation hooted heart-rendingly; the door of a
factor's shop banged in the wind. I had been in shift settlements like this often enough. In the heat of the last few years,
while the Arctic gasfields were being developed and while the
government was signing contracts with Western countries for
the delivery of Urengoi gas to Europe, the Soviet Arctic had
begun to languish for lack of qualified drillers, welders and
fitters. These specialists are held in higher esteem than
engineers, and a fast Arctic rouble isn't enough to entice them
to the tundra: you have to throw in a fully furnished apartment, a kindergarten, a school for the older ones and even a
cinema for the wife. But there's just no time to build cities with
central heating, hospitals, theatres and kindergartens — just no
time. The reserves of the Urengoi gasfields exceed seven and a
half trillion cubic metres — an ocean of gas — and in January
1984 it should and must flood into Europe. Needless to say,
with a deadline like that there's no way you can build settlements with all mod cons.

Then they introduced a different system of working — by
shifts. For the past five years planes have been ferrying work
teams to the Yamal tundra from all the oil- and gas-producing
areas of the country to work a fifteen-day shift. From Azer-
baijan, Tataria, Bashkiria and Moldavia workers fly in to shift
settlements like Yaku-Tur: a night's rest, then in the morning
out to the tundra, to the drilling installations or the pipe-
welding sites, for fifteen days and nights. Out there, it's a

sixteen-hour working day, tinned food heated over a primus for dinner and a short sleep in a railcar — in your clothes. Then back to work again till the arrival of the next fifteen-day shift. Naturally, every shift worker gets paid the earth: eight to nine hundred roubles a month — that's five times my salary. It's still worth it to the state, though — it means they don't have to build towns and settlements with the usual civilized amenities on the tundra. The main thing is more and more drilling tubes driving down into the permafrost like nails and thousands of tons of clay mortar to cork up the gas and prevent its eruption before the opening of the pipeline: all so that the pipeline rolls onward, across swamps and fenland, taiga and tundra, across the rivers and mountains of Siberia and Europe, ever onward to the West. Money meant nothing, money was paper, pay the toiling men in thousands, just so long as from January 1984 onwards our country supplies Europe with some forty billion cubic metres of gas annually and earns ten billion dollars a year!

True, after fifteen days' work on the open tundra, scoured by the icy wind, with the mortar and hydrochloric acid eating into your body and your soul and liver completely frozen, even a simon-pure Communist, once he gets back to the settlement, needs more than a bottle of vodka to console him and finds it hard to keep faith with a wife or girlfriend pining away somewhere in Moldavia. Women are worth their weight in gold — even Nenets girls in their filthy tents or prostitutes too worn out for the Black Sea resorts. And where there are vodka and women you get knife-fights, and where there are knife-fights that's where we are, of course — the militia, the CID.

Yaku-Tur was a typical shift settlement of the privileged type, so to speak; next door, about a kilometre and a half away stood a Nenets fish farm called Road to Communism. There the workers could always lay their hands on *stroganina*[1] made from pink and white salmon, which goes well with vodka —

---

[1] *Stroganina*: Freshly frozen raw fish, thinly sliced. Made of sturgeon, pink and white salmon, served with a dash of pomegranate sauce, tastes wonderful with vodka.

and Nenets girls. Which was why several of the railcar porches had stocks of frozen fish stacked up like firewood.

Our Sno-Cat rolled up to a railcar bearing the sign: 'Office of Yaku-Tur Seismic Research Expedition'.

Next to this, on the wall, there hung a red poster exhorting: 'LET'S GIVE THE COUNTRY ANOTHER BILLION CUBIC METRES OF YAMAL GAS!'

Near by snuffled two tracked vehicles and a KRAZ, their engines still running. There were no drivers to be seen. In these parts drivers don't switch off lorry engines in the winter, otherwise they'd have to warm them up with fires to get them started.

Orudjev threw open the metal door, and the fury of the icy wind stung our faces once more. It was a mere ten yards from the Sno-Cat to the railcar door, but to cover it you had to lean forward into the wind; you felt naked in that wind, your face, neck and knees freezing instantly. I again thought fleetingly of the escaping cons: how could they make the 140 kilometres from the camp to Salekhard in a blizzard like this?

Orudjev literally tore open the carriage door, so powerful was the pressure of that frenzied wind, and allowed me inside. Beyond the first, outer door was a second, padded with thick felt for warmth. Behind it, ragged singing could be heard, the sound of hoarse masculine voices:

Those were the days, my friend, I thought they'd never end,
O sing and dance for ever and a day....

I opened the felted door, and we found ourselves in reviving warmth and dense cigarette smoke underscored by the sharp smell of liquor. In this tiny room-cum-office, it seemed, the entire leadership of the Yaku-Tur seismographic research expedition sat behind a plank table: some twelve men and three women. They were all obviously drunk. There were already about ten empty bottles with white-and-green labels stating 'Potable spirit, 96°' alongside cut-glass tumblers with cigarette ends floating in them and slices of greasy pink salmon, long thawed, lying on a copy of the Tyumen *Pravda*. My sweeping glance automatically noted that patches of greasy dirt had disfigured the portrait of Andropov.

48

Our appearance cut short the song. The entire company turned in our direction, their liquor-laden bodies drunkenly swaying. A shortish fellow with pale, swimming eyes detached himself from his seat and strode forward to meet us. It was clearly taking all of his willpower to stay upright.

'W — What can I do for you, c — comrades?'

'Name?' I said, feeling some disgust.

'M — Mine? M — Malofeyev — '

'Your job?'

'M — Mine? Er, er — deputy manager in charge of c — commissariat. W — Would you take a seat?' He swayed, but leant an arm against somebody's shoulder.

'Anna Kovina, investigator Urengoi CID. We've come about Voropayev's murder. Where's the body?'

'Perhaps you'd care ... for a tot of vodka first? Must be cold.' Somebody said from the table: 'Drink to his soul, eh?'

I know realized that this booze-up was actually a wake for the murdered manager. Judging by the number of empty bottles on the table, it had been going on for quite a while — probably since morning.

'I said, where's the body?' I repeated coldly.

'What d'you mean, b — body?' Malofeyev tottered. 'I — It's in the coffin, where on earth sh — should it be? Outside, b — behind the office — '

'It's got to go to Kiev, by air. That's where his family is,' someone added.

Orudjev turned to me and asked:

'Where will you examine it? Shall I have it brought in here?'

I was desperate not to go out again into the icy blizzard, but I couldn't fetch the body in here, of course. Not on the table in front of this drunken crew.

▌Chapter Ten

Radio Message
To: Urengoi, head of Urengoi CID directorate, Major Zotov

In accordance with your directive, today 10 December 1983 at Yaku-Tur settlement I carried out an external examination of the corpse of the former chief of the Yaku-Tur seismic research expedition Voropayev and questioned his subordinates. In addition, together with the head of security at Camp no. RS-549, Major Orudjev, and using tracker dogs, a detailed search was made of the scene of the incident despite blizzard conditions. As a result of the said investigations the following has been established:

Early on the morning of 7 December Vitali Voropayev, aged thirty-seven, nationality Russian, was returning to the Yaku-Tur settlement from visiting his Nenets cohabitant Savana Pyrerko, about a kilometre and a half away at the Nenets encampment near the state fish farm Road to Communism. During questioning, Pyrerko (nineteen) stated that Voropayev had disappeared from her tent while she was asleep, in other words approximately between five and eight in the morning of 7 December. She was able to give details of clothing taken by the murderers: hat of young reindeer fur, light brown; tarpaulin jacket with wolf fur, with tarpaulin hood; dark blue dungarees, fur; flying boots, dog fur, black trim.

Additional questioning of the local population established that Citizeness Savana Pyrerko, nominally a member of the fish unit at the state farm Road to Communism, lives on income from prostitution, co-habiting with workmen and engineer-technical staff of the

Yaku-Tur shift settlement. A search of her tent revealed about three thousand roubles in cash and, in the vicinity of the tent, several cases of empty glass containers of spirit, vodka and eau-de-Cologne. Since the sale of spirits to the Nenets population is forbidden by law, there can be no doubt that liquor was brought in quantity by the clients of the said Savana Pyrerko, who visited her both singly and in groups.

I shall fill in the details. The body of the murdered Voropayev was discovered early in the morning of 10 December 1983 by a local inhabitant, Yakhano Tokho, a foreman at the Nenets fish unit Road to Communism; the corpse was about two hundred metres from Pyrerko's tent. So Voropayev, visiting Savana Pyrerko on the night of the sixth of December, was absent from work for four days, which naturally must have caused concern among his subordinates. However, Voropayev's deputy, Rodion Malofeyev, and other members of his staff stated that since all exploration work was suspended between December the sixth and the ninth owing to the severe blizzard, they did not want to disturb their leader, Voropayev, whom they supposed to be staying with Savana Pyrerko.

The Nenets Yakhano Tokho, aged sixty-three, testified that this morning, 10 December (he is unable to state the exact time since he does not wear a watch, but by my calculations roughly between six-thirty and seven a.m.) he took his dog team out of the encampment and headed towards Yaku-Tur to buy tobacco, flour and tea. On the way the dogs halted near a snowdrift, squatted down in the snow and began howling, while the lead dog started scratching away at the snow with his forepaws. Jumping off the sled, Yakhano Tokho dug into the drift and discovered the body of Voropayev. The corpse, in Tokho's words, was completely naked and frozen stiff, the sliced-off ears were frozen to the chest. In the groin, a frozen crust of blood surrounded the severed *khote*.[1]

---

[1] *Khote*: Male sex organ (Nenets)

Convinced that this was a punishment for debauchery inflicted by 'the tundra spirits at the behest of the great God of the tundra, Num', Tokho left the body untouched and raced his sled into Yaku-Tur to report his find to Voropayev's deputy, Rodion Malofeyev. He, together with his driver, Malyshko, and other assistants, set out into the tundra along the trail left by Tokho's dogs (the old man was terrified of the tundra spirits and refused to go with them), where they picked up Voropayev's body.

My external examination of the body showed no signs of decay, owing to the forty-degree frost. The bodily injuries, the severing of the ears and sex organ, had been carried out with a sharp, cold weapon. The same weapon was apparently responsible for the fatal blow to the heart. Voropayev's wrists and shoulders show clear bruising, which may testify to the victim's attempts to defend himself.

In my opinion, Voropayev left Savana Pyrerko's tent early on the morning of 7 December, intending to return to work. The blizzard did not stop him, since the night before he and Pyrerko had drunk between them three bottles of pure spirit. Two hundred yards from the tent Voropayev encountered his murderer or murderers: evidently the prisoners who had escaped that night from Camp RS-549.

However, in order to establish beyond any doubt the time of Voropayev's death and the exact sequence of events connected with his execution, an expert in forensic medicine must be sent to Yaku-Tur.

As far as the scene of the incident is concerned, I have to record that no trace of the criminal or criminals has been discovered at the scene of the crime.

I await your further instructions.

> Lieutenant of militia, investigator Anna Kovina
> Yaku-Tur settlement, 10 December 1983.

I reckoned my work-rate had put me one up on the best investigators at our Urengoi CID. Within a few hours of my arrival at Yaku-Tur and the fish farm I had gathered practically every scrap of information on Voropayev's murder — and in a snowstorm, what's more, when I had had to take statements not only from drunken Russians but also from Nentsi in their black tents reeking of dog.

Yet the brief reply to my radio message came not from my chief, Zotov, but from another quarter:

Radio message — URGENT:
To: Yaku-Tur, deputy leader Seismic Exploration Expedition, R. Malofeyev

Organize immediate departure of Urengoi CID investigator Anna Kovina to Salekhard KGB with all personal documents relating to escaped criminals and body of Voropayev. Inform Kovina that photographs of escapers in their papers absolutely necessary in pursuit and arrest of criminals.

To ensure safe passage in the blizzard conditions, send no fewer than three Sno-Cats with most experienced drivers. Report immediately on completion.

Chief of Salekhard KGB directorate,
Major Shatunov

▎Chapter Eleven

I took the summons to Salekhard, capital of the Yamal–Nenets district, as a fateful sign, whereas Orudjev reacted like a work dog hearing the command, 'Go fetch!' He seated himself at the steering gear of the leading Sno-Cat, and three tank engines revving up at full blast drowned out the roar of the storm.

Orudjev drove the Sno-Cats by compass-reckoning: straight ahead across the ice-hummocks, through the sparse tundra scrub, across frozen bogs and gullies. Because of the appalling shaking, Voropayev's coffin broke up in the first hour and the frozen corpse fell out onto the floor.

'Stop!' I yelled at Orudjev. 'Stop! You're spoiling my corpse. It's got to be medically examined! Stop!'

But Orudjev drove on without a pause. He didn't give a damn for forensic medicine or any such criminological refinements. Over there in Salekhard, or close by, he might find his escaped criminals and restore his unsullied reputation as one of the finest officers in the guard service.

Meanwhile, I almost wept with exasperation. Voropayev's murdered body was of unique value to forensic science since it had frozen instantly on the tundra, like the fish the Nentsi catch under the ice in winter. Once drawn out of the water, one touch of forty- or fifty-degree frost and the fish freezes in a fraction of a second; even the water has no time to drip off its slimy back. So Voropayev had frozen on the tundra, except that in his case instead of water around the gaping mouth with the *khote* thrust down the throat was a border of scarlet blood. The same icy loops of blood lay around the severed ears and the groin where the *khote* had been. At the time, no traces of decay; the corpse had lain four days on the tundra, as if in a refrigerator; the bruises on shoulder and wrist were ideally visible.

But now the jolting of the Sno-Cat was rolling the body round the floor.

Driving the dogs away, I somehow crammed the corpse back into the coffin with the help of two sergeants and strapped it round with our belts. The frozen body rumbled about in the coffin and I regretted not having wrapped it up in a jacket, but there was no opening it up again; it was all I could do to hang on to a metal stanchion for dear life.

I probably survived that journey without being sick only because I'd eaten nothing since the previous day and had nothing to spew up. Six times we overturned, skidding down the bank of a stream or the lip of a tundra gully. Four steel hawsers snapped while two of the Sno-Cats were putting the third back on its tracks after yet another capsize. During these operations, the tundra heard Russian, Ossetian and Ukrainian curses, the like of which I had never heard in all my years in the militia.

After three hours of this mad journey the engine of one machine overheated and began smoking, and an hour later the track of a second broke apart. We abandoned them on the tundra and all in one Sno-Cat rolled into the dark streets of Salekhard. The treads clanked along the frozen log roadway and the machine drew up outside the building of the local directorate of the KGB. I crawled out of the cabin only half-alive, with a frozen cheek and stiff, unbending legs. My back, shoulders and knees ached from the knocks they had received. Yet I was still able to help the soldiers drag the whimpering dogs out of the machine along with Voropayev's coffin.

'Leave that!' Orudjev pushed me away. 'In to Shatunov!'

In Shatunov's office sat about fifteen men: the entire Salekhard staff working on the detection of the runaways. Hudya Benokan was among them. Orudjev and I, swaying from exhaustion, halted in the doorway; I had the personal files of the prisoners in my hands. Major Shatunov, a fifty-year-old Siberian with a strong, weather beaten face and the white lashes of an albino, glanced at me approvingly:

'You got through, then?' He nodded to someone: 'Give her a chair, she'll fall over in a minute.'

Everyone burst out laughing. It's always the same — bugger

them! Do work three men couldn't manage, and all they can do is snigger.

Somebody got me a chair, took the personal files from me and placed them in front of Shatunov. I sat down and began to feel that the warmth was making me fall apart; a hiccup came to my throat. Hudya Benokan gave me a glass of strong tea. He had altered a lot over the four years. Before, at the university, he had been a buttoned-up Nenets with the artless face of a reindeer herdsman. But now something adult, harsh and weary had appeared on that face. No wonder, I thought: I just can't imagine how he got through his exams and sessionals in the university law faculty and look after a babe-in-arms in the hostel at the same time. When I was there I had my work cut out even without a baby to think of.

Shatunov meanwhile, without raising his eyes from the prisoners' personal files, asked Orudjev:

'Was it you who let these cons out of the camp?'

'It was, comrade Major,' said Orudjev, standing to attention.

'You'll be reduced to the ranks,' rapped Shatunov, still without looking at him. He tore the sheet of photographs from each folder and gave them to one of his assistants:

'Get these copied straight away and distributed to all concerned. I want posters with the murderers' pictures on every post within two hours!'

'Permission to wipe away the blame, comrade Major,' said Orudjev.

Only now did Shatunov raise his eyes.

'How do you propose to go about that?'

Orudjev's fancy white sheepskin was wet with snow, his face and hands a mass of bruises from banging against the windscreen; his right ear was frostbitten, and a dark stubble had sprouted on his unshaven cheeks. It was clear it was taking him all his strength to stay on his feet. Yet he spoke firmly, even brusquely:

'I'll get those bastards if I have to dig up the tundra!'

'Very well, go ahead and try —' replied Shatunov, and glanced in my direction. My hiccups were audible throughout the office.

He frowned, irritated and instructed Hudya Benokan:

'See her to a hotel.'

Benokan came over and made as if to help me rise, but I shoved his arm away and stood up on my own. That was all I needed — Hudya Benokan, of all people, to act the nursemaid to me. The most exasperating part, though — I could have cried! — was that after a whole hectic day spent on a hot job, after all my efforts in Yaku-Tur and that crazy drive to Salekhard, now came these idiotic, non-stop hiccups. With tears in my eyes I shot out of the office into the corridor. The door to the street was wide open as the soldiers carried in Voropayev's coffin, I couldn't stir for people. Why is it when somebody falls over or has the hiccups everybody thinks it so funny — even Hudya Benokan? He brought me a whole decanter of water, and said:

'Drink up, however. It'll help. Let's be off to the hotel — '

I rounded on him in a pause between hiccups, and said, full of hate:

'Listen! Piss off, will you — hic!'

He shrugged and went back to Shatunov's office.

▌Chapter Twelve

To: First Secretary Tyumen Province Committee
CPSU, Comrade Bogomyatov

IN REPLY TO YOUR EXPRESS TELEGRAM RE ARREST
OF PRISONERS ESCAPED FROM CAMP NO. RS-549 WE
REPORT:

IN SALEKHARD, ENTIRE AVAILABLE COMPLEMENT
OF LOCAL KGB, MILITIA AND MILITARY GARRISON
NOW MOBILIZED IN HUNT FOR CRIMINAL-
MURDERERS. SPECIAL OPERATION STAFF
HAS BEEN ESTABLISHED FOR THEIR
APPREHENSION. CAREFUL SEARCH BEING CARRIED
OUT OF ALL BUILDINGS IN THE TOWN, OF
LABYTNANGI RAILWAY STATION AND OF NEARBY
SETTLEMENTS, AIRPORT BLOCKADED, RAILWAY
BEING PATROLLED. DESPITE BLIZZARD URENGOI
CID INVESTIGATOR ANNA KOVINA HAS DELIVERED
PHOTOGRAPHS OF ESCAPERS FROM CAMP RS-549.
PHOTOGRAPHS HAVE BEEN COPIED AND
DISTRIBUTED TO ALL PATROLS. AT VERY FIRST
SIGN OF IMPROVEMENT IN WEATHER CONDITIONS,
AIRCRAFT WILL BE USED TO SEARCH
SURROUNDING TUNDRA.

CONFIDENT YOUR PARTY INSTRUCTION RE
APPREHENSION OR ELIMINATION OF MURDERERS
OF HEAD OF YAKU-TUR SEISMIC EXPLORATION

TEAM VOROPAYEV AND SENIOR CONSULTANT
SALEKHARD DISTRICT HOSPITAL HOTKO IS A
MATTER OF HOURS.

First Secretary Yamal–Nenets district committee CPSU
Pyotr Tusyada
Chief of operational staff, state security,
Major Shatunov

Salekhard, 10 December 1983

▌ Chapter Thirteen

Only a few minutes remained before the deadline set by
Bogomyatov, First Secretary of the Tyumen Province party
committee: 18.30 hours on 11 December. We — that is virtually the whole operational staff working on the murder hunt —
were sitting in the office of Pyotr Tusyada, First Secretary of
the Yamal–Nenets party district committee.

In anticipation of the arrival of the government delegation
and foreign guests for the pipeline opening the Soviet furniture
had been replaced by Swedish, the walls covered with Karelian
birch and an enormous relief map of the Yamal–Nenets
national district using green derrick-shaped markers to show
the gasfields and red lines to indicate pipelines. Small models of
reindeer, Arctic foxes and fish were used to show the other
resources of the Nenets tundra: reindeer ranches, fish-process-
ing plants, farms where fur-bearing animals were raised. The
map convincingly demonstrated that this wild Arctic territory,
one-and-a-half times the size of France, really was a unique
repository of 'blue gold' (gas), 'soft gold' (fur) and 'red gold'
(salmon).

And the titular master of this whole territory, Pyotr
Tusyada, First Secretary of the provincial party, a Nenets
specially appointed by Moscow six months earlier to demonstrate to foreign visitors the advancement of minority personnel to posts of responsibility, did indeed have something to
exhibit: the Nentsi of several exemplary fur-breeding establish-
ments and collective farms were hastily transferred from
reindeerskin tents to European-type settlements; the Nenets
song and dance ensemble Northern Lights learnt French,
German and Czech folk songs; and even the children of the
local school had devised a concert programme in four languages.

Nevertheless, at this moment Pyotr Tusyada was in no mood for French songs. A squat, thick-set Nenets of about thirty-six, he had been merely a manager of a Nenets fur farm before his promotion. He sat heavily in his leather armchair and slowly, after the fashion of his forebears, rocked his whole body backwards and forwards in time with his round, almost neckless head. His narrow eyes were open, but it was doubtful if he saw us. It seemed as if for the first time in the six months of his dizzy party career he desperately wished himself back on the tundra with his reindeer and his Arctic foxes. That went for the rest of the company as well: at that moment we all wanted to be as far away as possible from the red telephone on the table, the direct line to the Tyumen Province party committee. All the extraordinary measures for the detection of the escaped criminals had yielded no results. The blizzard had somewhat abated towards morning, and since then two polar aviation helicopters had been circling over Salekhard pinpointing every car, Sno Cat, even Nenets sled which left the town — all to no avail. The soldiers of the local garrison had combed every dwelling, every warehouse and hut, every habitable and uninhabitable corner, including the barges frozen into the Ob — all in vain. All over the town, the wind shredded and tore at hastily slapped-up posters bearing the portraits of the fugitive cons and the caption 'WANTED CRIMINALS'. On the railway, soldiers not only searched every carriage; they escorted the trains almost as far as the Urals. Sno-Cats quartered the surrounding tundra with a similar lack of result, visiting Nenets encampments near and far within a radius of fifty kilometres. The Nentsi greeted the soldiers with open derision:

'The Russians are looking for spirits, however. How can you find a spirit, however?'

In some unimaginable fashion the rumour that the tundra spirits had put to death two Russian officials had spread like wildfire across the Yamal peninsula. The Nenets bush telegraph at once adorned the facts with an incredible explanation: when the Russians first arrived in the tundra three hundred years ago to despoil the Nentsi of their fur and fish, the tundra spirits held their peace, the tundra spirits remained asleep beneath the earth. When the Russians began drilling the Nentsi

61

earth to seize the last riches of the native people — oil and gas — the spirits awoke. But the Russians did not release them from beneath the earth; they blocked up the holes in the earth with clay. Now, though, because of the opening of the pipeline, the Russians had begun to open up the bore-holes. The tundra spirits had burst forth from the earth and begun to take revenge on the Russians for having, they said, ripped apart the tundra with their iron machines, destroyed the reindeer pastures. Now there was nowhere a Nenets could graze his reindeer: they had killed off the rivers, polluted them with petrol, oil and hydrochloric acid. They had brought 'bad' diseases to the tundra: tuberculosis, syphilis, gonorrhoea ...

Needless to say, nobody on the operations staff gave any consideration to these rumours. We were concerned about something else: where on earth could the three escapers have got to? It wasn't spirits who had broken out of RS-549! Nearly five days had passed since they had absconded. They needed food, warmth, shelter, and yet along their entire route from the camp to Salekhard — a route marked by two corpses — there wasn't a single rifled shop, a campfire, nothing. And in Salekhard itself, not a single burglary, not a trace of any criminal on the run. After Voropayev had been killed in Yaku-Tur and Hotko in Salekhard, the fugitives had simply been swallowed up. Or had they, in some mysterious fashion, slipped past the railway patrols and got away to 'the mainland'?

Anyway, everybody gathered in Tusyada's office was depressed. It was at that moment that the door burst open and Orudjev propelled into the office two little Nenets boys wearing ragged reindeerskin *malitsas*. Everybody turned towards Orudjev, questioning and a little hopeful.

'Well?' said Shatunov impatiently.

'They'll speak for themselves, little shits!'

Orudjev jerked the boys roughly by the shoulder. His previous dash and polish had disappeared completely. A day and night of sleepless roaming around Salekhard had stiffened his face; his cheeks had caved in.

The boys said nothing, glancing at us with narrow, malevolent little eyes.

'Well, out with it!' Shatunov demanded of Orudjev.

'I caught them red-handed,' reported Orudjev. 'Writing in charcoal, little buggers, on the Lenin monument: "Russians, get out of the tundra!"'

'And that's all?' asked Shatunov.

'That's all, comrade Major. They'd started writing something about spirits — '

'Get lost!' said Shatunov softly.

'What?' Orudjev had misheard.

'I said, get lost!' Shatunov's voice broke as he shouted, 'Just fuck off!'

While all this was going on, nobody had noticed that the chief of the district militia, Colonel Sini, had hurried into the office. Although Sini had the rank of colonel and Shatunov was only a major, the latter as chief of operations and KGB representative acted as top man while the colonel simply tried to preserve his independence. Without looking at anyone, he went straight up to Pyotr Tusyada's desk and placed before him a typewritten sheet.

Tusyada read it without speaking, glanced briefly at Colonel Sini, then lowered his eyes once more to the paper. He then rose, and walked heavily on his short legs over to a wall cupboard which he opened. Hanging in there was a *malitsa* and other items of Nenets national dress. Tusyada removed his dark jacket with its supreme soviet deputy's badge, his tie and his white shirt.

We watched him in amazement. Was he going to strip off completely?

Meanwhile he was calmly putting a *yagushka* next to his bare skin; this garment was a shirt of reindeer hide with the fur inside. He then slipped off his fashionable shoes and, without rolling up his trousers, drew on some *ichigi* — fur stockings — and, on top of these, high reindeer boots or *kisi* and pulled them up above the knee by the laces. After this he neatly slipped into his *malitsa* with its all-enveloping hood and sleeves. And so, without a word, he walked out of the office, pausing only in a gesture of paternal authority to lay hold of the two Nenets boys by the hood and take them out with him.

'What's happened?' Shatunov looked at Colonel Sini, then leant across Tusyada's table and took the typewritten sheet. He had not finished reading it when, outside the window and illuminated by the bright streetlamps, Pyotr Tusyada hailed a passing Nenets reindeer sledge, took his seat and departed.

The clock on the wall showed eighteen-thirty. The red telephone on Tusyada's desk came to life with a soft, muffled ring. Nobody picked up the phone. The white sheet with its typewritten text passed from hand to hand to the rhythmical accompaniment of the phone. The contents were as follows:

Report

To: Chief of Yamal–Nenets directorate of militia, Colonel N. Sini

While carrying out routine patrol of Poluisky region of Salekhard, today 11 December at 18.10, duty patrol of three men under Militia Sergeant Orlov noticed that the wicket gate of the cottage belonging to Comrade P.R. Ryazanov, chief geologist of Yamal Oil and Gas Exploration Trust, was open. Upon entering the cottage yard the patrol discovered in the snow near the sauna the frozen naked corpse of comrade Ryazanov with marks of brutal violence — ears and sex organ cut off. The severed sex organ is in the mouth of the victim. Clothing and documents of the murdered man have disappeared. One metre from the corpse on the snow was discovered a tarpaulin mitten with a Camp RS-549 tag and the initials T.Z. written on the lining with a chemical pencil, which may prove that the mitten belongs to one of the three criminals from Camp RS-549, namely Timur Zaloyev.

While we were reading this, Shatunov was conversing with Colonel Sini in staccato phrases.

'Is the area cordoned off?'

'We're doing it now.'

'How many investigators at the scene of the crime?'

'From our Urengoi CID, Kovrov's just gone out there with Benokan and the dog-handler Telichkin.'

'How many dogs?'

'Three.'

'Okay. Mitten to Major Orudjev for identification. Nothing's to be touched in Ryazanov's house till I get there.' Having made these arrangements, Shatunov at last lifted the phone.

'Yes, Comrade Bogomyatov ... No, Tusyada's gone out, this is Major Shatunov ... No, unfortunately not caught yet, but they are in Salekhard ... I know because a third body's just been found. It's the chief geologist of Yamal–Oil–Gas, Ryazanov — '

Even from the impenetrable face of Shatunov it was clear that at the other end of the line the party terminology being used was weighty and a long way from printable. Shatunov could only get a word in now and again:

'No, they won't get away ... I understand, but now they won't get away — '

At last he had heard everything Bogomyatov had to say to him. He replied curtly, 'Very good, sir,' replaced the phone and turned to us:

'They've given us an extension till tomorrow morning. But if we don't get them — well, you don't need me to tell you. Now, all investigators follow me, to the scene of the crime!' He admonished the rest, who had risen noisily to their feet:

'There's bugger-all for the rest of you to do over there. Go and join the police cordon!'

∎ Chapter Fourteen

Meanwhile, what a few hours before had seemed a delirium of wild superstition unworthy of serious attention had turned, as soon as Ryazanov's body had been discovered, into something close to mass hysteria. Yes indeed, three murders in two days — and what killings! *Khote* stuffed down the throat and all. Well, a mob's a mob no matter how much atheism and materialism you teach them! That the tarpaulin mitten found at Ryazanov's cottage confirmed the murders as the work of the runaway cons not tundra spirits, nobody in Salekhard wanted to hear. 'The tundra spirits are punishing the Russians' was on the lips of everyone all over town. And the streets of Salekhard went dead. In their houses, the Russians barricaded doors and windows. Lights were on in the working men's hostels: the single men were packing their suitcases. Run! Run from the tundra! In Labytnangi, a settlement on the west bank of the Ob, there was a stampede at the railway station. Shift workers stormed the ticket office, those without tickets broke through the police cordon around the carriages on the platform and the Salekhard–Moscow train had to be delayed for three hours.

In the crush and fighting over tickets, a number of people were injured. About thirty were arrested for disorderly behaviour and obstructing the police.

Even that didn't help. A drunk climbed onto the rubbish bin next to the ticket office, laughing hysterically and yelling out over the heads of the sweating mob:

'Been out shagging on the tundra?! You running away from your sins? Who's grabbed sables off the Nentsi for half a litre? Is it your balls you're protecting? Ha — ha — haah! Which one of you tipped oil in the river, eh? Who's been banging little Nentsi girls? Now you're scared for your bollocks, you cunt-busters! Who brought syphilis into the tundra, I ask you?'

'Shut your mouth, shit-face! What about you?', someone yelled at him from the crowd.

'Truth hurts, eh?' responded the drunk cheerfully. 'Pity Jack London's not about. He could have described you lot — builders of Communism, tundra prick-swingers!'

'I'll slice your ears off myself!' Someone darted towards him.

'Hoboes!' cried the drunk gaily. 'What about me, then? I'm not denying anything — I've been whoring out there as well! I was a naughty boy as well! Just let him that is without sin cast the first stone! What? Nobody? Well I'm going to atone — to the tundra spirits, sod it!'

He fell, or jumped off the bin and dived through the crowd onto the station forecourt. He drew out of his jacket a thick wad of notes — a year's pay most likely — and began flinging them to the tundra wind: 'All of it! The lot! Keep it, tundra! Well now, who's brave enough to bloody well give back what he looted?'

He was arrested on the spot, of course, but even in the police station he turned out all his pockets, threw his last small change on the floor and went on acting the goat.

'What's the matter? I earned them here, I've thrown them away here! I've got the right! My bollocks mean more to me! I demand you write on the charge sheet: "Driller Trofimov redeemed his balls from the spirits of the Nentsi."'

Next morning, not a single Russian family let its children go to school and the majority of the Russian population of the town did not turn up for work. It was like Moscow in 1971, when the police couldn't lay hands on the sadist-murderer Idonesyan, who killed a child a day.

So as to stop the madness spreading across the territory, Shatunov ordered Salekhard and Labytnangi to be sealed off from the outside world: all mail was halted, no private calls were allowed to other towns, the airport was closed for outward flights and train schedules were suspended.

He referred to this action as 'psychological quarantine'.

Chapter Fifteen

Of course, nobody on the operations staff gave any credence whatever to these tundra spirits or any such devilry.

On the steep bank of the river Polui, a tributary of the Ob, Ryazanov's cottage had been cordoned off by the police militia; the yard was lit up by car headlights and searchlights positioned in the cottage windows. The cottage itself was located in a small modern development inhabited by the local elite; Salekhard residents had dubbed the place 'Laureateville' since nearly all its local leading lights were state-prize laureates and suchlike. Major Orudjev had already been toiling for three hours in the yard alongside Sergeant Telichkin, the local Salekhard police dog-handler. Orudjev took Zaloyev's mitten, found near Ryazanov's body, from its cellophane envelope and gave it to the dog to sniff. Then he described a wide circle with his arm, and said softly:

'Seek, Titan! Trace!'

Titan, a grey sinewy championship dog, knew what to do without being told. Lowering his muzzle to the snow, he moved round the yard in ever-decreasing circles before returning to the spot where the patrol had found the mitten several hours before. At this point he squatted down, yawned, and gave every indication that the search was over.

The same thing happened with the other dogs.

We were all crowded together at the doors and windows of the cottage watching Orudjev and Telichkin's vain efforts to find the faintest trace of Zaloyev's presence. It should be said that we investigators had got nowhere either. Hudya Benokan and his colleague from Salekhard CID, the criminal law expert Kovrov, had literally crawled on hands and knees around Ryazanov's cottage and the sauna building before reporting to Shatunov.

'That's it. You can go inside now. There are no prints or traces except for those of Ryazanov and his driver.'

Shatunov glared at them so savagely that the expert expanded on this, or rather added in self-justification:

'Nobody's lived in the cottage for a month. Everything's covered in dust, so fingerprints and other traces would be obvious. Ryazanov's prints are in the kitchen, on the refrigerator, on a bottle of cognac, a coat-hook and the hot-water radiator. His driver's prints are on two of Ryazanov's suitcases. That's the lot.'

Shantunov sighed and went over into the cottage, the rest trailed along behind him, myself among them.

I had never been in a millionaire's villa before, I'd only seen them in films; I'd known about government dachas only by hearsay. Now I was seeing with my own eyes what real luxury meant. Perhaps it's worth giving a few more details about Laureateville. Elite villages like this one are to be found in every development area of national importance: Bratsk, Ust-Ilin, the Viluisk hydro-electric project and up here in the north at Urengoi, Surgut and Tayezhni. I don't know who pays for the building in places like Bratsk, but up here they're obviously built with resources released by the 'shift method of developing the tundra': instead of being used for dwelling-houses, schools and hospitals in Yaku-Tur and similar working men's settlements all scarce building materials came here, to Laureateville. A special team of architects directed the building, adapting each cottage to the personal taste of its future occupant. At the same time, two camps' worth of cons laid out the streets and terraces, planted birches and pines from the taiga, constructed yacht-club moorings down by the Polui, a secluded swimming pool and two tennis courts, and fitted out each cottage with fireplaces, a sauna and similar Western-style comforts. Once ensconced, the owners began to compete over their furnishings: washable Finnish wallpaper that looked like leather, Swedish furniture, polar bear skins — even ancient Nenets idols — adorned the interiors of these villas.

Ryazanov's cottage was one of these. An enormous polar bear skin covered the parquet floor of the living-room. Light-coloured furniture matched the rug, while over by the fireplace stood three low stools with legs of walrus ivory; on closer inspection these turned out to be the core of walrus penises. (Because these animals mate in sub-arctic temperatures, nature has actually equipped their penises with a bone.) Doubtless at another time these penis legs would have given rise to ribald comment, but we were in no mood for humour: the 'comparative findings of the forensic medical examination' on all three corpses had arrived from the hospital.

'All three deaths,' Shatunov read out, 'came about as the result of a precisely delivered blow by a sharp piercing/cutting instrument in the neighbourhood of the heart. A fact meriting attention is that in all three cases, the depth of penetration is approximately the same, from 14.5 to 16 centimetres, which points to the same hand being responsible for all three wounds. . . . The nature of the cuts where the ears and sexual organs of the victims have been removed is likewise identical. This allows us to state that all the wounds were caused by the same sharp-edged instrument, most probably a knife . . . After comparative microscopic analysis of the wounds and cuts, and study of the dynamics of the infliction of body injuries, the examination concludes that the murderer possesses average strength and uses the right hand in a characteristic fashion: each slash is made by one abrupt blow from bottom to top, as indicated by the upward and outward direction of the slash lines where ears and sex organs have been severed — '

'The Tartar way!' commented Shatunov by way of conclusion.

'And the Nenets way,' I couldn't help saying. 'Nentsi butcher meat like that, I've seen them. They put one end of the fresh reindeer liver in their mouth and cut it with a knife from underneath.'

'So you're saying it's Nentsi who are doing the killing?' Hudya Benokan interposed vehemently, as if I'd insulted the whole Nenets people with my suspicion.

'Don't fight over it,' said Kovrov soothingly. 'Neither Nentsi nor their spirits wear camp mittens.'

'Exactly.' Shatunov went on reading the medical report: 'As a result of the extraordinary fast freezing of the corpses due to the low temperature of their surroundings, it is not possible to determine the exact time of death of Voropayev and Hotko by

70

bacteriological analysis. As regards Ryazanov, the exceptional weight of the deceased (140 kilos with a height of 1.67 metres) together with a thick layer of fat in the abdominal area partially retarded the freezing process. The autopsy has revealed unfrozen remains of food in stomach and intestine; this enables the moment of the attack to be fixed at three, three-and-a-half hours prior to the discovery of the corpse. The examination team would draw attention to the fact that there are no bruises or scratches on the bodies of Hotko and Ryazanov, while the preliminary external examination of Voropayev's body by investigator A. Kovina revealed scratches and bruises in the area of the right shoulder and the wrists, which may point to Voropayev's struggle for life. Unfortunately, inappropriate transportation of Voropayev's body from Yaku-Tur to Salekhard led to additional injury to the body and hindered the work of the team in determining the nature and location of injuries sustained while alive.'

Shatunov glanced at me with his white eyes. I shrugged:

'You don't get bruised wrists in a coffin.'

'Okay,' said Shatunov, and read on to the end of the report: 'The autopsy revealed a high alcohol level in Voropayev's blood. No traces of alcohol were found in Hotko. Signatures. That's it. Cretins!' said Shatunov without a pause, flinging the report onto the kitchen table. 'It seems two sober chaps — Ryazanov and Hotko — quietly let their penises and ears get cut off. Voropayev, drunk as a skunk, did put up some resistance. What does that tell us? Fuck knows. Right, Kovina, while those pricks are messing about with the dogs, tell us what you've got.'

He gazed around the kitchen and looked questioningly at Benokan and Kovrov.

'Can we sit down here? Have you checked the chairs?'

'Now we really are offended,' grinned Kovrov. 'You can even drink the cognac in that bottle — I've got all the finger-prints on film.'

Shatunov sat down at the kitchen table and poured himself half a glass of brandy, downed it at a gulp, grunted, took a sniff at his fist and gave me an interrogative glance: 'Well? Make your report.'

71

I wouldn't have minded a drink either, but it didn't occur to him to offer, though I'd been hanging about in the cold as long as he had.

I spoke:

'Ryazanov got into this business straight off the ship, so to speak. He only got back from holiday today, he'd been at a government sanatorium on the Black Sea. His wife and daughter stayed in Moscow to celebrate the New Year in the capital. He hurried back here for the pipeline opening, he even brought a whole suitcase full of whisky and cognac. Judging by the stamps on the labels, they're from the Gas Industry Minister's special supply — '

Shatunov didn't care for my informal tone, and interrupted:

'Keep it short! Stick to essentials.'

I got the record of my interrogation of Ryazanov's driver out of my briefcase and began to read:

'Ryazanov's chauffeur stated: "At two o'clock in the after-noon I met comrade Ryazanov at Labytnangi railway station. While we were crossing the frozen Ob from the left bank to the right, I told comrade Ryazanov about the escape of the cons and the two murders. Comrade Ryazanov knew both Voropayev and Hotko well, and was extremely upset. The "tundra spirits" business just made him laugh. "That's all we need, spirits cutting your balls off for a bit of humping!" was what comrade Ryazanov said. "Anyway, these Nentsi should be grateful for so-called debauchery: if it hadn't been for Russian sperm they'd have died out two hundred years ago!"'

'True enough,' grinned Shatunov. 'You've seen the children the Nentsi wives have got now?' Nearly taller than me. Fair lads, real Russkies.' Here he recollected that Hudya Benokan, the Nenets, was standing next to him, and said:

'Hmm. Just — er — strike those words about debauchery out of the record, will you?'

I nodded, and continued reading:

'"At approximately three-fifteen we drove up to Ryazanov's house in Laureateville. I took his two suitcases out of the boot of the Volga and brought them into the cottage after comrade Ryazanov. The path from the wicket gate to the porch had been cleared, the yard as well —"'

'Who cleared the path and yard?' asked Shatunov abruptly.

'I've checked. The caretaker swept both out at eleven that morning. He does it every morning for all the cottages. Shall I go on?'

'Yes, go on.'

'"Comrade Ryazanov opened the cottage door with his key and went in, I carried the two suitcases after him. Comrade Ryazanov took his things off and hung his sheepskin up on some reindeer antlers in the hallway. It was cold in the cottage — unheated — so comrade Ryazanov put his old sheepskin jacket on and turned on the central heating. I asked him if he needed me for anything else and whether he wanted the car that day. He said he was tired after the journey and was going to stoke up the sauna, have a bit of a steam, then go to bed. 'Come for me at seven in the morning as usual,' he said, and I drove away. I noticed nothing suspicious in the house. When I went out to the car, the street was empty. I saw lights in the cottages round about, but everything was quiet." Signature. Date.' I added, and placed the record in the briefcase. 'There's more, comrade Major. The sheepskin jacket the driver mentioned has vanished along with the rest of the things Ryazanov was wearing when he was killed. The picture begins to look like this: after dismissing the driver, Ryazanov opened that bottle of cognac over there; he drank fifty to eighty millilitres straight from the bottle and went out to stoke up the sauna. He did do that — it's still warm — then he came out again into the yard, where the murderer met him seven yards from the sauna. This was between three-thirty and four in the afternoon, that is in total darkness. I made the rounds of the neighbouring cottages where Ryazanov's chauffeur had seen lights. The ones to the right and left of Ryazanov's are about a hundred and seventy metres away. If Ryazanov had shouted loudly for help, he would have been heard. Both the men in those cottages were out at work, and the women say they heard nothing. Now I've got a question: does a man shout out when his — excuse me — sex organs are cut off, or are his vocal cords so constricted by pain and fear that he can't make a sound?'

'Don't know,' said Shatunov gloomily. 'I've never had anything cut off me yet. But if we don't find that Tartar by morning. I'll be able to answer that question tomorrow. Incidentally, ring those expert-pricks at the hospital. They missed out the main thing: what came first, the knife thrust to the heart and then the severing of ears and penis, or the other way about?' He rose, looked out of the window and shouted to Orudjev and Telichkin: 'Well? How long are you going to be with those dogs?'

Neither Orudjev nor Telichkin replied: both were watching intently as the last dog, called Carter, nosed about. For some reason, every militia unit has dogs named after American presidents or English prime ministers. It probably gives the soldiers a bit of pleasure to order about American presidents or English lords: 'Carter, sit!' or 'Thatcher, go get it!' On this occasion, though, Carter played a truly imperialist, anti-Soviet joke on Orudjev; not only did he fail to find anything, like all the other dogs, but in addition when he reached the spot where Ryazanov's corpse and Zaloyev's mitten had been discovered, he suddenly raised his hind leg and demonstratively pissed on the scene of the crime.

Any other time we would probably have fallen about laughing at this canine prank; now, we all kept quiet — except of course, Shatunov.

'Your dog?' he asked Orudjev, through the window.

'Yes,' Orudjev brought out in a low, crushed voice.

'The knacker's yard, boil him down for soap! And you as well — okay, take the dogs away, let's have the investigators examine the yard.' Here, Shatunov turned to Hudya Benokan and the rest: 'All snow in the yard to be gone through! With magnifying glasses!'

The sound of a helicopter drowned out his words. We stared into the dark sky. The aircraft was heading straight for Ryazanov's cottage using a powerful searchlight to search out a landing-place. At about sixty feet above the cottage, however, it hovered indecisively then turned away towards the street and put down on the snowy roadway. A small figure detached itself from the helicopter and I recognized it as my Urengoi chief, Zotov. Bending to the earth, he moved away from the aircraft, waving to the pilot to swing away. Two minutes later he was walking into Ryazanov's cottage, scraping his felt boots.

'Here we are,' said he, addressing Shatunov while shaking powdery snow from his fur jacket. 'Flown in from Urengoi to lend a hand. What have you got here? Any tea going?'

'Kovina can make you tea!' said Shatunov. 'A Pinkerton man from the sky, that's all I needed,' and went out into the yard to supervise the work of the investigators, who had replaced the dogs in scouring every inch of Ryazanov's yard and were actually using magnifying glasses.

I put the kettle on the electric stove and, while it was heating up, briefly told Zotov all I knew.

While he listened, Zotov took off his felt boots, undid the zip on the left side of his fur trousers and started rubbing his troublesome knee with that foul-smelling ointment of his. Afterwards he took a few calm sips of tea, lit his pipe and went to have a look around the cottage. He went outside, stamped about near the sauna, then came back in.

I spoke on the telephone to the hospital and learnt from the doctors that they were powerless to answer Shatunov's question on the method of murder. The doctors mumbled something about needing a specialist's opinion on vocal cords to determine whether or not the victims had cried out before they were killed. There was no such specialist in Salekhard; he would have to be summoned from the district centre, Tyumen.

'Well, now,' said Zotov, when I had put down the phone. 'Did you fetch Voropayev's clothes from Yaku-Tur?'

'You know they took all his clothes, stole them. What could I bring?'

'The rest of his stuff, from his flat — did you bring any?'

'What for?'

'Did you or didn't you?'

'No, of course not.'

'You're a fool, then,' said Zotov and turned to Shatunov as he came in from the yard.

'Before you started tormenting those dogs with Zaloyev's mitten, you should have put your brain in gear. If the murderer took the clothes off Voropayev and Hotko, he wasn't going to take them to market and sell them, was he? He put them on to keep himself warm, didn't he? Flying boots first of all. Now think: three made the break, but only one of them, according

75

to the medical evidence, actually did the killing. The first victim was Voropayev. Well, the killer would be the first in line for the clothes, right? Therefore that murderer came here in Voropayev's boots, yes? And what have you given the dogs to sniff? Zaloyev's mitten. There's no scent of Zaloyev's boots round here; he threw them away long, long ago in the tundra.'

My heart went cold. What a plain, simple idea it was! And I, like an idiot, hadn't even fetched a scrap of Voropayev's clothing, not even a handkerchief. There was no way I could avoid a ticking off from Shatunov now. There he was, looking at me now with his pale Gee Bee eyes!

'Don't panic now, Anna,' grinned Zotov, and slipped his hand inside his jacket. 'Why do you think I flew in from Urengoi? I made a stop in Yaku-Tur, it was practically on the way. And look . . .' With these words Zotov pulled out a cellophane package. He opened it and cautiously shook out onto the table a quantity of crumpled male underwear: vest, pants and a pair of long combinations.

'All Voropayev's, and all unwashed,' said old man Zotov with pride. 'Even I can smell the sweat on them. But before you start tormenting those dogs again you should get another lot like this from Hotko's flat. The murderer might just have put on Hotko's boots, hell knows.'

I went up to Zotov and gave him a smacking kiss on the cheek. Whether the dogs got on the scent from Voropayev's underpants or not, Zotov had saved me from disgrace for the moment.

Chapter Sixteen

Zotov's idea brought no results. Orudjev and Telichkin toiled away with the dogs for another three hours, giving them now Voropayev's, now Hotko's underwear, taken from his house here in Laureateville to sniff, but still no clues emerged.

'Zaloyev didn't get out of here by air, did he?' fumed Shatunov towards morning. 'He was walking about here on his feet, he didn't fly — dammit!'

'There's only one explanation,' said old Zotov, sitting by the fireplace puffing on his dead pipe. 'It wasn't Zaloyev. His glove was left here on purpose — '

'Oh, of course — it was the tundra spirits did it.' Shatunov smiled caustically. 'The tundra spirits cut Ryazanov's ears and balls off and dropped Zaloyev's glove in the yard!'

'If it was Zaloyev, his behaviour was illogical. Ryazanov was alone in the cottage and alone in the sauna. Any murderer prefers to do the job indoors, so that everything's nice and quiet and nobody sees. In that case we would only have found out about the murder at seven in the morning, when the driver came for Ryazanov. But instead of doing everything on the quiet, instead of getting Ryazanov's fine sheepskin coat and any other stuff, he kills him in the open yard, takes an old jacket and leaves a mitten on the scene of the crime for everyone to see. Like a challenge to a duel.'

'That's what drives me wild: he's making game of us, the son of a bitch!' said Shatunov. 'The only thing I don't get is, why?'

'He wants to show it's him, Zaloyev, doing the killing and not the tundra spirits,' said Hudya Benokan. 'That will help us quell the panic.'

'But why?' Shatunov repeated. 'Why bring it on himself?'

Hudya shrugged.

'Fame, however. There are such things as psychopaths. Hinkley, for example. Shot the president of America — for the publicity, the fame. Zaloyev could be one of those. Doesn't want to give the glory to our Nenets spirits, however.'

'However, however!' Shatunov mocked him. 'However, that break happened with your help. You're a know-all, aren't you? Hinkley!'

'It was I, however, who warned the camp commandant that a break like that was theoretically possible. Three weeks beforehand, however,' said Benokan, offended.

'Theoretically!' snarled Shatunov, since there was no getting round that: that was the fact of the matter, an ordinary police investigator — a Nenets at that — had warned the authorities at Camp no. RS-549, hand-picked KGB officers, that the high-tension cables could be used for an escape attempt and they hadn't taken a blind bit of notice.

'There is one point,' I said. 'We don't know why he's only killing high-ups. At the moment it looks like a string of coincidences — '

'Get on with it!' said Shatunov, irritably. 'Is this an idea, or are you talking for talking's sake?'

'It's an idea,' I said. 'Three got away. To get out of Salekhard they needed three sets of clothes and three sets of documents. One of the runaways had been an artist and icon-faker. It would have been child's play for him to take out the names of Voropayev, Hotko and Ryazanov and insert three different ones. Now they actually have three sets of clothes and documents. They've got no reason to hang about in Salekhard any longer. Even if this Zaloyev is crazy like Hinkley or a bloodthirsty maniac like Idonesyan, the other two must be trying to slip out of Salekhard on faked passports. And they'll be doing it now, today.'

'Good thinking,' said Shatunov. 'But the airport and railway are closed as it is, and winter roads are being patrolled.'

'There are other ways out of Salekhard in winter,' Kovrov remarked. 'The tundra's frozen solid now.'

'There are helicopters over the town,' said Colonel Sini. 'Not a mouse has got out of Salekhard tonight. Kovina's right, though: there's bugger-all reason for them to sit tight in town while we check every house. They've got to leg it out of here, and they'll try it today. The only thing is — how? You can't crawl across the tundra — '

'Huh!' sighed Shatunov. 'If I only had a couple of thousand soldiers — I'd turn Salekhard into a rat-trap! What can these villains do, though? Pinch a Sno-Cat? Don't make me laugh! We'd pick them off from the air like *kekliki*!'

'Or they you,' said Zotov suddenly.

We turned to him in amazement.

Zotov, sucking his pipe, enquired:

'Anybody know if there were any firearms in Ryazanov's cottage here?'

Shatunov screwed up his eyes, assimilating this new tack of Zotov's.

Meanwhile, Zotov continued:

'As my investigatress Anna Kovina found out in Yaku-Tur, Voropayev had a pistol with him when he went whoring with his Nenka[1] in the encampment. That pistol disappeared along with his clothes. The question is now: was Hotko carrying a weapon when they killed him?'

Of course I hadn't found out anything about Voropayev's pistol in Yaku-Tur — that was another of my slip ups — but Zotov was covering for me again. He certainly hadn't wasted his time going to Yaku-Tur! Any one of us knew there was a tacit instruction going back thirty years to Stalin's time that all leaders of tundra and taiga expeditions as well as all party chiefs, from regional committee secretaries upwards, were entitled to carry a personal firearm. In both cases it was in the event of workers rioting. Nobody has countermanded the order up to now, but today they only give pistols out to the KGB and even then on a strictly limited basis. So Voropayev, as the leader of an Arctic expedition, had a right to his pistol. Why the devil hadn't I thought of that in Yaku-Tur, fool that I was? I wondered if Dr Hotko had a pistol? If so, it was illegal.

'Hotko's pistol was removed by me from his apartment and

---

[1] *Nenka*: a female Nenets

handed in to the KGB,' said Hudya Benokan coolly. 'Which doesn't rule out the possibility of his having another one. Hotko's firearm was held illegally — even his wife didn't know about it. According to her, Hotko went out fishing with spinners, and a drill to bore holes in the ice. Three hours later the fishermen found him naked by the river. He hadn't started fishing — '

'Ryazanov had a rifle and a pistol,' said Shatunov. 'I went wild-reindeer hunting with him myself last year.'

'No such weapons were discovered during the search of the cottage,' said Hudya Benokan. 'No rifle, no pistol, no cartridges, no money.'

'Ye — e — s,' drawled Shatunov. 'That's spirits for you! That means the villains have now got a minimum of two pistols and a rifle. It could be quite a story arresting them! All right. If it's war, it's war — but where's the battle going to be? The sooner the better — '

'I think we can now give a material explanation for the mystical fact that only high-ups have been killed,' Zotov observed calmly. 'Spirits, spirits, the "revenge of the tundra"! All the criminals needed was arms and money. The top brass have got both.' Pleased with himself, Zotov got out his jar of smelly cream again.

But at that moment the echo of a deafening explosion rolled over Laureateville. We exchanged bewildered glances. Shatunov stretched out his hand to the phone, but it pre-empted him by ringing first. Shatunov picked it up. The longer he listened, the darker his face grew. Then he flung the phone from him and barked:

'The balloon's gone up! To your cars, philosophers! There's been an explosion at the Yamal-Gas trust.'

▌Chapter Seventeen

We raced along the empty streets of a darkened Salekhard towards the centre and the headquarters of Yamal-Gas trust, which stood on a street named after the Nenets national hero Vauli Piettomin. In the jolting Sno-Cat, no one spoke; we were amazed at the nerve of the criminals: three savage murders, and now an explosion in the main Yamal gas exploitation trust. The first thing that occurred to me was that they had blown up the trust to divert the KGB, police militia and duty helicopters to the town centre while they nipped out of Salekhard. Apparently everybody had the same idea: Shatunov leaned out of his Volga and started waving his cap at the helicopter which was following us:

'The tundra! The tundra, for fuck's sake!'

The pilot seemed to hear him; the helicopter banked and headed for the outskirts.

We rolled up to the Yamal-Gas building at about the same time as the ambulances and fire brigade. One look was enough to get the picture. The explosion had been at the entrance to the building not in the place itself. Fragments of a forty-ton Hurricane dumper truck were burning brightly in the roadway. Some little Nenets boys were dancing about and warming themselves by the fire, while the Hurricane's driver, a skinny middle-aged man, tried to chase them away with his fur hat.

The office workers inside, those who had nerved themselves to come to work that day, were scared to death. They peered timidly out of the shattered windows of the four-storey building and made no attempt even to catch the papers and drawings being carried out by the wind.

Naturally, we questioned the Hurricane driver on the spot. He began explaining that he was as innocent as a newborn

81

babe; he had popped into the trust offices on his way to work, just for a minute, about some meat coupons because his wife had given birth to twins a month ago and they weren't giving him any meat coupons for twins because, they said, they didn't need any meat, they were still on the breast — anyway, he went on describing how he had gone up to the first floor of the trust building to the accounts office: 'And then e — everything shook — look, I got cut on the cheek, maybe it was the petrol tank exploded — lucky I was empty. If I'd had a load on ...' and Shatunov was shouting down the phone to the airport chief: 'All aircraft, scramble! I don't need permission from the Moscow Aviation Authority, I'm the KGB and I order you to get those planes up! Or would you rather take the escapers' place in camp?' At that very moment there came a second blast.

Ten blocks away, by the main entrance to the headquarters of another trust, Northern Pipelaying, the director's official personal car had been blown up. The explosion was rather less severe than the first: only the ground-floor windows of the building had been blown out. Nevertheless, in the car boot there had been six crates of oranges and one of Heineken lager which the trust's director had obtained from the senior management special distribution warehouse. The oranges and aluminium cans of beer lay strewn all over the dark, snow-covered road.

'The bastards have bribed somebody to plant explosives, to keep us busy while they slip out of town,' perceived Colonel Sini belatedly as they got out of the car in front of Northern Pipelaying.

'They got hold of money from the victims — '

'Yes,' pronounced Major Shatunov pensively, gazing at the remains of the Volga, 'but this isn't fun and games, cutting off peoples' dicks. This is sabotage. And it's got a political smell about it.' He turned to me:

'That escaper Tolmachov's a political?

I nodded.

▌ Chapter Eighteen

After the two explosions, Salekhard was numbed.

People waited, holding their breath, for the next act of sabotage. Had there been air-raid shelters in the town, I believe the entire population would have camped out in them. In permafrost, though, you can't even dig a grave, never mind a bomb shelter, so people stayed at home with their doors and windows barricaded, waiting for the next explosion or the next murder. The radio called on the population to keep calm, but nobody listened to the radio. A lot of people reckoned the next blast would be at the power station or the waterworks, and started laying in supplies of water and retrieving candles and old primus stoves from store cupbards.

Meanwhile, we sat by telephones and radios in the local KGB building waiting for a message from the helicopter pilots telling us where the escapers were trying to break the militia cordon or what else they might have been getting up to in town.

But all was quiet.

After an hour of this, the nerves (and stomachs) of the workers in the hostels could hold out no longer. Workers and vagrants alike had been sitting starving since morning; they were afraid to venture out into the street to the diner. By about ten in the morning they had drunk up all their stocks of liquor on an empty stomach. There's never any food in the rooms of working mens hostels, but half-empty bottles of vodka and liquor can always be found. Now emboldened by liquor, with hunting rifles in hand, vagrants and workers began to dribble out singly and in groups towards the Wave diner-restaurant. (By day the place is open from seven onwards as a working men's café; after seven in the evening, it's a restaurant, that is the prices go up and vodka is sold.)

The Wave was shut, of course: none of the cooks had come out to work. The workers, about sixty in number, smashed the lock off the café door, poured in and set up a self-service system starting, of course, with the restaurant's stocks of vodka.

One hour later the whole drunken crowd of them, fearless in the face of tundra spirits or the devil himself, laid siege to the small single storey local KGB post. They smashed the panes in the barred windows and tried to unhinge the entrance doors, bawling:

'Give us a train! Shatunov, give us a train, you bastard! An express! To Moscow! Otherwise we'll rip your balls off!' Someone let fly with a sporting rifle at the window of Shatunov's office.

We lay on the floor and shoved the heavy steel security safes over to the window with our feet; Shatunov was shouting down the telephone to the chief of the town fire brigade:

'All fire engines over here! We'll turn the hoses on these pricks!'

A few minutes later, amid the roar of the crowd, the obscenities, the tinkle of broken glass and rifle shots, we heard the saving howl of the fire engines and the rumble of the three armoured personnel-carriers from the local military garrison. In another couple of minutes it was possible to look out of the shattered windows: the mob had dispersed, fleeing from the water lashing at them in powerful jets from the water cannon. Those who lingered were knocked off their feet and couldn't run away — at forty below, the water froze instantly and converted their clothing into icy armour, while their wet fur or felt boots froze them to the roadway.

'That's more like it!' Shatunov grated through his teeth as he rose to his feet brushing off the dust and glass splinters. 'This isn't fucking Poland!'

Through the window he shouted an order to the soldiers who were busy hauling the frozen workmen off to the Black Maria.

'Leave them! Let them lie on the ice. They'll sober up fast enough, fuck them. Then they'll show a bit of respect for

84

Soviet authority!'

He immediately seized the phone and dialled the airport chief's number: 'Agapov! Whatever happens in the town, even if — I don't know — even if they blow up the party committee, keep all aircraft flying! Got me? Not a mouse to creep out of town! What? Out of fuel? Nothing to do with me — get it from the emergency reserves.'

While radio messages about these events had been sent to Tyumen and Moscow and the first response received from Bogomyatov, secretary of the Tyumen Province party, we swept out the KGB offices and boarded up the smashed panes with plywood and display placards saying 'KGB — SHIELD AND SWORD OF SOVIET POWER'. Only then, an hour later, did Shatunov allow the soldiers and ambulancemen to pick up the frozen people from the road.

There now was no point in taking them off to the remand cell at military headquarters or to prison. They had been fatally frostbitten and were taken straight to the hospital.

Chapter Nineteen

Express Telegram
URGENT by Government Phototelegraph
Moscow, Kremlin, Central Committee CPSU

FORCES OF THE SALEKHARD KGB, POLICE MILITIA
AND MILITARY GARRISON UNABLE TO STEM
DISORDERS AND PREVENT POSSIBLE ANTI-RUSSIAN
ACTIONS BY NENETS POPULATION. TO GUARANTEE
SECURITY OF OFFICIAL OPENING OF
SIBERIA–WESTERN EUROPE GAS PIPELINE THE GOC
SIBERIAN MILITARY DISTRICT, COLONEL POPOV,
HAS, AT MY REQUEST, ASKED THE SOVIET ARMY
GENERAL STAFF TO PERMIT HIM TO TRANSFER
THE OCTOBER REVOLUTION PARATROOP DIVISION
TO SALEKHARD.

I REQUEST CO-OPERATION IN SECURING
IMMEDIATE PERMISSION OF GENERAL STAFF FOR
THIS OPERATION.

AT THE SAME TIME I CONSIDER IT APPROPRIATE
TO RAISE THE QUESTION OF POSTPONEMENT OF
OFFICIAL CEREMONY IN URENGOI OF
SIBERIA–WESTERN EUROPE PIPELINE.

V. Bogomyatov
First Secretary Tyumen Province Committee Communist
Party
Candidate-Member of Central Committee CPSU

Tyumen, 12 December 1983
12.30 hrs local time

Part Two
A Trap in Udmurtia

Chapter One

Central Committee of the Communist Party of the Soviet
Union
Member of the Politburo Central Committee CPSU,
Konstantin Ustinovich CHERNENKO

urgent
secret
special delivery

To Minister of Defence USSR, Marshal USTINOV: one
copy

To President of KGB USSR, Army General CHEBRIKOV:
one copy

I am forwarding to you a copy of the letter from First Secretary Tyumen Province committee, Comrade Bogomyatov. I support his request regarding the urgent transfer of forces to the Yamal–Nenets district. Order must be restored in Salekhard within twenty-four hours. There can be no talk of postponing the opening of the pipeline.

I request the KGB to take effective measures to prevent the leakage of any information to the West about disturbances in the Arctic.

Further details at the meeting with Comrade Andropov.

K. Chernenko

12 December 1983
9.00 hrs Moscow time.

The clock on the Kremlin's Spassky Tower showed nine-thirty-five. The black bulletproof Chaika with its government escort softly rolled out from the clocktower gates and cut across a snow-covered Red Square. A heavy wet snow was falling. It was the time of the thaw in Moscow, just before the Christmas frosts.

Konstantin Ustinovich Chernenko always felt lousy in damp weather like this; with his emphysema, it was hard enough to breathe in dry weather — only the upper half of his lungs took in any air — but in this ... And he was fed up to the teeth with this morning ritual: for three months now he'd been going to the Kremlin hospital every day for a conference with the dying Andropov. A man who had been head of the KGB for twenty years and with a stroke of the pen or a wave of the hand had consigned many a hundred to the next world at home and abroad, this man refused to believe in the inevitable reality of his own imminent death. Paralysed, his face grey and pinched, there he lay on the second floor of the Kremlin hospital looking down on Moscow with his washed-out eyes; and every morning, straight after the medical procedures, he would hold meetings of the Politburo or a conference with the state planning department, or with Gromyko or other ministers. In fucking charge! He'd even ordered the annual session of the USSR Supreme Soviet to take place on 28 December, the last day of the working year — hoping, no doubt, he would be up on the rostrum making his speech. Fat chance you getting up anywhere, arsehole! Communists don't believe in God — but there is one now! You brought two heart attacks on Brezhnev and sent him to his grave, but you're in a cot yourself not six months after!

Chernenko's limousine drove on down the central restricted lane of Gorky Street and turned off into Granovsky Street, closed to public traffic, where the Kremlin hospital stands.

A long line of government limousines and black Volgas were parked near the hospital. Of course they're all here, thought Chernenko, even though I'm twenty minutes early myself. There's Ustinov's car, Gromyko's; closest of all to the hospital entrance as the limousine belonging to Andropov's favourite, that upstart Gorbachev. Got here first, the son of a bitch! Maybe he camps out here at night?

The bodyguard opened the door and assisted Chernenko to

get out of the car. He conducted him by the elbow through a corridor of guards and up to the hospital door.

The warm vestibule was packed out with security men. Somebody took Chernenko's coat with the astrakhan collar and his fur hat. Chernenko feebly wriggled his shoulders, thinking to take a deeper breath at last, and at once caught a faint whiff of tobacco. Sods, some security man had been smoking again before his arrival! But finding out who . . .

Coughing, Chernenko surveyed the respectful poker-faces of the escort, shook his head reproachfully and passed on into the lift, taking small steps.

On the second floor, in a spacious hall decked out with potted palms and a Persian carpet on the floor, they were all sitting: Ustinov; Gromyko; the new KGB chief, Chebrikov; the new MVD minister, Fedorchuk; Tikhonov, President of the Council of Ministers — and Gorbachev, sufficiently youthful-looking to be out of place here. While waiting for the meeting to begin, they had not been wasting time: next to each stood a doctor — or even two. They were measuring Ustinov and Tikhonov's blood pressure, and Gromyko was having his head massaged. Fedorchuk was swallowing some tablets, and the octogenarian ancients, Politburo members Ponomaryov and Kuznetsov, were simply asleep. Next to these portly patriarchs of the Kremlin power structure (Kuznetsov had been in the Politburo back in Stalin's time, in 1952) the fifty-year-old Mikhail Gorbachev looked a mere stripling. He was the only one without a doctor. Bent over a thick notepad, he was writing something quickly and underlining it with sharp strokes. 'He's playing Lenin, the little shit,' thought Chernenko wearily. He gazed once more at the whole Kremlin senate and shook his head in despair: bugger me, the geriatric ward!

'Morning, all.' His bodyguard helped him to subside into an armchair between Ustinov and Chebrikov. Two doctors with pronounced Jewish features hastened over to him. One was holding the blood pressure apparatus; the other simply gently took him by the wrist ready to take his pulse.

'Fuck off!' Chernenko withdrew his arm.

'We have to check pulse and blood pressure, Konstantin Ustinovich,' the doctor said softly, as if to a naughty child.

'If you have to, check your own,' said Chernenko, gasping.

'Konstantin Ustinovich!' said the doctor reproachfully.

'Oh, all right. Here — ' Chernenko gave him his arm. 'Do they check Reagan every morning as well — damn and blast him? We're the same bloody age, and they shot that Hollywood dog point-blank, punctured his lung — he laughs it off, the bugger! He goes out horse-riding, the bastard — '

'He doesn't smoke and you shouldn't smoke, Konstantin Ustinovich. Categorically,' said the doctor. 'And you're smoking on the quiet, I can tell by your breathing. With your emphysema . . .'

Chernenko didn't bother to listen to the tedious medical rigmarole. He turned to Ustinov.

'You got my *tsedulya*[1] about the Nentsi?' Ustinov nodded. 'I've already given the order — to GHQ.'

Chernenko turned his head to Cherbrikov, at the same time noticing that Gorbachev was still scribbling away on his pad.

'Every measure will be taken at our end,' Chebrikov hastened to say. 'There's only one small point, Konstantin Ustinovich. Actually, I wanted to ask your opinion — '

'Well?'

'An hour before your order banning the entry of foreigners into Siberia, an American called Siegfried Shertz took a flight for Urengoi. You know him — '

'Who is he?' asked Ustinov.

Chebrikov quickly put Marshal Ustinov in the picture.

'He's the middleman between our External Trade Agency and the West European banks. A broker, in other words. Five years ago he helped us to get Western loans for the building of the pipeline. Not for nothing, of course: Leonid Ilyic gave him two and a half per cent commission on the deal . . .'

Chernenko knew Siegfried Shertz. This Shertz was a crafty animal who had conned Brezhnev into giving him two and a half per cent while the pipeline was still at the talking stage. It seemed Brezhnev's son, Yuri, deputy Minister for external trade, had introduced Shertz to Brezhnev and recommended

---

[1] *Tsedulya* = note (Ukrainian)

him as an outstanding broker: he knew Russian perfectly, had even been born in Russia to a family of Volga Germans before leaving the USSR as a boy. He was a German by blood and an American businessman to boot — nobody could be better as an intermediary between the USSR and the German banks. Later on, when the West German and French banks agreed to finance the pipeline construction, Brezhnev lit up and rubbed his hands: eighteen billion dollars they're giving — that's fucking fantastic! Maybe not all at once, never mind. We'll build the pipeline into Europe at their expense, and as soon as the French, Dutch or Germans start raising hell we'll just up and turn off the tap. They'll be left without gas, and all their industries will grind to a halt! Or we could raise the price, blackmail —'

'Right!' said Gorbachev loudly all of a sudden to the whole assembly, as he placed a fat full stop on his notepad. 'The question of the Salekhard disturbances has several aspects. First: on the seventeenth of December, when the pipeline completion protocol is due to be signed, the European banks must pay us the second half of the credit, that is nine billion dollars.' Here he turned to Tikhonov, 'Right?'

Tikhonov nodded.

'Recently there have been complications in getting these credits,' continued Gorbachev, glancing at his pad. 'In particular, due to the KGB allowing rumours to filter out to the West that political prisoners were being used on the construction work. Comrade Andropov did not punish anyone at that time; you know very well he covers up for the security organs. But if the West find out about the Salekhard disturbances now, you need have no doubt the Western newspapers will blow it up into hell knows what. Especially if they find out that troops have been sent in.

'You need have no doubts about the reaction of the European banks, either — they'll latch onto any excuse not to pay us the money. And that's not all!' Gorbachev raised an admonitory hand. 'The second aspect of the matter. I recall that the previous leadership had plans to build the pipeline into Europe with French and German money and then hold economic control over half Europe. But the French and Germans aren't idiots either. They financed pipelines from Algeria and Norway at the same time, and now it's not clear who's blackmailing whom. If we don't give them Siberian gas today, they'll go over to Algerian tomorrow and Norwegian the day after. And they'll be able to dictate our gas prices. Right?' He turned again to Tikhonov.

Tikhonov nodded once more.

'And finally, the third aspect. As you well know, comrade Andropov wishes to announce the completion of the gas pipe-line ahead of schedule to the Supreme Soviet. I therefore suggest that the Army General Staff should not only send the paratroop division to the Arctic but assume control of the entire Salekhard situation.'

Chernenko looked at Gromyko, Ustinov, Tikhonov and the other members of the Kremlin old guard. Nothing could be read in those faces: half-listening, half-dozing, but he well knew what lay behind the heavy, wrinkled features: fear. If Gorbachev took Andropov's place tomorrow, he'd swamp everybody with his businesslike calculations and sling the whole geriatric ward off the Politburo and onto their pensions.

And, more important, he's managed to reach the very top of the Kremlin power-structure in such a short time, the bastard. In a few years he has got himself to the top, when Chernenko spent his whole life climbing up to the same position. All because he exploited the fact that we are old and ailing, son of a bitch. He sat down there in the Stavropol regional party committee like any ordinary provincial secretary and showed no particular talent for anything. The collective farms in his region were in just as much of a mess as in the rest of the country — the harvest, when it exists, rots in the fields because the farm workers couldn't give a shit about it — they'd rather try to grow a few more tomatoes on their private plots to sell on the black market. . . . Gorbachev would never have risen from the position of a party pawn to the Politburo, if the leadership hadn't been suffering in their old age from all sorts of geriatric ailments, and hadn't gone to recuperate in the Stavropol region, where the main resorts — Mineralniye Vody (Mineral Waters), Kislovodsk (Sour Waters), Zhelezovodsk (Iron Waters), Yessentuki

— are located. It is the place for the government elite's best sanatoria and 'Kremlin' dachas. So it stands to reason that Gorbachev in the role of the hospitable host often met the visiting party bosses there, who came to convalesce or simply on vacation. He not only flooded their dachas and sanatoriums with the best food products, the freshest fruit and vegetables, but around the sanatoriums he established an entire area of exemplary collective farms which supplied them with milk, meat, apples, grapes, crab, fish. . . . These collective farms were provided with much more fertilizer than any of the others. They had the best equipment and the best agronomists in order to guarantee, as it were, sustenance for the Kremlin dachas and sanatoriums. But the second aim of this cunning Gorbachev was quite another story: when Grishin, Gromyko, Ustinov et al walked in the countryside around their dachas — or at least drove through it on their way from the airport — they would see what an outstanding leader Gorbachev was. And they took the bait! Even he himself, Chernenko, voted in the Politburo for the nomination of Gorbachev as the Minister of Agriculture. Who could have known then that Andropov and Gromyko were moving their pawn into a controlling position in the Politburo. . . . And now foreign journalists are sniffing all around Moscow like search-dogs for clues as to who is the most likely heir to Andropov's power. Chernenko, Romanov, Grishin or Gorbachev? Fuck him! For now, anyway, there is a majority in the Politburo from the old school, so that bald Gorbachev with the devil's mark on his skull can't get any further. We are not such fools as to not realise that any young General Secretary will drive us old men out.

'Apart from the fact that the army must take the situation in Salekhard under its control,' continued Mikhail Gorbachev to the members of the Politburo and Government while they were waiting for Andropov to appear in the lobby of the hospital. 'Apart from that, the KGB must ensure 100% secrecy of all events taking place in the Yamal–Nenets region. And having put a decisive end to the disturbances we must immediately open the pipeline. This opening must be celebrated by the whole country as proof of the triumph of our system . . .'

Chernenko smiled: the son of a bitch had said nothing new. All that had to be done was done already, and orders already issued. Without all these speeches and paragraphs, of course: quietly, without fuss.

Gorbachev clearly expected some discussion of his points, but Chernenko turned to Chebrikov and asked quietly:

'Well, what about Siegfried Shertz?'

'He was supposed to be going to the pipeline opening in Urengoi with the gas industry minister, Dynkov,' said Chebrikov. 'But Dynkov got the flu yesterday, so Shertz flew off on his own.'

'Did Dynkov get in touch with you about his health?' Gorbachev asked the doctors.

'No,' answered one of the medical men.

'I see!' Gorbachev smiled ironically. 'He's got flu like I've got labour pains. He's just scared to leave Moscow in case he loses his ministerial portfolio. For some reason everybody's convinced that comrade Andropov is about to leave us at any moment and government personnel will change straight away. Meanwhile, the doctors couldn't be more optimistic, isn't that right?'

'Absolutely! Absolutely!' The senior Kremlin hospital consultant hastened to his support. 'The haemoglobin levels in comrade Andropov's blood have returned to normal ...'

You're a crafty one, Gorbachev — my, but you're crafty! thought Chernenko. Just giving us the hint that we'll all keep our places if you take Andropov's place. Just you wait, though, we're a little bit craftier than you.

Paying no heed to the consultant's report on Andropov's state of health, he asked Chebrikov:

'Are there any foreigners up there in Urengoi, generally speaking?'

'Luckily, no', came the reply. 'There were some Frenchmen and Germans installing the computers and electronics at the compressor station, but they finished about a week ago. They'll be skiing in Switzerland now. There's just this Siegfried Shertz on his way there now. Do you want the aircraft returned to Moscow, or should he be put down somewhere in the Urals? If he's in Moscow, he'll mess about trying to get on another flight, I think. In the Urals, on the other hand ...'

'Yes, put him down in the Urals,' agreed Chernenko.

'Very good, Konstantin Ustinovich.' Chebrikov rose hurriedly and walked over to the lift.

'And as for ...' Chernenko chewed his lip, savouring the spoke he was about to put in Gorbachev's wheel, 'comrade Andropov's health — well, we all have faith in our doctors. Nevertheless, they'll hardly permit Yuri Vladimirovich to fly to Urengoi for the pipeline opening. Or me either — an old man, emphysema, it's bloody cold up there as well. So all things considered — why don't you go to Urengoi as the head of the government delegation, eh?' And Chernenko, for the very first time looked Gorbachev directly in the eye. His gaze was pure, gentle and benign. 'You are the youngest of us.'

Gorbachev got the point all right, but smiled as if nothing was out of the way.

'Of course I'll go. If comrade Andropov sends me.'

He suddenly rose, looking down the length of the corridor.

There the doctors were carefully wheeling a bed with a drip-feed along the parquet. On the bed, under a sheet, lay Andropov.

Gorbachev spoke quickly and softly:

'Comrades, please rise. Here is Yuri Vladimirovich.'

Chapter Two

'NO SMOKING! FASTEN YOUR SEATBELTS!' flashed the sign. Siegfried Shertz glanced out of his window, and at that very instant his stomach became aware that the plane was descending sharply. What the hell! They were still three hours' flying time from Tyumen, surely.

Beyond the glass, the sun was dazzling; below the aircraft lay Russia, white and snowbound with an occasional bare Ural peak and a frosty grey stubble of taiga. Siegfried was in no mood to appreciate the scenery. What were these blasted Russians up to? Maybe some drunken mechanic had made an error, or maybe the fuel tank had depressurized and they were about to blow up! Or the navigation systems had failed, like in that Korean airliner? Or all the pilots were drunk. He'd seen the captain at the airport: red nose, an obvious boozer — and now he was just diving the aircraft into the deck!

Siegfried knew he had aerophobia and was probably panicking over nothing; on the other hand, why were they going down so suddenly? Why hadn't there been an announcement? Why didn't that bitch of a stewardess come when he called? Two years before, thank God, the Soviet classless society had decided to introduce a first and second class. Not on Siegfried's account, of course; it was for their own top men, so they wouldn't have to fly in the same cabin as their people. Brezhnev's son, Yuri, used to laugh:

'We are the servants of the people, and servants should travel separately from their masters!'

Never mind first or second class, insolence was classless here. He'd been pressing the button for the stewardess for three minutes — and no stewardess. And if she wouldn't appear for the only first-class passenger on board that meant she hadn't time for passengers, the flyers were drunk! Heavens, do something! Why the hell had he gone on alone when his Moscow secretary-lover Tanya and the minister, Dynkov, went down with flu? Wasn't the flu a warning to him not to fly? Why did he have this stupid habit of always trying to outwit fate? That summer he'd gone into the Bermuda Triangle, even though practically all the yachtsmen of Palm Beach had warned him about the storm-force winds and the strength of the Gulf Stream in that region — but he'd gone. Naturally, he had had to demonstrate his audacity to his Siberian visitors, Bogomyatov, Salakhov and Ryazanov. He had brought them from Moscow to Florida at his own expense and organized a cruise for them round the Caribbean aboard his yacht, Dreamboat. Of course, thirty miles off the Bahamas his engine had started smoking and the navigational computer had gone wrong. At least then something had depended on him; he had been able to fight for life himself, and had brought Dreamboat to port — on one engine. But what could be done here? What the hell was the opening of the gas pipeline to him and all the millions he would get out of the 'project of the century' if now, at this very moment, they were falling, falling, falling in the middle of Russia, in the taiga, the Siberian snows.

'Attention, all passengers! Owing to weather conditions in Siberia, Tyumen Airport is closed. Our aircraft has landed in Izhevsk, the capital of the Udmurt Autonomous Republic. The temperature outside the aircraft is minus twenty-four degrees Celsius. Passengers are requested to remain in their places until the aircraft has stopped. Additional flight information will be announced by radio in the airport terminal building.'

So that was it; Siegfried breathed again. Tyumen was closed, so they'd landed in Izhevsk — wherever that was. Still, they could have said, dammit, they could have said earlier! These Russians always made such a botch of everything. It wasn't a country, it was a sort of gigantic safari: nobody gave a damn for anything, the people were so resentful that if you got on a bus or a tube wearing a sheepskin coat they devoured you with their eyes and looked ready to smash your face in. To them a sheepskin coat was a mark of class distinction: it meant you were either a 'lousy intellectual' or a 'black marketeer asking for it' — and that was in Moscow. Imagine what went on here in, what did she say? Udmurtia. Ah, there she was, the stewardess, fat-assed bitch! Turned up at last, with a miserable look on her face as well.

'What's the matter?'

Well, really! He'd called her up there, in the air, and she appeared when they were already rolling along the runway, and now a bad-tempered 'What's the matter?'

'How long will we be stuck here?' he asked in Russian. He had been born into a family of Volga Germans and had been eight years old before his parents had managed to get out of the USSR. With the usual German sense of thrift they had not allowed him to forget his Russian, and they had been right: in the years of détente, his translation firm — at that time very small made its first millions. Now, in perfect Russian, he asked this stewardess: 'Is Tyumen likely to be closed for long?'

'It'll be announced over there.' The stewardess, fat-assed insolence and all, nodded outside the plane and walked off. Bitch! If his Russian had contained the merest hint of a foreign accent, she would have been more polite; Russian women adore foreigners — he himself had made use of that fact more than once — but he wasn't going to mangle his beautiful Russian on account of that idiot.

'Passengers are requested to leave the aircraft. Do not forget your personal belongings,' said a man's voice over the radio. Immediately the searing frost and powdery needles of snow wafted in at the open door of the plane.

Siegfried donned his sheepskin, tied his fur hat on securely and settled his scarf around his throat. He was a seasoned traveller on Aeroflot; in his years of working with the Russians he'd done plenty of flying round the USSR. If Siberia is closed off because of the weather, he thought, I can imagine the number of passengers who've dropped out of the skies on Izhevsk — they'd be conducted across the bone-hard airfield on foot; there'd be no room to breathe in the airport buildings, there'd be children yelling, people sleeping on sacks and suitcases and some drunk puking up continuously in the toilet. No, one should never fly on Aeroflot international flights on one's own — not without Dynkov, Bogomyatov or some other

100

member of the government.

'Mr Siegfried Shertz?' a voice spoke in English as soon as he stepped off the gangway.

'Yes,' he replied in astonishment to a rather colourless thirty-year-old blonde in a dark grey provincial overcoat and felt boots.

'I'm your interpreter from Intourist, Vera Kolesova. Please — she indicated a black Volga standing by the gangway.

'I didn't request any interpreter.'

'I know. But as a foreign tourist first class you are entitled to an interpreter and special service in the event of forced landing. After you,' she inclined her head towards the car again.

Siegfried smiled to himself: it looked as if the KGB worked to a standard pattern throughout the USSR. They'd also palmed Tanya off on him in Moscow as an interpreter — and he the boss of the largest translation firm in the world, translating tons of technical documents from scores of languages into Russian and vice versa! Still, you had to admire the KGB's efficiency — even when an aircraft had to put down totally unexpectedly they kept their eye on you. If only their agriculture worked like the KGB!

Already eyeing this Vera Kolesova as his private property (Mm, yes, definitely not Brooke Shields — still, what do you expect in Udmurtia?) Siegfried smiled wryly as he got into the car.

'Does your Intourist happen to know how long Tyumen is going to be closed?'

'Yes,' replied Kolesova, getting into the front seat next to the driver. 'Three days, according to the forecast. There are blizzards all over Tyumen Province.'

Siegfried was aghast: these Siberian blizzards sometimes lasted a week. What about the pipeline opening in that case?

'What if I get a train? How long is it in the train from here to Tyumen?' he asked, as he watched the Volga come up to the freight compartment where men were offloading the passengers' baggage.

'Three days just the same,' replied Kolesova, 'but if the snowstorm intensifies the train could get stuck as well.'

No thanks; the prospect of being stuck in a train under a

101

Siberian snowdrift was not an attractive one. Fuck that. Of course Dynkov and Tanya's flu had been a sign to him to stay put. Now it was a case of sitting for three days in this crappy Izhevsk, and the best he could hope for in the way of amusement was this 'interpreter'. Naturally, she didn't have syphilis — you could bank absolutely on the KGB for that — but her English was terrible and she had two gold crowns in her mouth. Still, if she was undressed — hell knows, in Russia you could sometimes come across an Aphrodite in tarpaulin boots and quilted jacket with a metal crown on her front teeth!

Siegfried glimpsed his suitcase in the loaders' hands and pointed it out to the driver.

One minute later, the Volga was driving out of the airport past the one-storey lounge which bore an enormous portrait of Lenin on the pediment. Lenin's face was somewhat moon-shaped in this portrait, and Siegfried recalled that in every Soviet town he had been in Lenin looked different: in Georgia, he had looked like a Georgian; in Salekhard, like a Nenets; in Tashkent, he had resembled an Uzbek. Here, it would seem, moon-faced Udmurts resided. So it would have been better if the KGB had saddled him with some Udmurt girl instead of this Kolesova; it would have been a bit exotic, at least. Maybe I'll put in an order, he thought, grinning, recalling one of his earliest adventures long ago in Salekhard . . .

The Volga skirted the airport buildings and shot out onto the main road, hemmed in by huge snowdrifts. Above the drifts towered the supports of stereotype posters: exhortations to raise productivity and improve labour discipline. It was hard to imagine, thought Siegfried, why in a country plastered with slogans like this from Leningrad to Vladivostok general enthusiasm for work was not in evidence; what did prevail was a general obsession with sex and alcohol. Even Siegfried had become infected with it, whether he liked it or not. The Russians just couldn't understand business without vodka and women. Even when Brezhnev's son Yuri, deputy Minister for External Trade, had brought Siegfried out to the dacha to see his Dad, and said: 'Father, here's the man we've been looking for. He was born here, knows Russian, German and English, and he's an American citizen. Talented businessman, boss of the Globus translation firm. Ideal candidate for middleman between us and the European banks in getting a loan to construct the gas pipeline' — that very evening they had got as drunk as skunks, and Brezhnev had said, with alcoholic generosity: 'If you can screw a loan out of the European banks you're on two per cent commission.' 'Two and a half, Leonid Ilyich,' Siegfried had said cautiously. 'Up you! Two and a half!'

The car entered Izhevsk, a snowbound provincial city of one- and two-storey houses with peeling paintwork.

'Where are we going?' Siegfried enquired of his 'interpreter'.

'The Izhevsk Hotel,' she said.

Meanwhile at Izhevsk airport, twenty minutes after Siegfried Shertz had departed, a radio announcement rang out.

'Passengers for flight Moscow–Tyumen–Urengoi, please board the aircraft.'

All the passengers, blaspheming but overjoyed, returned to the aircraft. All, that is, except for the sole first-class passenger, the middleman between the West European banks and Soviet Extrade, Mr Siegfried Shertz.

The black Volga containing Mr Shertz drew to a halt before the entrance of the Izhevsk Hotel.

Chapter Three

KGB General Chebrikov's instructions to entertain Mr Sieg-fried Shertz in Izhevsk for three days placed Colonel Khanov, chief of the Udmurt Autonomous Republic KGB, in an impossible situation. 'He's got to be entertained so that he forgets about Urengoi for three days and nights. Think of something in the Intourist line, and make it snappy — the plane's landing in Izhevsk in thirty minutes. Report on action taken in two hours from now.'

Khanov didn't waste time explaining to Chebrikov that there was no Intourist in Izhevsk, a city closed to foreigners. Orders are orders. They couldn't very well take him to the Udmurt theatre — even the local populace didn't go to that! No excursions round the Izhevsk motorcycle factory, either: he would notice that the nationally famous IZH motorbikes were only a sideline of the giant tank factory.

Khanov said, 'Very good, sir,' to General Chebrikov and replaced the red receiver, the direct departmental link with Moscow. He at once picked up the local phone and dialled the foreign languages department of the teacher-training institute. He couldn't delegate an order from the KGB President; he would deal with this Shertz himself, personally. 'Khanov speaking,' he said, aware of the effect of his name on Udmurt citizens. 'Vera Kolesova, urgent!'

Eight years ago, when Kolesova had been a student at the teacher-training institute, she had angrily condemned 'certain students' who 'had sunk to the level of reading scum like Solzhenitsyn and Orwell behind closed doors.' Next morning in Khanov's office, Vera Kolesova had named those students; Khanov had encouraged her political vigilance and included her in the Udmurt youth delegation which travelled in the 'friendship train' around the fraternal countries of Eastern Europe. At this point, Kolesova had realized the advantages that a close working relationship with Colonel Khanov might bring. She became his main informer in the institute, and in consequence was taken on as a post graduate after completing her course. And she in turn repaid Khanov: now not just with official denunciations but with sexual favours. For which she had remained on the staff as a teacher and was on the point of becoming assistant professor.

'Hello!' came Kolesova's breathless voice on the line.

'Go outside. I'll pick you up shortly.'

'But I've got a lecture!' Kolesova was indignant, thinking Khanov was having one of his periodic lustful fits. That did happen with him; sometimes he just couldn't wait.

That wasn't the way of it now, though.

'No time to talk — this is business! Out you come!' he said.

A few minutes later, he was briefing Kolesova before her trip to the airport. 'It's an order from Moscow, you realize? The president of the KGB in person.'

'I won't sleep with a German,' announced Kolesova emphatically. 'I'm warning you straight away: both my grandfathers were killed in the war. So I can be a guide, but I'm not going to sleep with this German.'

'Hold on, what German? He's an American.'

'If he's called Shertz *and* Siegfried, he's a German. What's written in his passport doesn't interest me. I'm not sleeping with him.'

Khanov scratched his head, perplexed. As a rule, Kolesova's strong political principles appealed to him, but this time ...

'All right,' he said. 'Take him round the town, show him the centre then to the hotel — '

'And then?' Kolesova broke in with a sneer. 'Well, now we're at the hotel, how am I going to entertain him? I repeat: I won't sleep with him!'

Khanov regarded unflappability as the main feature of his character. Therefore, fingering his black, slightly curled moustache, he carried on speaking in the same calmly measured tones:

'In the hotel, in the restaurant you will introduce him to me.

105

As if by chance. Say I'm the director of the nature reserve in Zataika.'

Kolesova started in astonishment. Zataika was 120 kilometres from Izhevsk, in a nature reserve deep in the forest. It was one of the dachas belonging to the USSR Council of Ministers, and was famous for its elk-hunting and other legal and clandestine pleasures. Although nobody visited the dacha except Moscow ministers and Khanov himself, vague rumours circulated in Izhevsk about incredible orgies taking place there. Kolesova was therefore sufficiently intrigued to ask:

'Are you taking him to Zataika?'

'If he agrees to go,' responded Khanov. And thought: And if he doesn't agree, I can't really think what to do with him. Chebrikov is expecting my report in two hours' time . . .

Chapter Four

For two hours now Khanov and Kolesova had been driving him to somewhere in the back of beyond, deep into the snow-bound taiga. Siegfried, enveloped in his sheepskin, was half-dozing in the back of the car; the farther they travelled, the less he understood why all of a sudden the KGB should have turned so obligingly protective — an interpreter, a nature reserve, an elk-hunt! Of course, given the Russian mania for secrecy (which extended even to such things as the workings of photocopiers and the prices on the New York stock exchange) it was quite possible that this Khanov would regard an Udmurt toilet-paper factory as a strategic supersecret if its smoke could be seen from his hotel window. Khanov and Kolesova were taking him farther and farther away from Izhevsk and deeper and deeper into the reserve; and tomorrow they'd be drawing a bead on an aurochs or an elk ... Surely it couldn't be because Siegfried — heaven forbid! — might work out from the colour of the smoke what chemical poison they made at the factory along with the toilet paper?

That Kolesova was no part of Intourist service and Khanov was no nature reserve director Siegfried had realized from the first. One look at the military carriage of the moon-faced Udmurt, his jacket, all buttons fastened, like a uniform, his grey tie tight up against the collar of his white nylon shirt, his black typical-army shoes, and there could be no mistake: A Gee Bee — and no lower than a major, that was for sure.

But it was just because Siegfried recognized Khanov as a KGB officer that he had agreed almost without hesitation to go elk-hunting with him at Zataika. He had long ago got used to falling in with the KGB's little whims, having realized once and for all that what was convenient to them was convenient and advantageous to him as well. Did he regret having accepted Tanya as so-called interpreter six years ago? Even though it had been obvious from the start that she was an interpreter the way he was a soloist at the Bolshoi Theatre — and pointless, anyway, for someone who spoke fluent and literate Russian to have an interpreter at all. But it had been more convenient for *them* to follow his every move in Moscow and the Black Sea resorts through Tanya's eyes, and through her hands to fix the timetable of his working day. So what? Tanya had become not only his unpaid secretary but his beautiful unpaid lover. And what a lover! What a pity rotten old Moscow kept suffering from epidemics of Hong Kong, Afghan, hell-knows-what kind of flu! Otherwise Tanya would be with him on this elk-hunt . . .

Siegfried stirred, opened his eyes and looked out of the window.

'Nearly there,' said Kolesova from the front seat, noting that their guest had woken up.

'Beautiful, isn't it?'

It certainly was beautiful. Along the roadside the luxuriant, branching taiga was covered in powdery snow; on the left, a frozen brook sparkled in the sunshine, the snow just as pure; a bright ruddy sun fled through the gaps between the taiga pine trees as they tried to keep pace with the Volga. But why do Russians believe that such beauty exists only in Russia? Any forest near Munich or in Vermont looks as fine.

Round the next bend of the rutted roadway, Siegfried glimpsed Zataika: on the high bank of the river was a patch of forest, fenced off. Beyond the fence was a two-storey house with a smoking chimney. A Gazik pick-up stood by the front steps. A female figure quickly ran across from the house to a small structure on the very edge of the river, which also had a smoking stove-pipe.

'What's this? Are they stoking up the sauna?' asked Siegfried, reviving.

'Hmm,' drawled Khanov vaguely. 'Sauna, yes . . .'

He didn't care for people anticipating events. General Chebrikov had approved his actions; now the main thing was to carry it all out as planned. Some cheery surprises awaited Mr Shertz. Udmurtia would not disgrace itself in the sight of America.

Chapter Five

There was more food on the table than could possibly be eaten. One ample dish held mountains of hot curd dumplings, while another displayed baked carp; beyond were fish and caviar pasties, meat and cabbage pie, little marinated and salted mushrooms, a salad of fresh vegetables, a Russian salad and lots of other pies and bits and pieces to which Siegfried, connoisseur of Russian cuisine as he was, couldn't put a name. There was so much drink on the table that ten couldn't have put it away, much less the present three. There was cognac and vodka and champagne, wines galore and the plain white bottles Siegfried recognized from his trips to Urengoi, marked 'potable spirit 96°'. Yet the most remarkable feature of Zataika was not the food or drink; it was three sprightly round-faced, black-eyed Udmurt lasses — the cooks and waitressses. The expression in their eyes was so openly lascivious that Siegfried soon realized it wasn't just deer-hunting that lay in store for him. The movement with which one of them relieved Siegfried of his sheepskin was more pornographic than her cotton shift, which reached just below her bum and showed she hadn't a stitch on underneath. 'A brothel in Udmurtia,' thought Siegfried at once. He smiled inwardly: the KGB could read his mind. He'd hardly had time to think — and lo! Three Udmurt girlies. True, they were a good deal older than those little Nenets birds that time in Salekhard ...

'Well, now! A nature reserve indeed! But what have I done to deserve a licence?' he said smiling at Khanov, as if proposing a practical talk, one businessman to another.

'Ha ... yes. Hmm,' Khanov smiled into his dark moustaches and in his usual temporizing way said, 'Let's eat just now.'

'Take your places! Sit down!' The three little 'waitresses'

fussed around them, placing chairs for Siegfried, Khanov and Kolesova. Their youthful Udmurt flesh swelled out their abbreviated smocks so powerfully it seemed the buttons at the breast would fly off like pistol shots at any moment.

Gazing at these openly whorish girls, Kolesova was again reminded of the vague rumours of Zataika orgies and felt intrigued and excited. Meanwhile she kept her eyes studiously averted from Siegfried, as if embarrassed at the equivocal situation. At this point, however, Khanov filled her glass not with wine or brandy or even vodka, but with pure spirit from the bottle labelled 'Potable spirit 96", and Kolesova seized the wine glass by the stem as if taking a spear in her hand. All her self-consciousness evaporated. A veritable warrior maiden now sat next to Siegfried; she gripped the glass like a sceptre. She's an alcoholic, that's all, thought Siegfried suddenly.

'Well, now,' Kolesova turned towards him. 'Shall we try you on spirit, comrade Shertz?'

Her eyes, and her voice which had grown suddenly hoarse, held a challenge.

'Vera!' a sharp cry from Khanov, like a whiplash, checked her. He added in a milder tone, clearly for his guest's benefit: 'Mr Shertz isn't used to spirits. We'll all start with the vodka, eh?'

'I'll start on the eatables,' said Siegfried emphatically. He had learnt a lot of Russian habits over the last six years, but did not like the Russian tendency to get drunk even before supper, almost before touching the food.

'Now, you men, let's get on with it,' Kolesova grinned. Now that she had a glass of spirit in her hand she feared neither devil nor Khanov. 'You're not telling me you can't down a glass of spirit to the historic Russian–German–Udmurt friendship? And to, as they say, "great Germany" — conquered half the world during the war! God, what a pity we've got no schnapps!'

Siegfried was furious. So this idiot woman had some historical claims on Germany, had she? She needed putting in her place. He had never attached any significance to his nationality. Born in Russia, German by blood and American by passport, he regarded himself as a citizen of the world, a businessman outside racial and political prejudices; even his business was international. If you got tangled up in political games, racial barriers and whatnot — bang went your profits. But this . . .

He reached out for the bottle of spirit and, with everyone watching, calmly poured himself a full glass; he then clicked his lighter and brought the flame to the spirit, first in his own glass, then in Kolesova's. Both glasses spurted blue flames, which crackled in the silence. Now I'll teach you something, bitch! thought Siegfried, smiling grimly to himself as he gazed directly into Kolesova's astonished eyes. Raising his glass with its licking blue flames, he announced:

'I would like to say a few words. I have now been conducting business with the Soviet Union for over ten years. Of course, as president of my own firm, I could have sent a vice-president or some other subordinate to Russia. But I always come here myself. And do you know why? Because a trip to Russia is always an adventure! And the best thing about these adventures is — Russian women. They are always a puzzle one dies to solve! I want to drink to you, Vera, and in your person to all Russian women. I trust you won't refuse to drink to that?'

So saying, he lifted the blazing glass to his mouth and serenely drank down the blazing spirit. He had learned this trick when he first got to know Ryazanov, the chief geologist of the Salekhard Yamal-Oil-Gas trust. Ryazanov was a fat bon vivant greatly addicted to little Nenets girls. What you have to do as you bring the burning glass to your mouth is breathe through your nose onto the flame; that extinguishes it just before it gets to your lips.

The Udmurt waitresses burst into applause, but Kolesova did not risk drinking burning spirit; instead she gave Siegfried an ecstatic kiss on the cheek.

'Bravo!' said she. 'Where did you learn to speak Russian so well?'

'I was born in Saratov, on the Volga,' said Siegfried.

'So you're one of us, really!' She blew out the flame in her glass and downed what was left of the spirit in one gulp. Thus she abandoned her historical claims to Germany. Meanwhile Siegfried was thinking, there it is: the unique capacity Russian women have for adapting themselves to men. German, Swedish, French women and especially English or American women remain themselves with any man whatever and retain their internal autonomy, like Tibetan ladies in China. But Russian women are above feminism.

Inside twenty minutes around four bottles of pure spirit had been seen off in toasts to Russian–German–American–Udmurt friendship, to peace throughout the world, to women in general and every lady present individually. Kolesova put an Abba tape on the machine and insisted on Siegfried drinking *bruderschaft* with her. Pure surrealism, he thought with a wry smile, here we are in the Siberian taiga, an American businessman drinking spirit with KGB operatives and Udmurt whores to Swedish music. How true it was: every trip to Russia was an adventure!

He bent over to Khanov and enquired softly:

'Listen, Khanov, don't give me any more of that shit about being a wildlife supervisor. Just tell me honestly: what's this bloody piss-up in aid of? Why am I getting all this in Udmurtia?'

Khanov, however, only smiled into his little black moustache.

'I think we'll all go to the sauna now,' said he. 'The girls can give us a wash ...'

▌*Chapter Six*

The log bath-house stood by the river, and the red light of the setting sun illuminated the whole company as they slung on their coats and ran with a bottle of vodka and brandy each along the snowy path from the dacha.

Inside the sauna, in the dark changing-room, there were wooden benches, and on these cases of Zhigulyovsky beer. Warmed by the spirit, the excellent food and the mischievous glances of the black-eyed Udmurt girls, Siegfried no longer felt the slightest embarrassment as he undressed along with the others. It was the usual way of a brothel; only the ritual was different here, which is what made it interesting.

Quickly throwing off his clothes, Siegfried strode after Khanov into the steam room, still covering his lower belly with his hands in a reflex sort of way. And it wasn't a dry steam-room as in ordinary saunas, either. On the contrary, one of the waitresses was splashing jugs of water and beer onto hot sizzling stones; the air was heavy with fragrant white steam. Siegfried promptly climbed onto the upper bench after Khanov and felt he was getting drunk, but in a cheerful, boisterous fashion. Anyway, thought Siegfried, from the upper bench of a steam-room one does tend to view the world from a different angle. It was fun, for instance, to watch the frisky Vera Kolesova, instinctively rather than consciously, cover her breasts and gingerish pubic bush with her hands as she came in and forget her self-consciousness in no time!

Soon everything got pretty confused in there, anyhow. There was giggling and shrieking on the lower benches as the girls lashed one another with beer-soaked birch twigs, stoked up the heat and then rushed out into the changing-room for a gulp of cold beer. Four female figures with rounded hips and

113

bottoms and wobbling pear-shaped breasts swam out of the curtain of steam, then vanished into it again, only to reappear somewhere else with more giggles and shrieks. Then, after conspiratorial whispers, they climbed up to the upper benches and ragged Khanov and Siegfried down. They laid them face down on the benches below and began lashing their backs with birch twigs, wetting the leafy branches from time to time in a bucket of cold beer.

From the chastisement of these branches, whippy but not at all painful, somehow burning and relaxing at the same time, his body seemed to grow lighter, while the scent of birch leaves, beer and female hands running across his damp body caused his head to spin in a delightful floating fashion. While Siegfried was yielding to this ecstasy and floated above the world in body and spirit, hands turned him over onto his back and the burning-icy birch twigs flailed their trembling leaves against his chest, shoulders, belly and legs, as a result of which he felt an extraordinarily sharp and powerful surge of sexual desire. Without opening his eyes, just by listening to the voices and laughter around him, he realized that they had achieved the same with Khanov.

What followed was like a merry-go-round: three ravenhaired Udmurt amazons and one Russian blonde straddled the men in turn, not staying on each longer than a minute, but managing in that minute to exhibit individuality of temperament and experience. From this merry-go-round of sensation, Siegfried's soul had ascended into outer space, while his body emitted sighs mixed with groans. Then Vera Kolesova knelt down and washed his penis, now trembling in anticipation, using the same potable spirit; with a ritual solemnity in her severe blue eyes she slowly bent her head to this now pure and sterile flesh and began to suck it in. Siegfried, as he fainted away, distinctly felt his body winging its way upwards in pursuit of his soaring soul ...

Two hours later, Siegfried and Khanov continued their meal at the bountiful table. The waitresses had brought a sucking pig baked whole. Siegfried felt he could eat a whole boar.

'Not a rustle out in the garden now ...' he suddenly began singing spontaneously, as if the popular Soviet tune had just

114

been born inside him. 'Quiet till the dawn's early light . . .'

'If you only knew how I dream of you, and those wonderful Moscow nights!' Khanov, the waitresses and Kolesova at once joined in.

And they sang on and on that evening, sang and drank, and sang again, as if no sin lay between them, not to mention, as *Pravda* would say 'the fierce struggle of two ideologies'.

When Khanov was seeing him upstairs to his room, Siegfried addressed him with drunken docility:

'You know, old pal, even if you are a Gee Bee and took shots of me fucking about in the bath-house so as you can blackmail me, I don't care. It was fabulous, fuck me if it wasn't!'

Khanov merely smiled wordlessly into his moustache — he'd taken no photos, and had no intention of blackmailing Siegfried. He had honestly tried to amuse him, and next day they really were going elk-hunting. In the evening there'd be another feast and the usual booze-up, and so it would go on until the signal came from Moscow releasing Siegfried from his happy confinement. Everything had gone nicely according to plan, and Khanov had already taken a fancy to this gregarious American, much as a scientist becomes attached to his experimental animal.

Left alone in his room, Siegfried pulled his pyjamas out of his case along with a small, powerful Grundig transistor radio. Every night before he went to sleep, no matter where he was, he had to hear the share prices in New York, London and Hamburg and the rest of the political and economic news; otherwise he was unable to sleep. As he lay down he switched on the radio and at once got the voice of a Russian announcer:

'And now here's the weather forecast. Over the whole territory of Siberia from the Urals to Irkutsk, the weather has been fine, with no wind for the second day running. Temperatures today: Sverdlovsk minus twenty-seven, Tyumen minus thirty-two, Urengoi thirty-seven and Salekhard thirty-nine degrees below zero. The forecasters promise that clear, cloudless weather will continue tomorrow, though there is a chance of light snowfalls in places. Now we're presenting a programme of popular music for our boys working in the Far North:

'"We're not frightened of any ninth wave, or any permafrost we know!"'

a hearty Komsomol voice boomed out:

"For we're the brave lads, for we're the bold lads who work
on latitude seven-oh!"'

Siegfried turned it off. All the intoxication and other delights
of the evening left him instantly as his whole body grew stiff
with fear. So they'd lied about the weather in Tyumen. That
meant they'd taken him off the plane and carried him off to
this reservation deliberately so as to . . .

An icy suspicion gripped his heart. Of course: the KGB
wanted to deprive him of his profit! On December the seventeenth, when the international committee of experts signed the
pipeline protocol, the West European banks would hand over
nine billion dollars to the Russians, and Siegfried's commission
would be 225 million. But a generous promise of two and a half
per cent was one thing; paying out 225 million was another.
Siegfried had been in business a long time; he knew how reluct-
ant people were to part with money. And Russians surely love
money — especially foreign currency. They had needed him
earlier on, to extract such an enormous loan from the German
and French banks — eighteen thousand million dollars. Even
backed by government guarantees in France and Germany, it
had been no easy matter getting a loan like that, dammit!
Guarantees like that didn't grow on trees, either. Although he
was ignorant of the precise figures and had no real facts, he
had a strong hunch that somebody in the upper echelons of
government in France and Germany had been on his side in
the matter, that somebody there had been 'oiling the wheels',
as the criminal slang had it, for the USSR. True, after that the
French had realized the situation and Mitterand had thrown
out nearly a hundred Soviet spy-diplomats last summer.

Still, getting the banks' agreement to provide a loan to the
Soviets wasn't the end of the affair: the money was paid in
instalments every two or three months as construction work on
the pipeline progressed, so that payment was suspended every
time the Russians went about rocking the international boat,

now in Afghanistan, now in Poland; an attempt on the life of the Pope; exiling Andrei Sakharov, the Nobel Prize laureate, to Gorky; cons working on the pipeline; then the Korean airliner! Every time there was an international row the banks got nervous and wanted to stop payment of the next loan instalment.

The Economist — March 20, 1982

INTO THE VALLEY OF DEBT

... result of some political prodding. And Russia's request for an extra DM300m last December for financing the Urengoy Siberian gas pipeline sent the bankers scurrying to Bonn for consultations.

As bankers and governments become more aware that bankers' decisions to lend or not to lend, reschedule or not to reschedule are decisions of importance not only for banks' profits but also for their country's international relations, ...

U.S. News & World Report — April 5, 1982

FRANCE — IT'S BACK IN CHARACTER

... in a series of disagreements. Among other irritants:

*French cooperation in construction by Moscow of a trans-Siberian gas pipeline to Western Europe, a project the U.S. strongly opposes. Secretary of State Alexander Haig has said he is "appalled" that French banks, with loans guaranteed by the government, are helping finance the project. France dismisses U.S. objections that the pipeline will be a source of hard ...

The Economist — (c) 1982

April 10, 1982

RUSSIAN GAS PIPELINE; BANKERS TIGHTEN THE TAPS

The natural-gas pipeline to deliver, eventually, about 40 billion cubic metres of gas a year from Siberia's remote

Urengoi fields and Yamal peninsula to western Europe is catching Polish flak. West German banks are most at risk in Poland and experience there has made them leery about increasing lending to other communist countries, including Russia.

In consequence, when representatives of 20 banks met in Frankfurt this week to sign an agreement to reschedule Poland's debt, it very quickly became apparent in informal discussions that West German banks are most unhappy about Russia's recent request for an extra DM75m (about $30m) of unguaranteed loans for the trans-Siberian pipeline that is now under construction.

This sum will not make or break a project costing at least $15 billion. West German lenders have already extended DM2.5 billion in credits and are poised soon to announce agreement on a further DM300m the Russians asked for in December. Even so, the West German hesitation is significant because it reflects a general dampening of enthusiasm that may delay completion of the pipeline.

The DM2.5 billion loan was extended by a consortium of 16 West German banks and largely guaranteed by the state export credit insurance agency, Hermes. It was founded on a promise by the Russians to make a 15% down payment from their own resources. In December, the Russians said they could not keep their promise, and asked for another DM300m.

Members of the banking consortium were divided over what some of them saw as a dangerous breach of principle. Bankers say the credit is likely to go ahead once niggling over interest rates is over; but some banks, led by Bayerische Landesbank, may opt out.

These banks were particularly annoyed by Russia's request for the extra DM75m early this year. Even the big banks, Deutsche, Dresdner and Commerzbank, are not keen to lend a lot more money unguaranteed. There have been three main reasons for the shift from the go-go fervour of a year ago, when there was talk of DM10 billion in German financing alone.

First, the collapse in Comecon creditworthiness has chilled enthusiasts. The rescheduling of Poland's and Rumania's debt has made bankers fretful about the size of the Soviet Union's pipeline borsize of the Soviet Union's pipeline borrowing. Repayment of the loans (from gas sales) is still supposed to be assured, but delays in construction could mean expensive delays in repayment.

Second, America's opposition to the project found more effective expression in President Reagan's post-Poland trade sanctions. The American export ban blockaded one of the pipeline's vital turbine parts, to have been manufactured in the United States. This slowed the pipeline more than any amount of political jawboning.

Three European firms — AEG Telefunken, Nuovo Pignone and John Brown Engineering — that had signed contracts last autumn to supply 125 turbines based on the American General Electric's rotary parts are hunting for ways round the ban — and so are the Russians. According to the Swedish consulting firm PetroStudies, the Russians have brought forward their pipelaying schedule; and have accelerated programmes designed to give them the capacity to manufacture near-substitutes for the American-designed turbines. Reliance on Soviet manufacture, however, would set completion of the project back far beyond the 1984 target date.

Third, as oil prices have dropped and gas supplies increased, European consumers are no longer in quite such a hurry to sign long-term contracts for Soviet gas. Two other new gas pipelines are on the way: Algeria's to Italy via Tunisia (now completed) and Norway's from the North Sea (to be ready by the mid-1980s).

Only West Germany and France have signed firm supply agreements with the Russians. Italy's state-owned utility, Eni, put together an agreement in principle last year, but has yet to get government approval. Holland, Belgium, Switzerland and Austria are still talking. Russia was expected to receive between $8 billion and $10 billion a year from sales of 40 billion cubic metres a year. Firm contracts to date guarantee Russia less than half as much income than that.

RISING HOPES

West German banks agreed to lend Russia $1.13 billion for the Siberian gas pipeline.

There had been several such episodes in the history of the construction of the Siberia–Western Europe gas pipeline, and on each occasion Siegfried had dashed around, flying between Moscow, Paris, Urengoi and Bonn and spending incredible amounts of money in order to save the situation. It was only the Russians who believed he had pocketed the first half of the commission himself. Who had organized that trip to Urengoi for French bankers so they could see there were no cons there? And who was still retaining agents at the Algerian and Norwegian construction sites to report on exactly when the competition went on stream and which firms they had contracts with? And who had gone without sleep at nights these last four years getting the Russians their regular three to five million dollars every three or four months? Then, of course, they were all over him and rolled out the red carpet: he got the best girl in Moscow as a mistress, booze-ups at government dachas, free holidays at Black Sea resorts and no customs inspection at airports — take icons out, if you want! And that was nothing to Urengoi, Salekhard and Tyumen. There he was a king, the bosom friend of party members and Gee Bees, and the chief geologists of the territory. But now — that was all over. The pipeline was built; in three days' time the commission would sign the protocol bringing it into service and the Russians would get their nine billion. That's why they were in such a hurry to get it over with, and he, Siegfried, had been a complete idiot giving them the chance to entice him into this Udmurt trap. Khanov was nothing, a minor official of the Udmurt KGB — but tomorrow the boys from Moscow would be rolling up. They would show Siegfried a photograph album of his whoring exploits in the USSR: with Tanya in Moscow and on the Black Sea, those mulatto girls in Alma Ata, and the Udmurt girls today. They would show him the album and say: either you sign over your 225 billion voluntarily to the International Movement for Peace and Disarmament or tomorrow these photos will be sent to *Der Spiegel* or *Playboy*. And if — God forbid! — they knew about that business in Salekhard five years ago as well, they wouldn't stand on ceremony with him at all. They would just sling him into one of those Arctic camps he'd asked to have moved well away from the eyes of West European bankers. American citizenship would be no help whatsoever — the KGB know how to frame foreign nationals too. Incidentally, they had a camp for foreigners somewhere round here — was it Udmurtia or Mordovia? He'd read about it in the papers. Indeed, they'd wrapped him round their little finger and no mistake. For six years they'd allowed him the freedom of the store, let him make hay with the Russian girls while they put together their little album and laid their trap in Zataika.

Siegfried lay there, petrified by the awareness of inescapable disaster. Even if he ran away from the dacha this instant, they would pick him up as soon as he got to Moscow; he wouldn't make it from the airport to the embassy. The bastards, the lot of them! Even Tanya, the KGB bitch — her and Dynkov's flu, all lies. Got to do something. Now. But what? Nip out to the bath-house and check for hidden cameras?

The door opened part-way, and the figure of one of the waitresses slipped into the room without knocking. She was wearing a transparent nightdress and carrying a bottle of champagne and two glasses. Placing them on the bedside table she scuttled into bed, although Siegfried was lying with his eyes closed pretending to be asleep. She pressed up against him with her glowing body and kissed him hungrily on the lips. But now even her youthful, juicy flesh evoked in Siegfried nothing but disgust. No doubt Khanov had sent her, so as not to leave him on his own even at night. Siegfried moved away, mumbling:

'Don't . . . I want to sleep.'

The girl froze, in astonishment, where she lay.

'You want me to go?'

'Yes. I'm tired.'

She sighed.

'Oh, dear! And I won you for the whole night.'

'What do you mean, won me?' Siegfried was astonished.

'Well!' she said, relaxing onto the pillow. 'Only old farts come here from Moscow — ministers. It's really boring with them. They keep us shut up here, like in a harem. So we have to throw ourselves at some old man who can't even get it up. And suddenly we get a young, hunky fella — an American to boot — knocking back spirit better than a Russian. So us girls drew lots for all three nights. Is it because you don't like me? Should I send somebody else?'

'No. I'm just very tired. Let's postpone it till tomorrow — '

'It's not my turn tomorrow,' she said, rising from the bed. 'Do you want the other one, the Russian? She's busy with Khanov, anyway.'

'No. I'm going to sleep.'

'Should I come back near morning?'

'Thank you — no.'

She looked at him with desolate regretful eyes and even shook her head. She gave a profound sigh of sadness and went out, disappointed. As she left she contemptuously clicked off the light.

Siegfried lay listening intently to the noises of the house. It took about twenty minutes for everything to quieten down in the waitresses' room below and in Khanov's on the first floor; yet he stayed there for another good hour, to make sure everyone was asleep. He had worked out a plan of escape. He got up, got dressed and went quietly downstairs, fearing his every step would creak. If they found him here, it would be all right; he could say he was looking for something to drink.

But the house was absolutely silent. Siegfried reached the hall, slipped on his sheepskin coat, hat and shoes, and wrapped his scarf around his throat. He just wanted a breath of fresh air, didn't he?

He didn't need an excuse, anyway: all the house's other occupants were asleep.

Siegfried rummaged through the pockets of Khanov's coat, which hung close by, and removed the keys to the black Volga. From this moment on there was no going back. He got a sharp knife from the kitchen and slipped two unopened bottles of vodka into his coat pockets before going outside.

The Volga was standing by the gate next to the pick-up in

which the waitresses had doubtless arrived earlier on. Beyond the cars, the gates were closed, not locked. Past the gates, he recalled, there was a slope down to the river where the road ran into the town.

Of course, he could run along to the bath-house and check if there were any cameras hidden somewhere under the ceiling — but was it worth wasting time? Even if there were no cameras, that didn't mean there hadn't been any three hours ago, during that mindless orgy.

Siegfried approached the pick-up truck slowly, as if out on a stroll; he walked all round it slitting each tyre with the kitchen knife. The pick-up settled quietly into the snow. He waited several seconds: would a light flash on in the house? He then climbed onto the dacha fence, reached out for the telegraph pole and cut the wires with his knife. The end of the wire fell inside the fence, onto the snow. Siegfried climbed down and sliced it off close to the house. About thirty metres of telephone wire now lay on the snow. He coiled it up and placed it in the black Volga. Like his German parents, he always did everything thoroughly, thinking out every detail. If his flight was discovered, Khanov would have no pursuit car available and no telephone to raise the alarm in Izhevsk — not, at any rate, for some time.

Now for the opening of the gates. They creaked a little, but to Siegfried the noise seemed loud enough to wake the whole planet. Still no one woke in the house. Too much to drink, Siegfried grinned to himself.

Growing bolder, almost scorning concealment, he put the Volga's gear lever into neutral and, holding onto the wheel with one hand, put his shoulder to the door and rolled the car through the gates and down the hill towards the river and the forest road. The car rolled easily down the slope and was soon moving by itself. Siegfried jumped in as it was going and taxied along as far as he could go. Only when he was down by the river and shielded from the dacha by the snow-covered pines and cedars of the taiga did he switch on the ignition.

The Volga leapt forward and raced along the taiga road in the darkness. The souped-up engine, custom-made for Khanov at the Izhevsk tank factory, enabled Siegfried to squeeze up to a hundred kilometres an hour even on a track deep in snow.

At first the road lay empty under the night: no oncoming cars, no lights of villages or settlements. Along either side of the road the headlights picked out only the dark snowy shapes of cedars and pines. It was as if he were speeding along through the unpeopled Siberian taiga alone.

Yet half an hour's driving brought him out onto a main road only partially cleared of snow and just as dark and poorly lit. There were no road signs whatsoever: Russian roads are very different from American highways. Siegfried had no idea in which direction Izhevsk lay. Fortunately, the headlights of some sort of lorry appeared in the distance.

Siegfried pulled up and jumped out of the car; he quickly lifted the bonnet and burnt his hands unscrewing the radiator cap. Hot steam belched out from beneath the bonnet. He jumped out into the middle of the road, waving his arms at the approaching vehicle.

The lorry stopped, and the driver stuck his face out of the cabin.

'What's up?'

'Fucking radiator's leaking.' He said this in the true Russian manner, switching at once into truck drivers' obscenities.

'No, get stuffed! I'm not towing a Volga,' the driver said at once. 'I've got a trailer already — can't you see?'

Sure enough, there was a trailer on the back, some sort of container; but Siegfried was not interested in towing the Volga anywhere.

'I can see. Just drop me off at Izhevsk, the airport. I'll pay — look!' Siegfried pulled the two bottles of vodka from his coat pockets. 'There's cash in it for you as well. My wife's flying in, see. If I'm not there to meet her, she'll smell a fucking rat, say I was on a screwing expedition ...'

Male solidarity combined with cash and two bottles of vodka carried the day. An hour later, the lorry rolled up to Izhevsk Airport.

The terminal building was cold and empty. There were, of course, no passengers from yesterday's Moscow–Tyumen–Urengoi flight: they had left the day before. Nor were there any groups of passengers in transit, as happened in bad flying

124

weather. This was one more confirmation for Siegfried that yesterday's 'forced landing because of blizzard' had been merely a KGB ruse to lure him off to Zataika. 'Boarding is proceeding for flights Izhevsk–Moscow and Izhevsk–Siktivkar,' came the radio announcement. 'Passengers are requested to board the aircraft. I repeat . . .'

Siegfried restrained himself. His first impulse was to make a dash for the Moscow flight, but Moscow was now the most dangerous destination of all. It was nearly four hours' flying time to Moscow; by then, news of his flight would surely have reached them and a detachment of Gee Bees would be waiting for him by the gangway. No — anywhere but Moscow!

'How long is it to Siktivkar?' he asked the drowsy cashier.

'An hour and five minutes,' she answered.

That was what he wanted. An hour from now he'd be in Siktivkar. Once there, change planes straight away and off somewhere north, preferably into the tundra or the taiga where no one would think of looking for him. In a couple of days, when dozens of foreign journalists would be flying into Urengoi for the opening ceremony — he would drop in out of the blue. He would be inseparable from the pressmen and fly out of the USSR along with them. In front of Western newspapermen, of course, the KGB wouldn't lay a finger on him.

Now it remained for him to do one more thing — get a ticket for the airplane without showing his foreign passport and without saying his last name.

'How much is a round trip to Siktivkar?' he asked.

'74 roubles . . .'

Siegfried pulled out a hundred rouble bill, and put it down in front of the cashier and said: 'Keep the change.'

The fat woman cashier, wrapped in a heavy overcoat, raised her sleepy eyes at him in surprise. It was simple arithmetic — 26 roubles tip — Reason woke her up.

'Passport,' she said, getting the form for the ticket out of the drawer.

'That's the point, honey!' said Siegfried, pushing the hundred rouble bill towards her. 'That's the whole point! I'm flying in order to retrieve my passport! A drinking buddy of mine flew off to Siktivkar wearing my jacket, and in the pocket of the jacket are my passport and all my papers. And today I need them right up to here' — he held his hand up to his chin, showing that he needed his documents, on fear of death — 'I'm signing up for work here at the paper factory — that's why I'm going there and back. When I return I'll show you my passport, I promise! Give me the ticket! I tell you — keep the change.' He again moved the 100 roubles nearer the cashier and beseechingly looked her in the eye.

She looked over him for a few seconds. Siegfried's eyes shone with absolutely genuine sincerity and his whole appearance — sheepskin coat, expensive fur hat, his clean, sober face — suggested that he was a respectable person, an engineer, and not some kind of criminal who the police could be looking for.

The cashier silently hid the hundred rouble note in the drawer of her table, then holding pen above the empty ticket asked: 'Last name?'

'Thanks!' Siegfried said. 'Ivanov, a simple last name. Ivanov Boris Ivanovich.'

▌Chapter Seven

Only when he was on board the plane, a little forty-seater Ilyushin, did Siegfried allow himself to draw breath. He reclined limply against the head-rest and thought, horrified: What have I done? On the run from the KGB, and where — inside the USSR!

While he'd been driving the car away, hurtling desperately through the taiga at dead of night, getting his ticket and boarding the plane, everything had been wound up inside him by the sheer dynamics of physical action, while his thoughts were totally occupied by the need for self-control — not to give himself away, not say a word out of place, make no suspicious gesture. But now that they'd taken off and nothing depended on him any more, and all he had to do was wait passively till they reached Siktivkara, his fear returned. And all his aerophobia, he thought, was nothing compared to the terror he felt now.

He looked about him. The plane was in from the south, the Caucasus, and was packed with black-moustached Georgians in huge cloth caps. They were talking noisily among themselves in Georgian. There was also a strong, unpleasant smell of sweat, garlic and *chacha*[1], and as well as the cases in the baggage compartment everybody carried an extra bag or box of tomatoes, mandarins or flowers under his seat. What had happened was that for the first time in all the years he had been coming to the USSR, Siegfried had descended from the high standard of living enjoyed by the privileged Soviet elite to the normal, everyday level. The abundance of Georgian black

---

[1] *Chacha*: grape vodka

127

marketeers on the plane and the fact that the stewardess had obviously been bribed to let them bring their heavy sacks and boxes into the cabin reassured Siegfried most of all; it meant that at least there were no KGB operatives on board. His Georgian neighbour took his shoes off, and the air at once grew thick with the smell of long-unwashed feet — so, what the hell! Better freedom and the smell of sweat than the fresh air of the game-trap at Zataika. And anyway, thought Siegfried suddenly, in a couple of days I won't smell any better: my case is back in Zataika, and you can't buy deodorants in Russia ...

His neighbour, meanwhile, now shoeless, had dragged out of a voluminous wickerwork bag a roast chicken wrapped in a greasy copy of the evening edition of *Tbilisi*: to be more precise, it was a 'chicken *tabak*' smelling sharply of garlic and spices. Out of the same bag appeared a large bottle of red wine, a round of fresh cheese, some greens, ripe tomatoes.

Siegfried had a sudden piercing pang of hunger, so much so that his mouth was filled with saliva. The Georgian, as if reading his thoughts — or more likely out of Georgian etiquette — broke the two-pound chicken apart and offered half to Siegfried.

'Go on, go on!' said he in a Georgian accent.

'I'm Soso from Tbilisi. You?'

'My name's Siegfried,' said Siegfried indistinctly as he tackled the chicken.

'A Jew?'

Siegfried, sinking his teeth into juicy chicken flesh, mumbled something between confirmation and denial.

'What's your line of work?' asked Soso, pouring wine for both of them into plastic cups.

'I'm ... a translator,' Siegfried managed to say.

Soso grinned:

'You're a translator and I'm a transporter!' and lifted his cup of wine. 'Okay! Your health, friend!'

They drank, and the garrulous Soso asked:

'What language do you translate from, *genatsvali*[1]?'

---

[1] *Genetsvali*: dear (Georgian)

'English, German — ' said Siegfried.

'Oh dear, dear, dear!' said Soso, distressed. 'If you know languages like that, why didn't you go off to America when Brezhnev was letting the Jews out?'

Siegfried was beginning to regret having accepted the chicken and getting drawn into this conversation. He shrugged vaguely.

'You're sorry now, of course' said Soso confidently, pulling a packet of Marlboro from his coat and proffering it to Seigfried. Siegfried declined: he didn't smoke. 'I was a fool too,' continued Soso. 'In Tbilisi, you could marry a Jewish girl for ten thousand and get away. But I just sat thinking: go or not go. If I went to Israel — a totally different country; if I went to America, I'd have to know the language, right?'

'Right,' confirmed Siegfried.

'Wrong!' Soso contradicted emphatically. 'I should have gone! There's no living here. None at all, know what I mean? Here's me taking mandarins up north. Before, when Brezhnev was in charge, I made my eight thousand on a trip like this. So what, in Georgia you give the police a sweetener to let you take the stuff out, so in Urengoi or Norilsk you do the same and they keep their hands off. Two, three thousand I lose. But I still had five thousand, I could live! Now? Now I'm risking my life when I fly. Even if I give out half my profit in bribes, there's no guarantee I won't land up in jail! Andropov!' Soso heaved a sigh. 'No, we missed our chance, missed it. Should have gone without thinking. I'd be in America now driving a Cadillac.'

Before too long, Siegfried knew a good many details of the clandestine market in fruit, vegetables and flowers in the USSR. The cost of these goods rose with the polar latitude, but there were differentials even beyond the Arctic Circle. 'You can't take fruit into Murmansk now,' pursued the voluble Soso. 'The whole police force has been changed over because Andropov banished Brezhnev's son-in-law there as militia chief. Not one policeman takes bribes in Murmansk now; they're scared. There's no business in Archangel for us, there's no money about. Different matter in Urengoi or Surgut! The geologists are well-heeled, and your ordinary working man rakes in up to a thousand roubles a month. Risky, of course. Shatunov, the KGB chief in Salekhard, is a real brute —' No, thought Siegfried, the undercover fruit trade in the USSR was not much different from the traffic in arms or drugs: the state had a trading monopoly and was unable to run it properly. It persecuted its competitors as if they were selling people pistols and grenades instead of flowers and mandarins.

'Have you heard the latest one about Andropov?' said Soso, chattering on. 'As soon as everybody on the Central Committee had voted for him as General Secretary, Andropov says: "Voters, you may lower your hands and move away from the wall!" Later on, at a press conference, some foreign correspondent asks Andropov: "Comrade Andropov, are you confident that the Soviet people will follow you?" "If they don't follow me, they'll follow Brezhnev!" answers Andropov. Do you know what Andropov's New Year TV message will be? If he lives till then, of course. "Dear comrades, Happy New 1937!"'

'FASTEN YOUR SEATBELTS,' the red sign lit up. The aircraft banked and swiftly came in to land in Siktivkar, capital of yet another ethnic mini-republic, the Komi ASSR. And now a double terror gripped Siegfried's heart: aerophobia and fear of the KGB.

The aircraft skis scraped along the snow-covered landing strip and the plane taxied briefly before coming to a stop. Siegfried looked fearfully through the window. Needless to say, if a black Volga appeared by the gangway, it was for him.

But no one met him by the gangway.

From the wall of the concrete airport building a gigantic portrait of Lenin, now resembling the slant-eyed Komi rather than the moon-faced Udmurts, gazed serenely down on the Georgian black marketeers as they dragged into the terminal their boxes of fruit, flowers and suchlike bounty from the Soviet subtropics.

Siegfried gave his new friend Soso a hand with hauling his cases of fragrant mandarins and chrysanthemums.

As soon as they had traversed the frozen nocturnal airfield and entered the terminal, they were assailed by a wave of stale air. The building held several hundred transit passengers: shift

130

workers along with the Caucasian fruit merchants. Both groups had to get to Salekhard — the workmen to the boring-sites and the pipeline, the traders to their market. Salekhard, however, had been closed to passenger flights for two days now on Shatunov's orders. In winter, bad flying weather and post-poned flights are no rare thing in the north, so the workmen slept as usual side by side — on the floor and on the window-sills. The black marketeers stayed awake, worrying over their perishable goods. The arrival of another thirty Georgians raised a gale of laughter; the traders hailing from the 'frater-nal' republic of Armenia found this especially funny. Armen-ians and Georgians love one another like the Flemings love the Walloons.

'Get in the queue for Murmansk, *genetsvale!*' shouted a young Armenian to the newcomers.

'Why Murmansk?' said another. 'As a matter of fact, Georgians can fly to Salekhard. They've got nothing in their pants anyway, they're in no danger.'

A burst of laughter drowned the end of the sentence.

The new arrivals looked everywhere in their embarrass-ment. At last an old man took pity on them and put them in the picture:

'In Salekhard the tundra spirits are cutting Russians' cocks off. That's why they're not letting anybody in or out of Yamal, so the panic doesn't spread.'

'What tundra spirits?' asked Soso.

'Nobody knows,' said the old man, and pointed into the air: 'Spirits, know what I mean? They're — nothing! But they're going round cutting Russians' balls off!'

'Thank the Lord,' said Soso.

'What do you mean, "Thank the Lord"?' The old man was puzzled.

'Thank Him for starting the operation,' said Soso. 'Pity He started in the north, though. Couldn't He have made a start with our Russians in Georgia?'

Now everybody laughed, Georgians and Armenians together. Of course nobody believed a word of the 'tundra spirits' business, but with the great love the Caucasian peoples bear to their 'Russian big brother', everybody listened to the fantastic rumours about Russians being punished in this 'interesting manner' with keen enjoyment.

Siegfried, though, was in no mood for jokes or stupid stories about tundra spirits. He left the Caucasian company and walked out of the terminal onto the airfield, deeply depressed. When Khanov woke up he could easily find out which were the flights out of Izhevsk that night, and this meant he had to disappear out of Siktivkar urgently, at once. There was only one flight timetabled in the next three hours: Siktivkar–Izhevsk–Tbilisi, the same one Siegfried had used to get here.

The realization that once again he was in an even worse trap than Zataika clouded his brain as if he had been involved in a heavy boozing session. He looked about him.

To the right, a few metres from the terminal building stood a small two-engined Anton with a red stripe along the fuselage. It was equipped with skis. Near it was a lorry bearing the word 'MAIL'. A young lad in a fur flying suit — a pilot or a mechanic — was throwing sacks and boxes out of the lorry and through the open door of the aircraft. In there, hands were catching the boxes and stowing them further inside the plane.

Siegfried approached slowly. Now he could make out the addresses on the parcels: 'Novy Port', 'Amderma', 'Dikson'. Novy Port — that was on Yamal, roughly a hundred and fifty kilometres north of Salekhard . . .

The boy loading the mail onto the plane wiped the sweat from his brow.

'Haven't got a smoke, have you?' he asked Siegfried.

Siegfried didn't smoke and, for the first time in his life, regretted the fact poignantly.

'Hold it!' he said to the boy. 'Hang on a minute!'

And raced back to the airport buildings. As he ran he was pulling out Soviet money from his jacket pocket. Since there are no credit cards or cheque system in the USSR, Siegfried always changed ten or fifteen hundred dollars into Soviet roubles whenever he visited Moscow and always carried a thick wad of banknotes in his pocket. Now he peeled off two hundred-rouble notes as he rushed up to Soso, who was sitting on his boxes noisily playing backgammon with his associates.

'Soso, be a pal!' said Siegfried excitedly. 'Sell me some mandarins, ten kilos.'

Soso looked at him in amazement. Siegfried lied fluently:

'I've just met a friend. It's his wife's birthday. And those American cigarettes I saw you had — sell me a packet, ten roubles!'

Inside a minute he was picking his way to the exit, with Soso's wicker bag stuffed with mandarins and a packet of Marlboro in his hand. As he emerged onto the airfield he saw the little mail-plane. Both engines were running and the propellers turning; the young lad was standing in the doorway dragging a metal gangway inside. Siegfried ran up, holding out the packet of Marlboro.

'Catch! Take the lot!'

'What do you mean?' The boy was surprised. 'No, I only want one.' He explained, 'I've given it up, that's why I've got none myself.'

'Go on, take the whole packet! American!' Siegfried thrust them at him vigorously. American cigarettes are rare in the USSR.

'Well, shit!' grinned the youth sheepishly. 'How can I give up smoking at this rate?' He lit up with evident enjoyment and stowed the cigarettes in a pocket of his flying suit. 'And whereabouts are you flying?' he asked Siegfried.

'Novy Port,' said Siegfried and opened his bag of mandarins as if by accident. On glimpsing this subtropical 'baggage', the lad glanced furtively around to check if there were any bosses or witnesses about. He then addressed Siegfried in rough haste:

'Well, get in then. Look bloody sharp! What are you fucking waiting for?'

One minute later they were taking off into the dark polar skies.

Siegfried was jubilant: it was six in the morning, and even if Khanov roused the entire KGB, who would think of looking for Siegfried Shertz in Novy Port in the Yamal tundra?

When the aircraft was on course, the young fliers, pilot and mechanic, munched their oranges with relish and confided to Siegfried:

'You were in luck, pal, with us — too bloody true you

were! A mouse couldn't get into Yamal now. Everything's sealed off.'

'Why's that?'

'The place is a shambles, the Nentsi are in revolt. You don't believe it? Fuck me! A few days back, three cons made a break for it out of camp and sliced up three geologists or something on the way. They cut off their balls, and their ears. Fuck me, it was the airport chief himself told us. But that's not the funny part. The funny bit is, the Nentsi decided it was the tundra spirits doing it, giving them the signal to rise up, and they've started massacring us Russians all over the tundra. In Salekhard they've even caused two explosions. Stuff them, though, our paras are going in today. They'll restore law and order — and bloody how!'

And it suddenly dawned on Siegfried: so that's why they'd held him back in Izhevsk, that was the reason for Zataika and its unlooked for delights — a revolt on Yamal! But, hell's flames, this ridiculous revolt could disrupt the pipeline ceremony. That made his trip to Urengoi even more urgent. He was simply a genius escaping from Zataika! If the European banks didn't pay the nine billion to the Russians because of the uprising — goodbye to Siegfried's millions. No — nuts to them — no KGB was going to stop him now!

Part Three
Ice-drift in December

▮ *Chapter One*

Government telegram

Urgent
Secret

TO: Salekhard, district committee CPSU

TODAY 12 DECEMBER OCTOBER REVOLUTION
PARATROOP DIVISION UNDER THE COMMAND OF
MAJOR GENERAL GRINKO IS ARRIVING TO PUT
DOWN THE DISTURBANCES IN YOUR DISTRICT.

THE SECOND SECRETARY OF THE DISTRICT
COMMITTEE, COMRADE ROGOV, IS TO TAKE OVER
THE DUTIES OF THE FIRST SECRETARY AND
MOBILIZE THE TOWN PARTY ORGANIZATION AND
ALL RESOURCES OF THE LOCAL KGB AND POLICE
MILITIA TO ASSIST THE MILITARY FORCES ON THEIR
ARRIVAL. FORMER FIRST SECRETARY PYOTR
TUSYADA IS TO BE EXPELLED FROM THE CPSU FOR
ABSENTING HIMSELF FROM HIS POST WITHOUT
LEAVE.

COMRADE BOGOMYATOV, FIRST SECRETARY OF
TYUMEN PROVINCE PARTY COMMITTEE, IS
APPOINTED AS PRESIDENT OF THE PARTY
COMMISSION FOR THE ELIMINATION OF DISORDER
IN THE DISTRICT.

A. Yeremin, Head of personnel administration,
Central Committee CPSU

Moscow, Kremlin, 12 December 1983

Chapter Two

At four o'clock in the afternoon a cavalcade of official cars and Sno-Cats, escorted by the three personnel-carriers of the military garrison, set off from the District Committee building. The new First Secretary, Vladimir Rogov, the chief of Salekhard KGB Directorate, Major Shatunov, the local chief of police militia, Colonel Sini, and other top brass were on their way to the airport to meet the October Revolution paratroop division. Shatunov promised to drop me off at the hotel on the way: a night spent investigating Ryazanov's murder meant I'd had no sleep at all; then there were the two explosions at Yamal-Gas and Northern Pipelaying — followed by the attack on the local KGB headquarters by mobs of workmen. After all I had been through, coupled with the lack of sleep, I was almost collapsing on my feet.

A full moon, red because of the frost, hung over Salekhard. Beneath it, in the black skies of the polar night, three helicopters and three Annushki of the local Arctic air service circled over the town.

But the escapers made no attempt to slip out of Salekhard, even during the two morning explosions. In fact, not a single Sno-Cat or Nenets sledge had left or even attempted to leave that morning.

We drove through the streets of Salekhard — empty, as if frozen solid — past buildings defaced by anti-Russian inscriptions and drawings. As a rule, from four to seven in the evening was the liveliest time of day. The shops — hairdressers, the café, the post office — were open, and there was the usual urban hustle and bustle on the main thoroughfare, Lenin Street, with its bright streetlamps. Up to three days ago that's how it had been, especially since the Yamaltrade and Yamal-

138

store trusts, as was usual before public holidays — in this case, the pipeline opening — had supplied the shops with imported boots and shoes, ladies' underwear, Finnish-made men's suits, transistor radios and tape recorders (the food stores had real butter and even chickens!). Naturally, the streets of Salekhard had filled up at once with sledges loaded down with weighty bags of goods obtained by queuing. It took more than a snowstorm to remove from these people's faces the smiles of happiness which seemed to say: 'We've come through, we've tamed the tundra, and now we've got something to celebrate with!'

But today all that holiday bustle had gone from Salekhard. The town was under siege, something like Beirut during the Israeli occupation: only armed police patrols, tracked vehicles — and hordes of Nenets youngsters. Since their Russian teachers and boarding-school staff had not turned up for work, the children went tramping round the central streets or riding in dog-sleighs; some even attached themselves with metal hooks to the backs of Sno-Cat and slid, laughing, behind them along the icy roads. Nenets teenagers, sixteen or seventeen years old, strolled around the streets in festive *malitsas* and *kisi*,[1] jeering at the police patrols and Gee Bee Sno-Cats in their own language. What they were saying practically none of the Russians understood, but their gestures were eloquent. As if by chance, as soon as a patrol or Sno-Cats got near, they would draw a handsome bone-handled knife (an essential part of Nenets national trappings) from the sheath on their belt; this done, they would pretend to test the edge with their thumb to see if it was sharp or not. Needless to say, inscriptions such as 'Russians, get out of the tundra!' and 'The tundra spirits are with us!' were their work, as were the drawings of blood-dripping male penises disfiguring the faces of Russian tundra-tamers on the triumphal posters.

The motorcade halted by the North Hotel, a three-storeyed building with a façade freshly painted for the arrival of the European visitors and bearing an enormous plywood sign declaring, in scarlet letters: 'THE PARTY: MIND, CON-

---

[1] *Kisi*: thigh-length boots made from deer fur

Shatunov got out of the car with me, and we went into the hotel. In the middle of the empty lobby, Major Orudjev was playing cards with a police-patrol detail: an extremely young sprig of a lieutenant and two vigilantes. Two guard dogs from the camp were dozing by Orudjev's feet.

On seeing Shatunov, the police detail and Major Orudjev sprang to their feet in alarm. The young lieutenant rapped out in a loud voice:

'Comrade Major, permission to report! All quiet in the sector entrusted to me, nothing to report!'

Shatunov nodded sourly towards the manager's counter.

'Where's the hotel manager?'

'The hotel staff have not reported for work, comrade Major,' the lieutenant informed him, and added with a smile: 'They're sat at home barricaded in, comrade Major. Scared of spirits.'

'I see,' said Shatunov. 'And who do you think is going to look after the military commanders here? Pushkin? Look sharp and get hold of a Sno-Cat and get round the houses! Everybody is to be at their posts within half an hour! Clean linen in all bedrooms! The Divisional Staff are going to be based here, understand?'

'Very good, comrade Major. Permission to carry on?'

'Carry on.' Shatunov's eyes followed the policemen as they rushed out of the hotel. Then he turned to Orudjev. All this time he had been standing to attention by the counter. 'Why haven't you gone? You should be back at the camp, otherwise all your cons will be doing a runner.'

'There's no diesel fuel, comrade Major,' said Orudjev. 'Can't go without it. The KGB transport stores won't refill us and neither will the police, they haven't enough for us. They won't even give me any meat for the dogs. They haven't eaten for two days.'

'They haven't earned any meat, your dogs, that's why!' said Shatunov. 'All right, while they're collecting up the hotel staff you can sit here on guard. Later I'll issue an order for the diesel fuel. And then out of my sight straight away, understand?'

'Very good, comrade Major.'

Shatunov sighed, gazed round the hotel lobby and went out without a word. His Volga at once shot off towards the airport to meet the parachute division, and Orudjev and I were left alone in the hotel. I started to climb the stairs to the second floor. Even through my back I could sense the beseeching, dog-like gaze of Orudjev. A single gesture on my part, a mere turn of the head, and he would have flown up those stairs to my room. But I did not look back. All that had been between us only three days ago in Camp no. RS–549, stayed there — on the straw mattress in the room where prisoners were allowed to meet their close relatives. There it had been one Orudjev; here, quite another. Let him thank his lucky stars for what had happened.

I went up to my room and turned the key twice in my lock just to be on the safe side. I hadn't the strength to take a bath; I wrenched my boots off, discarded my sheepskin, pulled off my fur coveralls and flopped into bed. The last thing I heard was the heavy drone of aircraft away out over the Ob.

■ Chapter Three

Operational Report

Special military communication

To: Minister of Defence, USSR
    Member of Politburo Central Committee, CPSU,
    Marshal Dmitry Ustinov

From: Commander October Revolution Paratroop Division,
    General Grinko

In accordance with your orders, today 12 December 1983 at 16.30 the October Revolution paratroop division, consisting of three parachute regiments, two independent armoured battalions and nine helicopter squadrons disembarked at Salekhard Airport.

After an examination of the strategical situation I decided to surround the town with the military forces at my disposal and tighten the ring gradually, entering the town and searching every house, leaving patrols beyond the town limits and using observer-helicopters.

The division completed the operation by the time comrade Bogomyatov, First Secretary of Tyumen Province party committee, arrived from Tyumen with his entourage, that is at 20.40 local time.

As a a result of the operation the following have been arrested:

(1) Forty-two traffickers in fruit, all persons of Caucasian origin, present in Salekhard with intent to sell fruit and vegetables brought in from the Caucasus at black market prices.

(2) Thirty-nine youths aged 17-18, all persons of Nenets origin, for venturing disparaging remarks during the operation and other anti-Russian activities.

(3) Prostitutes, 132 in all, living in Salekhard without a permit.

(4) Seven persons of Tartar origin, resembling one of the wanted criminals to wit T. Zaloyev (all seven subsequently released after careful police enquiries).

Despite the meticulous care taken during the operation, the criminal-murderers were not discovered in Salekhard.

Jointly with the province party leadership from Tyumen and with the assistance of the chiefs of the local KGB, police militia and CID, we are proceeding to widen the sphere of operations across the Yamal-Nenets district.

General V. Grinko

Salekhard, Divisional HQ, North Hotel

12 December 1983, 21.30 hours

▪ Chapter Four

I'd managed to get in exactly three hours' sleep before the hotel became full of the crashing of army boots and voices issuing military commands. It was the staff of the paratroop division getting settled in at the hotel.

I got out of bed and took from my rucksack a pair of calf-leather boots, grey uniform skirt, officer's shirt and tie and tunic with its militia lieutenant's epaulettes. There was nowhere to iron them, but if I dabbed a little water on the creases my tunic and skirt would hug my figure — by no means the worst in the world — and everything would be okay.

I got dressed, put on my eye make-up, had a good look at myself in the mirror and went downstairs to the lobby.

So recently empty and quiet, it now resounded with the rumble of male voices, the crackle of radios in constant communication with the helicopters circling above the town, the to-ing and fro-ing of messengers, and that peculiar army smell: a complex mixture of male sweat, soldiers' tarpaulin boots, shag tobacco and the squeaky leather of officers' shoulderbelts.

Far down the lobby, officers of the militia and KGB were questioning those who had been arrested: Georgian and Armenian fruit traffickers, prostitutes, Nenets youngsters, and Tartars who did or did not resemble Zaloyev's photo. Many of the young Nentsi were stubbornly refusing to talk to the investigators in Russian.

Aware of the interested eyes of the paratroop officers on me — my dress uniform hadn't been a waste of time! — I walked the length of the lobby to Major Zotov's table and saluted:

'Investigator Kovina present and reporting for duty.'

'Had your sleep out?' He asked and, without waiting for an

144

answer, looked at the four arrested persons: three lads and a girl. They were standing in front of his table, pale and scowling, narrowing their already slit eyes.

'Who's been writing "Russians, get out of the tundra"?' asked Zotov in Russian.

There was an answering silence. I translated the question into Nenets: in my four years spent working on Yamal I'd become fluent in that rather simple language. This was hardly surprising, though to be honest I'd not once opened the copy of *Nenets Fairy Tales and Legends* that Hudya Benokan had given me as a present.

'You think they don't understand Russian?' Zotov smiled. 'The inscriptions are in Russian, no mistakes.' He addressed the boys again: 'Why have you got knives?'

Silence. I translated the question again.

'Nentsi have always carried knives,' the eldest answered me in Nenets. 'A Nenets would be lost without a knife in the tundra, however.'

Zotov understood the reply perfectly, but asked in Russian nevertheless.

'This is not the tundra, however. This is the town. Why do you need a knife in town?'

Silence.

'The Russians brought you out of the tundra and into boarding school, taught you to read and write, gave you electric light,' said Zotov. 'Why don't you like Russians? Me, for example?'

'The Russians gave us light and took away the tundra, however,' grinned the youngest, aged about fourteen.

'They kidnapped me on the tundra and brought me into boarding school, the Komsomol. And then the Komsomol secretary wanted to shag me in his study!' said the girl; she would be about sixteen, no more.

This pronouncement was no news to us. Every autumn before the start of the new academic year, people from the district education department went out in helicopters to the Nentsi grazing their reindeer on the most northerly areas of tundra, close to the Arctic Ocean. Nentsi won't part with their kids over eight or nine for the world: they're the best hands

145

with the reindeer and about the house. Any ten-year-old Nenets knows how to lasso a wild reindeer, deliver a reindeer calf or find a runaway animal on the tundra, and much else besides. So the education department people apply a simple method which has stood the test of time: they get the obstinate parents drunk on vodka, both father and mother. After that, they exchange the children for bottles of vodka — one bottle per child. The youngsters are carried off to boarding schools in Salekhard, Nadym and Urengoi. There, from time to time the Komsomol leaders (and sometimes non-Komosol at that) allow themselves a little fun with the young Nenets girls. Needless to say, from a legal point of view even a sixteen-year-old Nenets girl is theoretically below the age of consent; yet on the other hand the Nentsi themselves give their daughters in marriage at thirteen, sometimes even at eleven! Generally speaking, up till relatively recently our men had no trouble sleeping with a Nenets girl. Any Siberian who's been around will tell you about the Nenets hospitality ritual: the head of the family would tuck up his own wife in the bed of any Russian visitor who happens to be staying the night in his choom — a treat. He would even be insulted if his 'treat' was declined. As little as fifteen to twenty years ago, women in Nenets settlements, on seeing a helicopter full of Russian geologists, would run out to meet them with joyful cries of : '*Lyucha*[1] have come! Now we'll have some fucking!'

But over recent years the situation has begun to change. This is due either to the arrival of a new generation of more or less literate adult Nentsi or to the fact that the demand for women has risen incredibly with the influx into the sub-Arctic of hundreds of thousands of single men and the Nenets girls have suddenly discovered their market value; most likely a bit of both. Some young girls at the boarding schools have stopped being pushovers in this sense; come to that, on several occasions our town court in Urengoi has settled alimony claims made by under-age Nenets mothers against local geologists and engineers!

---

[1] *Lyucha*: Russian (Nenets)

146

I glanced at Zotov, wondering how he would react to the sixteen-year-old's statement. At another time, probably, he would have tried to discover the name of this corrupt Komsomol secretary who had tried to seduce her in his study; now, he merely gave it up as a bad job.

'All right, let them go. Write her name down and we'll sort it out later.'

I wrote it down on my notepad: 'Ayuni Ladukai, sixteen years, eighth class, Boarding School no. 3, 9 Gagarin Street.'

▌Chapter Five

Everything was quiet by the time Bogomyatov arrived at the hotel. Ye gods, the faces of our party leaders have certainly begun to change over the last few years! There's no comparison between Andropov, Aliev and Gorbachev and those who were in the Politburo before. If you made a composite picture of a typical member of our old governments, putting together Kruschev, Brezhnev, Podgorny, Bulganin and the rest, whose pictures have followed me since I appeared in the world, you would get a well-fed, rosy-cheeked face with a double chin. The eyes would be devoid of any hint of intellect, romance or even any basic strength of will. I remember when I was about twelve or thirteen this used to annoy me a lot. For our country, building a new road into the bright future for the whole world, I wanted leaders who were handsome young men, like Vyacheslav Tikhonov, the film star who played Prince Bolkonsky in *War and Peace*.

Bogomyatov, First Secretary of the Tyumen Province party committee resembled neither a prince nor a film star. But he was clearly a man of a new mould — *ours*. I mean he's older than me, of course — about fifty — but he doesn't have that Kruschev–Brezhnev 'falling apart' look in the face. He has the intelligent, forceful, even harsh, face of a leader who knows what he's about. He wasn't wearing the standard short overcoat, either; instead, he had on a becomingly fashionable well-cut sheepskin. With swift steps he and his entourage — the chiefs of the Tyumen Province KGB and police militia — passed through the lobby and went up to the de luxe suite of General Grinko, commander of the paratroop division. There the secretary of the Yamal-Nenets district committee, Rogov, Major Shatunov and Colonel Sini were due to report to

148

Bogomyatov on the current situation in Salekhard. Ordinary investigators like us — and that included Zotov — were not invited to this conference, needless to say.

Yet I had no time to feel a pang of annoyance or hurt vanity, because into the hotel came Rasim Salakhov. The man was a legend: the geologist who had first discovered oil in Western Siberia twenty-two years before. Rasim Salakhov is a separate page in my biography — a special page, I should say. Now they make films and write plays about him, now he's the manager of the Tyumen Oil-Gas trust, Lenin Prize winner and hero of socialist labour. Only eight years earlier, though, he had been merely the head of one of the geological expeditions. Our affair then didn't reach the bed stage only because I was an eighteen-year old idiot, a virgin all atremble over my innocence. I can still remember that taiga clearing above the Irtysh river, when the air was heavy with summer heat and taiga flowers. Salakhov, with typical Caucasian ardour, covered me with his body and I convulsively pressed my legs together, whispering for shame: 'Anywhere but there! Anywhere but there, please!'

Of course, if I'd been brought up in somewhere like Moscow or Paris that stupid stopper wouldn't have been there — at all events, by the age of eighteen it wouldn't have been there any more. But it was my first year at Moscow University and I was still the provincial girl from Voronezh with the powerful volley-ball player's legs. So Salakhov didn't go in 'there' — something I think I still haven't forgiven him for. All the rest did happen between us; in fact, I myself was half-dead with desire and my hands held his hot prick to me, caressing all round my fuzzy maidenhead.

Having come on my belly, Salakhov calmed down, laughing at my 'daftness' and, possibly to distract himself from another onset of desire, started telling me the story of the discovery of Tyumen oil and gas.

During those feverish white summer nights in my confusion of thoughts and desires I scarcely listened to him and remembered nothing apart from isolated episodes from his adventures over twenty years in the wild Siberian taiga and the Nenets tundra. Apparently, as long ago as the thirties the celebrated geologist academician Gubkin had predicted the discovery of

149

oil in Siberia. Going on certain resemblances between the geological structure of the West Siberian platform and other oil-bearing regions of the world, he calculated that there ought to be oil in the taiga. But where? Where should searches be made? That the academician did not know. But Siberia is vast: the Yamal-Nenets national district alone is larger than France in area. True, Salekhard is not Paris; the taiga and tundra can't be compared with the Bois de Boulogne and its neat gravel paths. Geological parties wandered through the impenetrable wilderness for thirty years, drowning in the summer bogs and freezing in the polar night. For thirty years the state threw money away on exploratory bore-holes which yielded nothing apart from disproving the celebrated academician's theory. Among these failed geologists was the young, twenty-three-year-old Rasim Salakhov from Baku. On his chestnut stallion, Kazbek, he wandered through the taiga and the tundra, feeding the mosquitoes with his young blood, falling into swamps, fighting with his workmen, former criminals, of course — who else worked on taiga expeditions in those days? With true Caucasian stubbornness he squeezed out enough money in Moscow to equip new expeditions.

Nevertheless, in 1960 all this came to an end. The Ministry of Geology halted oil prospecting in Siberia as being completely hopeless. The last geologists abandoned the taiga. Autumn navigation barges ferried out drilling rigs and the rest of the bulky oil prospecting equipment. There was only one drilling derrick they couldn't manage to get out: ice had gripped the tundra river Plotva. Salakhov kept the Moscow evacuation order from his workpeople and sank a last bore-hole near Surgut — but nowhere near where the geologists had said it should be. 'Ya see,' he told me in his Caucasian accent, 'oil is lighter than water and geologists had always found it in the anticlines of oil-bearing strata. But here there was no oil in the anticlines. For thirty years people drilled bores into those domes — and no oil, no nothing! But at least a century ago the Nentsi had seen "greasy patches" on the lakes. They reckoned it was the "earth sweating". But that was oil, *oil*! Well, so I decided to go against the rules, and not drill into the domes but at the very base of the anticline.

'For five months the drilling went on — imagine, five months! In winter, with no wages, no bread — we just ate venison. I don't know how many times the workers wanted to murder me — I had some canisters of spirit and I swapped it for reindeer meat from the Nentsi. Well, the workmen wanted the spirit as well — the lot at once ... In March 1961 the bore exploded in an oil gusher, the drilling rig collapsed and such a torch of burning oil roared out over the tundra that six Nenets camps up and bolted while we jigged about round the blaze and rubbed oil over each other ... Now they want to make a film of it all — some writer even flew out from Moscow to see me. They'll never do it like it really was! They'll never put on the screen that I was held by the KGB for six months while they tried to pin sabotage charges on me — who gave *me* permission to set light to the oil, national property?'

We sat there above the Irtysh, Salakhov smiling bitterly as he remembered the past and I smoothing his curly hair, black but with a hint of grey, kissing his prickly moustache. In a few minutes we were rolling around again among the fireflowers and willow herb. Yet when it came to sex, Salakhov was not so invincibly persevering as he had been when searching for Siberian oil, and I left my first student practice a virgin. Two years later the film about Salakhov, *The Land of the Long Winter*, was released and then there was a play, but needless to say neither film nor play contained the KGB episode. Either the writer had been scared to put it in, or the censor had cut it out.

Another two years after that I got my law diploma and requested a posting to Tyumen Province — not without a certain amount of romantic daydreaming. When I arrived in Tyumen, I discovered that Salakhov was now the chief geologist of Western Siberia, head of the Tyumen-Oil-Gas trust and Lenin Prize laureate. How could I, just one of thousands arriving in the taiga in those days, fight my way through to such giddy heights of authority? And what reason could I put forward to get an appointment? Report to him that I was no longer a virgin but that I'd dreamt dozens of times in the students' hostel at Moscow University of being with him in that clearing above the Irtysh filled with fireflowers and willow herb?

I spent a week in Tyumen, striding about like a complete idiot under the windows of Tyumen-Oil-Gas in all my non-working hours. I was rewarded by a glimpse of Salakhov arriving at the trust in his personal Volga. He walked into the building three paces from me, hurrying as usual. Naturally, he didn't notice me, with all those passers-by. And no doubt after me there had been plenty of probationers in those clearings with him, and not so stubborn either. After all, Salakhov was now a celebrity, hero of stage and screen ... To cut a long story short, I applied that very day to the Tyumen Province police chief requesting a transfer to some newly-built tundra settlement as far as possible from Tyumen.

And now the romantic hero of my girlish dreams was walking into the lobby of the North Hotel. Short sheepskin coat, tarpaulin trousers beneath a fur coverall, dog-fur boots and the same stiffly curly hair, now completely grey and beautifully barbered, above dark Caucasian eyes. A number of people, evidently from Tyumen, were coming in after him, but I only had eyes for Salakhov. A sort of oppressively warm wave of tenderness and sadness swept over me from head to foot.

'*An torovo, hasava!*'[1] was his loud and cheerful Nenets greeting to one and all.

'Well, now, are these "tundra spirits" giving you a hard time?'

Of course, only Salakhov could permit himself to clown about in a situation like this! He was at once surrounded by the heads of the local geological authorities, who had drilled in here under various pretexts but really for the protection of the paratroops. He shook hands with them, joked, clapped someone on the shoulder — and then caught sight of me standing among the others. For several oppressively long seconds he looked into my eyes; then he abruptly moved someone aside and walked straight towards me. In those moments it seemed that his gaze caressed my hair, shoulders, eyes ...

'Anya?' he said as he approached.

Close to, I could see how he had aged over the years.

---

[1] *An torovo, hasava*: Hello, friends! (Nenets)

Wrinkles and furrows had creased his brow and face. In his eyes lay the deep weariness of an ageing man.

'What on earth are you doing here?' I asked quietly.

'It is Anya, isn't it?' he asked again, switching his astonished gaze from my face to my militia lieutenant's uniform.

'Yes, I'm Anya. I'm an investigator now. But what are *you* doing here?'

He seemed to understand what lay behind my question.

'I?' he said cheerily for the whole lobby to hear. 'I'm just getting a bit closer to the Nenets spirits. I mean, if they're castrating the people who discovered oil and gas here, they should have started with me! The point is, I want to take a walk by myself round Salekhard. Just to show there's no such thing as these ridiculous tundra spirits, and put an end to the panic. People have stopped work all over the Yamal. But you can keep me company if you like. I don't think a woman will frighten the spirits off. Will you?'

'What do you mean — are you serious?'

'Of course I am!' he added softly. 'None of my expeditions have been operating for three days. People are on the run from Urengoi, Tarko-Sale, Nadym — imagine what that means. Are you coming?'

I shrugged. Perhaps he was right. Maybe if they wanted the panic to stop, the top people shouldn't be hiding in here under the wing of the paras; they should be out on the streets. But only Salakhov could hit on the idea; tomorrow the word would go round the whole territory that Salakhov *himself* was strolling around Salekhard freely and without any bodyguard — and that no 'spirits' had laid a finger on him. This would bring Russians and Nentsi to their senses.

Of course, as an atheist I've got no time for mystical nonsense, and, anyway, when you've got a good hundred of our gallant paratroop officers around you the devil himself wouldn't scare you, even if his existence were scientifically proved. So Salakhov and I left the hotel as if we were on a lyrical stroll — accompanied by jokes from those present.

'Have you got your pistol with you?' asked Salakhov in the doorway.

'Yes.'

'Leave it here.'

'Why?'

'Leave it, I said.'

I pulled my TT out of its holster, and in front of the paras, investigators, geologists and youthful Nenets prisoners I handed it over to Zotov.

'Ah, the purity of the experiment above all!' said one of the geologists. 'But we should check if Salakhov has got his male tool with him!'

Out on the street in front of the hotel, the engines of the paratroopers' personnel carriers were snarling and wreathed in grey exhaust fumes. Beyond them, though, the street was empty and dead. The frost nipped at our faces and the snow crunched under our feet.

'Scared?'

'I should think not,' I lied, because in actual fact the further we got from the hotel the more uncomfortable I felt inside. I believe I began to understand those people who had so easily panicked. You can be an atheist a hundred times over, but when you're face to face with a dead, frozen town in the dark of the polar night every rustle, every dog coming round the corner can seem like a ghost, a murderer, a tundra spirit.

'Okay,' said Salakhov, taking my arm. 'Tell me about yourself. How long have you been in Salekhard?'

'This is my second day. Actually, I work in Urengoi. Five years now.'

'And never phoned once, never called in ... You married?'

'No'.

We let a patrolling armoured car pass along the road, then I asked:

'Are *you* married?'

'Yes, I've got three children already. Making up for lost time. You frozen?'

'Not yet ... Look!'

An extraordinary display of northern lights had begun above us, above the town and the Yamal tundra. It doesn't matter how many times you've seen it, there's no getting used to a sight like that. The dark sky suddenly seemed to fly up from the earth — up, up and up! And at every corner of this huge and instantly luminous heaven appeared broad, shining, ghostly-icy multicoloured bands of flickering fire. They resembled shining ribbons fluttering across the sky, constantly changing altitude, tone and colour. And all this in total silence, soundless as if it really were what the Nentsi say, the spirits of the dead flying through the sky . . .

The ever-changing hues of glowing yet lifeless light illuminated the squat snowbound houses of Salekhard, its dark dead streets and, directly in front of us, on the wall of some official building a large red poster. It bore the legend 'THE RICHES OF THE TUNDRA — FOR OUR BELOVED HOMELAND!' The poster was of the standard type; beneath the slogan was a picture of a young workman with a clear and open Russian face. He stood against a tundra backdrop, with oil derricks scattered over the landscape. The workman's face had been disfigured in the usual obscene manner: a bleeding penis had been drawn onto his mouth. In rough, uneven lettering the inscription read: 'RUSSIANS, OUT OF THE TUNDRA!'

Salakhov inspected the poster in silence.

From round a corner a sudden rush of feet, voices — low as if stifled — and the sound of muffled blows. Salakhov and I raced wordlessly in that direction, rounded a corner and saw what was happening.

Under the Northern Lights, beneath the windows of a working men's hostel, about ten of them were beating up a Nenets. The latter was a short fellow, in all probability drunk — he didn't cry out, and was putting up no resistance. Wrapped in his thick reindeer *malitsa* he kept falling down like a sack under the blows, but they pulled him up again and hit him with savage enjoyment, using fists and feet. The shapes of approving spectators stood at the hostel windows.

As Salakhov and I ran up, the crowd took us for their own and stood aside for us to do our bit; but, of course, Salakhov didn't start hitting the Nenets. He seized somebody by the collar and asked brusquely:

'What's up?'

'Nothing! Thump him!' The inertia of the fight caused the workman to tear Salakhov's hand from his coat collar and rush towards the Nenets again. The rest, meanwhile, carried on

155

hitting him. Someone held the Nenets up by the *malitsa* so he wouldn't fall over.

'Stop this!'

Amazed at my feminine voice (here, in winter clothes a woman can easily be mistaken for a man), they let the Nenets go for a moment and he fell like a sack of potatoes.

'What's he done?' asked Salakhov.

'Ah, nothing! He's a Nenets, the shit! We'll show them tundra spirits now!' and he slammed his boot full force into the recumbent Nenets.

The same second Salakhov slashed the workman with his fist so that he fell onto the ice-covered pavement with his legs kicking in the air.

'What're you hitting your own for, bastard?' The rest rushed towards Salakhov, and I at once regretted leaving my pistol in the hotel.

'Stop! This is — Salakhov!' I shouted at them.

'We don't give a shit for Salakhov or whoever he is! We were thumping a Nenets — why the fuck's he interfering? We're going to squash the lot of them now, the shits. With tanks — our troops have arrived!' They shouted, keeping up the heat.

Yet the legendary name of Salakhov, familiar to every worker in the tundra, led them to restrain their knotted fists.

'Are you really Salakhov, *the* Salakhov?' someone asked, calmer now.

'*The* Salakhov ...' he brought out, lifting the Nenets from the ground.

His eyes were closed; the broad face with its prominent cheekbones was smashed and a thin fountain of blood had spurted from his mouth. His head lolled forward onto his chest, like a doll's.

'You've killed him,' said Salakhov, lowering the Nenets to the ground.

'Well, fuck him!' said the one Salakhov had knocked down. He was now on his feet.

'One wog less, who cares!'

But he didn't manage to finish the phrase. A blow from Salakhov flush on the teeth made him choke off the last bit and crash into the roadway again next to the dead Nenets.

'What's up, chief? Have you gone bloody barmy?' said one of the workmen, astounded. He pointed at the man Salakhov had twice struck. 'What's he done to you?'

'I'm a "wog" too!' Salakhov shouted at them, and for the first time in my life I saw a furious Caucasian. He walked towards them, shouting: 'I'm an Azerbaidjani! To you Russian pigs I'm a wog, like that Nenets! Well, who's going to hit me, eh?'

'Come on, all right, all right, chief, cool down!' They were backing off and turning away from his fists. 'Nobody means you. Nobody's touched you —'

But if I hadn't intervened and hung onto Salakhov he would have provoked them to another fight. But no problem: I had been taught in the police how to grab a man from behind so that he can't move.

'You cheap bastards! Strong if you've got tanks.' Salakhov was struggling to be free and suddenly shouted at me: 'Let me go, dammit, Russian idiot!'

I shuddered as if I'd been slapped, and let him go.

He turned and spoke to me face to face.

'Should have fucked you that time, no pity! All of you should be —' he went off without finishing. Again I regretted leaving my pistol at the hotel. At that, I would hardly have dared to shoot at him, Salakhov! Besides, at that moment the echo of another explosion rolled out over Salekhard.

■ *Chapter Six*

From the Operational Log of the October Revolution paratroop division:

On the evening of 12 December, after operational units of our division had entered Salekhard, local working men in a drunken state began to seek out and assault Nentsi. Six cases of fatal assault were registered and twenty-three of grievous bodily harm.

At 22.17 hrs local time a twelve-year-old Nenets youth, a pupil of Boarding School no. 3, Vauli Litkoi, set fire to a personnel-carrier parked near the North Hotel by dipping a smouldering bundle of reindeer hide in the petrol tank. The explosion damaged the hotel building. Seven soldiers and two officers were wounded.

Immediately after this, assaults on Nentsi became extremely widespread ...

Chapter Seven

We ran up to the North Hotel before the powdered snow raised by the explosion had had time to settle. Fragments of the destroyed personnel-carrier were still burning at various points on the roadway, along with the placard: 'THE PARTY: MIND, CONSCIENCE AND HONOUR OF OUR EPOCH', which had tumbled off the hotel façade.

The pale faces of the party leaders peered out of the shattered hotel windows as soldiers hauled the wounded indoors.

In the lobby, paratroops, geologists and police stood in a dense crowd by a sofa on which lay a mortally-wounded Nenets boy, twelve years of age. I pushed through the crowd after Salakhov and saw: the boy's shoulder and side had been mangled by splinters from the destroyed vehicle. His tattered old *malitsa* was drenched in blood. The paratroop medical officer stood up and waved the stretcher-bearers away: no one could help the boy now. The last signs of life were quickly fading from the broad, high-cheekboned face. Nevertheless, Hudya Benokan, kneeling in front of the boy, cried:

'Why? Why did you do this? Who put you up to it?'

The boy opened his narrow eyes and — or so it seemed to me — even smiled slightly.

'Vauli —' he replied softly.

'Vauli who?'

The boy was clearly gathering his breath to answer. We froze.

'Vauli Piettomin,' he brought out. 'He has come.'

One of the paratroop officers next to me asked:

'Who's this Vauli? One of the escapers?'

'It's their national hero,' said Zotov. 'Like Spartacus. Two hundred years ago he raised a rebellion against the Russian tsar. He was caught, escaped from forced labour, fomented another rising and was killed. But the Nentsi believe he will return —'

'And the other two explosions — was that you?' Benokan asked the boy.

'Us ...' sighed the boy, and in that 'us' there was pride.

'But why? Why?' Benokan cried out again in despair.

'Because I ...' the boy muttered in a feeble voice. 'I am Vauli. But you ...' Here, with his last reserve of energy, he was clearly intent on spitting in Hudya's face. His strength failed him, though: the bloody spittle froze on his lips and his eyes closed. The doctor took his hand and felt the pulse.

'All over,' he pronounced after a few seconds.

Hudya Benokan rose and surveyed us all with his narrow eyes, now almost white. He seemed to shout something at us, or say something. But without uttering a sound he walked with the slow, heavy waddling gait of all Nentsi through the crowd, which made way for him, and out of the hotel door into the street.

In the ensuing silence the words of the duty staff officer sounded crisp and clear. Clutching a number of radio messages in his hand he went up to the paratroop commander, General Grinko, saluted and said:

'Comrade General, permission to report. Aircraft have observed three drilling sites on fire in tundra regions Anaguri, Nugma and Yunarta. None of the three have responded to radio calls ...'

Three sites on fire! At any other time one fire would have been enough to set off a general commotion, but now the news made no special impact on us. Only Shatunov sighed and said:

'It's started. This is what I've been afraid of.'

Lakes Anaguri, Nugma and Yunarta lay at widely separated points on the Yamal peninsula, three hundred — even four hundred kilometres — to the north of Salekhard, so there could be no thought of escaping cons being responsible for the fires. They had only lit the fuse of Nenets hatred for us Russians, bottled up for centuries.

I saw Salakhov go pale and approach General Grinko:

'Connect me to your airmen, the ones who can see the fires.'

'Why?' asked the General.

'If it's only the derricks ablaze, that's not so bad. If there's been a gas blow-out —'

'I think we'd better get out there in any case,' said the General, and turned to a youthful colonel. 'Scramble three squadrons on operational alert!'

▌Chapter Eight

Anybody might envy the efficiency of the paras in action. Within minutes the military helicopters had taken off from Salekhard Airport and set course for Anaguri, Nugma, and Yunarta. At the same time three enormous MI-10 helicopters put down close to the hotel, right on the snow-covered wooden roadway; they picked up the investigation teams and all possible top brass, including Shatunov, Salakhov and Zotov. I wasn't in any of the teams investigating the fires. Zotov hid his eyes as he said to me:

'Kiddywink, you've worn yourself out these last few days. Besides we have to find out urgently who's been spreading rumours among the Nentsi that their Vauli Piettomin's come back.'

'You've got Hudya Benokan for that!' I answered, furious. 'It's his field, let him do the job. Especially as he's a Nenets.'

'I don't trust him,' said Zotov.

'Really?'

'You saw what he was like when that kid died? No, it's better if you deal with these Vauli rumours. Who's putting them about? Why? Go round the schools, you can speak the language. The children will talk better to a woman.'

The assignment, of course, was just a way of keeping me away from the fires. Even though it was obvious that these were more serious crimes than a boy setting an army vehicle alight — but no, we men will deal with that, you stay in Salekhard and do a bit of snooping on the Nentsi ...

Zotov apparently read all this in my eyes as he added, hastily:

'If there's anything interesting at the fires I'll send for you, kiddywink, honestly!'

I snorted contemptuously and went back into the hotel and up to my room.

Once there I plonked myself down on the bed and bawled my eyes out. Not at all because Zotov hadn't taken me with him to investigate the reason for the fires; it was because of what had happened between Salakhov and me two hours ago. Come to that, I was unable to have a proper cry anyway, given that thirty degrees of frost was blowing in through the window, smashed in the explosion. I got up off the bed and wiped away my tears as I walked over to the window to shove a cushion in it. Outside, the last MI-10 was taking off, its engines roaring. Bastards, the lot of them, bastards — Zotov, Salakhov, Hudya Benokan, the whole blasted lot!

I opened my rucksack and drew out my emergency store — a bottle of Stolichnaya vodka, poured out half a glass and tossed it down.

Now I could carry on working and do Zotov's bidding. The twelve-year-old Vauli Litkoi who had set the personnel-carrier alight had been a pupil of Boarding School no. 3.

I took out my notepad. According to this Ayuni Ladukai, the sixteen-year-old girl who had told Zotov and me that some Komsomol secretary had tried to rape her was resident at the same boarding school. All right, it was a perfectly good pretext for paying this Ayuni a visit and taking a look round the whole school at the same time.

▉ Chapter Nine

A fat little puppy dog, falling about on uncertain legs, came running joyfully towards me along the corridor as soon as I opened the door of Boarding School no. 3. In the empty corridor, half-filled with battered school desks, a boy's voice, high and breaking, echoed and re-echoed.

'And like wolf-packs on their quarry
There came streaming like a river
Russian hordes upon our homeland,
Pushing up away to northward,
Far off to the Icy Ocean,
Stripping us of all our pastures,
All our rivers, all our fishing,
Beasts and fowl and all our reindeer,
Everywhere intent to ravish
Wives and sisters and our daughters . . .'[1]

'So-o-o! Some poem!' I thought, as I closed the outer door. Carefully, so as not to step on the silly pup or knock against the stuff piled up in the corridor: boots, *malitsas*, a punctured globe and so forth, I moved along the corridor towards the classroom from where the boy's voice was coming.

'Hear us, hear us, Lord Almighty —
This is the voice of all thy peoples,
All thy peoples now in bondage,
Worn out by the weary burden —

---

[1] Here and elsewhere: these are genuine verses from 'Yangal-Maa', a nineteenth-century Nenets ballad. This was only published once in Russia, in 1933.

By the battle never-ending
To sustain a bare existence.'

I glanced in at the partly-opened door. It was a normal school classroom with all its desks apparently thrown out into the corridor. Yet the blackboard remained, and on it were chalked the words: 'RUSSIAN OCCUPIERS, OUT!'

A short, slit-eyed boy of about thirteen was standing beneath the blackboard holding an exact copy of the book Hudya Benokan had once given me — *Nenets Ballads and Fairy Tales*. He was reading from memory, though, not looking at the book:

'Well thou knowest Lord Almighty,
How the strangers came among us
Into our beloved homeland
Came the Rus with fire of cannon,
Came with axe and deadly poison
In he came with priests of cunning
Rus came thieving — took with iron,
Priest — with cross and honeyed speeches ...'

Yet the most remarkable thing in that classroom was not the boy reciter or even the sacrilegiously defaced portrait of Lenin on the wall; it was the audience. They were sitting on the floor, densely packed together — about two hundred people. There were children eight to ten years old and youngsters of sixteen, seventeen or eighteen. They wore reindeer *yagushki*[1] unbuttoned in the heat and had long hair, broad cheekbones, slit eyes. Their figures were bent towards the reader in what seemed one concerted movement. Their eyes were riveted on him and his words:

'Then the Russian war detachments
Conquered us with swords of iron,
Did away with all our elders
Put in posts of power above us
Many bloodsuckers and bandits
Holding court, dispensing justice,

---

[1] *Yaguskhi*: shirts made of reindeer suede

165

Taking from us furs in tribute
And dishonouring our women!
These days all our wives in childbirth
Bear us feeble, breeding weaklings,
Like the seventh pup, the last one,
Born in an old bitch's litter —
Far too weak to rise in anger
Strike for freedom ...'

At this point the indescribable took place. A cry of savage anger, 'No-o-o!,' rose suddenly from every throat. Part of the audience leaped up in fury; somebody rushed towards the declaiming boy, seized the book from his hand, tore out the page and angrily ripped it into pieces, shouting:

'That's it! Enough! That was before. Now — that's it! Read on from here!' He showed the boy another page.

The boy raised his hand for quiet, but the hall was still seething with angry exclamations. Then, like an experienced orator, the boy uttered in a low voice:

'Nut i shar! — the bear's my witness!
I would wish that every Nenets
Shout out loud with voice triumphant:
"Death to the insidious strangers!
Nut i shar!"

By the end of the first two lines the hall had fallen silent, and after 'Death to the insidious strangers' had been pronounced calmly and harshly, the audience spoke as one voice with the boy's:

'Nut i shar! The bear's my witness!
Yamal will one day see its peoples
Seize again their ancient freedom!
Nut i shar!

They leapt to their feet, eyes blazing, their broad faces alight. Among them I recognized Ayuni Ladukai. Of course, any 'heart to heart' talk with her was now out of the question; she was swearing, along with all the rest:

'Nut i shar! The bear's my witness!

166

Times of terror! Keep your courage!
Death will be there, fire and famine;
From the old crone's scarlet death-grin,
Like a pack of wolves in panic,
Leaving all, from tundra flying,
People running for the mountains —
Russian people from destruction!
Nut i shar!

Above the loud chorus rose the high, breaking voice of the reciting boy:

'*Nut i shar!* The bear's my witness!
I can see the glow of fires,
Smell the burning, night draws nearer,
Smoke in clouds blots out the heavens
As the hated Russian bandits
Flee in terror from our forests!'

He seemed to have gone into a trance, a shaman's ecstasy. His whole body shaking, he shouted forth his prophecies:

'*Nut i shar!* The bear's my witness!
After this will come the dawning
Of an age that's new and other
Time of justice and of freedom
From the God-accursed Russians!'

'A tambourine! Fetch him a tambourine!' someone shouted.

A youth sitting by the door jumped up and rushed into the corridor — and stumbled over me. Nor did I have time to jump to one side or hide behind the door. I was discovered, and for a second everything went silent and still as in a theatrical pause. But in the next instant they had recognized me and the roar of voices shook the school.

'Russian! Spy! Bloodhound! Grab her!'

The older lads, around eighteen, flung themselves upon me. Their narrow eyes made me realize that this was no place for joking or for words. I grabbed my pistol.

'Stop — or I'll fire!'

The boys halted.

167

I began to step slowly backwards towards the corridor.

But the corridor was obstructed by broken school desks and other school equipment; it was hard to back off in a straight line, that wretched pup was getting tangled round my feet. Suddenly behind the backs of the senior boys there rang out the voice of the boy reciter, who was walking directly up to me, reciting loudly:

'Go on, shoot, yes, shoot, you bastard!
Nenets oil is not sufficient?
Nenets furs are not sufficient?
Nenets fish are not sufficient?
Let my blood then flow in rivers
Nut i shar! Then shoot, you bastard!'

He was clearly in the same kind of trance that Nenets shamans used to induce in themselves at one time. But I couldn't shoot a boy. I turned away and ran towards the exit.

The leather lasso caught me just by the door, the noose lashed around my neck. Well, those Nenets youngsters know from childhood how to bring down a healthy bull reindeer at full gallop. I felt a sharp tug as if my throat had been cut, and lost consciousness as I collapsed to the floor.

▌ Chapter Ten

'I see the glow of fires': this prophecy of the little shaman from Boarding School no. 3 came true that night with alarming speed.

From *Urgent Report of Party Commission for Suppression of Disturbances in the Yamal-Nenets District to the Soviet Government and Politburo of the Central Committee of the CPSU*

'It was not possible to approach the drilling sites or to execute a parachute drop: at all three sites, gas flares 150–300 feet in diameter are burning to a height of 700–1000 feet. For a radius of 1200–2000 feet around the flares the permafrost has melted, as have the swamps and lakes. An aerial survey of the burning sites showed that all equipment, including the derricks, has been destroyed and the site workers either killed in the fire or drowned in the melted permafrost and swamps.

Owing to the intensity of the flares at the sites, the investigation teams are not in a position to determine how or by whom the fires were started. However, the pre-meditated character of the fires is shown by their simul-taneous incidence in widely-separated parts of the Yamal tundra. At 4.15 in the morning information was received concerning similar fires at drilling sites in the region of Lake Mirigi, the river Haide and near Kamenni settle-ment.

Geological specialists have calculated that the burning fountains are consuming thousands of cubic metres of gas per minute, but the flares can only be extinguished by

169

drilling inclined bore-holes to conduct gas away from the vents which are on fire. Drilling shafts of this nature will take no less than three to four months.

Simultaneously with the occurrence of the fires, a mass flight of workmen from the tundra has been observed, which has resulted in a cessation of drilling operations, the freezing of the clay compound in bore-holes and twenty-two drilling sites being put out of action. Losses are being estimated at millions of roubles a day, and rumours of the 'white terror of the tundra' are threatening to bring the territory's entire Russian population to a standstill, provoke uprisings in the labour camps and prevent the Siberia–Western Europe gas pipeline from coming into operation.

According to the heads of the local KGB and police militia, the arson is being carried out by the native inhabitants of the territory: the Nentsi, influenced by rumours of the return of Vauli Piettomin, who twice led the Nenets people in uprisings against the Russians in the last century. It cannot be ruled out that the escape of the three prisoners from Camp RS-549, the brutal murders of pipelaying and geo-survey chiefs, the explosions in Salekhard and the firing of the drilling sites — it cannot be ruled out that all this is a planned operation on the part of American intelligence aiming to disrupt the Siberia–Western Europe gas pipeline project.

Bearing in mind the above, the Party Commission suggests that the October Revolution paratroop division is by itself *patently insufficient* to restore order speedily throughout the district. The Commission judges that to prevent a total revolt of the Nenets population and the spread of such a revolt to the Khant-Mansi, Taimyr, Evenki and other neighbouring districts populated by northern national minorities, and also to prevent uprisings in labour camps and the threat of the destruction of the gas pipeline and gas enterprises, *it is essential for additional military units to be transferred to the Yamal-Nenets district immediately and to occupy all — repeat all — inhabited points in the district with these forces, to prohibit*

170

all movement across Yamal on the part of the local population'

President of the Party Commission,
First Secretary Tyumen Province Party Committee,
Bogomyatov

Salekhard, 13 December, 5 a.m. local time

Chapter Eleven

I regained consciousness to a familiar combination of pain and pleasure. Next to me, literally by my ear, a tambourine was beating loudly and rhythmically, and in time to the beat a man forcibly entering my body, producing both pain and sexual languor. I automatically wriggled my body to escape my assailant, and only then realized what was taking place.

I was lying absolutely naked on some sort of table; arms, legs, and head were roughly bound to this table with narrow leather thongs, my eyes were heavily bandaged, and I was gagged. I could not move or shout, and I couldn't see who was violating me. It was only the weight on my body and the fact that the emission occurred very quickly that told me it was a boy of about fifteen.

'Next!' said a girl's voice in Nenets.

I was horrified: surely they weren't all here, the whole school, girls as well?

The next boy came into me and, ignoring the tambourine rhythm, finished literally in a second — a twelve-year-old, most likely.

'Next!'

Now something enormous — like an elephant's — was forcing its way into me, literally tearing my insides apart. My shriek must have penetrated the gag. Yet the pain subsided as instantly as it had begun, as he spurted the scalding liquid of his sperm into me even before he had fully entered.

'Next!'

And all of a sudden, through the incessant rapping of the tambourine, a quiet boy's voice, the familiar voice of the boy reciter:

'I don't want to —' he said, in Nenets.

'What?' the girlish voice screeched in indignation.

'I won't do it, however —'

'Oh, fuck you!' swore the girlish voice in pure Russian. 'And yet Russian men can fuck *us*?! I've already had two abortions. They sent Okka to the next world! But you, you cowardly son of a crow, scared to touch a Russian woman. Now, then, where's your *khote*? Soon you'll be able to manage anything, however. I sure learnt a lot from those Russians!'

I didn't see what happened next; I only heard general laughter and the steady beat of the tambourine. In half a minute, no more, the next boy's *khote* entered my body and spent itself at once.

'Next!'

I swore to myself that if I survived I would kill that little girl; the others as well, but her first.

The beat of the tambourine was bursting my brain.

Yet another almost instant injection of sperm. I'd already lost count ...

In fact, it was this inability on the part of the boys to sustain sexual activity for long that saved me that evening from severe injury or, as they put it in forensic medical reports, 'damage to internal organs'. The youngsters simply spurted the load they had been accumulating in their scrotums, swollen by the erotic dreams boys have; the table under my buttocks was very wet already. No doubt the moisture had even dripped onto the floor — I suddenly heard a muffled blow and a squeal of protest from the puppy as it flew off out of the way. The same little girl's voice gave instructions:

'Get rid of the dog, however! Otherwise it'll get used to licking up sperm!'

The tambourine clashed.

The next *khote* entered my body.

Close to my ear, the same girl's voice sounded:

'Well, Russian bitch? How do you like it, however? That's the way you've been fucking us for three hundred years now. Nice? Me as well they —'

She was interrupted. There was a distant clashing of doors, the tramp of running feet, and a voice — the voice of Hudya Benokan!

173

'Stop this!' he bawled.

The tambourine was silent.

I couldn't see what was happening. The one thing I realized was that belated salvation had arrived; I could let myself go and sink into oblivion. It would have been even better, I thought, if I could have lost consciousness an hour ago so that I wouldn't have had Hudya Benokan, who had been head over heels in love with me five years ago, see me, naked and tied to a table, being raped by a load of schoolboys.

I did not lose consciousness. I waited for the boys to go rushing off at the sound of Hudya's voice, but that didn't happen either. All I felt was my hands, head and legs being freed from the thongs. Hudya, moving round the table, cut through them with one swift movement of his sharp knife. While he was at it, he shouted:

'Why?! Why did you do this?! You'll all go to gaol, the lot of you!'

Sensing that my body was now clear of the straps, I turned over on one side and crossed my legs as I curled up tightly. Hudya drew the gag out of my mouth and cut through the bandage around my eyes. I didn't cry out or weep: I was trembling violently and in dire need of a drink. But I was too weak even to ask for water. I didn't want to open my eyes, either — I didn't want to see, to know, to live.

But I saw and heard all the same.

That same sixteen-year-old Ayuni Ladukai whom Zotov and I had interrogated in the hotel lobby went up to Hudya and said, in that voice which I would never mistake for any other in the world:

'We were avenging Okka! You're not a man — you can't take revenge on the Russians yourself. Just the opposite: you serve them like a faithful hound, however! Huh!'

I don't know who her spit was aimed at, me or Hudya; probably at both of us. But I clearly recall that Hudya made no reply to her. He bent down to retrieve my clothes lying about on the floor and glanced inside my holster. It was empty.

'Give her pistol back!' he said harshly — so harshly, in fact, that one of the boys gave him the gun without argument. Hudya replaced it in the holster; then, wrapping me in my sheepskin, lifted me and carried me in his arms out of the school into the street.

'And we're not scared of Russian courts!' Someone yelled after us. 'There are no prisons beyond the tundra, anyway.'

The thirty-degree frost burnt my lungs and froze my knees sticking out from under my coat. But it cleared my head, and I revived. I burst out crying and buried my head in Hudya's chest. Still holding me in his arms, he quickened his pace.

There was no one about on the empty street: Salekhard seemed dead, numbed.

Chapter Twelve

Hudya took me home with him. He lived three blocks from the school, on the second floor of a concrete building raised on piles; his tiny one-roomed flat was clean, with reindeer skins on the floor and books lining every wall. There was no furniture whatever; just the skins on the floor as in a Nenets choom. Probably taking the place of a hearth, a home-made Dutch stove stood in the middle of the room with a metal pipe leading out through a window.

Hudya bore me through into the bathroom, sat me down on a little stool, turned the shower on hot and left, closing the door behind him. I threw off my sheepskin and forced myself to get up from the stool and step under the spray. I hadn't the strength to stand, though; I sat down in the bathtub and listened and listened to the warming, reviving water flowing and flowing over my skin. I sat motionless — like a mummy, a statue — except for the tears that flowed, unbidden, from my eyes. The water washed them from my face.

About ten minutes later, Hudya knocked anxiously on the door.

I made no reply, didn't even budge — I felt utterly indifferent; it was as if I were stupified, totally deaf and blind.

He opened the bathroom door and saw me sitting motionless under the shower in the overflowing bathtub, just sitting and silently crying. He came up to me and started washing me with soap and a flannel, talking to me softly:

'Never mind . . . never mind, however . . . Forget about it — it never happened. Shall I tell you a fairy story? One of ours, Nenets. About how a little mouse talked with the whole world. Listen, then. A little mouse had a hole right on the bend of a river. In spring, the sun came out into the sky at last and began

176

to warm the whole earth. The snow began to melt on the ground and the ice on the river. And ice floes floated down the river and ran into one another with such a crashing, it was like thunder or someone firing a rifle, however. The little mouse got frightened and came out of his hole and said: "Hey, ice floes, float away! You'll break my house down!" At this, the ice floes spoke up: "Hey, little mouse, what are you talking about? We're ice floes! If we're going down a river, nobody can stop us and nobody can tell us where to float! If there are mouseholes in our way, we'll break down mouseholes as well!" Now the little mouse said, "Hey, ice floes who do you think you are, however? Throw you on the bank and the sun melts you . . .'"

I knew this Nenets fairy tale: it had often been on the radio. The little mouse talks in turn with the ice floes, the sun, the clouds, the mountains and so on, defending its hole. Now the tale had taken on a secondary meaning, a subtext about the crushing passage of the ice floes which nothing could now stop. Yet the thought kept coming and going, fading and getting lost on the rim of consciousness — probably because Hudya's warm, slightly hoarse voice and rough, hairy hands so cautiously touching my back and shoulderblades made me feel cosy in a poignant sort of way, as in childhood. And it really came as a surprise to myself that I suddenly turned my head, caught his hand on my shoulder and pressed my cheek against it. I used to press my father's hand against my shoulder like that when I was a child.

'What made you come into the boarding school?' — I asked.

'I was going round all the boarding schools. Our children had been left alone without supervision as all the teachers had run away. I wanted to tell the children to stop blowing up cars and armoured trucks.'

'Where is your daughter?'

'She is in the tundra, staying with my parents . . .'

Later, wrapped in a sheet, I lay in his room on the floor, on reindeer skins, covered by the hide of a polar bear. Hudya didn't have a bed: like all Nentsi he still preferred sleeping on the floor, despite all his attempts at getting used to one in his student days. I half-lay on the skins while Hudya fed me strong tea from a saucer and firewood crackled cosily in the Dutch stove.

Thinking it over now, I am struck by the complete illogicality of my behaviour. By rights, once I'd recovered from my humiliating violation I should have rushed back to the hotel, to the paratroop division HQ, got hold of a company of paras and arrested the whole bloody school, all the Nenets boys in one go! And there I was, lying and drinking tea from Hudya's hands. Why? Very simple. How could I, the 'Urengoi Alsatian' go to divisional HQ or the CID directorate and say: 'I've just been raped by some Nenets boys!' How could I say that? Who could do it? In spite of the fact that the law and official public morality were on my side, I would still have been a laughing stock in the eyes of the whole CID and everybody else in Salekhard and Urengoi.

It is because of these hidden sneers, this silently contemptuous attitude of the public towards rape, that thousands — even tens of thousands — of women and young girls in the northern hostels, and throughout the country, don't go to the police or even to hospital after being violated. The Moscow prosecutor Malkov revealed an interesting statistic to us when we were on investigator practice: in 1979, seventy percent of women claiming to have been raped were — wait for it — prostitutes using this as a means of settling accounts with clients or lovers.

The average woman finds it easier to endure and suffer the act of rape than expose herself openly as the victim to public — what, scrutiny? No — virtually always, secret mockery. In the heat of wild booze-ups in the men's and women's hostels where the young tamers of the north reside, not a night goes by without a rape, most often a gang — but even from the victim of a gang rape you'll never get honest evidence.

Now I had joined the number of women shielding rapists from justice. But I honestly gave no thought to it that night in Hudya Benokan's flat; I gave no thought to anything. I just drank hot tea from Hudya's hands and in a way that seemed almost natural felt myself to be a little, put-upon girl — not a CID investigator.

Hudya sat in front of me on the floor, tucking his legs beneath him, Nenets fashion; he poured the tea into the saucer and brought it to my lips. I drank, my eyes half-closed, and with the hot strong tea my heart recovered and the pain in my lower belly eased. Hudya's quiet voice was unhurried; like all Nentsi, he softened the 'd' till it almost sounded like 't' — an added charm, as if it weren't an adult but a child telling you an interesting story, soothing away the pain, the Salekhard explosions and the rapes.

'When I was just a little lad,' Hudya was saying, 'my grandfather Eptoma often used to tell us about a certain country. If you can cross the ice floes and keep heading north and pass through a wall of circling winds, you get to people who love one another and know neither enmity nor spite. But those people have only one leg each, and none of them can move independently. Yet they love one another and walk about embracing, loving one another. The more they love, the tighter they embrace and the better they can walk — and even run, faster than the wind. But when they stop loving, then they immediately stop embracing and they die. When they love, they can achieve miracles. So my grandad used to say. And I always used to dream of heading north, getting through the wall of circling winds and finding that land where there is no enmity, no spite, only love ... Are you asleep?'

'No, Hudya. Talk some more.' I stretched out my hand for his and stroked it. 'Please ...'

Hudya got up and put some dry birch logs on the dutch stove. The fire raced swiftly over the birch bark. Hudya put the light off; now only the orange glints from the stove lit up the dark walls and windows. Hudya, without undressing, lay down beside me on the skins.

'Good. Listen,' he said, putting his hands behind his head and lying down next to me at an elbow's distance. 'Only this is not a fairy tale; it happened to me when I was a kid. These last few days I keep remembering the story —'

'Is it frightening, Hudya?' I curled up and snuggled close to him just as I had done long ago in childhood, when I used to get up on the settee and arrange myself at my father's strong officer's shoulder. He was a military man, had worked his way up to lieutenant-colonel, and now lives quietly on his pension in Voronezh.

'No, it's not frightening. Lyrical ...' Hudya, it seemed to me, smiled in the darkness. 'One summer we had brought the reindeer up to the very north of Yamal, to the shore of the Arctic Ocean. There were good grazing grounds there. Not like now, however. I was a boy, ten years old. We had a large herd of animals, two thousand reindeer we had. The dogs knew their job, though, so I could leave the herd and go walking on the tundra. I used to go off from the herd to the shore of the ocean. There you could find something interesting every day. After a storm all kinds of things get thrown up on the beach. I've found American whisky bottles, coloured buoys with yachts' names on and even rubber sneakers — torn, of course. The main thing I was searching for, however, was planks with nails in. Nails and screws, that's what we're short of here — real riches ... You asleep?'

'No, Hudya. Go on.'

I thought I had never felt so warm, uncomplicated and cosy — not with a man, I mean. I lay on Hudya's shoulder, feeling his unshaven cheek on my temple, glints from the fire drifting across us. I knew Hudya was trying to take my mind off what I had been through, to help me to fall asleep with his stories. But no matter how comfortable I was in those moments, I could not sleep. Inside me, apart from enormous weariness, pain and weakness there was some nervous thing beating in my pulse and temples which would not let me sleep. So I just listened.

'So one day after another ocean storm,' said Hudya, 'I found two seagulls on the beach — ocean gulls. There are a lot of birds on the north Yamal — whole bazaarfuls of auks and geese — but we don't get many gulls. These two were lying quite still on the shore; one of them was already dead. The second, the male, was still alive. But so weak it didn't stir as I came up to it. Just looked at me with his round eye and, I well remember, there was already a kind of quiet death film in that eye, however. I'd found dead seagulls before and didn't pay them too much attention — so one had died, the other would lie for a while then fly off. But I came the next day and found the two seagulls in the same place. The live one was sitting motionless next to the dead one. When I got near he tried to rise; but he hadn't the strength to stand up, even though he used his beak to balance on. I ran off and came back with a small fish. I wanted to feed her — that is, him — you haven't

180

got a word in Russian for a male gull. We have, though. Anyway, he wouldn't eat. I pushed the fish into his beak, but he just took it and threw it to one side. He didn't want to eat. If he'd had the strength, he would probably have pecked me, but he hadn't enough even to get up on his legs. Still he refused to eat. And then I understood what was going on: he wanted to die next to his mate. He had decided to die next to her, and even I with my tasty bit of fish couldn't make him change his mind. I realized what had happened to these seagulls. Out over the ocean they had run into a storm. She had succumbed and hadn't made the shore, just fallen onto the water unable to fly. He had likely flown round and round above her on the stormy ocean, crying to her, calling. Have you ever heard gulls crying in a storm? They're crying to those who've given in and fallen onto the water and can't fly, however. But they don't abandon their loved ones. The one I found on the shore, he perhaps flew all night above the waves, over the body of his beloved, watching the waves tossing her, covering her in foam and carrying her closer and closer to the shore. And he flew to that shore, reaching it with his last strength, and saw that the waves had tossed her onto the land. At first, breathless, he lay near her and waited for her to get up. But then daybreak came, the ocean retreated from the shore, and the storm died down; he realized his beloved would never rise again. It was then that he decided to die near her. If he'd been old he'd probably have died the first day. But I came to see him for a whole week — every day — and brought him fish and water. On hot days I bathed him in sea water and kept trying to feed him. But he kept throwing the food away and wouldn't drink the water. On the sixth day, a storm rose during the night. When I ran to the shore after the storm, I couldn't find either him or his dead mate. The storm had carried them back whence they had flown. And he — he had achieved his death next to her, just as he wanted, however. And I realized that the country my grandad Eptoma had spoken of actually did exist. Those two seagulls were from there: that's why they died together. You asleep?'

'Yes, Hudya ... I'm quite, quite asleep,' I whispered, and asked him:

'Hudya, do you love me?'

Hudya was silent.

I had never asked any man that question before. Especially in bed. If only because once you're *in* bed, a man will tell you anything you like to get everything that enters his head that night. The more varied his desires, the more lies he'll tell.

That day I couldn't have satisfied even the most basic of male desires: all my insides were twisted and ached like one big wound, now slightly less painful but still open. And yet I don't think Hudya had that on his mind just then.

'Yes, I love you,' he pronounced after a pause — pronounced calmly, the way they announce an undisputed fact in court. 'I've loved you for four years — even longer, however. That's why I didn't go with you to the concert that time. I didn't want to give in to that love. But I named my daughter Anna after you. And now sleep, however, please.'

'However!' I raised myself on my elbow and kissed Hudya's stubbly cheek. And then — on the lips. His lips were dry, and tightly shut: they did not respond to my kiss. Hudya lay like a stone; not a muscle moved in his face.

I lay back. No, I was not after sex — how could I be, after all that had happened just a couple of hours ago? But surely he could have just moved his lips a little in response? It wasn't my fault I'd been raped — I wasn't a leper, was I? Even for a Nenets. This was the second time this Hudya had said 'no' to me, the second time! A mixture of wounded female vanity and exasperation made me clench my jaws to stop myself from bursting into tears.

And then I felt his hand on my cheek: dry, rough, hairy. I turned my head sharply away. No, I didn't want his sympathy, no patronizing caresses!

'Anya,' he said calmly, in darkness now, as the wood in the stove had burnt through. 'You don't understand. I can't say more than I have said. But what I have said is the truth, however. I had no right to love you in Moscow, and I don't have that right now. And now sleep, please . . .'

At that a furious wave of anger lifted me, no, jerked me upright on the skins. A simple idea had occurred to me and harsh, angry words flew automatically from my tongue —

182

faster than I was able to think.

'You're lying! It's all lies!' I shouted. 'About love and your seagulls — lies! You're just scared I'll arrest those snivelling school rapists — and you're buying me off with your fairy tales and lying! But really you're a coward — a coward, yes! You fell in love with me in Moscow, yes — but not to conquer me, oh no! You ran off into the woods. Let other people sleep with me, let Moscow fat cats seduce me, let officers in the zone sleep with me, or rape me! But not you, you pure romantic — on one leg!'

I didn't know what I was saying myself, but what lay buried within me, beneath my officer's uniform — the simple dream every woman has of loving and being loved and cared for by one man, the dream I had concealed from myself and dissipated, like some prostitute, in bed with the likes of Orudjev, proudly thinking it was not them seducing and using me but I them — that dream suddenly burst through in the form of spiteful insults at this man who could probably have become that one and only if he had but been willing to try. For it was only with him, of all the men I had had, that I felt at ease and cosy as if he had been my own father. That feeling, that instant of perception, means more to a woman than sporting with twenty stallions like Orudjev. That was why I was shouting now at Hudya as I got dressed, shivering, in the dark.

'You prevented yourself falling in love with me in Moscow not because it stopped you studying! No! You think I don't remember how you looked at us when that Nenets kid was dying at the hotel? You hate us Russians; you're a racist — yes, you are! Know what you are? You're a racist and a murderer! You murdered your love because I'm Russian! Then you go and call your daughter Anna in honour of that love. You're a masochist, that's what you are!' In the dark I slipped on the soft skins, swore and fiddled about with my hand for the light switch: I turned on the light.

Hudya was lying on the floor, on the skins, motionless.

I had already put my tunic on when he spoke:

'You're not leaving here. The door's locked, however. The key's in my pocket. You're going nowhere.' The words were spoken simply and convincingly as if stating an obvious fact.

I stood stock-still. Surely he didn't intend to keep me here by force? The nerve of it!

He lifted his arm and glanced at his watch.

'Yes, you're not leaving here for two hours, minimum. Because the boarding-school lads are on their way out of town. I don't want them to be caught.' He got up from the pile of skins with the look of a man who had decided exactly what he was going to do in the next minute. Most probably he simply intended to tie me up. Good God, that meant I was right — in the heat of my anger I had guessed the truth!

Hudya hadn't even got to his feet when a powerful blow landed on his cheekbone. *I* had punched him! I hit him the way they do in the police, they way they *teach* you in the police. I've got trained hands, believe me.

Hudya made no attempt to dodge the blows, though I put all the force of my resentment into them. The swine, swine and bastard! Carried me from the school, told me fairy tales of love, gave me tea, told me he'd loved me for four years — all that, just to let those boy rapists slip out of town quietly and unnoticed. Of course! Who's going to stop youngsters when they're looking for escaped cons?

I hit him, and Hudya stood there like a bull, legs firmly apart holding his squat, sturdy frame craned slightly forward. My next blow took him along the eyebrow, and blood flowed from the cut. I felt a sharp pain in my wrist and realized I'd dislocated it. The bone of his eye sockets must be hellish hard, my God!

'Cretin! Give me the key, I'm getting out —' said I, doubled up with pain.

'I've told you once: you're not leaving. Go to the bathroom and wash your hands. They're all covered in blood —'

Blood was seeping in a thin rivulet from his cut brow onto his eye, but he seemed insensible of it. He looked at me calmly, his eyes perhaps just a little whiter, the swellings under his cheekbones tensed.

'You look as if you've dislocated your wrist. I can put it back.'

'Oh yes, right away,' I sneered. 'What are you talking about?' But I was going round the room in circles from the pain

184

in my hand. At last I took the plunge and tried to set the joint myself, but my wrist responded with such a fierce stab of pain that I exclaimed softly.

Hudya strode over, took my hand and gave a short pull. I cried out again, but the joint had gone back in. Hudya was squeezing my wrist softly with his strong, dry hands, talking as he did so:

'You can believe me or not, it's up to you of course. I told you the truth. About the seagulls I found that time, and about us. I loved you and still do, however.'

'Who's Okka?' I asked, suddenly remembering Ayuni Ladukai's words to Hudya in the school: 'We're avenging Okka! You're not a man — you can't take revenge on the Russians yourself. Just the opposite: you serve them like a faithful hound!'

Hudya went on squeezing my wrist, saying nothing. Then he went into the bathroom and returned with a bandage. The blood from his brow had reached his chin but he paid no attention to it and began binding up my hand.

'So, who's Okka?' I asked again. With my free hand I wiped the blood from his face almost automatically.

'That I can't tell you,' he pronounced. 'Go to bed. I can't let you out on the street alone at night. There are villains out there.' A brief smile touched his lips. The first time in the whole evening, I believe.

'Oh, I won't give your youngsters away!' I said contemptuously. 'That's all I need, for the CID to know I was raped.'

'I thought as much. But in any case I told them to get out of town. That's it.' He neatly tied the bandage with a bow and tucked the ends underneath. 'That bandage will remind you of me for a couple of days. You won't be able to break the door down with one hand, and the key's in my pocket. So let's sleep.'

With these words he lay down on the floor again on the skins, stretched out at full length and closed his eyes.

I stood in the middle of the room, feeling helpless and ludicrous. It was true I couldn't break the door down with one hand; nor had I any need to hurry to the North Hotel, where there were tons of army and police bigwigs. I really did look as if I'd been raped now!

Tapping my foot, I sighed, put out the light and began to undress. Although the room was in total darkness I said to Hudya:

'Turn away.'

In the darkness, I heard him turn on his side.

I got my clothes off and guessed my way to where I had been lying before. And, needless to say, stumbled over Hudya: I trod on his back and toppled over. His arm caught me and cushioned my fall, but I caught my shoulder badly just the same. Hell's bells, I was really in the wars that night! That stupid fall was probably the last straw as far as my endurance went. I sat down on the floor holding my injured shoulder with my dislocated hand and just began to whimper like a puppy — mournful, tearful and forlorn.

Hudya put his arm round me and laid me down next to him. I lay on his arm and he pressed me to him, all of me from head to foot, my breast to his, and my tears flowed across his unshaven cheeks and the lips with which he gently kissed me.

'Sleep. Please, sleep . . .' he kept saying softly.

I don't even remember when or how I dozed off.

Chapter Thirteen

The characteristic click of a yale lock woke me up; I guessed
this was Hudya closing the outer door. What a great idiot I
was, when all was said and done! If he had a yale lock on his
door, that meant I could have just walked out during the night.
Hudya didn't have any key in his pocket; he was just playing
with me, like a child!

But I no longer felt any anger towards Hudya. Quite the
opposite: I had slept half a night on his shoulder, and a quiet
sense of peace and happiness had come to dwell in me despite
all the humiliation I had undergone at the school. I was even
grateful to Hudya for deceiving me and not letting me go
during the night. Now he had quietly departed and I didn't
need to talk to anyone. He had given me the time to come to
my senses so that I could lie here on these skins and cherish
within me that rare feeling of having discovered *my* man, as a
mother cherishes the baby at her breast.

I lay like that for about twenty minutes. All the turmoil and
frenzied activity of these last days, all the murders, explosions
and the rest of the nonsense, glided away from me into
nothingness, became totally insignificant. No, I hadn't fallen in
love with Hudya that night, but I felt the way I suppose
composers feel when the first notes of a new melody rise up in
their mind ...

About twenty minutes later, I got up all the same and put on
the light. My watch showed ten-forty a.m.; beyond the window
were the polar night, darkness and some sort of vague rumb-
ling. I put the kettle on the electric stove and switched on the
local radio receiver. The set exploded into a hearty youthful
melody:

'We're not frightened of any ninth wave,
Or any permafrost we know!
For we're the brave lads, for we're the bold lads
Who work on latitude seven-Oh!'

I switched it off, revolted; these pseudo-hearty songs
seemed repulsive to me now! I wandered about Hudya's little
flat and examined the bookshelves. Everything connected with
Hudya's personal life had become interesting to me now; I even
kept repeating his name over and over to get used to it.

There were lots of law books on the shelves, virtually all the
leading lights in criminology I had ever heard of. There was
also a whole shelf of books on Nenets history, Nenets fairy
tales, legends — even anthropological research on the Nentsi.
Yet the experienced eye of the 'Urengoi Alsatian', that specialist in sniffing out anti-Soviet literature, at once recognized
among the spines of Soviet books such anti-Soviet editions as
George Orwell's *Nineteen Eighty-Four*, V. Bukovsky's *To Build A
Castle*, A. Abdurahman's *The Technology of Power*, Menachem
Begin's *White Nights*.

Now, fancy that! I thought. I had often seen anti-Soviet
works — Solzhenitzyn or Orwell, for instance — despite the
fact that even possessing such writings could be punished by
prison sentences of up to three years. But party leaders and
KGB men of high rank even have *The Gulag Archipelago* on
their shelves at times, just to show their friends how much they
are trusted by the party!

My Hudya Benokan was not a party bigwig or even a KGB
operative. He was a militia investigator, like me — and a
Nenets to boot. Naturally I wouldn't inform on him, but I
would have to have a talk with him about it: anybody might
drop into his flat for a cup of tea or a glass of vodka and then
inform the KGB — and that would be it, his whole career over.

I drank up my tea and got dressed. Curses, Hudya didn't
even have a mirror: I couldn't check what I looked like! A night
like that, and not take a look at myself in the mirror! Beyond
the window came the heavy, intensifying roar of aircraft. Hell,
that night it was as if I'd dropped clean out of the stream of
events and hadn't a clue as to what was going on in Salekhard.

I pulled on my sheepskin, but before going out into the hall-way I went to the bookshelves again and took out all the anti-Soviet stuff — Bukovsky, Abdurahman, Orwell and Begin — and looked around. Hudya had no furniture, as I've mentioned before. So I just shoved the books under the reindeer hides lying on the floor. In a few minutes I would see Hudya at Operations HQ and tell him to be a bit more careful with his 'literature'.

I buttoned up my coat and went out into the tiny hallway.

Only as I came up to the outer door did I see a note pinned up next to the yale lock. Written in a hurried but firm hand were the words: 'Goodbye, and, please, go back to Russia. Hudya'.

Part Four
Hände Hoch!

▌Chapter One

On winter nights, Moscow is deserted. Even in the city centre, life dies down around one a.m., when the underground stations close. Only the duty traffic policemen stand about at the downtown crossroads and stare intently at the rare passer-by hurrying for a taxi or stamping their freezing feet at a trolleybus stop. At one-thirty the doormen-cum-bouncers turf out the last drunken clients from the restaurants and get them a taxi for a three-rouble consideration and for another ten smuggle them out a pint of vodka for the journey.

Towards two, the city is sunk in sleep. Only the snowstorm scours round the deserted frozen streets like a hungry beggar: fluttering the ripped newspapers in the garbage bins, probing under doorways or bowling a tin can along the roadway.

It was on such a night, at two-thirty a.m., that three government limousines raced at high speed along a deserted Kutuzov Prospect, left the city confines then turned sharply into Rublyov Highway, kept meticulously clear of snow, narrow as it was. Here there were police posts every two or three kilometres in the shadow of snow-laden pine trees. As the black limousines proceeded the duty militiamen would pop out of these posts, fully alert. They wore fur jackets, and none of them was below the rank of major. At the approach of the government vehicles they drew to attention and saluted. The limousines, without reducing speed, swept on, shrouding the sentries in slipstream and powdery snow.

Ten minutes later the cars reached a long, high brick wall snow-speckled and crowned with three tiers of barbed wire. This wall stretched on for many kilometres, with its watchtowers and high steel gates, an entry and exit barrier and close-circuit television concealed in the trees; it surrounded the group of government villas closest to Moscow. The top-security system which obtains here is very reminiscent of the camps, the only difference being that in the government 'camp' the inhabitants are not prisoners but the nation's leaders and bosses. Though which side of the wall is the camp compound is a relative concept; it all depends on your point of view.

However that might be, around three in the morning three government limousines bearing the number plates MOSH-006, MOS-009 and MOS-012 rolled under the raised barrier, negotiated hastily-opened gates and found themselves in the Christmas peace of a pinewood park, with snowy paths sprinkled with yellow sand leading off into the interior of the little settlement. The cars turned confidently onto one of the paths and, much more slowly now, approached the last control point in front of the two-storey dacha of Konstantin Ustinovich Chernenko. Here the limousines' occupants, Marshal Ustinov, General Fedorchuk the Interior Affairs Minister and General Chebrikov, President of the KGB, got out and walked the last twenty yards to the porch. A tall Christmas tree half-decorated with coloured lights stood in front of the dacha; next to it was an unfinished snowman with a child's sledge, a box of Christmas-tree decorations and a toy tommy-gun of obviously foreign manufacture. Two of Konstantin Chernenko's bodyguards were stamping their feet on the porch. One of them opened the door for the nocturnal visitors.

Chernenko was sitting in the drawing-room on a low stool by the fireplace, where crackling birch logs burned fiercely. Bending towards the fire, he was smoking slowly and with enjoyment; it was the only cigarette he allowed himself per day, unbeknown to his doctors, and he listened with repulsion to the hoarse bubbling sounds his chest made in response to every draw. He was at pains to direct the smoke up the chimney. On seeing the visitors enter, he furtively threw the cigarette into the fire and covered it over with birch embers. Then he grew ashamed of the gesture and made a wry face.

'There you are. Shit, I smoke as if I were thieving something! Sit down. Kolya, tea for everybody and a bite to eat.'

'Kolya', a six-foot bodyguard, went out into the kitchen while the guests sat down in armchairs by the hearth.

'Well, what do you make of it? The balls-up with these

Nentsi? A-ha-hem —' Chernenko began a fit of coughing and rubbed his chest with a pudgy hand.

'We could put another few divisions in there,' said Ustinov, when the paroxysm was over.

'Divisions ... You're pretty free with your divisions — and what if the Americans pick up troop movements by satellite? They'll prick up their ears straight away — what the fuck do they want troops on the pipeline for, they'll ask.'

'In the first place, it's the polar night up there now,' said Ustinov. 'Secondly, the forecasters guarantee total cloud cover in the area for the next three days. With cloud like that, especially at night, no satellite's going to see a fucking thing, even an American one.' He took a glass of tea from the tray which the bodyguard Kolya had brought, but his gesture had been irritable and the tea spilt onto the hand-woven Persian carpet. Everyone pretended not to notice this — everyone, that is, except Ustinov himself. The marshal stared demonstratively at the damp stain on the carpet and even rubbed at it casually with his black leather boot. Chernenko's indecision exasperated him. An hour ago, when Bogomyatov's telegram concerning the scale of the situation in Salekhard had arrived, the marshal had rung Chernenko to inform him that he was sending in another four divisions. Chernenko, however, had put a stop to this and asked him to come and see him at the dacha. Any fool could see that delay in putting down this stupid Nenets rising was dangerous, not only because the contagion of rebellion might spread, as Bogomyatov had said, to other national districts or disrupt the opening of the gas pipeline. That was bad enough. Yet something else was a good deal more important: hesitation and the half-measures now being employed in Salekhard by the local authorities and the October Revolution division were giving trump cards to Gorbachev and the entire echelon of 'young' men backing him up: Marshal Ogarkov, Aliev, Dolgikh and that Siberian party upstart, Bogomyatov himself. This was all they needed: to catch 'the old men', that is Chernenko and himself, unable to cope even with Arctic Nentsi!

'N-yes,' Chernenko chewed his lip. 'Forecasters ... Cloud cover —' and glanced at the head of the KGB, General Chebrikov. 'Well, what have you got to say? Will they get wind of it in the West if we open fire in Salekhard?'

'I guarantee — no!' Chebrikov said hurriedly. 'We shall take measures. If we send in our special security division alongside the army —'

'I would like the police militia to take part,' broke in General Fedorchuk, Minister of the Interior. 'In Voronezh there's the advanced police academy: thirteen hundred men. Hand-picked officers as highly trained as paratroopers. After all, there will be lots of visitors, we have to guarantee security—'

Ustinov smiled mockingly at the zeal of Chebrikov and Fedorchuk. The police and KGB had failed to notice the start of this rebellion; now they wanted to get in on things.

'That should have been guaranteed before now —' he said.

'N-yes,' Chernenko sighed again. 'With things as they are we'll have to get the Politburo together and discuss the operation, then report to Comrade Andropov. But that's two days, maybe three, not less. And Bogomyatov says we can't wait, eh?' Chernenko looked demandingly at the servile Chebrikov. 'Or is he trying to provoke us into overreacting, the son of a bitch?'

At long last he'd come out with what had been tormenting him since the arrival of Bogomyatov's telegram. After all, it wasn't out of the question that this Bogomyatov was deliberately exaggerating the danger of the Nenets revolt. He'd even slipped in 'plots by American intelligence'; he was either over-insuring himself — the sod — or deliberately driving him, Chernenko, to extreme measures. And if it should turn out that there was nothing at all going on there, a few drunken hooligans and he, Chernenko, had sent in thousands of soldiers, a KGB division, a police academy — all that without the knowledge of Andropov and without the Politburo's permission! Gorbachev, the very same, would make a laughing stock of him, not to mention Andropov! 'He can't stand the heat,' they'll say. 'Scared stiff when the chips were down.' And the whole implication would be that comrade Chernenko couldn't be considered for the post of head of state after Andropov died — lost his bottle in his old age. And what if American intelligence starts stirring it up — not in the Far North with a bunch of lousy Nentsi, but nearer Moscow? What then? Will comrade Chernenko start an atomic war straight away?

On the other hand, suppose the action in Salekhard really was American intelligence at work? You couldn't put anything past Reagan. Off his rocker since we crapped all over his sanctions and built the pipeline without American know-how — suppose he sent a couple of spies into Siberia to touch off a Nenets uprising and, under cover of the uproar, blow up the pipeline? The Americans had been telling the world for long enough that the Soviet Union was about to split apart because of internecine hostilities. And now, at the moment of decision, Chernenko's dragging his feet, displaying a lack of character, hesitation. The young ones will be in for the kill all right, and Ustinov for one will change sides like a shot: 'I was the one who advised decisive measures, etc., etc.'

'Bogomyatov's not provoking anything,' said Ustinov edgily. Meanwhile, though, Chernenko had made a point of addressing Chebrikov. 'I was talking to General Grinko, the commander of the October Revolution division, and he reckons the situation is extremely serious. The rising's only just starting, and the district's extensive — bigger than Poland. You can't get by on one division —'

'Major Shatunov has also reported to me ...' said Chebrikov. 'A mob of drunken workmen attacked our KGB directorate in Salekhard, smashed the windows and broke the doors in —'

'They did right!' grinned Chernenko, looking him straight in the eye. 'What's the point of us having a bloody directorate in Salekhard if we get no early warning on the mood of the population? Kick the lot of them out on their arses — understood?'

'Very good, Konstantin Ustinovich,' said Chebrikov hurriedly, realising that if the Nenets rebellion lasted another week it would be his turn to follow Shatunov.

'So then —' Chernenko rose heavily. 'So, we all agree decisive measures are called for — yes or no?'

So that's why you called us out here in the middle of the night, Marshal Ustinov smiled grimly to himself. Of course! It won't be Chernenko who takes the decision to squash the Nenets rising with the might of the army, the KGB and the police; it'll be a joint decision made by the Minister of the Interior, the President of the KGB and the Defence Minister. The crafty old fox! And there was no evading a direct reply: those watery little eyes were staring hard at you, awaiting the answer.

'Yes,' said Ustinov.

'Absolutely,' Chebrikov at once chimed in. Fedorchuk simply nodded.

'Well, now,' Chernenko's puffy lips smiled in relief. 'As comrade Lenin said on the night of the storming of the Winter Palace in 1917: "Yesterday was too early, tomorrow will be too late." All right, then: Ustinov will send in the nearest troops to Salekhard he's got, Fedorchuk his police academy and Chebrikov his KGB Division — what's more, he'll fly out there himself, this minute. And tomorrow it's all got to be over — got it?' He stared hard at Chebrikov, who had leapt to his feet and was standing to attention. 'And the vital thing is: not the slightest leakage of information to the West, is that clear? Did you manage to nab that American, Shertz?'

'Of course, Konstantin Ustinovich. He's in Udmurtia, in a nature reserve,' he glanced at his watch. 'Right now he's either sleeping off a hangover or banging one of the girlies there, a cook —'

'The way some folks live!' Chernenko declared enviously. 'And here there aren't any girlies and I haven't even got time to make a snowman for my grandson. Incidentally, Fedorchuk, your grandson gave mine a bloody nose here yesterday over some toy. That's all right, boys will be boys, a bit of fighting. What's not all right is him going round all the dachas boasting about it: "I'm the one who punched Chernenko himself on the nose!"'

Everybody laughed except Fedorchuk.

'The scamp!' said Fedorchuk, flushing. 'I'll give him what for! Can we go now?'

When the door had closed behind Ustinov, Chebrikov and Fedorchuk, Chernenko stamped around the fireplace, raking about among the burning logs with the steel tongs as if hoping to find his half-smoked cigarette there. The butt had long since burnt up, and Chernenko turned to his bodyguard.

198

'Kolya, can you give me another one?'

'Not on any account, Konstantin Ustinovich,' came the reply, stern as if to a child. 'We agreed —'

'But I didn't finish this one ...'

The bodyguard shook his head.

'Well, fuck me!' grinned Chernenko. 'Well, all right then, fetch me my boots. Let's go and finish the snowman.'

A minute later an outside observer (if such a thing were possible in a Soviet government villa complex) would have seen a very odd picture indeed: at the dead of night, at twenty below zero, Politburo member, Secretary of the CPSU and soon-to-be head of the Communist Party of the Soviet Union Konstantin Ustinovich Chernenko, wearing felt boots and a Siberian fur coat constructing, with the help of his two bodyguards, a snowman for the grandson who had recently been hit on the nose by the grandson of General Fedorchuk. He knew very well that from the minute Ustinov and the others got into their cars their radio telephones would buzz into action and terse coded instructions would start winging their way to all corners of the sleeping land. These instructions would set in motion the vast and mighty machine of Soviet power. Red-alert sirens would go off in paratroop formations, at the Voronezh advanced police academy and the Dzerzhinsky KGB special division. Night-shrouded aerodromes would resound to the roar of aircraft and helicopter engines; thousands of soldiers were already being issued with ammunition — live rounds. All in the cause of preserving Soviet authority in the Far North, protecting the Siberia–Western Europe gas pipeline and foiling the intrigues of American intelligence ... But no, Chernenko was no longer thinking of that.

'Anyway, you —' he was saying to his bodyguard, who was adjusting the snowman's head. 'You were the one who promised to teach my grandson self-defence. Why the fuck didn't you?'

'I did teach him, Konstantin Ustinovich, honestly,' said the bodyguard. 'He just panicked.'

'Just panicked!' mocked Chernenko, nettled. Surely his own irresolute nature hadn't been transmitted to his grandson? 'You teach him to keep his head, all right?'

▌Chapter Two

The frost had already penetrated his sheepskin and trousers, and the chill was heart-stopping. Siegfried kept jumping up and down on the spot and flapping his arms, all to no avail. He felt that if they didn't open this bloody trading post in another ten or fifteen minutes his legs, face and ears would just drop off. He did not suspect that at that very moment in a still-dark Moscow, Chernenko himself was envying him, given that Chebrikov, head of the KGB, did not yet know of Siegfried's flight from a warm bed in an Udmurt nature reserve.

Next to Siegfried, a Nenets hunter rolling a plug of chewing tobacco behind his lip, spat on the ground — or rather on the snow, criss-crossed by sledge tracks. The spit froze in flight and struck the snow as a lump of ice, rebounding like a stone: minus fifty Celsius, he calculated. At one time, in those great days when he had been an honoured guest of the Tyumen territory bosses, Bogomyatov, Salakhov, Shatunov, Ryazanov and the other party, Gee Bee and administrative chiefs of Siberia, it had been the height of cool to walk out of a warm hotel, just like that — casual, Siberian-style — and calculate the temperature with one spit: if it landed on the ground without freezing, that meant it was less than forty below; if it froze in flight and didn't bounce off the frozen tundra, it was minus forty-five; but if it froze before it hit the ground and bounced like a piece of ice, then it was all of minus fifty Celsius. After that, Siegfried would get into the waiting managerial Volga and admire the beauties of the Siberian winter and the polar tundra from the safety of a warm car.

Now, though, there was no cosy hotel or managerial Volga. In fact, Siegfried Shertz had hardly jumped out of the mail-plane onto the snow of the Novy Port aerodrome when his self-confidence declined sharply. It was one thing to be without lines of communication or contacts (but with credit cards in your pocket) somewhere in Alaska, Taiwan or even Honolulu; in five minutes, Hertz would hire you any car you liked, from a cheap Toyota to a Mercedes. And if you had a pilot's licence, you could rent an aircraft or a helicopter. While you were filling in a few formal bits of paper you would get coffee and, in between times, book a room in a hotel. All this standard Western comfort and convenience was so much taken for granted by Siegfried that even though he knew of the total absence of such service in the USSR he couldn't imagine what it was really like to do without a hotel, a car, a telephone, hot coffee and a warm toilet. The toilet in Novy Port was a decrepit plank nesting-box raised above the permafrost on little wooden stilts. Leading to this edifice through the snowdrifts was a well-trodden path bordered with ornamental yellow initials. In the few minutes anyone needs to adjust their dress, everything that had to be exposed in that nesting-box was liable to be frostbitten. It was this first contact with unexhibited, un-touristy Russia — with everyday Soviet reality, in fact — that utterly shook Siegfried's faith that with one youthful bound he could board a passing Sno-Cat and hurtle down from Novy Port to Urengoi or Salekhard.

But there was no going back now. Anyway, if a Nenets uprising was threatening the life of the pipeline, to hell with these Russians and their playing at secrecy! The pipeline wasn't just the Gee Bees' private property; there were 225 million dollars of Siegfried's in there. So he had to get to Urengoi urgently — now — to see with his own eyes what was going on.

Yet there weren't any passing Sno-Cats going to Urengoi, or to anywhere else. Novy Port is the most northerly river port on the Ob — above the Arctic Circle. It is out of action during the winter and wrapped in the pale, frosty phosphorescence of the polar night. Nonetheless, the ice-bound jetties, the frosted cranes, and the barges and tankers sunk in the yard-thick ice of the Ob did not mean that the port was in a state of total hibernation. No, indeed, the settlement lived in winter too: there were the aerodrome, the technical workshops, a club, a trading post. Most importantly, it was from the warehouses here that daily convoys of trucks set out by the 'winter roads' across the frozen tundra swamps with food, clothing and technical equipment for geologists, oilmen and gas-pipeline workers out in the depths of the tundra. Doubtless at any ordinary time it would have been easy to fix something up with the lorry drivers and, for a couple of bottles of vodka or spirit, go with them to any of the tundra settlements.

Today the 'winter roads' were deserted, still.

Armed guards were strolling about near the port warehouses, kitted out in long-skirted fur overcoats, fur hats with ear flaps and felt boots. They were stamping their feet, hugging their Kalashnikov automatic rifles to their chests and glancing suspiciously across the road at the score or so of reindeer sledges by the trading post. The owners of these sledges, Nenets hunters and fishermen dressed in bright *malitsas*, were grouped around the closed doors of the trading post waiting patiently for it to open. And Siegfried stood with them. Unshaven and short of sleep, his sheepskin coat stained and baggy after the long journey from Zataika to Novy Port, he no longer looked like a prosperous foreign businessman; it was a lot easier to put him down as a hard drinker dying for the shop to open so he could get drunk again. There are enough of that sort in the north, and such people as the Nentsi and the armed warehouse guards no doubt took him to be one.

Siegfried had no need of liquor, though. He wanted food, and Novy Port had no restaurant, no diner, and the tiny buffet at the aerodrome was shut, like everything else today. There remained this shop, which should have opened an hour ago. Siegfried waited impatiently, and marvelled at the unshakable calm of the Nentsi. If everything the helicopter pilots had told him about the Nenets uprising was true, these Nentsi here should have disarmed the food-store guards — surely a trifling matter for polar hunters like them — and rifled the stores, rather than wait for the shop to open. Seizing supply dumps was the first act of any uprising, thought Siegfried.

Yet the Nentsi seized nothing. They talked quietly among themselves in Nenets, smoked their pipes and chewed tobacco. Close by, the harnessed reindeer snorted and twitched. Their breath rose in clouds of steam above their branching antlers as they cocked their dark sloe-eyes in all directions, jaws phlegmatically chewing on wads of dried lichen. As was usual in the vicinity of Russian food shops, stray dogs were wandering about rummaging in the snow and also casting glances at the closed doors of the trading post. The chimney on the post's roof was giving out smoke, and the fact that the stove was going inside gave Siegfried, the Nentsi and the dogs hope that sooner or later the shop would open up.

Compelled by a lack of anything else to do, Siegfried glanced over at the Nentsi: the usual old-man-Eskimos, looking like Japanese. Squat, powerful frames, calm wide-cheeked faces framed in fur hoods frosted by their breath. Their *malitsas* gave off a penetrating whiff of dog.

'Your Russian cheeks is white, however,' said one of them in Russian to Siegfried. He bent down, scooped up a lump of snow and held it out: 'You should rub it with snow, however.' He pronounced the letter 'd' like 't', which softened his speech and made it sound childlike.

'Thank you,' Siegfried took the snow and said: 'I'm not Russian, I'm an American.'

The Nentsi stared silently at him with their narrow eyes.

'I'm from America. A translator,' said Siegfried, rubbing his cheeks with the snow. These savage Nentsi were hardly likely to run off and report him to the KGB.

'Oh, America!' exclaimed one of them. 'America — good, however. America lives good law: it sells vodka to anybody. No different there, white man or Nenets, sells vodka to everybody — *savo!*'[1]

'And you like vodka?' asked Siegfried, interested.

'My likes vodka very much, very much!' The Nenets even screwed up his eyes, so much did he like vodka.

Just then a stout Russian wife emerged from a wing of the shop to one side and headed for the door, crisscrossed from head to toe in fluffy grey shawls. On her appearance, the stray dogs at once scampered up to the porch and the Nentsi clus-

---

[1] *Savo*: good (Nenets)

tered closer. She opened the sizeable barn-lock and thrust the dogs away with her foot.

'Get lost!' She then turned to the Nentsi: 'Don't push now! No pushing!'

Opening the frosted door, she entered the shop in proprietorial fashion. Nentsi and dogs followed, with Siegfried bringing up the rear.

It was warm inside the shop — well and truly heated up — and Siegfried drew a blissful breath. The Nentsi, meanwhile, were crowding round the counter, inspecting the shelves. The shelves held nothing except pyramids of tins labelled 'tourist breakfast' and cans of eggplant and peppers.

A subdued grumbling began among the Nentsi.

The shopwoman disengaged herself from her fluffy coverings and approached the counter.

'Well? What do you want?'

One Nenets indicated the shelves.

'Nenets can't eat that, however. Give bread, give tea, give flour. Gun powder also give.'

'At once! I'll run and get it!' sneered the lady. 'They burn our oil sites and we give them bread! Take what there is, while it's still there.'

'Nenets can't eat this,' said the Nenets again. 'Such law not, not sell flour to Nenets. Only for vodka is such law. Not for flour. You will give me as much flour as I give you money, macaroni you will give also . . .' At this, he pulled a bundle of rags from the leather bag at his belt. Undoing it, he placed money on the counter. 'Take money, give butter, give flour, tea —'

'Come on. Don't fuck me around' said the shopwoman. 'You'll get no flour and no butter! Do you want the tins?'

The Nentsi became noisy and started jabbering among themselves in Nenets.

'Well?' said the woman impatiently. 'I'll be shutting up the shop in a minute.'

'Such law not — close shop —' the Nenets began again.

'Don't "the law" me! That's it, shit! Out of here!' she waved her arm in the direction of the door and picked up the lock from the counter.

The Nenets sighed, took four sable pelts from his bag and placed them on the counter. But she thrust them away decisively.

'No! You should have come before with this. I've got instructions now: for you — just that.' She indicated the pyramids of cans. 'Take them while you've still got the chance.' Her regretful gaze followed the pelts which the Nenets was tucking back in his bag. She took the money from the counter, swiftly counted it and announced:

'There's enough for three cases. Which'll you have? One of each?'

The Nenets nodded wordlessly.

In twenty minutes or so the Nentsi had cleared the shelves. They hauled sackfuls of dusty 'tourist breakfast' out of the shop as well as the prehistoric tinned eggplant and peppers. The woman was flushed with her exertions, the counters on her abacus going like a machine-gun, and Siegfried suddenly realized that this old woman was not only offloading old stock on the Nentsi but robbing them as well; uneducated as they were, how could they check her lightening arithmetic?

Now only perfume remained on the emptied shelves: dusty cakes of fragrance soap, Pomorin toothpaste and Red Moscow scent.

'Scent also give,' said one of the last clients.

'I won't — you'll drink it,' replied the woman, tired now.

'My won't drink,' said the Nenets. 'My old woman give present, however.'

It was only now that Siegfried perceived that the *malitsa*-clad figure standing next to this Nenets was indeed female.

The shopwoman, if only to rid herself of this last Nenets, handed him a bottle of scent. In one second the Nenets had unscrewed the plastic top from the bottle and given it to his wife; before Siegfried's astonished eyes she drank half of it down, gurgled and returned the rest to her husband, who finished it off.

'Drunkard!' sneered the shopwoman. 'And you want freedom as well. If you did get freedom you'd drink yourselves to death! Huh!'

'It's you, *lyucha* made the Nenets a drunkard, however,'

said the Nenets peaceably. 'When the *lyucha* didn't come to the tundra, the Nenets was a hunter, never see vodka.'

'All right, all right, on your way! No meetings here,' she interrupted roughly. 'This isn't the town council, making speeches!'

'Never mind,' the Nenets went on. 'Soon Vauli will come here as well ...'

The Nenets couple left the shop, towing the last case of tinned goods behind them. The shopwoman seated herself on a stool, wiped the sweat from her brow and unhurriedly retrieved a round of sausage from under the counter; she broke a piece off and trimmed it, throwing the skin to the dogs.

'Well? And what do you want?' she asked Siegfried ungraciously.

'I'd like some sausage as well — and a bottle of vodka. Two would be even better.'

'There's no vodka and no sausage,' she stated, gnawing at the hunk of sausage, only now staring at Siegfried with her prominent, brazen blue eyes.

He calmly withstood her gaze. He well knew that from Moscow to Kamchatka there wasn't a shopwoman in the USSR who didn't have at least two or three bottles of vodka tucked away.

'I'll pay triple,' said Siegfried and placed a brand-new hundred-rouble note on the counter.

They continued to look each other in the eye for several instants, during which time the woman's gaze took on a liveliness, intrigued — not by the hundred but by Siegfried himself. Then, with a sigh, she rose from the stool and went into the back room, wiggling her powerful hips coquettishly.

'Four bottles!' Siegfried called after her.

▌Chapter Three

A few minutes later he walked out of the shop carrying a heavy bag. Out in the street, the Nentsi were busy round their sledges, tying on their sacks and cases of provisions.

Siegfried went over to the Nenets who had advised him to rub his cheek with snow and put his bag on the sledge.

'I am Siegfried. What's your name?'

'Ani-Opoi,' said the Nenets.

'And where are you going?'

'Over there . . .' The Nenets pointed in the direction of the tundra.

It was fifty below, a temperature unsuitable for subtle diplomacy. Siegfried spoke directly:

'If you take me to Urengoi, we'll drink a lot of vodka.'

'I can drink a lot of vodka,' said the Nenets. 'I can't go to Urengoi, however.'

'Why can't you?'

'Today I have to catch fish, however, to feed children. Ani-Opoi is not kill Russian boss, Ani-Opoi not set fire to Russian gas site. But Russian shop give nothing to Ani-Opoi, however.'

The situation was desperate: this Nenets was Siegfried's last chance to nip out of Novy Port and reach Urengoi.

'All right,' said Siegfried. 'Today we'll catch fish, tomorrow you take me to Urengoi. In Urengoi we'll buy flour, we'll buy tea, we'll buy butter and we'll drink a lot of vodka.'

When all was said and done, it was an adventure: riding with Soviet Eskimos some three hundred miles on a reindeer sledge across the Arctic tundra. Later on, he would be able to give an excellent interview to the *New York Times*, or even *Playboy* . . .

'I want to drink a lot of vodka, I want very much,' the Nenets said, almost dreamily. To look at he would be about sixty, short with an expressive, wrinkled high-cheekboned face. 'Can't go to Urengoi all the same. Mighty long distance,

207

however. Three changes of reindeer. Ani-Opoi poor, Ani-Opoi no monies change reindeer three times.'

Siegfried felt he was freezing again in this damned frost. Stamping his boots on the snow, he enquired:

'How much does it cost to change reindeer?'

'Dear, mighty dear,' replied Ani-Opoi, putting the last few items on the sledge.

'Well, how much?' Siegfried persisted.

'Maybe three hundred roubles ...' said Ani-Opoi thoughtfully. Maybe one hundred and twenty!'

Siegfried realized that the commensurability of figures was a relative affair for this Nenets. He asked:

'Would they change reindeer for vodka?'

'Oh yes,' Ani-Opoi answered joyfully. 'Of course they will, however!'

'How much vodka?'

'One bottle!' the Nenets said quickly. 'Don't give more! If there's more, we'll drink it ourselves, however. We'll drink as we go!' He screwed up his face in anticipation of delights to come. He then surveyed Siegfried from head to toe, and added despondently: 'You won't get there alive, however.'

'What?'

'Your parka's thin. Can't go tundra with such parkas. With such parkas you go to *khalmer*.'[1]

And although Siegfried didn't know what *khalmer* meant, he got the gist from the serious way the Nenets was regarding his clothing.

'Never mind,' said the Nenets. 'Now you be running behind *agish*,[2] mighty warm will be. When we come choom I will give *malitsa, pimi*[3] also *ichigi*.'[4] He sat down on the empty space in front of the sledge free of provision sacks. He pulled a long stick out of the snow, brought it down on the crupper of the lead reindeer and shouted: '*Hokh! Ho! Otte tsort!*[5] *hokh!*'

---

[1] *Khalmer*: cemetery (Nenets)
[2] *Agish*: sledge
[3] *Pimi*: boots made from reindeer hide, furry outside
[4] *Ichigi*: fur socks, furry inside
[5] *Otte tsort*: Bloody hell!

The reindeer four moved off in mettlesome fashion. Stunned by such a simple turn of events, Siegfried had nothing more to do than run after the sledge holding tightly onto his bag.

They had barely turned off the street onto the tundra, which began immediately where the town ended — since Novy Port was really all one long street lining the banks of the Ob — when Ani-Opoi also leapt down and ran alongside Siegfried.

'*Hokh! Ho!*' he shouted to the reindeer.

Siegfried thought of taking the Nenet's place on board, but the whole sledge was bumping so heavily on the rough patches and ice-hummocks that had he done so he would hardly have been able to keep his seat. He was forced to run, and found himself sinking through the brittle, frozen crust. The insides of his boots became packed with snow; yet he was steaming — soaked in sweat — and unfastened his sheepskin as he ran.

'*Savo!*' shouted a broadly-smiling Ani-Opoi to him as they ran. '*Savo*, tundra warm!', and struck his reindeer with the switch: '*Ho! Hokh!*'

▌ *Chapter Four*

The spike, a special seventy-pound gouge with a weighted end, echoed and boomed on the ice of the river, chopping out large jagged fragments.

Ani-Opoi stood chest-deep in the excavated hole, lifting the spike with both hands and driving it down powerfully, gouging and gouging into the river's icy armour. His face was pitted and cut by flying splinters of ice, blood was trickling down his cheek and forehead, but he went on furiously smashing the ice. The last dark layer was quite close now, and he had no intention of giving up the spike to anyone else, though another dozen Nentsi were standing round the rim. But it was he, Ani-Opoi, who had brought his camp folk here — the whole Haryuchi clan — and it was he who had promised them that at this very point there would eventually be fish.

A few days before, while tracking a marten — a rare animal nowadays, driven out of the tundra like all the rest by the roar of Russian tractors and the reek of petrol — Ani-Opoi had stumbled upon the Techida, right at the brook's source. He had been drawn to it at once on account of its clean, untrodden snow. That whiteness of snow, with no trace of soot, not one speck of dust, had typified the whole tundra thirty years before. Only dog and reindeer sledges had disturbed that whiteness then, while Arctic foxes, martens and squirrels wove upon it a *tynzei*[1] of spoor. But no beast nor bird nor reindeer sledge had spoilt the tundra, and even reindeer hoofs had not sullied it the way the iron tracks of Russian machines, stinking of petrol, had disfigured the landscape. The smoke from these machines

---

[1] *Tynzei*: a woven leather belt (Nenets)

settled on the tundra as soot. Wildlife fled from the smell, and men fell ill from the airborne dust.

The Techida, however, lay far from Russian roads, hidden away among frozen bogs, and the snow on her banks was clean and white. Ani-Opoi even stopped tracking the marten, kicked off his broad, fur-covered skis and set to work digging up the snow on the bank and on the river's icy plating, sniffing it and even tasting it on his tongue. No, the Techida didn't smell of oil! So that meant there must be fish in the Techida. When he had been a small boy there hadn't been a Nenets in the tundra who hadn't had as much fish as his heart desired — and no ordinary fish, either: sturgeon with caviar, Siberian salmon both pink and white. Dogs had been fed on dried salmon; they had refused to touch pike or catfish. Dried pike had been used to light campfires. And there had been a particular abundance of fish in winter, when the pressure of the ice in the Ob had forced them out into the smaller streams where they could be netted or even scooped up by hand.

But the Russians had come to the northern tundra and begun pouring petrol, oil and other filth into the Ob and other rivers, and fish had begun floating belly-upwards on the waters of the Ob. And now there wasn't enough fish for the people, never mind the dogs.

Yet there ought to be fish in the Techida, Ani-Opoi informed his children and all his clan, the Haryuchi, named for the proud crane. Would a strong crane-like man give up the gouge to anyone else when at any moment water might spurt up: dark, living water bearing oily, precious caviar-rich fish. When this non-Russian guest had asked him for transport to Urengoi, Ani-Opoi's first thought had been to take a caviar-fish along and get plenty of provisions in exchange: the Russians were avid for caviar-fish.

The spike suddenly broke gently through the ice and almost slid through into the water, so carried away was Ani-Opoi by his thoughts. He had even forgotten his non-Russian guest, who was standing with all the rest of the Haryuchi above the hole and watching him at his work. But Ani-Opoi kept hold of the spike, pulled it out of the water and flung it to one side; then he immediately sank to his knees feverishly, tearing off his fur mittens and, scooping up the dark water, brought it to his lips.

The clansfolk watched him tensely. If Ani-Opoi declared the river water to be living water, they would at once cut another hole about ten metres from the first and lower nets between the two on a long pole. Some hours later, if Num, God of the tundra, was merciful to the Nentsi, they would, as in years gone by, haul from the water an enormous sturgeon with a belly full of caviar. The sturgeon would smash its tail furiously against the ice, but Ani-Opoi, as was his right as first provider, would still it with a blow on the head from the spike before slashing its belly with his sharp knife. From the opening would pour the dense mass of caviar to fill the bucket placed at the ready. Everyone would pull a spoon from the top of their boots, and the caviar would be eaten up faster than a fox can run from one river bank to another. Then, thus fortified, they would haul from the river nets filled with sturgeon, salmon and beluga, drive new holes and again lower the nets. Ani-Opoi, meanwhile would be resting on the bank, shouting: 'Eh? Ani-Opoi knows where to find living water!'

But Ani-Opoi was in no hurry to gladden his relatives. He drank all the water from his palm, cupped up more and swirled it round his mouth. His ice-pitted face was covered in blood, but he was indifferent to that.

'Well?!' Someone's patience broke. 'Tell us! Is it living water?'

Ani-Opoi made no reply. He peeled back his *malitsa* and, on all fours over the hole, sank his bare arm up to the elbow in the river's dark waters. Down there, he broke off a piece of dark ice and drew it out. Oblivious of the water that was literally freezing on his arm, he began examining the ice fragment from all sides, even sniffing it.

At last he straightened up, threw the ice away and scrambled out of the pit. He shouldered the spike in silence and headed off upriver without a word.

The Nentsi followed him, and so did Siegfried. The latter was already kitted out Nenets fashion in fur socks or *ichigi*, fur boots or *kisi*, suede shirt or *yagushka*, and on top, a *malitsa* and a *sokui*, a sort of heavy suede smock worn only on long

212

journeys. Still, Siegfried was warm in this get-up. His feet no longer froze in his fur boots with the straw insoles, while the Arctic-fox edging of his hood protected his forehead and cheeks from the tundra wind.

Ani-Opoi went about three hundred paces upstream, halted, and crashed the spike onto the ice, starting another hole. Ani-Opoi did not like the water he had just tasted at the first hole. The Techida water was dead — not because it was polluted with oil which might have seeped in with the spring melt-water but dead from a cause Ani-Opoi did not want to — could not believe. This was why he had begun so desperately to gouge out a second hole.

After an hour of this exhausting labour, many of the Haryu-chi had already driven off on their dog- and reindeer-sledges back to the encampment. Ani-Opoi took the spike from Sieg-fried, who had been awkwardly pecking at the ice, swiftly excavated down as far as the water and scooped up a handful. Blood from his lacerated face dripped into the liquid, and he poured this away to one side, onto the snow, before trying again and raising the new draught to his lips. He held the water in his mouth for some time, swilling it this way and that with tongue and palate before spitting it out and reclining against the cavity wall.

'Well, then? Tell us!' said someone.

Ani-Opoi looked up. There was such profound, unaffected grief on that old, wrinkled face with its dried crust of blood that Siegfried for the first time experienced a genuine compassion for these people. Six years earlier, when Bogomyatov, Salak-hov, Ryazanov and Shatunov had ferried Siegfried by helicop-ter round the Yamal and shown him the Nenets herders, hunters and fishermen, he had seen them, in their reindeerskin garments, as quaintly exotic, no more than that; rather as if he had been taken on a tour of Disneyland and shown models dressed up in Eskimo clothing. A little later, five years ago, the fat bon vivant Ryazanov, chief geologist of the Salekhard Yamal-Oil-Gas-Exploration trust, had 'treated' Siegfried to a twelve-year-old Nenets girl from a Salekhard boarding school. This little thing had had no difficulty in convincing Siegfried that she was no ice maiden. She had been alive, a savage of

213

wondrous flesh with a bronzed body, a warm little bosom, provocative grey eyes and a scalding hot slit under a tiny black pubic scut. Siegfried, try as he might, was unable to recall the name of that grey-eyed twelve-year-old, though at the time, five years ago, after that first night in Ryazanov's cottage, she had come to Siegfried every night in the North Hotel — and that had been one of the sweetest weeks in his experience as a man. So sweet, in fact, that at the farewell party — again at Ryazanov's cottage — he had behaved in a proprietorial way, like a lovelorn boy: he had turned down every suggestion on the part of that small male company that he should share the girl for group sex and they had had to make do with someone else, another Nenets girl.

Convinced though he was — in the most direct manner possible, so to speak — that the Nentsi were a living people of flesh and blood, Siegfried had never regarded them as 'people' in the full sense of the word, as human beings like ourselves. As a result, when some eighteen months later on a routine flight to Salekhard he learnt from Ryazanov of the tragic death of his 'sweet Nenochka' — she had died immediately after Siegfried's departure, of an asthma attack according to Ryazanov — Siegfried, inasmuch as he looked on the Nentsi as a sort of polar Papuans, didn't so much feel pity for the girl — hell, what was her name? — as disappointment that this trip would bring no more of such nocturnal delight. In any case, Ryazanov, with the aid of his contacts, easily made good the loss with another Nenets Lolita, no whit the worse between the sheets than the first had been. Siegfried had decided that these ten- to twelve-year-old Nenets girls had a primitive or, more precisely, a savage lack of inhibition as far as sex went, and an almost prehistoric temperament; so it followed that these people were a kind of Arctic neanderthal with sensual, early-maturing young girls. He was even proud of his strikingly original anthropological analysis.

Now, though, after half a day with Ani-Opoi, observing his exhausting toil and even assisting in it himself, Siegfried regarded these 'polar savages' in a somewhat different light. They lived in the snow of the tundra in chooms, alongside their dogs, with no light or electricity, and obtained their food through labour: using a seventy-pound spike in minus fifty degrees of frost. And the result of this labour? Nothing: only grief and despair on the face of Ani-Opoi.

'Water dead,' said Ani-Opoi. 'All dead. Even no grass under water, however. Even no air in water, however. They killed water.'

He didn't know how to explain to his non-Russian guest that when the weeds die in a river that special taste which distinguishes river water from melted snow disappears; that this means not just the destruction of a river but the death of everything round about. Birds would no longer come to rest on the water, animals would desert the water-holes and perish without finding fresh water elsewhere, because the Russians had poisoned the other rivers too, and the reindeer pastures along the river banks would also die out. And without fish, without birds, without reindeer and without animals, death would come also for all the crane-like race of the Haryuchi . . .

He could not explain all this to his non-Russian guest; he had neither words nor desire enough to do so. Yet this non-Russian guest seemed to have understood everything without a word being spoken: he took a bottle of vodka from his bag, tore off the aluminium top with his teeth and held out the bottle to Ani-Opoi.

Chapter Five

But perhaps Ani-Opoi and the whole crane-like Haryuchi clan need not wait till the Russians poison all the rivers in the tundra, destroy all the reindeer pasture with their tractors and drive out all the wildlife down to the last lemming? Perhaps Ani-Opoi should abandon his choom and go where three days ago his eldest son, Sanko, and five other lads from the Haryuchi and neighbouring clans have gone — to help the spirits drive the Russians from the tundra? But no, the young folk wouldn't take oldsters like him; they'd laugh. 'You've drunk a lot of Russian vodka,' they'd say. 'How can you fight against the Russians now?'

Ani-Opoi stood in the path of a reindeer herd being driven towards him by husky dogs and his camp neighbours. A long *tynzei* plaited from leather thongs lay coiled in his hand; his eyes sought out a female deer yearling. Of course he could have killed some draught bull reindeer from those which had had their day or were lame, but the meat of draught and working animals was stringy and tasteless. One couldn't entertain a guest on meat like that, especially this guest — from America!

Ani-Opoi had wanted to work a crafty one: ride to Urengoi at this American's expense, exchange his fish for a huge quantity of foodstuffs and drink a good deal of vodka with this Siegfried — that's how Ani-Opoi had laid his wicked plan! For that the tundra spirits had punished him at once, had not given him fish in the Techida. But Seigfried didn't even know how Ani-Opoi had wanted to trick him and had given Ani-Opoi vodka to drink. Now it was an urgent matter to recover the goodwill of the spirits: they had to be placated by the sacrifice of a female deer yearling, and all his encampment neighbours, plus Siegfried, had to share in this animal.

Oh, Siegfried's vodka was lovely — how lovely it was! Of course he'd take him to Urengoi, the very next day. He'd take with him a sackful of squirrel furs, four fox pelts and seven martens from the stocks he kept lying in his choom against hard times. And he would take his son and his son's companions a month's supply of provisions so that they would fight well against the Russians: butter, salt, sugar — and maybe tobacco and gun powder. How else could an old man help his children, when the three-sided arrow was flying across the encampments with its signal for revolt — and all must go to the battle, both valiant warrior and common man?

The thud of reindeer hoofs rolled ever nearer. The grey mass of the herd bore down on Ani-Opoi pulverizing the tundra snow. Beneath the blows of those hooves, the frozen tundra rang like a shaman's tambourine. The branching antlers rolled above the herd like the wave of the Ice Ocean. Like a little boat, they disclosed, then obscured a beautiful yearling with a graceful breast and head held high. Ah, if all the Nentsi could have gathered together into such a herd to fall upon the Russians and with one blow hurl them out of the tundra! But only Vauli, the legendary hero — Vauli Piettomin — had known how to drive Russians out of the tundra with one blow. And that had been long ago — long, long ago, when the Russians had no aeroplanes or tanks. And now, said Sanko, the Russians had to be defeated another way: they had to be so scared that they would flee the tundra of their own accord, like animals fleeing a forest fire. 'How can you frighten them?' Ani-Opoi had asked his son. 'The spirits have taught us how,' Sanko had grinned, and reminded his father of the old Nenets fairy tale Ani-Opoi had heard from his own grandfather as he had from his. 'From their living enemies they cut off the ears and *khote* and made them eat their own *khote*. Thus the fathers avenged their blood; thus do the sons likewise.'

The herd was almost level with Ani-Opoi: about twenty metres remained. Ani-Opoi must stop thinking; Ani-Opoi must coil himself like a spring, as if he himself, and not his leather *tynzei*, were to swoop on this beautiful deer with the large black eyes and tender ears. Now!

The lasso flashed in the air like a snake and lashed round the yearling's neck.

As if cut down, the yearling collapsed into the snow and turned head over heels, dragging the Nenets after her with her whole body weight. But Ani-Opoi's arm was strong, as were his legs: even after a glass of vodka he can lasso a reindeer and keep his legs! Sanko should not call him an old man.

The herd raced past; only the lassoed yearling remained, and got to its feet. Two Nentsi, assisting Ani-Opoi, rushed towards her, threw another loop of the *tynzei* round her neck and stood at either side of her head. Each held one end of the *tynzei* in his hand. One quick, powerful tug on these ends, and the yearling, which had suffocated instantly, with neck outstretched and hind legs buckling, subsided heavily onto the snow.

Only now did Ani-Opoi take the hunting knife from its carved sheath of walrus ivory. Those Russians slaughtered their domestic animals with knives or — as Ani-Opoi had heard — even axes! Tormenting animals and spilling valuable blood needlessly. No, not a single Nenets would kill a reindeer with a knife: that would be a sin in the sight of the tundra and its spirits.

Swifly and neatly, Ani-Opoi made an incision in the hide of the suffocated reindeer from fore to backleg, and continued it to the end of the body. No drop of blood issued from this cut: Ani-Opoi cut only the hide, not the meat. He inserted his knife in the incision and began to prise the skin away from the carcass, his left hand tugging at the skin while his right fist pressed down on the meat where the hide was being detached from the muscles. Under his deft hands the skin came off easily, like a dress.

Siegfried watched this virtuoso performance with a mixture of squeamishness and curiosity.

In a few minutes the entire skin of the reindeer lay on the snow, fur side down, without a single piece of subcutaneous tissue adhering, and no blood either — just clean, smooth hide. On the hide, as if on bedding, lay the naked carcass of the deer.

The Nentsi seated themselves around this original table.

218

'Ho!' Ani-Opoi hurled his *tynzei*.

'Come here, however! We're going to *aurdat*!'[1] shouted Ani-Opoi to Siegfried, as he carefully opened the animal's abdominal cavity and ribcage with his knife. A second cut near the backbone, and the entire flank of the carcass came off along with the ribs; and in another minute Ani-Opoi had tipped the innards out onto the snow. Once more, no drop of blood was spilt.

One of the Nentsi dragged the guts off and gave them to the dogs.

Meanwhile Ani-Opoi sank to his knees in front of the carcass and plunged his arm in somewhere under the yearling's throat. A strong tug, and from the torn windpipe of the animal came a fountain of scarlet blood; it quickly filled the abdominal cavity, where the heart and lungs floated in it like soup. Steam rose above this scarlet 'soup': the blood was still warm — no, hot ...

Women and children came running from the encampment to this festive board and formed a noisy circle round the felled reindeer. Each one had a knife and kept looking at this enormous dish with anticipatory relish; yet Ani-Opoi raised an admonitory hand.

The hubbub ceased. Ani-Opoi pulled out the liver from the carcass, neatly sliced off a long thin piece and proffered it to Siegfried.

'*Savo Syunze!*'[2] said he. Seeing that Siegfried was regarding the morsel with evident distaste, he dipped the liver in the warm blood and again held it out: 'Eat, eat! The girls will love, however! Your dick will stand good.'

The Nentsi fell about laughing — men, women, and children. Siegfried, under the gaze of all those present, took the piece of liver and nibbled it. It was warm and seemed to him tasteless. Nevertheless, as soon as he had received the dainty from Ani-Opoi's hands everyone else eagerly set about eating the reindeer flesh still warm and raw, dipping it in the blood.

---

[1] *Aurdat*: eat raw meat (Nenets)

[2] *Savo Syunze!*: from all my heart

'Ah, ah, ah, tasty!' the children kept repeating. 'Siegfried, take salt — salt for meat. So tasty, however!'

The Nentsi were amazingly neat in their eating habits. Each person would take a piece of blood-dipped flesh in one hand and seized one end of it in their teeth, but without biting through. In their other hand, everybody carried a knife as sharp as a razor. Using this they made a quick cutting stroke upwards and sliced off the meat, almost grazing their chins and lips. Siegfried thought they were going to injure their noses or lips, so close did the knives pass in front of the face — a literal millimetre.

Of course, Siegfried had often heard of Eskimos drinking reindeer blood and eating raw reindeer flesh and so protecting themselves from scurvy. Still, it was one thing to hear about it and quite another to be the guest of honour at such a banquet. To an outside observer it would doubtless look most picturesque, he reflected: a group of Nenets families in motley reindeer *malitsas* sitting on the snow round a freshly-slaughtered reindeer and wolfing down raw meat with scarlet drops of blood raining onto the snow like strawberries. All around stood the dogs, impatient for their turn. Close by, a couple of dozen conical chooms made of reindeer skin and, near every choom, harness gear and several draught animals; a three-year-old had harnessed a half-grown pup to a washing trough and was now riding and laughing over the snow. A real patriarchal idyll! On the other hand, how on earth could these patriarchal, savage Nentsi ever raise a rebellion against the Soviet empire?

Later, in Ani-Opoi's choom, reindeer meat boiled on the hearth in a blackened cast iron pot in honour of Siegfried, unaccustomed to eating raw flesh. The hearth divided the choom into two parts; in the front area nearer the entrance lay an old, dark, foot-worn reindeer hide; here the dogs slept during snowstorms. In the rear part of the choom, beyond the hearth, lay mats of soft grass and clean reindeer skins: beds for Ani-Opoi and five of his children, four daughters ranging in age from five to eleven and his two-year-old son. Now all his children apart from the eldest one present, eleven-year-old Melkune, were lying there tucked up in skins and peeping out

220

at Siegfried in the half-light with curious little eyes. Melkune was waiting on the adults. From the left-hand corner of the tent, where all the crockery was kept along with stores of dried fish, tea, salt and sugar, she fetched a large glass cup which she wiped energetically inside and out with tarpaulin strips, filled with strong, brick-coloured tea and then handed to Siegfried. The rest of the Nentsi, including Ani-Opoi, drank tea from plain aluminium mugs. Siegfried, as a guest, got the glass one.

The smoke from the hearth went out through an aperture in the choom roof, the fire gave out heat, and the Nentsi, copper-faced in the firelight, sat cross-legged close to the hearth. They had taken off their *malitsas* and were half-naked in their suede pants and vests. They smoked pipes, placing their chewing tobacco behind their lip. They drank tea not with sugar but with dried fish, which now lay in front of them in a wooden basin. Though they studiously kept off the subject of recent events in the tundra, Siegfried was determined to raise it.

'I've heard somebody has been setting fire to the drilling rigs on the tundra,' he said.

The old men said nothing, either glancing questioningly at Ani-Opoi or averting their eyes altogether as they spat tobacco juice. Ani-Opoi replied diplomatically:

'Nenets knows nothing. Nenets wanders over tundra, grazes deer. Tundra spirits set fire on Russian sites.'

'Why?'

'Don't know why,' Ani-Opoi turned his eyes away. 'Russian peoples came, lots of bad did to tundra. They killed rivers, frightened animals, made little holes in the ground — woke up the spirits altogether, however. While these little holes were not in the ground, the spirits couldn't get out, they stayed under-ground. Now Russian peoples wanted to drive the spirits out of the tundra through a tube. They opened little holes in the ground and started driving the spirits into the tube, like into a trap. So the Nentsi would have no friends left. But the spirits broke out and punished the Russians . . .' Here Ani-Opoi noisily sipped tea from his mug.

'Not a bad interpretation of the Siberia–Western Europe gas pipeline issue,' smiled Siegfried to himself. Aloud, he spoke otherwise:

'When the Russians reach the gas under the ground, the tundra will be warm and light. The Russian people will build you warm houses, power stations.'

'Then the Nenets will be dying altogether, however,' sighed one old man, and even began rocking his body as one doomed.

'But why?'

'The tundra will be altogether dirty. While Russian peoples don't come here, the tundra was clean, Nenets was never ill. But Russian peoples came and brought many of their spirits to the tundra, however.'

'But surely they built hospitals, schools, boarding schools — I've seen them myself in Salekhard and Urengoi.'

'Hospitals — huh!' said another old man in sudden indignation. 'They don't cure you at all! My belly hurt, very bad — they took my one reindeer to hospital, to Novy Port went. Doctor says give him a sable, he will give medicine. I say, you give me medicine, I will go choom, I will bring you sable. No, he says, first give sable, however. So he not give medicine till I went choom ill stomach, get sable for doctor.'

'Now it's all like it was before the Revolution, long long ago,' said a third old man. 'Even got worse, however. Russian peoples don't give us Nentsi passport. Without passport police not one town allow to live. To Moscow not allow to live, Leningrad — even Salekhard not allow. Tundra live! But how tundra to live? In shop you give sable; shop give you nothing. Flour don't give, tea don't give, butter don't give. Only paper monies for sable give. Nothing nowhere for paper monies. Mine daughter went trip Moscow, says to me: Moscow even for Russian peoples no meat, however! My old head don't understand: if Russian peoples for selves nothing, why Russian came to tundra? Nenets can't feed all Russian: few Nenets, very many Russian peoples, however.'

The dogs came running into the tent through the entrance flap to get out of the wind which rose on the tundra towards nightfall. Lolling out their tongues, they settled down on the tattered skin, glancing now at the heat of the fire, now at the Nentsi and Siegfried. Droplets of melting snow glinted silver on their bushy coats.

'Russian peoples bad peoples, bad head,' the oldster went on

222

to explain: 'Dog, see? My dogs right dogs: herd the deer, attack wolfs — mighty likes children, however. Russian peoples not so — others lands war, build a camp for themselves in the tundra, prison! And other Russian peoples they put in camps — own peoples put in camps, prison! And spoil dogs, teach fight men however.' The old man shook his head disconsolately, a head which had never considered such savagery — teaching a dog to attack a man and put other men — his equals — in gaol, like a marten in a cage!

'You talk a lot, Labuta,' Ani-Opoi chided him, clearly not relishing the direction the conversation was taking.

'My name means that: "talk a lot",' replied the old man. He asked Siegfried, 'And what means your name?'

Siegfried shrugged.

'Nothing ... Just a name.'

'It can't be nothing. Every name means something, however. Teta, for instance ...' — Ani-Opoi became more animated, obviously delighted at this chance to turn the conversation, and pointed at the old man whose doctor had demanded a sable in return for treatment — 'Teta means: "has lots of reindeer".'

'Now not so many,' said Teta. 'Now *lyucha* has spoiled the tundra, no moss for the deer. Many deer die, however.'

'So your name is wrong now,' said Ani-Opoi and indicated Labuta. 'But his name is right. "Talks a lot", it means.'

'And what does your name mean?' Siegfried asked Ani-Opoi, placing the next piece of boiled venison in his mouth and sipping his tea.

'My name means "one more",' said Ani-Opoi. 'My father called his children so: first-born, Opoi. One, that means. The second was born: Side. "Two," that means. Third was born, Nyagar: "three". So seven children were born. So when I was born he began again: Ani-Opoi. "Another one," it means ...'

The Nentsi laughed indulgently, as if all of them had been qualified mathematicians.

Siegfried looked with something approaching astonishment at their open, childlike laughter.

'And where is your wife?' he asked Ani-Opoi.

'My old woman gone to the *khalmer*' said Ani-Opoi, at once

saddened. He explained to the uncomprehending Siegfried: 'My old woman was bearing a son. The Russian doctor took five sables, but he still cut her belly open and then sent her to the *khalmer*. Didn't give sable back, however.'

All the Nentsi grew sad at once: their faces were filled with sympathy for Ani-Opoi.

'Two years I live alone,' he went on. 'Eight children to feed — very hard, however. Therefore five children here, one son is hunter in tundra and two older daughter gave to boarding school. Didn't want to give: there Russians men will spoil, fuck them. But eight children Ani-Opoi cannot feed: tundra became very bad — no animal, no bird, no fish also, however ...'

The old Nentsi men took to sighing noisily.

'What do they call your two eldest daughters?' asked Siegfried with inner misgivings.

'Tadane and Padane.'

Siegfried took a relieved breath: that hadn't been her name. He asked, 'Why did you make so many children?'

'What else to do?' his eyes glinted slyly. 'No television. No light also, however.'

Once again all the Nentsi burst out laughing: a gay, frank, childlike mirth.

All of a sudden the dogs leapt out of the choom barking loudly. Ani-Opoi and the other Nentsi rose to their feet and, pulling on their *malitsas* as they went, followed the dogs out.

Siegfried remained alone with the five children. Melkune, the next-eldest daughter, was busy in the corner. Out of pieces of fur and cloth she had neatly fashioned a tiny figure in *malitsa* and *kisi*.

'What is it?' asked Siegfried.

'It's a doll. A toy for youngest sister, however,' responded Melkune, eyes lowered.

Bloody hell, thought Siegfried, dirty, unwashed living with dogs and reindeer, these people are also — people! Of course, that didn't mean that for their sake the pipeline should be cancelled and 225 million lost — not that it was in his power to cancel the project anyway — but sacrifice a hundred and fifty to two thousand on some tundra Disneyland for these kids, that he would do right away. Especially as something had to be

224

written off for tax purposes in any case.

Unexpectedly, one of the child's heads poking up from the skins asked:

'Siegfried, are you going to sleep with us?'

He shrugged his shoulders.

'Probably . . .'

'Will you sleep with Melkune?'

'Why Melkune? I'll sleep on my own.'

'Alone, sleep bad. Cold, however. You sleep with Melkune, be warm. Take Melkune for wife, good wife will be. You want to take Melkune for wife?'

'What's your name?' smiled Siegfried.

'Me you can't take for wife yet. You have to wait three years for me, I am only eight years old. My name is Okka.'

Siegfried felt it like a whiplash: Okka — that had been her name, that had been the name of that twelve-year-old five years ago! Hearing the name again drove him to recall that week of delights, that fervent, wild, debauched and innocent Nenets Lolita . . .

He got up, pulled on his *malitsa* awkwardly and left the choom. About ten paces to one side near the sledges, still unloaded, on which Ani-Opoi and the other Nentsi had brought from the factors their sacks and tins of 'tourist breakfast', something was being discussed. At Siegfried's approach, however, everyone fell silent. He saw the figures of six young Nentsi he did not know. They had hunting rifles, and their reindeer were breathing heavily.

'Why did your coming out of the choom?' Ani-Opoi asked Siegfried. 'Your better sit in choom, drink tea.'

'I came out for some fresh air,' said Siegfried.

The Nentsi began talking among themselves in their own language. It seemed to Siegfried that the young lads were speaking out, displeased with the old men: Ani-Opoi appeared to be defending himself. Then the lads harnessed fresh draught animals to the sledges laden with provisions and, shouting '*Ho! Hokh!*' drove off into the tundra night. The dogs accompanied them to the outskirts of the encampment, then returned to the Nentsi old men who stood and watched in silence as the sledges pulled away.

'Who are they?' Siegfried asked Ani-Opoi.

'My son Sanko, hunter,' said Ani-Opoi unyoking the weary reindeer from the sledges left behind by the visitors. 'Gone to find squirrel, long way tundra. You go choom, however. Sleep, however. Tomorrow we go Urengoi, *savo?*

He looked embarrassed, and lowered his eyes.

'*Savo*', said Siegfried.

Chapter Six

From Operational Report to Government

From: President of KGB, General Chebrikov

SECRET
URGENT

I bring to your attention several points from Operational Reports received from various regions of the Yamal-Nenets district:

POINT 1
(1) In extending the search area for the criminals who burned the drilling rig at Lake Mirigi, Lieutenant Zvyagin, commanding a helicopter squadron, noticed from the air the tracks of reindeer sledges leading away from the lake in a north-westerly direction along the bed of the river Techida. Following these tracks, Lieutenant Zvyagin's squadron of three helicopters observed and detained in the tundra six reindeer sledges along with six Nentsi. During questioning the detained persons stated that they were on a hunting expedition in the tundra. According to them, they heard the explosion and saw the fire rising over the tundra near Lake Mirigi. Deciding that this was the 'tundra spirits' blowing up the drilling sites, they left their hunting area and were proceeding home. A search of the sledges revealed hunting rifles, eighteen squirrels and three martens: an extremely small amount for such experienced hunters as the local Nentsi. The hunters explained, however, that as a result of the laying

of the pipeline the catch of fur-bearing animals in the tundra has sharply diminished and that the traps and nooses they had set near the lake perished, in their words, from the fire.

Although the presence of the Nenets hunters close to the scene of the incident raised Lieutenant Zvyagin's suspicions, their statements and the absence of direct evidence of their involvement in the arson compelled him to release the detainees.

(2) Similar tracks of dog-sledges were observed by helicopter crews in the area of site no. 727, near the settlement of Kamenni. The investigating team, led by experienced detectives who came with me from Moscow, followed these tracks to a Nenets state fur farm called Dawn over the North. In the words of Nentsi questioned here, a group of hunters from the fur farm had actually been near site no. 727, following a wolf pack. The Nentsi affirm that the development of gasfields has caused 'all beast gone from tundra', and the wolves, for lack of other food were attacking not only reindeer but also Nenets encampments. Here the Nentsi showed a child bitten by wolves and three pelts of wolves they had killed. A search of the encampment yielded no evidence of the involvement of Nentsi in the burning of Site no. 727. Nevertheless, another detail merits attention. In connection with the forthcoming visit to the district by members of the Soviet Government and foreign journalists Dawn over the North Farm was selected as a showpiece and a month ago all the workers were moved from their chooms into snow-shielded houses. The team of investigators has discovered that the Nentsi have dismantled the interior walls of these houses and erected their chooms inside. They are now living in their chooms and burning the wooden house partitions and the furniture on their hearths. In reply to questions on the reasons for such behaviour, the Nentsi stated that they did not wish 'to live Russian-style'. Similar information concerning Nentsi moving back from the houses to their chooms has also begun to come in from other parts of the district.

(3) In the areas of site fires, namely Lake Anaguri, Nugma, Yunarta and river Haide, no tracks have been discovered, but pipelayers on the Anaguri–Urengoi section say that they saw several dog- and reindeer-sledges on the tundra some hours before the fires occurred.

(4) In the Nenets settlement Red North, the former First Secretary of the Yamal-Nenets District party committee, Pyotr Tusyada, has been discovered and arrested. During questioning Tusyada stated that he had deserted his post because he considered that the exploitation of the tundra gasfields would bring disaster on the Nenets people and that he did not wish to be involved in this 'crime'. Explaining the firing of the gas rigs, Tusyada stated that the oil and gas of Yamal belonged to the Nenets people and that the people had the right to burn the gas as they saw fit. In saying this Tusyada indirectly confirmed that the Nentsi are responsible for the arson attacks . . .

All these points: the demonstrative mass exodus of Nenets from houses to chooms; their open declarations of the harm done by the pipeline; the traces of their presence in the vicinity of the site fires as well as all the preceding incidents in Salekhard and the rumours of the return of Vauli Piettomin — leader of anti-Russian rebellions in the eighteenth century — testify, in my view, to an *organized conspiracy among the Nenets people* against Soviet power in general and the construction of the pipeline in particular. It is perfectly obvious that the Nentsi have selected the tactic of 'invisible terror' in subverting Soviet authority: in other words, using the polar night and their excellent local knowledge, they attack the drilling sites, kill the workmen and cover the traces of their crimes by setting the place alight. On returning to their encampment the criminals melt into the general mass of Nentsi, while the crimes they have perpetrated create panic among the Russian population of the territory.

In view of the need for an immediate end to the disorders, now taking on the character of a national anti-Soviet uprising, the joint command of the army, KGB and police in Salekhard, together with the party leadership of Tyumen Province, have taken the decision to carry out a series of punitive operations in various parts of the Yamal tundra.

▌Chapter Seven

The snow crunched beneath the runners. Siegfried sat on the sledge behind Ani-Opoi, trying to ape his pose exactly. The compact figure of the Nenets in his dark *sokui* clung tightly to the sledge; no hummock disturbed his balance. With his right leg tucked under him and his left stuck out, Anoi-Opoi poised himself on his toe-end on the sledge close to the runners. In his left hand was an eight-metre stick with which he not so much beat as frightened the reindeer, crying 'Ho! *Hokh!*'; his right hand held the rein of the lead animal, and with it he guided the team.

How Ani-Opoi found his way through the icy silence of this totally monotonous tundra shrouded in polar darkness, with its lightly phosphorescent spurs of blue-white hummocks Siegfried did not know and did not attempt to understand. There are situations when you can neither control events nor even guess at their logic and direction; the only thing to do is relax and go with the current, as the Russian poet has it: 'whither the destiny of events draws us on . . .'

It was only some twenty-four hours back that Siegfried had fled from Zataika, his soft warm bed and the hospitable Khanov, yet it seemed to him now that it had been long, long ago, almost in another life. The monotony of the tundra, its pure frosty air, the rhythmic thudding of reindeer hoofs and the warm fur clothing he wore — all this prompted him to doze off. Hell's flames, he hadn't slept for three days now! — you couldn't call his night's stay in Ani-Opoi's choom sleep, could you? Siegfried slept fully clothed on reindeer skins covered with furs, but even through the skins his body, unused to such a bed, sensed beneath it the yards-thick layer of permafrost with its icy strength. Apart from which Ani-Opoi had snored all

231

night, the dogs had fidgeted about and whined in their sleep by the choom flap, and in the middle of the night the two-year-old, Ani-Opoi's youngest, had suddenly got out from among the pile of sleeping children and made his way on unsteady legs to the flap, raised the curtain and stood there barefoot on the snow, piddling straight onto the tundra. Gusts of wind had carried spray and snow back into the choom as the child had got back under the furry hides, but the entrance flap had remained open and slapped in the wind like a sail, wafting a whole snowdrift into the choom before Siegfried, cursing, had crawled out from beneath his coverings and closed it. Ani-Opoi's family had seemingly slept on as if nothing had happened; but on the way back to his place Siegfried had suddenly encountered the fixed, expectant gaze of Melkune. He would not have laid a finger on her for all the money in the world: in the choom, next to her sisters, her snoring father and the whining dogs — no way!

But now that he was in the sledge, alternately dozing off and being jerked awake by the next ice-hummock, Siegfried bethought himself, not without a certain feeling of self-satisfaction, of the mature gaze of the eleven-year-old Nenochka.[1] Who knew: perhaps in a year or two he would chance to be in this part of the tundra again on business? Melkune in a bath of shampoo — she was a minor, of course. Oh come on, he said to himself, what was wrong with making love to a twelve-year-old girl if she herself was begging for it? That meant she was ready for it: they matured early in these parts. That other one — Okka — hadn't been a virgin at twelve. She had been uninhibited and insatiable — how did it go in Baudelaire? 'Like a frenzied Jewess spreadeagled on the bed . . .'?

The roar of helicopter engines drew him out of his sweet reverie. Both Siegfried and Ani-Opoi looked up into the sky.

Three machines were flying south to north, intersecting Ani-Opoi's route. Nose and tailplane were brightly lit, and searchlights probed at full power. These made the helicopters look like huge birds of prey with white legs thrust out ahead,

---

[1] *Nenochka*: a little Nenets girl (term of endearment)

prepared to seize their prey in their powerful talons.

Me! thought Siegfried, terror-stricken. It's me they're looking for, the Gee Bees! They'll land in a minute, pick me up and have a good laugh at my Nenets fancy dress, and then . . .

But the helicopters passed on and went away to the north, the rumble of their engines dying away behind a distant hilltop.

Ani-Opoi brought his reindeer to a halt and anxiously raised himself to his full height on the sledge, even craning in the direction the machines had gone. He listened intently. He then sprang down off the sledge, threw back the hood of his *malitsa*, lay down on the frozen ground and placed his ear to the ice. The resting reindeer pulled to a bare patch of rock amid the snow cover where some frozen lichen stalks could be seen.

'What's the matter?' asked Siegfried, but Ani-Opoi only waved his arms as if to say, 'Quiet! Let me listen to the tundra.'

Abruptly he sprang up from the earth — sharply, with his whole body, as if he had been struck. His face was utterly transformed. Now it was cruel: the eyes, dark and narrow enough before, were now slits. He jumped onto the sledge, struck the lead animal sharply, and roughly wheeled the whole team in the direction taken by the helicopters. Siegfried, hanging onto the sledge with both hands, could barely maintain his grip.

'What's happened?' he yelled again.

But Ani-Opoi paid him no attention whatever. He was standing bolt upright bawling at his reindeer and driving them with all his strength across the tundra in the wake of the helicopters. The reindeer had probably never seen their master in such a state. With quivering ears and tails almost vertical from fear, they literally floated across the tundra, snorting and turning their thick muzzles towards their master.

Siegfried, to stay on the sledge, simply lay down, tucking beneath him his bag of vodka bottles and the sack of squirrel and sable pelts Ani-Opoi had been taking to Urengoi.

After some twenty minutes of this frenzied progress, when Siegfried felt his arms and legs could no longer keep him on board the sledge and Ani-Opoi, indifferent to the foam-flecked muzzles of his beasts, continued to beat them mercilessly with his stick, crying '*Hor! Hor!*', the roar of helicopter engines became audible once more. They were now flying from north to south towards Ani-Opoi's sledge and a great deal lower than before.

Unexpectedly, one of the helicopters detached itself from the trio, dropped still lower before switching on its searchlight, and with a deafening roar hurtled straight for the sledge.

The reindeer, blinded and deafened, veered to one side, snorting with fear. Ani-Opoi controlled them by a miracle, but the aircraft came lower and lower as if intending to ram.

Recoiling from the helicopter coming straight at them the reindeer trampled backwards onto the sledge as the powerful blast of the rotors flung the maddened reindeer, men and sledge in all directions.

Siegfried, deafened, leapt crazily to his feet, waving his arms and shouting: 'Stop it! What are you doing? There are people here!'

The helicopter banked to one side, and then came straight for him, Ani-Opoi and the overturned sledge. 'Stop!' yelled Siegfried. 'I'm Shertz! I surrender! You've no right! I'm an American!'

The down draught from the rotors once more swept him from his feet, but as he fell he managed to catch a glimpse in the aircraft's cabin of the young, laughing face of a pilot in army uniform.

The helicopter then soared aloft and flew off to catch up with his army pals.

Ani-Opoi got up from the snow, looking about him. The sledge was overturned and badly damaged; the reindeer, with broken reins, were racing headlong in all directions across the tundra.

Ani-Opoi dragged off his heavy *sokui*, threw it onto the snow and without a word to Siegfried ran off across the tundra in the direction the helicopters had just come from, the north. Siegfried, totally at a loss, ran in pursuit shouting: 'What's up? Where are we going?'

He was soaked inside his *sokui* and tried to take it off, but at that moment they came up onto the crest of a hill and what they saw below made them both freeze to the spot.

A bloody jumble of human bodies, dead reindeer and tins of

'tourist breakfast' and marinaded peppers machine-gunned from the air lay below on the white snow of the tundra.

Ani-Opoi fell to his knees and crawled towards the shambles. His eyes had already found the body of his son, slashed by bullets. Sanko's *malitsa*, like those of the other five Nenets boys, was peppered with bulletholes as if the helicopters had circled around over the dead bodies and fired off all their ammunition into them, to the last round. The same machine-gun bursts had mutilated the reindeer, who looked as if they had tangled with a drunken butcher.

Around these fragments of human and reindeer flesh from which steam was still rising, punctured tins of 'tourist breakfast' lay like a garnish. There was not one tin left intact, as if the gunners had been competing among themselves as to who could hit the most tins from the air.

Chapter Eight

From instructions to the October Revolution paratroop division:

Carrying out the Government's operational orders, the third helicopter regiment of our division successfully conducted an operation in defence of Socialist property and the Soviet system in various parts of the Yamal-Nenets district.

As a result of the exemplary conduct of the operational mission, I order: that the commander of the helicopter regiment, Major Strigunov, squadron commanders Lieutenants Zvyagin, Akhmerov, Ignatyuk and Shevchenko be promoted to next-highest officer rank; machine-gunners taking part in the mission are to receive official thanks and ten days' leave.

Divisional Commander
Major-General Grinko

Salekhard, 14 December 1983

▌Chapter Nine

Siegfried did not think he would survive to reach any sort of habitation in the tundra. But whenever he fell helplessly onto the snow, Ani-Opoi lifted him up roughly by the collar of his *malitsa* and hauled him along the ice until he recovered himself and begged: 'Let go! I'll manage!' Ani-Opoi himself did not stop once, not even to thrust a piece of ice or snow into his mouth to relieve his thirst.

After two hours of this cross-country run across the brittle snowcrust, they saw the rows of snow-powdered open-air wired cages of the Nenets Bright Way fur farm: light-blue Arctic foxes, chocolate-coloured mink and silvery dark foxes. Behind the cages rose the living quarters of the farm and chooms, reindeer sledges, children in *malitsas*.

Siegfried pitched forward onto the snow.

Ani-Opoi went on alone to meet the huskies that came running towards him from the encampment.

An hour later, Siegfried regained consciousness to the clatter of a tambourine, the glare of a bright light and a feeling of lying on something warm and soft. Unsure whether he was dreaming or not, he ungummed his sticky lashes and screwed up his eyes at once: it really was electricity — fluorescent lighting. Shading his eyes with his palm, he gazed about him.

He was lying in a large, elongated room that was completely unfurnished, apart from a long table and portraits of Marx, Lenin and Andropov on the walls. Yet the room's main distinguishing feature was the fact that the whole place, the long table and the entire expanse of floor, was filled with heaps of sable, fox and mink pelts. He himself was lying on several piles of sables, hence the extraordinary feeling of soft, gentle warmth.

Siegfried stirred and at once heard a man's voice: low, cigarette-hoarse.

'Aha! So we're coming round?'

Siegfried turned his eyes towards the voice. To one side, by the small, dark, sightless window stood a tall, husky old man of about eighty: one of those old thoroughbreds that no amount of time and toil can ever really age. He had a narrow, thin face, a powerful nose and a grizzled comb of a moustache; his teeth, large, powerful and tobacco-stained, were clamped on an empty amber cigarette holder. He wore a voluminous thick grey sweater under a fur jerkin, along with trousers and high *kisi.* From beneath grizzled bushy eyebrows he gazed keenly and cheerily at Siegfried with his light blue eyes.

'Come on, up you get, up you get!' said he. 'Or you'll miss the whole show!' He nodded towards the window where the tambourine was getting louder and some sort of lights were flashing. 'You don't see this kind of thing too often. Get up!'

Siegfried looked around. There was literally no room to put his feet because of the pelts that covered the floor. The old man said: 'It's all right. Walk straight over the furs, don't be afraid! Let me introduce myself: Geizenrikh — Lev Nikolayevich, fur expert. I'm buying furs for the international fur auction in Leningrad, in January. And your name, if you'd care ...'

Everything was unusual about this old man: the old Russian aristocratic 'if you'd care', the surname that was clearly un-Russian (and un-Nenets), his direct social manner, not to mention the fabulous riches of this interior where his feet trod on Arctic fox and mink.

'Siegfried Shertz,' he said, stepping uneasily over the furs. 'But where am I?'

'Wh-a-at?' the old man interrupted, raising his brows in astonishment. 'You're Siegfried Shertz?' he switched at once into German: '*the* Siegfried Shertz, the middleman between the USSR and the Western banks? I hope you speak German?'

'Yes,' said Siegfried, astonished in his turn that an old man living in the depths of the tundra should know German.

'I've heard a lot about you, my friend,' Geizenrikh went on meanwhile, 'but how did you turn up here with the Nentsi?'

'It's a long story,' said Siegfried evasively. He had only now perceived the strong Russian accent of the old man's German and the fact that his sentence structure was the old, literary, high-flown style of Schiller's time.

'Well, tell me later!' said the old man complaisantly and pointed to the window. 'Go and look, go and look! Even I rarely see it now, and I've been in the Arctic sixty years. You're in the director's office of the Bright Road fur farm. Roads, it's true, I don't see, but there's plenty of bright light — look!'

Through the double glazing of the window it certainly was light, coming from an enormous bonfire which the Nentsi had built on the wide, snowy square in front of the farm director's hut. Near the fire, on six sledges, lay the bodies of the six dead Nenets hunters which had been brought in from the tundra. The bodies were wrapped in coarse cloth; by each man's right hand lay his smashed hunting rifle; by the left his portable cooking pot, knife, box of matches, packet of shag tobacco — all a hunter would be likely to need in this life and the next. Near these sledges, prepared for the men's last journey, stood a crowd of Nentsi bearing torches. By the bonfire, on a reindeer hide, sat a man in a strange costume: a handsome suede shirt with red cloth epaulettes edged with the same red piping and tufts of red hair. His entire face was covered with a piece of scarlet material, and on his chest hung a kind of silver plate. A large tambourine was in his hand.

Geizenrikh smiled: 'The shaman. Soon he will *kamlat*, that is commune with the spirits. Just now he's warming up the tambourine to stretch the skin, make it resilient.'

In fact the shaman was moving the tambourine towards the fire, holding it there for a while; then, taking it in his left hand and a wooden stick in his right, he began striking the tambourine quietly and rhythmically, listening intently like a musician tuning his instrument.

'Of course he's not a real shaman,' said Geizenrikh. 'It's Vaska Nogo, a veterinarian; he's about forty. But his grandad and great grandad were real shamans, it's their costume he's got. Didn't drink it away, at least,' he concluded, in near-astonishment.

'Are you German?' Siegfried enquired finally.

'My ancestors came to Russia from Bavaria in the seventeenth century,' said Geizenrikh casually and turned back at once to the window.

There the shaman had apparently decided that the tambourine was 'tuned'. The blows on it became powerful, delivered with all his strength, and faster too; and as they increased in frequency so the shaman rose from his reindeer skin part-dancing, part-performing what seemed like ritual twitching movements. The Nentsi clustered closer round about, their cheekbones lit by the glow of fire and torches. The shaman struck his tambourine and leapt, now approaching the sledges bearing the dead men, now retreating from them, shouting out in time to the beat: '*Go-o-o-oi! Go-o-oi! Go-oi! Goi!*'

'He's calling up the spirits,' Geizenrikh informed Siegfried. 'By the way, his great-grandfather really did that, I saw it myself . . .' Since Siegfried was now looking at him in surprise and curiosity, Geizenrikh willingly amplified: 'I've been spending a few months a year here since 1923. I'm a furrier by profession or, if you like, a fur expert . . . Well, Vaska, come on! Let's see what you can do!' he said through the window, nimbly scrambling onto the sill and opening a fanlight to hear the shaman better.

The frosty wind and the smoke from the bonfire stole into the room. There, beyond the window, the shaman suddenly stood stock-still and, throwing back his head, began shouting out something in Nenets.

'Shall I translate?' asked Geizenrikh.

'Yes, please.'

'He's asking the spirits of the dead: "Who killed you, men?",' and Geizenrikh began a simultaneous translation of the shaman's exclamations; he was now questioning the spirits of the fallen and immediately shouting out their answers:

'Airmen killed us — Russian airmen.'

'Why did Russian airmen kill you?'

'Because we burned the drilling rigs.'

'Why did you burn Russian drilling rigs?'

'Because the drilling rigs are killing the tundra and all our people on the tundra.'

'Is our hero, Vauli Piettomin, far from you?'

'No, Vauli is not far from us — he is here!'

'What do you say to us, Vauli Piettomin?'

'The Russians are killing you from their aeroplanes and heli-copters, like hunting down wolves.

'My spirit walks the tundra and seeks a bodily form, to avenge on the Russians the death of Nenets men. I have loosed the triple-edged arrow across the Tundra with the signal for revolt, and all must go to do battle, both valiant warrior and common man. But are there still among the Nentsi men whose hands will not tremble and whose eyes will not blink as they shoot at the Russians? Are there?'

The shaman accompanied each question with a blow on the tambourine and, running towards the Nentsi, shouted in their faces:

'Are there still men among the Nentsi? Vauli himself is asking you. Vauli himself! Who will go to wreak revenge on the Russians?'

'I will!' said Ani-Opoi in a low voice as he stepped forward from the ranks of bereaved relatives. 'I will set fire to one drill-rig. For my son, however.'

'I also,' someone else strode forward.

'And I also, however.'

Eight men moved out from the crowd and stood eyeing one another. Then the shaman leaped high in the air before crash-ing to his knees and yelling: 'Earth!' A crash came, on the tambourine, then: 'Bear them well on thy back, do not overturn them!' — crash. 'Kingfire! By thee we live, we are warmed by thee!' — crash. 'Keep wolves far from them, devour the Russians' drills with mighty fire!' — crash. 'Drive the Russians from our land!' — crash. 'To our tundra without Russians make haste and come!' — crash. 'We beseech thee, O Sun, light of the earth — we wish to live! To see our dear ones well! To graze our reindeer! To catch our fish in the rivers! To hunt down our wild animals in the tundra!' The shaman quick-ened the tempo of his invocations, struck his tambourine faster and more resoundingly; his jig became ever more vigorous and his shouts louder: 'Let the Russian people run away. Let them fly away in their aeroplanes! Let them depart with the night! With evil spirits let them depart! With their diseases let them depart! With their tractors let them depart! With their socialist

241

commitments let them fly away! The tundra cannot live under socialism! There is nothing in the tundra as it is!'

Here Geizenrikh burst out laughing and stopped translating — not that there was anything to translate; after a few more invocations, the shaman collapsed onto his reindeer hide and fell silent. The Nentsi touched the animals harnessed to the sledges bearing the bodies, and the long funeral procession, accompanied by children and dogs, melted away into the polar night, the glint of torches still visible in the distance. The last to go was the weary shaman; he had already taken the cloth from his face, but his shoulder now bore a Kalashnikov submachine gun.

'Oho!' Geizenrikh at once grew serious and screwed up his face, saying 'I'm afraid there isn't going to be an official opening of your gas pipeline on the seventeenth of December . . .'

▌Chapter Ten

'Fur is — romance, my dear fellow,' said Geizenrikh euphorically some time later, offering him strong tea with real Moscow *sushki*.[1] He took a pelt from one of the piles of mink or fox and jerked it about in the air as if shaking it out; then he turned it towards the bright fluorescent lamp and said: 'See the play of colours? The height of fur? The density? But that's only a third-rate one. For the home market. Export begins with first-class furs, but there is something above first-class: the 'extra–1' and 'extra–2'. Not the farm-bred fur, not those beasties you saw in the cages — the wild animals, from the tundra.' Here Geizenrikh walked over to some bundles of gorgeously luxurious furs and picked up a blue fox pelt, lovingly ran his palm along the fur and proffered it to Siegfried. 'Have a feel. Know how much a pelt like that would fetch at auction? Fifteen hundred dollars! Now cast your eyes round this room, my friend. There are up to a thousand pelts. In other words, you and I are sitting on a millon fur dollars, that's all. And that's the income of just two fur farms: a hundredth part, perhaps, of what will be on show at our January fur auction. That's why even Stalin, when he put an end to all private trading in Russia, didn't stop the Leningrad fur auctions — currency, pure hard currency! Every year the furriers from all over the world come to Leningrad for furs. And leave several million dollars behind in just a few days! Where else in the USSR can you see that, a real auction with bids in hard currency?

---

[1] *sushki:* small dry bread rings

Soviet roubles are never even mentioned — good money only. But I was talking about romance, wasn't I? Romance, not money ...'

The old man had clearly been starved of an audience — one that understood his native German, too! Siegfried, warmed by the tea and feeling he was back in civilization once more, soon took on his former image of self-confident businessman, calmly and smilingly indulgent towards his companion — just as a ship entering safe habour after a storm turns from a windblown, waterlogged shell into a proud, majestic vessel. Siegfried felt he had reached harbour, sailed through the icy sea of the tundra if not quite as far as the mainland of civilization, then at least to one of its islands.

'Romance lies in the furs themselves,' old man Geizenrikh was going on. 'Fur — is love. Yes, yes, don't laugh! I've had six wives, my dear fellow, all of them Bolshoi ballerinas — that's what fur is, my boy! Of course, your pipeline will kill off the tundra and there'll be no more sables, foxes or ermines here. And that's stupid. You can find gas in the Sahara or somewhere. Anyway, using oil, coal and gas is characteristic of barbarous civilizations. In about twenty years, thirty at best, man will be extracting energy from the sea — All right, say a hundred years! But you won't get an ermine or an Arctic fox from sea water or a nuclear reactor. Anyway, do you know what the tundra is? The tundra is the only health resort on earth, where as recently as twenty years ago the air was totally free of harmful bacteria! People terminally ill with asthma were cured here in a week. Yet instead of building health resorts here, they built labour camps!' grinned Geizenrikh. 'Truly, the USSR is a land of paradoxes. Stalin killed millions of his own citizens; there isn't a family in Russia which hasn't had at least one relative driven off into the camps by him. I — if I might mention it — did time here from '38 to '46, as a German-Japanese spy,' he smiled bitterly, 'but it was easier for me than the others. I was used to the tundra. But the others ... Every year here, even now, when the swamps melt, human bones and skeletons float in the quagmires ... And the Russian people still yearn for Stalin, "the boss", as they call him. His pictures all over the country again, in any bus you get on. Even

244

Zinoviev, the dissident, calls him "a great man"!'

Siegfried noticed that a sort of fiery glint had kindled in Geizenrikh's eyes. Clearly it was the first time the old man had come across someone he could tell everything without holding back — pour out his soul, as the Russians say.

'Still, no nation in the world knows how to draw lessons from history,' Geizenrikh pursued. 'A separate individual, yes — a single individual — learns from his mistakes: a child doesn't put his hand in the fire twice. But peoples are amazingly forgetful, that's the paradox of humanity. You want examples? Permit me: Israel exports flowers to Germany. No, just think; Israel exports flowers to Germany, and Germany sends army uniforms to Israel. And you say, lessons of history!' And although Siegfried had said nothing of the kind, the old man continued: 'It's because nations have no memory that I don't believe Soviet power will ever be overturned in Russia, or that any sort of democratic reform will ever come about in this country. The Russians don't know what democracy is: they're afraid of it, they need "a boss". That's why the authority that's driven the population of the whole country to semi-starvation — that power is today the most powerful in the world. No dissident can stir the people to general revolt: no Solzhenitsyn, Sakharov, Bukovsky can do it, for all their quixotic heroism. Even during the hunger strike in Novocherkassk there was no rising, even in the towns and villages round about! The Russians just don't have any experience at fighting for democracy — if they ever did rise up, it was for a "good" tsar! The Nentsi, though ... Of course they're a savage people, uncivilized and backward. But that's to their advantage, too: they haven't got a historical slave complex. Until they were enslaved by the Russians they lived here as a primitive commune. They didn't have tsars, kings or even princelings: their judges were the elders, who owned nothing, neither land nor people. I've studied this territory in Miller, Milton and Georgi[1] — I know

---

[1]Milton and Miller were famous seventeenth-century ethnographers; Georgi, one who lived in the eighteenth century. All three were celebrated for their journeys through Siberia.

what I'm talking about! Nowadays just travel about the USSR and look: in every national republic from the Baltic to Georgia, Russians are regarded as occupiers. The Russians know this, so they're always on their guard. The government stations troops in every republic, in case of an uprising. But here, in the tundra — well, who could have foreseen that Nenets savages would rebel?! Nobody even regarded them as people; the British probably thought the same about the Jews in Palestine in the 1940s. Having just destroyed Hitler in Africa, how could the British army and its generals regard ringleted Jews as serious opponents? Now, remember the tactics the Jews used to gain the victory in Palestine, how they drove out the British. After all, in Israel, just like here in the tundra, there are no forests, no jungles for guerrilla warfare! Just like here, the whole country and its population wide open like the palm of your hand. Yet, nevertheless, in the course of a few months the Jews had thrown the British out of Palestine. How? What with? Terror! Simply by using terror they brought the British to a point where their army sat shamefully in barracks, too scared to poke its nose outside their stone walls. After that they fled the country altogether —'

He's just a maniac, thought Siegfried suddenly. He's a madman, dreaming mad dreams about overturning Soviet power in the tundra.

'I don't know who organized the Nentsi for this uprising,' Geizenrikh continued, '— if they have a single organizer at all — but things are developing in the tundra now almost like in Israel before the British fled: first individual acts of terror directed against prominent people, then scattered acts of sabotage, finally followed by sabotage across the whole territory: firing the drilling rigs. You follow my train of thought?' he abruptly demanded.

'Yes, but I ... I didn't think it was as serious as all that. So far as I've heard, it all started with murders committed by escaped prisoners. What have the Nentsi got to do with it?'

'You think that, do you?' the old man smiled grimly. He walked across the furs to a corner of the room and removed a pile of sables from a cupboard from which he took a little book with a well-worn cover, bearing the title *Nenets Legends and*

Fairy Tales. The middle of the book held a paper bookmark. Geizenrikh perched his pince-nez on his nose, opened the book at the place and said to Siegfried: 'There's an excellent legend here about seven Nenets hero-brothers and their seven sisters. One day, returning from a hunt, the brothers discover that enemies have destroyed their chooms, driven off their deer and violated their sisters. The brothers leap onto riding reindeer, overtake their enemies and ...' here Geizenrikh raised a finger and read: 'however many there were of the enemy, all were slain. While they were still alive their ears and *khote* were cut off and they were forced to eat their own *khote*. Thus the fathers avenged their blood and disgrace, thus do the sons like-wise! You know what a *khote* is? It's what you've got between your legs, my boy. Now, you tell me, what would be the point of escaped Russian prisoners carrying out the precepts of Nenets legends, especially so closely and accurately, and cut-ting off the ears and sex organs of such lovers of Nenets girlies as Ryazanov, Hotko and Voropayev —'

'What? What was that?' Up to now Siegfried had been listen-ing rather patronizingly to the old man, as to one slightly off his head, but now his whole body shot forward. 'Did you say, Ryazanov? Which Ryazanov?'

'Pyotr Ryazanov, chief geologist of Yamal–Oil–Gas Explor-ation,' said Geizenrikh, and looked at Siegfried with interest. 'Did you know him, then?'

Did Siegfried know Ryazanov? Yes indeed, he knew all three: Ryazanov, Hotko and Voropayev. They were the ones who had been in Ryazanov's cottage five years before at that very leaving party for Siegfried, when he had refused to let his Nenets Lolita, Okka, be passed round the circle. Then they had consoled themselves with another young Nenets girl, doing hell knows what to her — and it was those three the tundra spirits had killed, and how!

'Do you — are you telling me they killed them and cut off their ... because they —?' Siegfried brought out, almost stam-mering.

'I don't know the precise order of events,' smiled the old man. 'Whether they killed them and then cut or cut first and then killed. The legend in any case definitely says: "While *alive*

247

their ears and *khote* were cut off."' Geizenrikh again stared hard at Siegfried. 'So you knew Ryazanov?'

'N–yes,' said Siegfried, embarrassed. 'Not too well ...'

But his knees came together from very fear. This instinctive gesture of self-protection did not escape Geizenrikh's keen eyes. He laid the book aside and said with a soothing smile:

'All that is just purely literary conjecture. You've got nothing to worry about, in any case. You're just a visitor.'

I do just have something to worry about, thought Siegfried as the sordid picture of group debauchery that drunken night swam up before his eyes. But, God, he hadn't had any hand in what Ryazanov, Hotko and Voropayev had done with that Nenochka! He'd only made love to his Okka. And anyway, it was all rubbish about 'tundra spirits', Nenets legends, and this old tundra hand with the piercing eyes, bookish German, anti-Soviet speeches and portentous literary deductions. He'd had six wives himself, shouldn't wonder if he's had his good times in Nenets chooms with the likes of Melkune — and Okka — but he's not scared, and he's not running either.

Nonetheless, that cursed sense of fear had taken root in Siegfried's mind; a cold foreboding of disaster and catastrophe, like in a plane when a new fit of aerophobia struck. All three of them had been in Ryazanov's cottage that night, and now the 'tundra spirits' had executed the three; logic suggested that it was the turn of the fourth — *his* turn. More than anything at the moment — more than his 225 million dollars and the opening of the pipeline in the company of Western journalists — Siegfried wanted to be lost in the snows back at Zataika with KGB Colonol Khanov, so solicitous, so reliable ...

But outside the window was the polar night of the Yamal, and the Nentsi coming back from the *khalmer.*

'Have you got a line through to Urengoi or Salekhard?' he asked Geizenrikh.

'No telephone, of course. There's the radio,' he replied, and indicated with his eyes a tall pile of fox furs by the window.

Siegfried went over and removed the furs from some bulky object, and noticed that it was a low stool with an antediluvian radio of the type known in Russia as the Harvester. He picked up the receiver and began turning the handle of the dynamo, listening intently to the crackling sounds in his ear. He would call up the Urengoi or Salekhard KGB directorate, say who he was and surrender himself into their trusty arms. That would put an end once and for all to his delirious flight into the tundra and to the mystic threat of retribution for what five years ago had been a passing peccadillo with a twelve-year-old Nenochka.

But before the distant female voice of the radio telephonist sounded in his ear, he caught the boom of helicopter engines outside the window. He glanced outside as Geizenrikh came over.

In the dark sky of the polar night could be seen the signal lights of heavy MI-10 paratroop helicopters. They were swiftly descending towards the Nenets encampment of the Bright Way fur farm. Siegfried's ears were overwhelmed by the heavy booming sound, while outside reindeer were breaking their tethers from fear, chooms swayed in the blast of the rotor blades above them, and in the cages and enclosures mink and Arctic foxes raced around deafened and terrified. It seemed inevitable that at any moment automatic weapons and machine guns would open up.

But no: the figures of army paratroops began leaping soundlessly out of the aircraft. Using the butts of their rifles, they drove the Nentsi onto the square in front of the farm administration building.

One of the helicopters landed right by the porch of the building, where Siegfried and Geizenrikh waited. Loud, hurrying footfalls echoed along the corridor, and one of the paratroopers kicked open the door of the fur-sorting room.

Struck by the unexpected sight — the bright fluorescent light and the abundance of furs on the floor — the young paratrooper in his khaki jacket stopped short, rigid with surprise, in the doorway.

'*Hände hoch*,' said Geizenrikh quietly to Siegfried, to make him put his hands up.

At these words in German — familiar to every Russian through films about the Second World War — the young para's

249

eyes flashed triumphantly. Keeping his rifle trained on Geizen-rikh and Siegfried, he turned towards the corridor and shouted:

'Boys! Hoorah! They've put us down in Germany!'

Part Five
Fire in the Tundra

Chapter One

It was only as I was leaving Hudya's flat for the street that I realized what the heavy drone of aircraft rolling over Salekhard actually meant. Inside, the noise had been muffled by the double glazing.

In the time I had spent drinking tea, inspecting Hudya's bookshelves and suffering my astonishment initially at his reading anti-Soviet books and then at his strange note on the door, 'Goodbye and, please, go away to Russia', the droning had reached such an intensity that hundreds of people were spilling out of the houses and waving arms and caps at the sky.

Dozens of transport aircraft were roaring overhead. The powerful drone of their engines rolled like a wave over the town from the west, north-west and south-east. The semicircle of their landing lights shone out as they blinked in the darkness.

Behind the aeroplanes came the enormous freight and paratroop helicopters. Over Salekhard itself the air brigades split up. The planes went on to land at the airport, while the helicopters put down close by the river jetty near the Wave Restaurant, on the thick ice of the frozen Ob.

These were the reinforcements sent by party and government orders into Salekhard to assist the October Revolution paratroop division; from Moscow, the special Dzerzhinsky division of the USSR KGB; from Voronezh, thirteen hundred students at the advanced police academy; from Murmansk, two divisions of marines, and from Khabarovsk a paratroop brigade and special troops for guarding targets of particular importance to state security. Units of these forces had already fanned out across the tundra, dropping paras at oil- and gas-drilling sites, pipeline sections, shift settlements and Nenets encampments. But even those operational units which had now arrived in Salekhard produced a stunning effect on the inhabitants by their numbers and the military strength they disposed.

I imagine the Czechs experienced a similar shock in their time, when our paratroops rained down on Prague during the airlift. The only difference was that the Czechs were unlikely to have been so pleased to see them as was the entire Russian population of Salekhard.

Hell, it feels good all the same to be a citizen of a country that's got military strength like ours! Never mind the rationing, or that there's no meat or butter in the shops. At least we can sleep securely knowing we need have no fear of any Chinese, American, West German or Israeli aggressor. My heart warmed to see the huge, potbellied Antons disgorging tanks, armoured cars, tracked amphibians straight onto the frozen Ob. With revving engines they formed up into columns ready to storm through tundra, taiga or desert, wherever the homeland should require ... If I were a sickly 'intellectual' or a college kid, what had happened to me yesterday might knock me right off balance for at least a year, if not for the rest of my life. There are women who go crazy or become lesbians after the shock of being raped. I can't say I'm made of iron but I'm not made of wet rags either. After all, I've been in the police force for four years and this kind of work certainly strengthens your nerves and character — believe me. And now, looking at the might of our armed forces and joining in the general sense of excitement in the streets, I almost completely forgot about what happened to me only one night before. A sense of jubilation rose up inside of me as I felt a flood of renewed strength.

▌Chapter Two

A euphoric atmosphere — literally festive, in fact — prevailed at the North Hotel too. Here, right in the hotel lobby, were located the joint operational staffs of the army, KGB and police. Radio operators dictated to staff officers the reports they had received.

'Police militia landing at Dawn over the North!'
'Marines have taken Road to Communism!'
'KGB forces have blocked off Ilyich's Legacy!'

Nobody latched on to the double meanings of these phrases; the staff officers quickly inserted coloured flags into a huge map of the Yamal–Nenets district, denoting the areas now securely sealed off by the troops sent in.

'Yes, our military machine works like a Singer, no problems! These Nentsi — huh! We'll snap them in half, the wimps!' These big words were uttered in the hotel dining-room by a husky 23-year-old Ukranian tank commander helping himself to a large plateful of 'navy style' macaroni. The restaurant had been converted into a staff canteen and was now crammed with officers from all arms of the services. 'If we don't cope with that lot, I'll telegraph my brother — he's in the special units preparing a drop into Sweden,' the Ukrainian went on. He addressed the cook through the serving hatch. 'Chef, are you a local man?'

'Yes I am. Why?'

'Listen, is it true what they say about the Nenets women having their cunts sideways on?'

This ludicrous idea dates back to prehistoric times, that Nenets vaginas are placed differently from everyone else's. This hoax gets passed on, in some totally mysterious fashion, from one generation of men entering the north to the next. There's not been a man yet who hasn't fallen for that one as soon as he arrives.

I ordered millet porridge with bilberry jelly — I can't eat 'navy style' macaroni first thing in the morning! There were no free tables, but three groups of officers immediately offered a seat at their table. I accepted the one where the cloth was cleanest. Of course, I was now the centre of attention. After a brief, lightly flirtatious introduction ceremony, one of them decided to get everyone's attention — mine included — by saying:

'Listen, boys, have you heard the one about how Vanya Bugayev, one of the Khabarovsk paras, caught two German saboteurs? No? Well! It's the biggest laugh of the day. The whole of HQ knows! Listen. Two Germans — one of them was a Russo-German, something to do with the fur trade and the other wasn't a German at all, he was an American of German descent, but that's not it — anyway, two foreigners were at this Nenets farm, Bright Way, before our boys arrived. There they were, sitting quietly having tea and sushki, when suddenly the Khabarovsk paras drop out of the sky onto the tundra. Among them Ensign Vanya Bugayev. I should say, Anechka (this was just for my benefit) that they collected all these paras, Bugayev included, on operational alert in the middle of the night and shoved them into MI-10s while they were so dozy they were wrapping their footrags round their boots — they hadn't a bloody clue where they were going to fight! Anyway, Vanya Bugayev jumps out of his helicopter onto the tundra, bursts into the farm admin building half-asleep, and these two foreigners, as soon as they see a soldier, come out with "*Hände hoch!*" — sheer habit. Of course they said it to each other, but Vanya Bugayev went barmy as soon as he heard "*Hände hoch!*" and bawled at the top of his voice: "*Hitler — kaput! Hitler — kaput!* Hoorah!"'

After everybody had finished laughing, the storyteller added, with a smile:

'Do you think Bugayev got torn off a strip for that? Not on your Nelly! He only got official thanks from the KGB, that's all! It turns out that this American German or German-American — who the hell knows, anyway, one of these

Germans — is some sort of VIP. He's called Siegfried Shertz. The Udmurt Gee Bees let him slip and he got into the tundra. Decided to take a stroll round the Soviet Union, the son of a bitch! But Vanya Bugayev grabs him by the collar. "*Hitler — kaput!*" he shouts ... Anechka, where are you off to?'

'Business,' I smiled. 'Thanks for the company'.

I had no time to sit about in a restaurant listening to army tall stories. I had to find Hudya Benokan. He wasn't in the restaurant, or in the lobby either; nor was he in the staff rooms on the first and second floors. However, when I opened the door on the second floor I came across my boss, old Zotov, and the head of Salekhard KGB, Major Shatunov. I was flabbergasted: amid all these events, at the very centre of HQ bustle and tense operational activity, these two looked like holidaymakers. They were sitting in their underwear in the middle of a double hotel room, unshaven and playing cards. On the table were an empty brandy bottle and the remains of a snack. Of course they'd been eating — ugh, nothing could be worse! — tinned herring in tomato sauce.

'Good morning,' said I. 'You haven't seen Hudya Benokan?'

'Eh? Are you still here?' said Zotov vaguely. 'I thought you were back in Urengoi —'

'Yesterday you yourself ordered me to look into the rumours about Vauli Piettomin here —'

'Ah, yes, so I did,' he recalled. 'But you look different somehow ... Anything happen?'

What did I look like, I wondered. I went through into the bathroom to take a panicky look at myself in the mirror. My face, it has to be said, wasn't as fresh as it might have been — but nothing drastic. And yet Zotov, the meticulous old man, had spotted straight away that something had happened to me that night. I soon got busy with my make-up, and heard drifting in: 'King of diamonds! Nine! Queen of trumps ...' Hell, why weren't they working, when all this was going on round them? Having powdered over the dark rings under my eyes, I emerged from the bathroom.

'There's women for you!' said Shatunov. 'A spit and a dab and they're as fresh as a daisy, good enough to eat!'

Even the style of the sentence was extraordinary coming

from Shatunov. Yesterday he had been a smart, brusque, taciturn KGB major; but now, as if making a show of it, he was playing cards with Zotov in front of the whole hotel — in his underclothes, unshaven, with brandy on the table. His talk was no longer businesslike, it was normal everyday chat. So I asked him frankly, matching his tone:

'What're you up to here, playing about?'

Zotov, about to play his next card, held his hand above the table and looked at me in surprise.

'You don't know?'

'What should I know?'

Instead of playing his card, Zotov lowered his arm and turned to face me, sneering:

'And just where did you spend the night?'

I forced myself to grin.

'W-well, that's my business.'

'I see! Of course, there's been a clear-out of officers ...' Zotov mumbled, returning to the game, adding, as if it were a minor detail: 'We've got the sack.'

'Wh-at?' My astonishment was so loud both of them looked at me and Zotov added:

'It's all right, now. When guns speak, you know, the muses are silent.' And he turned to Shatunov: 'Your go, major ...'

Abruptly I covered the cards with my hand.

'Will you explain what's happened — properly?'

'Your officers are pretty decisive characters.' Shatunov smiled at Zotov, and then addressed me.

'It's all very simple. The head of the KGB himself, General Chebrikov, flew in from Moscow and immediately relieved me and your chief of all duties. And after the army restores order here, we'll be court-martialled —'

'What for?'

'For not catching the escaped cons. For not discovering that a Nenets rebellion was brewing and nipping it in the bud. In a word, for the whole shambles. Somebody's got to be the scapegoat! Chebrikov and Bogomyatov have decided on us, Major Orudjev, Pyotr Tusyada and Colonel Sini. The longer the list, the more solid the case.'

'Don't you worry, kiddywink,' added Zotov. 'You're not on

the list, so you can fly off to Urengoi; they'll have appointed somebody in my place already, I expect. At the same time you can tell my old woman not to worry: they won't give me a stretch because of my age. They'll just cashier me good and proper and I'll lose my officer's pension. Well, fuck it!' At this, he slapped a card down on the table and swore: 'What a fucking system it is: you serve all your life — like a dog; then one thing goes wrong, and the boot goes up your arse — no pension, even!'

Yesterday if anybody had dared say such a thing about our Soviet system in the presence of KGB Major Shatunov, I have no doubt that he would have spent the remainder of his life in places far away from central heating and other comforts of civilization. But today, Shatunov did not raise an eyebrow. He played his next card:

'Jack of spades.'

I began to feel sorry for them, both Zotov and Shatunov, sitting there together, putting on the swagger, drinking cognac and playing cards. In fact, if Bogomyatov himself and the head of the KGB had selected Shatunov and Zotov as being responsible for all that had occurred in the tundra, the matter would not rest with reduction to the ranks and loss of pension. But why should I speak to them about that and make their already miserable mood even worse.

'Men,' I said with affected carelessness. 'Have you had any breakfast yet? Or have you been living on brandy all night?'

'Hm-m,' coughed Zotov. 'We're ... not hungry.'

Well it was clear enough: for all their old-soldier manner they couldn't go to the officer's canteen for breakfast — the finger would be pointed at them there. So there they were, sitting in their room eating herrings and swigging brandy.

'Stop lying! Not hungry!' I teased them. 'Just say what you want brought from the canteen. I saw navy-style macaroni there, reindeer goulash and millet porridge. And tell me, please, if you've seen Hudya Benokan today?'

'I believe I did ...' said Zotov vaguely. 'Yes, he popped in an hour or two ago. But there's all this army business going on here. So if you need him, better look for him at he local CID.'

I went downstairs to the restaurant, and it was only when I

was coming back bringing Zotov and Shatunov two portions each of macaroni and goulash (honestly, even under a microscope you couldn't tell the difference!) that a new thought occurred to me and brought me to a halt. Of course — why hadn't I thought of it before? If Shatunov and Zotov were put on trial, one of the first questions put to Zotov would be: 'And who was sent by you to Camp RS-549 to ascertain the circumstances of the break-out? Investigator Anna Kovina, of course! Splendid! And why, comrade Kovina, on your arrival at Camp RS-549 at two in the afternoon didn't you interrogate the escapers' room-mates the same day and again the next morning? You must surely have realized that a group escape, especially on the eve of the official pipeline opening, was an unusual occurrence? What were you doing in the camp all that evening, that night and the following morning?' That was all — and I was already involved: I was already 'on the list', as Zotov had put it. They'd put more pressure on. I know our judicial system all right. It's one thing when you're inside the machine and do as you like in its name: then minor peccadilloes are forgiveable, they turn a blind eye. It's quite another matter when the machine starts working against you. The night I had spent at Hudya Benokan's would simply be put down as 'corruption while carrying out official duties'; as for the night spent with Orudjev in the meeting room at Camp RS-549, enough said! These two facts were more than enough for the judicial findings to say: 'The Urengoi and Salekhard CID operatives have been wallowing in debauchery, which explains the absence of professional and party vigilance with regard to the anti-Soviet mood of the population of the Yamal-Nenets district.' And if, in addition, they found anti-Soviet literature in Hudya Benokan's flat ...

I went cold inside. Doubtless Hudya, like me — known throughout the territory as the 'Urengoi Alsatian', a sniffer-out of pornography, narcotics and anti-Soviet writings — had confiscated the books from local dissidents. Yet he had not handed them over immediately to the KGB; he'd concealed them. If there was an anti-Soviet uprising in the district, how could Hudya prove that he had not disseminated anti-Soviet literature among the young Nentsi? And that was an official offence. Article 118 of the Criminal Code, point three: use of official position for the subversion of Soviet power, minimum sentence ten years' strict regime — in practice, the uranium mines in the Pamir, where no one survives more than three months.

My first thought was to run over to Hudya's place, break into his flat and burn the books in the Dutch stove.

But with all that was whirling about in my head in these minutes I realized that to break down the door of what, after all, was someone else's flat in broad daylight just wasn't the thing to do.

▌Chapter Three

The whole ground floor of the Salekhard CID was crammed with arrested Nentsi. The entire town seemed to have been raked through, along with the encampments on the outskirts. While waiting their turn to be questioned they sat on the floor, which was the standard brick-brown colour to hide the occasional bloodstain. Guards stood over them having a smoke. Still higher, on the walls of the corridor were photographs of the escaped cons from Camp RS-549 bearing the inscription, 'WANTED CRIMINALS', and a decorative poster bearing the full text of the moral code of a builder of communism. Behind the doors of the interrogation rooms, investigators flown in from Moscow and Tyumen were conducting their ceaseless questioning. Their main object was to find out who was the leader of the Nenets rebellion, who had spread the rumour of the return of Vauli Piettomin across the tundra and who had fired the drilling rigs.

Stepping across the legs of the seated Nentsi, I glanced into all the ground-floor offices. No Hudya. In an office on the second floor, however, the directorate secretary tore herself away from the continual ringing of telephones to look at me, harrassed.

'Hudya? He flew to Urengoi half an hour ago.'

'Why?'

'Well, who knows? In this madhouse, everybody does what they want!'

Odd, I thought. Hudya flies to Urengoi and leaves me that stupid note: 'Goodbye, and, please, go away to Russia.' Why should I up and go to Russia for no reason at all, and why 'Goodbye' if I live and work in Urengoi and that's exactly where he's gone?'

262

I walked, puzzled, along the second-floor corridor. It was quieter here, with fewer detainees. I had already reached the down staircase when the door of the nearest office opened and out came Ayuni Ladukai — the same Ayuni who had led the boys of Boarding School 3 in raping me the previous night.

We both froze. I was on the landing preventing her escape, she was in the corridor. The radiant smile slowly left her face: she'd obviously been set free after questioning.

My first desire was to pull out my pistol and shoot the bitch on the spot. My hand went for the holster automatically.

But it was then I recalled the words she had hurled at Hudya Benokan when he broke into the school and interrupted the violence. Glancing swiftly round at the Moscow investigators and guards, I quickly seized Ayuni's elbow with my trained hand twisted her arm in a painful hold so that she could neither run nor resist.

'Come with me,' I said in a low voice.

All the offices were occupied by crowds of investigators, but I had to interview this little cunt as soon as possible, interrogate her alone and in secret. So I pushed her roughly into the ladies' toilet, so quickly that no one paid us any attention.

There were only two cubicles in the loo, and both were dirty; still, they were empty. I pushed Ayuni into one of the cubicles and closed the door behind me. It seemed the girl could feel the iron grip of my fingers even through the sleeve of her *malitsa*, and I twisted and twisted her arm to a point where the piercing pain stops anyone even contemplating resistance. Most probably the bitch never thought of resistance anyway, but last night she had shown no pity towards me — why in hell should I feel sorry for her today?

Raising the arm she had twisted behind her back, I forced Ayuni's face almost into the lavatory bowl, yellow from old urine and excrement, and only then released her and said:

'Who is Okka?'

The girl was silent. She wore a fine *malitsa* and was of middling height, shorter than me but strong-boned. I didn't expect her to talk straightaway. Zotov had told us investigators that under interrogation Nentsi are secretive and reticent, like getting blood out of a stone. But yesterday, at the school, she had been taking her part in the general boys' chorus of: '*Nut i shar!* Death to the Russian occupiers!'

'Who is Okka, for fuck's sake! Or I'll break your arm,' I said crudely and jerked her elbow upwards to hard that her face splashed into the lavatory bowl. But I forced her up again. 'Well?'

All of a sudden, with an adroit movement she twisted her whole body and I felt her elbow slipping out of my grasp, leaving me with just the empty sleeve of her *malitsa*. This was something they hadn't taught us at police school: ju-jitsu grips when your opponent is wearing a *malitsa* made of slippery reindeer fur. Another fraction of a second, and she would have broken free of my hands altogether. But nuts to that, she'd chosen the wrong one this time!

Using my free hand, I gave her a powerful backhander across the nape of the neck. I followed it up by gripping her wrist in both hands and forcing it so far up her back that I heard the crunch of her shoulder joint quite clearly. The girl gave a suppressed scream, and I saw red: not only had the little sod organized a queue of rapists for me the night before, now she was forcing me to torture her in real earnest.

But I had no time for niceties. I forced her face still deeper into the loo and held her under till she gurgled and tried to say something, her whole body writhing. Then I released her contorted limbs and allowed her to straighten up and draw breath. I kept standing behind her and didn't see her dirty face, smelling of urine, but I could guess how the beat of her suffocating heart must be deafening now and how she was gulping in air with her wet, gaping mouth. Well, the previous night they had tortured me worse — till I had lost consciousness. Now she and I were almost quits, but I still needed to know the Okka for whom I was being raped. After all I had been through, I had the right to know that!

'Well? Will you say who Okka is? Or —' I began to squeeze her arm again, giving her to understand that nothing would stop me from drowning her.

We were alone in the toilet and — I don't know, perhaps at that moment of bitterness I really could have killed her and left her there, suffocated.

Yet she suddenly spoke.

'I'll talk ... I'll tell you —'

I kept her bent over the bowl.

'Talk!'

'Okka is Hudya Benokan's sister.'

In my astonishment I released her hands, and she turned on me her dirty wet face in which her narrow eyes shone with hatred.

'Okka ... is Hudya Benokan's sister,' she said with a crooked smile. 'Five years ago she died, however. She choked on Ryazanov's sperm, however.'

'How do you know that?'

'I saw it myself, however. I was eleven years old; she was twelve. Hotko was the senior doctor in charge of our schools, and he took Okka and me out of school saying we were going to the hospital. He brought us to a drinking party at Ryazanov's however. There was Ryazanov, Voropayev and some American. They filled Okka and me up with alcohol and fucked us. Ryazanov, Hotko and Voropayev fucked me, but Okka had taken the American's fancy and he didn't let them fuck her. But in the morning he flew to Moscow, however. Then all of them started fucking Okka together. From behind, in front and in the mouth at once, however. When they stopped, they found that Okka had choked to death on Ryazanov's sperm. Nothing happened to them over that. They sent me home to the tundra straight away. Now the tundra spirits have taken revenge on them; it's only right. Only the spirits can't reach the American. Pity, however ...'

'When did all this happen?'

'I told you: five years ago, May, before the end of the school term —'

'You mean, you think the tundra spirits killed Ryazanov, Voropayev and Hotko because of Okka?'

'What else, then?' she smiled bitterly, washing herself in the hand basin. 'Not Hudya Benokan, was it? If he'd wanted to kill them, he'd have done it five years ago, however. But he went to Moscow to study, the shameful son of a dog —'

'Why did the spirits wait five years, then?' I smiled.

'They were shut up in the ground, however. And now your

265

drills have let them out, they've taken over the cons and the cons have started ripping up our enemies. This is only the beginning, however. Well, can I go?'

'Wait a minute ...' I said, thinking. 'What was the American's name?'

'Siegfried, they called him.'

'Siegfried Shertz?' I said, recalling the surname of the American VIP the paras had captured at the Bright Way fur farm.

'Don't remember. Perhaps, however —' she said indifferently, and for lack of a towel wiped her face on her *malitsa* sleeve, then spat contemptuously on the floor of the toilet and went out.

I did not hold her back.

I remained alone in the toilet and walked over to the window.

Along the dark Salekhard streets moved personnel carriers and army lorries filled with paratroopers, marines and police. Patrolling soldiers with dogs could be seen on the icy pavements. The air was filled with the drone of military helicopters and aeroplanes.

Surely all this — the Nenets rising, the firing of the drilling installations, the occupation of the territory by KGB, police and marines — surely all this couldn't be happening, just because five years ago in May 1978 Ryazanov, Voropayev, Hotko and some visiting American had overdone their bit of fun with a couple of Nenochkas? Why did nobody know about this story — not even Shatunov? He would certainly have connected the three murders with the death of this Okka long ago. And how, how had it happened that the avengers were cons escaping from Camp RS-549? The idea of tundra spirits taking them over was crazy, of course ...

And suddenly — it was as if a bit of electricity went through my head, lighting up the events of the past few days. Like a word turning up among a jumble of blocks, even if a letter or two were missing.

I remembered how five years ago, in the summer of 1978, the whole of Moscow University had been agog over 'some Nenets', Hudya Benokan, who had practically galloped into Moscow from the tundra on a reindeer. He had joined the law faculty in order to become an investigator.

I remembered Major Orudjev had kicked the base of the electricity pylon in Camp RS-549 and explained that it had been Hudya Benokan who had said in front of the cons how escape from the camp was feasible — by way of the power lines. After that, three cons had indeed used that escape route, mysteriously disappeared in the tundra, survived a severe blizzard and executed, one after another, the murderers of Hudya Benokan's sister.

And I remembered that the first investigator on the scene at the murders of Hotko and Ryazanov had been — who? None other than Hudya Benokan!

▮ *Chapter Four*

I was still unsure of myself; I didn't allow myself to believe that Hudya was a murderer or an organizer of murders and the fomentor of the Nenets rebellion. Even on the way to the local register office I kept trying to find another explanation for what had happened, damping down my feverish imaginings.

The register office was two blocks away from the Salekhard CID and police station; in provincial towns like Salekhard, all the municipal institutions are located next door to one another in the centre of the town.

I went practically at a run. Of course, it was empty and quiet here: these mad days nobody was registering marriages, divorces, newborn babies or even deaths. Yet the head of the office was on duty, the first sign of the return of law and order — people were going out to work again. Another two or three days, and this office would see life back again with a vengeance. The youngsters would be registering marriages, divorces, babies; champagne corks would be smacking the ceiling on any pretext; cognac and vodka would be flowing generously onto the floor from overfilled glasses and crystal goblets smashing musically on the stone porch. The job of registrar required either a strict teetotallar to withstand the assault wave of liquor gifts or someone with the constitution of a horse, to drink to the newlyweds every day.

The Salekhard incumbent clearly belonged to the second category. A hale old man in a wolfskin jacket, he looked up at me with the frank thirst of the alcoholic as soon as I entered. Realizing I was an investigator and not a newlywed, however, the old man subsided and at my request produced with a scuffling of felt boots the *Civil Status Register for April–May–June 1978.* This book contains all births and deaths taking place in the town.

I opened the book, and at the page dated 19 May found the entry:

'Benokan Okka Nogovna, born 1966, died on the night of 17–18 May from an asthma attack. Buried in the Nenets cemetary. Based on: medical certificate no. 852/6 18 May 1978.'

From an asthma attack! So that was how the three had covered up the murder. Even if you exhumed the corpse and conducted an autopsy — after five and a bit years! — you'd hardly find traces of Ryazanov's sperm or lung infection. But to dig down to the truth I had no need to drag out the girl's remains from her tundra grave.

'I need the medical findings on her death,' I said to the registrar.

The old man shuffled over to a tall cupboard with a card index. Having fussed about for ages with the bar that locked all the drawers at the same time, he finally pulled one of them out and picked up a hefty folder bound with twine. On it was written boldly in ink: 'April–May–June 1978' He undid the twine, licked a grimy finger and began to leaf through the sheaf of medical reports. It took him a minute — the longest minute of my life — to extract a piece of paper and hand it to me.

It was not a medical report. It was the standard form of the Salekhard police militia directorate CID. On it was a short typewritten note:

Declaration no. 774, 2 July 1983

I, Hudya Benokan, investigator CID Salekhard Police Directorate, hereby declare:

For official purposes, the medical report no. 852-6 supplied 18 May 1978 by V. Hotko, senior physician at Salekhard Municipal Children's Hospital, has been removed from the records.

H. Benokan

2 July 1983

These few lines removed any lingering doubt. The twentieth of June is the traditional date for defending one's diploma thesis at Moscow University; the twenty-fifth sees the official award of the diploma, followed by a banquet in the evening. The train from Moscow to Salekhard takes three days. That meant that no later than 29–30 June 1983 Hudya had returned to Salekhard from Moscow and taken up his duties as an investigator with the Salekhard police force. And the first thing he had done was extract from the registry the medical report on his sister's death, signed by one of his sister's killers. Was this not the reason why Ryazanov, Hotko and Voropayev had failed to cry out or shout for help when their murderer had cut off their genitals and ears — was it not because the murderer had held that fake medical certificate in front of their eyes?

I went over to the registrar's desk and picked up the telephone.

'Operator? Give me the North Hotel, duty staff officer.'

A second later and a clipped voice came on.

'Staff duty officer, Colonel Khropachov, here.'

'Comrade Colonel, this is CID investigator Anna Kovina speaking. This morning your paratroops captured an American called Siegfried Shertz at the Nenets Bright Way fur farm. Do you know where he is being held?'

'Why is the CID on about him again? I told your investigator this morning: he's been taken by the KGB to Urengoi. Doesn't your left hand know what the right one's doing, or something?'

'What investigator did you inform?' I asked, growing cold. 'What was his name?'

'Fuck knows what his name was! Some Nenets name —'

I opened my mouth and gulped some air. There was only one investigator in Salekhard with a Nenets name. Hudya Benokan. Hudya, who according to the secretary of CID, left for Urengoi an hour earlier ...

'Comrade Colonel,' I said beseechingly. 'Could you possibly get in touch immediately with Urengoi KGB and find out exactly where this Shertz is now?'

'It's a madhouse in Urengoi at the moment — they're getting ready for the Government flying in for the pipeline opening. If you like, I can connect you with the Urengoi Gee Bee on our radio and ask them yourself.'

'No thanks, no need', I said quickly. No KGB operative would tell me over the phone what they were doing with Shertz or where they were holding him. And tell them that I suspected Hudya Benokan of intending to kill Shertz? — no thanks, I hadn't come to that yet. 'Comrade Colonel, when is your next plane to Urengoi?'

'Two planes are getting ready to leave right now, off in about twenty minutes —'

'Comrade Colonel, dearest,' I tried to put all my feminine charm into my voice, plus a hint of flirtation. 'Couldn't you just hold one up for about ten minutes? I'm in the centre of town, I need about half an hour to get to the aerodrome —'

'Hold up the aircraft?' The colonel was astounded. 'Well, sweetheart, that's asking a bit too much! Do you know how many passengers there are — important people, too!'

I didn't let him finish. I dropped the receiver and raced out into the street.

An armoured personnel-carrier was bowling along the roadway, probing the polar night with powerful headlights.

I ran out into the middle of the road, practically under its tracks, and waved my arms.

The carrier stopped, and a youthful, hook-nosed face poked out of the cabin and, needless to say, bawled out a few obscenities.

'What's the matter with you? Off your fucking rocker?'

I ran up to the cabin and thrust out my red police identity card.

'Dear heart! I'm a police investigator! I have to get to the airport, urgent!' Without waiting for an answer I crawled up on the track.

'What's up? You giving birth or something?' asked the driver, stupefied.

'Almost! Drive on, step on it to the airport, sweetie!'

'A kiss, then!' said the driver, and stared at me with cheerful insolence.

Without thinking, I kissed him on the lips and made him gasp for breath and shake his head. Eventually he said admiringly:

'Well, shit! Never thought I'd ever kiss the police!' and he pressed the pedal down to the floor.

▍ *Chapter Five*

Government Telegram

Urgent, Secret

Government special service

To Comrade Chernenko, Kontantin Ustinovich,
Secretary of Central Committee CPSU,
Member of Politburo Central Committee CPSU

IN ACCORDANCE WITH GOVERNMENT ORDERS AND
YOUR PERSONAL INSTRUCTIONS, JOINT FORCES OF
THE ARMY, KGB AND POLICE HAVE DURING THE
LAST 24 HOURS OCCUPIED VIRTUALLY ALL MAJOR
INHABITED POINTS, WORKER SETTLEMENTS AND
NENETS CAMPS IN THE TERRITORY OF THE
YAMAL–NENETS NATIONAL DISTRICT AND PLACED
UNDER GUARD ALL GAS PIPELINES AND ALL GAS
AND OIL INSTALLATIONS ON THE YAMAL
PENINSULA. SPECIAL MEASURES ARE BEING TAKEN
TO EXTINGUISH EIGHT GAS FLARES BURNING IN
THE TUNDRA. KGB AND MVD FORCES ARE
CONDUCTING ACTIVE OPERATIONS TO BRING TO
LIGHT THE FOMENTORS OF THE DISTURBANCES.
THE SECURITY OF THE OFFICAL OPENING OF THE
SIBERIA–WESTERN EUROPE GAS PIPELINE IS
GUARANTEED.

President of KGB USSR, Army General Chebrikov
First Secretary Tyumen Province Party Committee,
CPSU, Bogomyatov

▌ Chapter Six

'It's to Urengoi we're going, tundra round us as we pass ...'

A freckle-faced lad was singing this in the plane to the tune of the old colonial song, 'It's to Uruguay we're going'. He was accompanying himself on a guitar. The whole plane joined in the chorus:

'Night complete with snowstorms blowing
Watches over Nenets gas ...'

There were none of the usual passenger seats in an AN-24 paratroop transport aircraft. Instead of seats, there was a row of aluminium forms along the sides and a sort of rail overhead for the parachutists to secure their straps on. Now the entire plane was crammed full of people who in two days' time were going to stand round the government rostrum in Urengoi as heroes and guests of honour. Here were the drillers from Baku, Ufa and Kishinyov who had bored the first exploratory and the first industrial wells on the Yamal a few years back. Here the first welders and pipelayers were playing cards and dominoes. The builders of the first tundra settlements, specialists in capping oil gushers, shift workers who had been stuck for a few days at the airports in Siktivkar and Naryan Mar — all were singing, eating and drinking as they sat on the aluminium forms, on suitcases or on the floor. Here also, along with all the others, were five Georgians in enormous cloth caps, with cases of oranges and flowers. How the black marketeers had managed to get onto a military aircraft and what bribe had been required, God only knew; but after all, Georgian black marketeers had also done their bit towards the building of the pipeline. As one of them said: 'Without our vegetables and fruit you'd have been on a prison diet here!'

274

'It's to Urengoi we're going,
Silent night, like ammonal . . .'

Yes, everything was returning to normal: life, with its gaiety,
noise, songs, silly jokes, and the Caucasian oranges was rolling
back aboard military transport aircraft into the Yamal tundra,
so that in a few days all the deaths, the explosions, the whole
Nenets revolt would be forgotten and disappear as if they had
never been. Along the whole five-thousand-kilometre length of
the gas pipeline from Urengoi to West Germany and France,
adjuster engineers were checking the readiness of compressor
stations to receive the first of the Yamal gas. In Moscow,
members of the government delegation and foreign guests were
doubtless already packing their suitcases, making sure to
include three pairs of warm woollen underwear. The guitar
twanged:

'Just be careful, friend,
Because nobody's ever yet been —
In that mysterious land, that's called Yamal . . .'

I was sitting in a festive atmosphere, but I was on tenter-
hooks, glancing at my watch every minute. I tried to imagine
what Hudya Benokan was doing right now in Urengoi. Surely
he wouldn't risk penetrating the KGB to finish off this Siegfried Shertz? Bloody hell! We had gone chasing after the
escaped cons, thinking up the most unlikely scenarios about
how they managed to kill Ryazanov, Hotko and Voropayev —
Zotov even brought Voropayev's sweaty underwear from
Yaku-Tur! and all the time Hudya had been next to us, sitting
alongside us, leading us by the nose, even tossing us Zaloyev's
tarpaulin glove to keep us on the false scent. But who really did
do the killing? Hudya himself — or did he just help the cons to
escape on condition they did the murders?

We were coming in to land at Urengoi. Beneath us lay the
tundra gas installations, the frosted filaments of the pipelines
and the Urengoi main compressor station, the working heart of
the pipeline. Just as in the body blood flows to the heart and is
pumped out in massive spurts to all parts of the organism, so
this station collects gas from all over the Yamal and in two
days' time with its gigantic, super-powerful turbines will begin

sending it along the eightfold pipeline into Europe. Deep in the polar night, lying on the white dish of the tundra, the station resembled an extra-terrestrial building put up by some superior civilization centuries ahead of humankind.

The aircraft banked to the left and came down to land on the Urengoi landing strip, swept clear by the ground wind.

I was literally feverish with anxiety. What was waiting for me in Urengoi? News of the arrest of Hudya Benokan while attempting to get through to Siegfried Shertz? Or — if Hudya had succeeded in duping the Gee Bees — Shertz's corpse with ears and genitalia severed?

▋Chapter Seven

There were no taxis at Urengoi Airport, but calling up an official car at CID would mean losing forty minutes at the very least. That left the bus.

The Urengoi streets were thronged with people, despite the thirty-degree frost and a gusty wind. It was the first time in several days, that people had come in numbers without fear, to form queues in the shops. On the eve of the official opening, just as in Salekhard, goods that were scarce had appeared — real milk even, not the sour acidophilus stuff. People were in a hurry to buy, not just for the holiday but to stock up for the New Year. There was even a queue in the hairdresser's, and I had the fleeting thought that — good heavens! — it really was the holiday in two days, and when on earth could I get to the hairdresser's?

The crowds of citizenry on the streets slowed the bus down though, and I grew more anxious with each passing minute — well, come on, come on! Why the hell are we waiting for that old biddy running for the bus with two heavy string bags!

At last, the square in front of the town party committee building and the government rostrum. This was draped in red calico and decorated with pine branches and government portraits: Andropov, Chernenko, Ustinov, Gorbachov, Gromyko. Carpenters were swarmimg round the rostrum, tacking up an enormous placard: 'TO YOU, HOMELAND, SIBERIAN GAS!' The Moscow architect was also fussing about here.

I jump out of the bus and cross the square at a run to the white two-storey building which houses the local KGB. Before the door, a moment to catch my breath, get a hold of myself, appear calm and collected. I pushed the door on its heavy spring; behind it, of course, the checkpoint with its armed guard.

'Who do you want?'

I thrust my police investigation identity card over.

'I want to see Major Gromov.'

The guard picks up the phone. The Urengoi KGB's a bit different from Salekhard: the building's new, and they even have an internal telephone.

A minute later they let me through and I run up to the first floor, noting in passing how the Gee Bees have tarted themselves up for the celebrations: red carpet strips along the corridors, red placards declaring 'KGB, SHIELD AND SWORD OF SOVIET POWER', and, of course, Andropov's portrait festooned with red ribbons. (Why shouldn't they decorate him — after all, he did raise their pay, didn't he?) And all around, the KGB's now virtually the supreme authority in the country. The dirty work gets done by us, the police militia.

Now the office of Major Gromov, deputy chief of the directorate. Behind the door, the peck of a typewriter. I straightened my fur jacket and hat and knock briefly.

Major Gromov, seated at his desk, typing; next to him is a tape recorder.

I speak formally.

'Comrade Major, permission to speak. Investigator Kovina from CID –'

'Okay, Anechka,' he smiles. 'At ease. Take a seat. What can I do for you?'

'Oleg Borisovich,' say I, to show that we in the police know their first names too. 'I'm looking for Siegfried Shertz, the American picked up by the paras at Bright Way. The duty staff officer in Salekhard said you had him.'

Gromov says nothing, smiles faintly, but even his cocky little smile makes me feel relieved: at least Shertz is alive, otherwise Gromov wouldn't be smiling. Naturally, Gromov wants to know what the hell this American is to me; but he wants to demonstrate his shrewdness so he asks a typical man's question.

'Good looking, is he?' Gromov lights a cigarette, his voice even holds a note of jealousy.

278

Okay, think I, we'll play it your way, you asked for it.

'Not bad, considering ...' I speak eventually, never having seen the man. 'Have you still got him?'

'You mean, you've flown here from Salekhard to defend this Siegfried?'

Defend? Does Gromov know everything already? But I continued the game and asked: 'Why defend? Has he done anything?'

Gromov bursts out laughing — frank, open laughter.

'You're wonderful! Armed reconnaissance! Brilliant! All right, relax. He has done something, of course, but not here; in Udmurtia. He made a monkey of the Udmurt KGB chief — took his car for a ride. Want to hear?'

Gromov pressed the 'rewind' button on his tape recorder and ran the tape back a little way. While he was thus occupied his face bore — how shall I put it? — a certain satisfaction that some American had outwitted the chief of the Udmurt KGB. Gromov stopped the tape and pressed the 'play' button. He seemed to know the tape by heart (he wasn't transcribing it was he?), as if he knew the exact spot.

'If comrade Khanov had told me he was chief of the KGB ...' came a masculine voice from the recorder. I marvelled at how well this American spoke Russian. 'But judge for yourself, comrade Major! That Kolesova, the interpreter, tells me that a snowstorm has covered the whole of Siberia for three days; then she introduces me to this guy in Udmurt and they cart me off to some hideaway in the taiga and start to get me drunk. It struck me as suspicious from the very start. You hear stories like that every day in the West: bandits kidnap millionaires and demand a ransom. You've heard of Heineken beer? Well, not long ago Heineken himself was kidnapped in Holland. Anyway, when I heard on the radio that there wasn't any blizzard in Siberia, I decided straight away that they'd kidnapped me — Kolesova and this Udmurt. I'm a millionaire as well, you know. Not as rich as Heineken, but still ... Well, I got up in the middle of the night and quietly split. I drove the car away, but bear in mind I didn't run off to Moscow to our embassy, I didn't ring up any Western newspaper correspondents. I flew on here to Urengoi, to tell you and comrade Bogomyatov the

279

whole story. As regards material damage — the punctured tyres and the telephone wire I cut — I'll pay for that. How much do I owe? Three hundred roubles? Four hundred?'

Gromov switched off the recorder.

'Did you follow all that?' he asked me, smiling. My face obviously registered total blankness and he condescended to clarify matters:

'General Chebrikov ordered the Udmurt, Colonel Khanov, to delay this Shertz of yours and amuse him while we sorted things out here. But Khanov got plastered — so much so that,' he pointed at the recorder, 'he'll get the push.' He raised his eyes to me and at once became serious. 'So, Anya. You know very well that we don't encourage contacts with foreigners. However, I'm prepared to turn a blind eye on your affair with this Shertz, if you'll do me a favour. Find out from him, little by little, what he saw when he was with the Nentsi. He tried to tell me here that he saw nothing, no rebellion, but ...' here Gromov again smiled grimly, 'I'm not Khanov, am I?'

'Where is he now?' I asked, ignoring the grimy hint of an 'affair' with Shertz. 'You've got him, haven't you?'

'Well, we can't hold foreign subjects,' smiled Gromov. 'He's in the Polar Hotel, catching up on his sleep —'

'How long?' I moved impatiently towards the door. This self-satisfied idiot had let Shertz go to a hotel, alone, without protection!

'Well, not so long ago ... about three hours ago. You understand what I asked you to do?'

I didn't hear him as I rushed out of his office, though there was still one more question I was dying to ask: had the Salek-hard investigator Hudya Benokan shown any interest in Shertz? But maybe, after all, that was now a purely academic question!

It was only three blocks from the KGB to the spanking new Polar Hotel, and I set off at a run.

■ *Chapter Eight*

If I'd had the time to complete an interrogation statement from
the duty manager of the Polar Hotel, it would have gone something like this:

> Duty manager of the Polar Hotel, comrade B. Mironov,
> stated:
> 'At approximately twelve noon, on the instructions of
> KGB major comrade Gromov, Siegfried Shertz, a US
> citizen, was accommodated in deluxe suite no. 29 on the
> second floor of the hotel. Mr Shertz was brought to the
> hotel in an official KGB car. He was wearing Nenets
> clothing: *malitsa* and *kisi*. He looked very tired and
> unshaven, and smelt like the Nentsi. On receiving his key,
> he stated that he was going to bed and did not wish to be
> disturbed. He expressed an interest in knowing when we
> were expecting the arrival of foreign journalists. Since
> this information is no secret I told him that the govern-
> ment delegation would be coming today and tomorrow
> and the journalists tomorrow and the day after. Mr
> Shertz said he hadn't slept for three days and would prob-
> ably sleep through till tomorrow. He therefore asked me
> to put no phone calls through and allow no visitors. After
> that, he went to his room.
>   Roughly two and a half hours later — that is at three in
> the afternoon — a CID investigator from Salekhard came
> to me. I have forgotten his name, unfortunately, although
> he did show me his official identification. This investiga-
> tor, a Nenets in appearance, asked me the number of Mr

Shertz's room. I told him that Mr Shertz did not wish to be disturbed for any reason whatever. The investigator told me that he had urgent official business with Mr Shertz. Ten minutes later the investigator and Mr Shertz left the hotel together, got into an official police car and went off, in which direction I do not know. I noticed nothing suspicious in their behaviour. The car in which they left was a 'Gazik' with 'MILITIA' written on it, I don't remember the number.

I repeat: I kept no official record of my conversation with the hotel administrator — no time for that! I glanced at my watch. Hudya had taken Shertz out of the hotel thirty-eight minutes ago. I raced out of the hotel and, still at a run, hurtled into our police directorate. In thirty-eight minutes, I thought on the way, the American could have been taken out onto the tundra and had everything cut off!

Near our directorate building stood an official Volga. I didn't go into the directorate to find out from the duty officer what pretext Hudya had used to get a police Gazik out of him. I didn't care whether Hudya had given him an official 'requisition for automobile transport' or a couple of sturgeon.

I tore open the Volga door. Sergeant-Driver Krylov was sitting there: the same 'Uncle Kolya' who had taken me to Urengoi Airport on the ninth of December on my assignment to Camp RS-549. In the four years I had worked with the Urengoi police I had ridden often enough with Uncle Kolya to dispense with the niceties. Anyway, I was in Urengoi, wasn't I? My own patch!

'Cheers, Uncle Kolya! Go and report to the duty officer that I've taken the car for twenty minutes. Don't ask me anything, it's urgent and I'll take the responsibility! Well, move it, move it!' I almost pushed him bodily out of the car, took his place at the wheel and stepped on the gas. It was warm in the car: Uncle Kolya never switched off the engine or the heater in the Volga. On the radio, one of the policemen out on patrol was calling for first aid in Working Men's Hostel no. 7: The usual booze-up and brawl, I thought briefly, as I cornered at full

282

speed and almost rammed a municipal bus. The yelling mouth
of the driver flicked by as I wrenched the wheel; one more turn
and I was in the local schoolyard. The second-shift pupils were
already at their lessons, and the yard was empty: just what I
needed.

I picked up the mike. It was really because of the radio that
I had turfed Uncle Kolya out of the car. Now the main
business was at hand. The flight from Salekhard to Urengoi,
the talk with Major Gromov at the KGB and the questioning
of the Polar manager — all of that was child's play. I
took a deep breath, as if about to jump into water. I then
pressed the switch on the mike, put the radio onto 'transmit'
and spoke:

'Hudya, Hudya! It's Anna, it's Anna! Hudya, it's Anna! I'm
in Urengoi! Come in, I implore you! Over.'

Instead of Hudya in the crackling ether, there came the
indignant voice of the duty officer, Captain Shevtsov:

'Kovina, what's all this then?! Why have you taken the car?
Who's this Hudya you're after?'

'Boris Markovich, dear, get off the air — it's a matter of life
and death!' I spoke pleadingly into the mike, secretly overjoyed
that Shevtsov had come on the air. Hudya's Gazik had a
similar radio, and he'd most likely got it switched on to find out
what the police were up to and whether he was being sought.
Now he knew that I was in Urengoi, that I knew almost everything and that all the police cars in the town were listening in.
If Shertz was still alive, this might restrain Hudya from the
final step. 'Boris Markovich, clear the channel. Hudya, Hudya,
it's Anna! It's Anna! I know everything! Now, please come in!
Hudya, dear, come in! Over!'

I can imagine the 'duty' and the other police cars pricking
up their ears hearing that 'dear' and 'implore'. What did I care!

I switched over to receive and froze in anticipation. After a
pause, a calm voice sounded:

'Anna, Hudya here. Over.'

'Huddy, dear, sweet, darling! Is he still alive? Is he still alive?
Over!'

'Anna, do you want to talk to him? Over.'

'Yes, I do! Of course I do! Over.'

Lord, that meant Hudya hadn't killed the American yet!

Now I heard the same masculine voice I had heard in Gromov's office.

'Hello, over.'

'Are you Mr Shertz? Over.'

'Yes, I'm Siegfried Shertz. Over.'

Well, I thought, go for broke; nothing else for it.

'Mister Shertz, I am CID investigator Anna Kovina. I am charging you on two counts. First, five years ago, in May 1978, you took part in the group debauchery of a twelve-year-old Nenets girl named Okka and an eleven-year-old named Ayuni Ladukai. As a result of the orgy at the villa of Pyotr Ryazanov, chief geologist of the Yamal-Oil-Gas Exploration trust, Okka died. What have you got to say on the matter? Over.'

I'd never preferred charges by radio before — a foreign subject, at that! I can imagine Captain Shevtsov and the rest going crazy. I wondered if it would occur to Shevtsov to switch on the tape recorder?

The calm voice of Siegfried Shertz came on again:

'I would like to hear the second charge. Over.'

Bloody hell, that American had nerves of steel! Or did Hudya have a gun on him and it was him dictating the questions?

'Certainly,' I said. 'So at Ryazanov's villa you, Ryazanov, Hotko and Voropayev took part in the debauching of Nenets girls. The other three men have been killed over recent days. You must have connected the circumstances of their death with that orgy and Okka's death. The Nentsi didn't know the real reasons for the murders of Ryazanov, Hotko and Voropayev; they took it to be the 'tundra spirits' signal for an uprising, but you *did* know the truth! Yet you concealed that truth from the police and even from the KGB, although you were with KGB Major Gromov only three hours ago. In our country, non-disclosure is equivalent to a crime — especially in a situation like this. I accuse you of withholding information of importance to the state. Over.'

It seemed to me that even the atmosphere had died out. At any rate, neither Captain Shevtsov nor anyone else butted in.

'The business of the tundra spirits killing Russians and cutting off their genitals,' said the unhurried, almost deliberately slowed voice of Siegfried Shertz, 'I heard while I was still in Siktivkar, at the airport. But it was just a rumour, a joke — nobody believed it there. That it was Ryazanov, Hotko and Voropayev who had been killed I only found out this morning. Mr Geizenrikh told me, you can check with him. Yes, I did connect their murders with that evening at Ryazanov's dacha. Moreover, I thought that I was in danger myself. But it wasn't so easy to give evidence against myself; at any rate, it isn't done in America. The main point is, I didn't seduce Okka. Yes, there was a booze-up: my send-off, to be exact. I was flying out of Salekhard the next morning. Ryazanov brought the girl Okka to me a week earlier. He brought her to me at the hotel, and she herself, of her own free will, stayed in my room, you may believe it or not. She wasn't a virgin; in fact she was already — how can I put this? — an adult, even passionate, woman. I am trying to explain this to investigator Benokan, but he hasn't read Nabokov's *Lolita*, so I can't explain to him what sort of a girl Okka was. She was a depraved Nenets Lolita. She came to me in the hotel by her own decision all that week, every evening, and stayed the night — you can check that with the staff at the North in Salekhard. I think her sexual education had been expertly supervised before me either by Ryazanov, Hotko or Voropayev — maybe all three, I don't know. That evening you and investigator Benokan are talking about, when Ryazanov organized my send-off, Dr Hotko brought another little girl: I don't know what her name was, maybe it was the one you mentioned. She was just as depraved as Okka, though it seems she was even younger. They wanted to organize group sex straight away: two girls to four men. And, by the way, both Okka and the other girl were agreeable, to say the least ... But I didn't agree. You may believe this or not, but I was in love with this Okka–Lolita, honestly. She was a beautiful little girl, and I didn't give her to them — I mean, I didn't give her to them for group sex. In the morning they took me to the airport and I flew to Moscow and later to the US. It was only a year later when I was back in Salekhard that Ryazanov told me that my Okka-Lolita had died of asthma. That's all I know. Over.'

'Hudya! Hudya! Now listen carefully. Everything he said is the truth,' I said into the microphone, putting my soul into it. My main job, after all, wasn't to interrogate Shertz or make accusations against him — what in hell did I want with Shertz? No, the main thing was to keep Hudya from committing a fourth murder. 'Hudya, can you hear me? I questioned Ayuni Ladukai. She was the second girl that evening. She also confirms that when Shertz left for the aerodrome Okka was still alive. It all happened after that, when the three men had intercourse with Ayuni and Okka, all three at the same time. Can you hear me, Hudya? Over.'

'I hear you', Hudya's reply was muffled. 'Have you finished questioning Shertz? Over.'

'No, I haven't finished! Hudya, please, dear, don't switch off! Mr Shertz, one more question: do you know the surname of that girl, Okka? Do you know her surname? Over!'

Of course, I was more interested in where they were, Hudya and Shertz. But neither I nor Captain Shevtsov nor even the local KGB could pinpoint their position in Hudya's Gazik: we just didn't have the equipment. Maybe the paras had — in fact they were sure to have — but it would hardly occur to Captain Shevtsov to get in touch with them.

'No, Anya, he doesn't know Okka's surname yet. Over.' Hudya Benokan's voice came dryly through the radio. I realised he had taken over the microphone from Shertz.

'Hudya, where are you? I'll come to you straight away! Dear, tell me where you are — over!'

'Anya, did you read the note I left you on the door?'

'Yes, I read it, Hudya. Over!'

'If you *immediately* do what was written on it you will have the chance of speaking to me again. That's all. End of transmission.'

'Hudya! Hudy–a! I don't understand! *Hudy–a*!' I yelled into the microphone, but the only response was a faint crackle of interference: Hudya had switched off his radio.

I slumped dully behind the wheel. All around was the blackness of the polar night; the Volga's headlights still probed into the snow-laden wind.

The urgent voice of the police duty officer, Captain Shevtsov, jerked me out of my trance:

'Kovina, what's going on? Can you explain? Over!'

'Just — all of you, fuck off!' I said to the microphone, tossed it onto the seat and began to swing the car round. The sense of Hudya's last reply began to trickle through to me. 'Goodbye, and, please, go away to Russia' — that's what the note said. There's no railway in Urengoi. That meant I could only go to Russia from the aerodrome. If so, Hudya had made an appointment to see me at the airport. 'Immediately,' he had said.

I shot the car out of the schoolyard, switched on the siren and the distance headlights and sped off towards the airport.

The siren scared away the oncoming traffic, and the people shopping; even the paras' armoured personnel-carriers gave me the right of way.

I was driving in third gear: I couldn't use fourth on the slippery roads, I wouldn't have reached the airport in one piece.

About ten minutes later, I saw that on my tail were two blue police Volgas and a black one with no markings — Gee Bees. I didn't care, I paid them no attention.

We raced out of Urengoi along the airport road. Because of the government delegation arriving today from Moscow the road had been meticulously cleared of snow; machines had raked up walls of snow on both sides of the road, and on some stretches bulldozers were still chugging along.

I changed up to fourth and gunned the engine, hanging grimly onto the wheel. Captain Shevtsov's voice broke in over the radio.

'Kovina! Go easy, Kovina! Have you gone crackers? Kovina, I'm ordering you: reduce speed! You'll kill your fucking self!'

In the rear-view mirror I saw that one of the blue police Volgas had skidded off at a sharp bend and buried itself up to the windscreen in a snowdrift.

Just then, the cortege of black limousines and Volgas of the town party committee came into view in front: it was the local party and military chiefs on their way to the airport to meet the government delegation from Moscow. Hearing my siren, the limousine drivers pulled over to the right as I rocketed past. Out of the corner of my eye I glimpsed the astonished, bewildered faces of Bogomyatov, Salakhov, the grey astrakhan hats of KGB General Chebrikov and the paratroop commander, General Grinko.

▌Chapter Nine

As I tore up to the airport terminal, my headlights picked out a figure in a *malitsa* standing by the entrance.

There was no sign of any police Gazik or Hudya. I left the car and ran into the terminal. The Nenets by the entrance barred my way:

'Are you Anna Kovina?'

'Yes, I —' I made to run off.

'But the Nenets grabbed me by the arm.

'I'm Siegfried Shertz.'

'You?'

It was only then I remembered that the Polar Hotel manager had described Siegfried Shertz as being dressed in Nenets national clothing. 'But where's Hudya?'

'Stop! He's gone.'

'Where?'

'I don't know. He dropped me off here and asked me to give you this,' Shertz handed me a sheet of paper, torn out of a notebook.

In the light pouring through the terminal windows I read:

'ANYA, I'M LEAVING HIM ALIVE - HOWEVER. GOODBYE. I AM NOT A COWARD. THE REST YOU WILL HEAR ON THE RADIO. HUDYA.'

The police and Gee Bee Volgas skidded to a halt next to us, and Captain Shevtsov, Major Gromov and a number of other officers spilt out. Gromov grabbed Hudya's note out of my hand, read it and asked:

'What does all this mean?'

'You heard my conversation with Hudya Benokan on the radio?' I asked.

'Not the beginning, but Captain Shevtsov patched me in at

289

the most interesting part. Well?'

'The surname of the Nenets girl Ryazanov made a present of to Mr Shertz five years ago was Benokan — Okka Benokan. She was Hudya's sister.'

'You mean, the murders of Ryazanov, Hotko and Voro-payev were his work?' Gromov didn't even wait for my answer. He nodded to his Gee Bees. 'Into the car, the radio!'

The heavy drone of aircraft drowned his last words. Above us in the dark polar skies a TU-104 with the government delegation on board was coming in to land.

The motorcade of VIP limousines and Volgas was approaching the aerodrome.

One of the KGB officers of Gromov's group dived into the Gee Bee Volga, while Gromov himself got into the one I had driven to the airport. He issued his orders: 'Call him up, your Benokan!'

I obeyed reluctantly. Behind me, Siegfried Shertz seated himself in the rear without asking permission.

'Hudya!' I said into the microphone. 'Hudya, it's me, Anna! We're at the airport. Over.'

The extraneous conversation of the police patrol still in the hostel kept breaking in.

'. . . No need to secure him. He's drunk as a skunk as it is . . .'

Gromov smiled unpleasantly.

'"We"'!' he mimicked. 'Are you informing him you're not alone?' He took the microphone from me and spoke into it himself: 'All radios off the air! All off the air! Benokan! Benokan! This is Major Gromov, state security. I'm asking you not to do anything else stupid. No more nonsense! If you give yourself up we'll look into all the circumstances of the case.' At the same time, Gromov was following the TU-104 with his eyes as it descended towards the illuminated landing strip. 'Give yourself up, Benokan. We'll look into all the circumstances of the case, favourably! I promise — the word of an officer! Over!'

The TU-104 touched down on its skis, raising a snow tornado behind it. After taxiing a short distance it swung round and approached the terminal building. The gangway was hurried out to the aircraft, followed by the motorcade of limousines and black Volgas containing the town party committee and the military chiefs.

'This is Hudya Benokan,' came through the radio. 'There will be no official opening of the gas pipeline. Do you hear me? Over.'

'I can hear, Benokan. Don't be a fool. I've told you: I guarantee a favourable review of the case. Over!' Gromov cocked an eye towards the neighbouring Gee Bee Volga, where his officers were talking to somebody on their own Gee Bee radio.

'This is Hudya Benokan,' came over the radio. 'Five years ago Ryazanov, Hotko, Voropayev and Shertz killed my sister. I swore then that I would become an investigator and bring them to court in a show trial. I was a boy, of course, a provincial member of sub-Arctic Komsomol. I believed in your slogans and your Soviet legality ...' Hudya spoke in a calm, even voice, as if dictating his will. 'But five years at Moscow University and practice in your Russian courts showed me what your Soviet legality really is. If I had instituted proceedings against those four men, you would have expelled me from the force, however. Nobody would lay a finger on VIPs like Ryazanov — laureates, all of them — on account of one little Nenets girl! You want to know how I killed them? No, I didn't kill them; I arranged a show trial for the whole tundra, as is the way of my people. Yes, I organized the escape of the three cons from Camp RS-549. Every camp has at least one con ready to escape, because the swan waits for spring and the con waits for freedom. I noted cons like that in Camp RS-549; the rest was a technical matter, as the Russians say. Tolmachov, Shimansky and Zaloyev agreed to make a break during the first snowstorm. At night I waited for them outside the compound with a team of good reindeer, food and warm clothing. I gave them a compass, and they went off on good reindeer into the storm — beyond the Urals, however. I think they are now on a sunny beach by the Black Sea. The rest you can imagine. It was I, instead of the cons, who went on the dog-sledge to Yaku-Tur and from there to Salekhard. Voropayev was the first: I dragged him, drunk, out of the choom of that Nenets slut; I dragged him out because it is our Nenets custom not to kill one's enemies in their chooms.'

The door of the TU-104 opened, and the Moscow visitors stepped onto the gangway. They all wore deerskin and astrakhan hats, warm overcoats with astrakhan collars. Their faces were — ministerial. The head of the government delegation, Secretary to the Central Committee of the CPSU Mikhail Gorbachev, gave a firm party handshake to the party bosses and the joint chiefs of staff of the army, KGB and police, who had so effectively restored order to the district.

Gromov, meanwhile, took a swift look at his Gee Bees in the next Gazik. They nodded in confirmation.

'I tied Voropayev up and dragged him across the tundra,' Hudya Benokan continued, as calmly as if he had been merely testifying as a witness. 'That's why you found bruises on his wrist and shoulder, Anya ... Then came Hotko and Ryazanov. *Nut i shar!* I organized a show trial for them — but I was just fulfilling my vow, I didn't know that my people would take it as the tundra spirits' summons to revolt. But you've taken everything from us Nentsi: rivers, land, sky and even the gas under the earth. You have killed us, you have killed my people and bred a few hundred 'exemplary' Nentsi. And I was one of them, however. Think of that: the first Nenets investigator in the CID! Our own trained Nenets, however — yes? No, not true, however. The swan awaits the spring! I avenged my sister, but I was also thinking of my daughter, who would fall, in ten years' time, into the hands of your Ryazanovs and the rest. Just as Okka did, and my wife, and Ayuni Ladukai, and hundreds more. It helped me to grip the knife firmly ...'

I couldn't understand why Gromov had made no move to interrupt Hudya; nor did I understand why Hudya was speaking so calmly and for so long. Nonetheless, Gromov's silence was explained a minute later: two military helicopters suddenly flew over us, almost touching the car roofs. They flew off ahead of us across the airfield in the direction of the compressor station. Gromov started up his car and shot away after the helicopters. Only now did I realize why Gromov had chosen not to interrupt Hudya. On Gromov's orders the paratroop radio operators had fixed the place from where Hudya was broadcasting, and two helicopters with what must have been hundreds of soldiers on board were now on their way there, just as we were — two Volgas full of police and Gee Bees. Towards us came the motorcade of black government cars: in one was seen the puzzled face of Salakhov; in another sat Bogomyatov and Gorbachev.

And Hudya went on talking calmly, as if he had been wound up, not suspecting that any minute he would be grabbed.

'But my people understood me. They made a new Vauli Piettomin out of me, though none of the Nentsi knows yet that the new Vauli Piettomin is plain Hudya Benokan. But I, I know. That's important, however ...'

I was unable to sit quiet a moment longer; I twitched towards the microphone to shout to Hudya about the helicopters, to tell him that his position was known. But Gromov jabbed the barrel of his pistol in my side: 'Sit still! Take it easy! Let him talk ...' He smiled grimly, gripping the wheel powerfully with one hand, his eyes glued to the helicopters up in front. This time his smile was quite different from when he had flirted with me in the corridor of the CID: this was an evil smile, steely.

We sped across the airfield. Ahead of us, in the tundra, lay the compressor station.

Still Hudya went on, and his voice grew louder, higher-pitched:

'When a man is driven to the wall, even a coward bites back, however. My people have been driven to the wall: you Russians have driven them there. And they have made a Vauli Piettomin out of me. And now I know that the death of that boy who blew up your armoured vehicle is on my conscience. Even the hooligan behaviour of those young people at the boarding school is on my conscience, Anya! I brought about this revolt — I alone. Of course we cannot overcome you Russians: we're illiterate, backward and sick. There are few of us, only thirty thousand in all! Even a very large people like the Poles can't defeat you yet. But the time will come, however! There will be other times. The swan waits for spring, and the prisoner waits for freedom. Small and big, sick and well, literate and illiterate — all the peoples you have robbed of oil and diamonds, rivers and mountains, life and liberty will rise up against you! They will all rise — you hear, Anya? And woe will come upon your people, woe, however. As is said in our old songs, "*Nut i shar*, the bear's my witness. I can see the glow of fires." I can see the glow of fires, and you also will see it, now, at this moment. You will not get the gas of Yamal. That's what little Vauli, who died in Salekhard, wanted. That's what those lads wanted, those you shot in the tundra. And I, Hudya Benokan, will do what he must do. You remember, Anna, I told you about the sea gull ...'

We had almost run up against the wire fence of the compressor station. Close by, the two helicopters were hovering over a police Gazik — Hudya's Gazik. A para officer was running towards us from the car.

Gromov leapt out, I followed him, and both of us raced towards the Gazik; but the para halted us.

'It's empty. There's a tape recorder working ...'

We still ran on to the abandoned Gazik. On the front seat, an old reel to reel tape recorder lay next to the microphone. The spools were turning, and Hudya's voice spoke straight into the radio mike:

'... Seagulls choose their own way to die. I also. Goodbye, Anna. And, please, go away to Russia ...'

Gromov looked about him, at bay.

'We need dogs! He can't have got far.'

So that was why Hudya Benokan had spoken so calmly, so evenly: we had been listening to a tape, not to him.

I drew breath with a kind of inner relief. Hudya had gone away. Into the night of the tundra, the ground-hugging wind ...

But Gromov was already shouting down the radio mike. 'Dog-handler and tracker dogs! Dog-handler and tracker dogs! Call out the compressor station guard — red alert! Call out ...'

A deafening explosion at the far end of the compressor station interrupted him. The blast rocked me where I stood, and even the cars and helicopters swayed from the shock wave.

An immense pillar of fire rose over the compressor station, bathing in orange light that triumph of Russian, French and German technology: six square kilometres crammed with rectifier columns, turbine-section housings, cooling substations and its electronic control room.

The enormous spherical compressed gas holder had blown up — or rather, Hudya Benokan had blown it up.

There were twelve such gasholders towering above the compressor area — thousands of cubic metres of gas under pressure — and after the explosion, two more began to sag towards the ground on their silver-steel supports.

The fire was spreading: it was already licking along the pipe-line and along the earth itself towards the control room and the turbine units.

Another blast shook the air as a second gasholder sagged to the fire and detonated at a touch. A minute later and the heat was breathing in our faces, a fleeting breath which melted the tundra earth beneath yet another gasholder; it collapsed. A third explosion ...

The compressor station was blazing, fire hummed across the entire area — a fire from which no one could be saved, including, of course, Hudya Benokan. The helicopters lifted away from the tundra into the sky.

Gromov jumped into the Gee Bee Volga and pulled away from the fire in reverse. Siegfried Shertz and I leapt into Hudya Benokan's abandoned Gazik and tore off, near-suffocated by the heat and smoke, into the tundra.

Away to one side of us, halfway between the airport and Urengoi, the motorcade of black government Volgas had halted. The Moscow and Tyumen VIPs had got out, and all of them, including Gorbachev, Chebrikov, Bogomyatov, Grinko and Salakhov, were rooted to the spot, staring at this tundra firework display put on in honour of the pipeline opening, not by the Moscow architect but by Hudya Benokan.

Yet further off, in Urengoi, people were spilling out of the houses, gazing at the enormous pillar of fire, tearing into the black polar sky above the main compressor station. In the tongues of that fire, it seemed as if the tundra spirits were dancing ...

I stopped the car and fell limply forward onto the wheel. I had no tears. There was an overwhelming emptiness inside, an overwhelming emptiness. Ahead lay the Yamal tundra, dark and silent; behind lay the burning compressor station. And for some reason, relevant or otherwise, this irritating jingle swam in my mind:

> It's to Urengoi we're going,
> Tundra round us as we pass.
> Night complete with snowstorms blowing
> Watches over Nenets gas ...

The light gusts of the tundra blew oblique strands of white
snow through the beams of my car headlights. It always does
that when a blizzard is on the way.

▌Epilogue

From AP, UPI and Reuters news agencies and accredited Western correspondents in Moscow:

Moscow, 11 January 1984
'On 15 December 1983 a fire occurred in the region of the Urengoi gasfields as a result of which important electronic equipment was destroyed, and the delivery of Siberian gas via the new pipeline to Western Europe has therefore had to be postponed for a considerable period. The *Washington Post*, quoting informed circles in Washington and Paris, says that the fire destroyed the compressor station in Urengoi. Moscow representatives of Western companies supplying equipment for the pipeline have declined to comment officially on this, though they have confirmed that the Trans-Siberian gas pipeline will become operational only after many months.

Moscow, 12 January 1984
Soviet information and propaganda services are attempting to rebut stories of a fire and explosions on the Siberian pipeline. The official Soviet information agency, TASS, has published an interview with the Soviet gas industry minister, Vasili Dynkov, who stated that 'rumours put about by bourgeois mass media are false and have no foundation in reality'. Dynkov denies that there has been an explosion on the Siberia–Western Europe gas pipeline, admitting, however, that a fire did

take place at the Urengoi compressor station. He attempted to minimize the scale of this fire and stated that the equipment damaged as a result of the fire would be replaced in the immediate future.

In the opinion of Western diplomats in Moscow, the damage to the pipeline caused by the fire is more significant than the Soviet minister has admitted. In view of the prestige of this installation, however, and the passions aroused by it, the Soviet Union does not wish to disclose the true facts.

Time magazine January 23, 1984

INCIDENT AT URENGOI

For the Soviet Union, the building of a 2,759-mile natural gas pipeline from Siberia to Western Europe has become a test of technological prowess and a national crusade. Over the past two years, the Soviets have raced to finish the $18 billion project on schedule and prove that U.S. economic sanctions aimed at delaying the pipeline have had no impact.

With an air of satisfaction and triumph, Moscow announced two weeks ago that Siberian gas had started to flow into France on Jan. 1.

But even as the Soviets were proclaiming their success, reports were swirling in Moscow that the undertaking had suffered a setback. A fire at a compressor station in Urengoi, Siberia, was said to have damaged essential equipment.

Western experts contend that the fire at the Urengoi station, the largest of 41 planned compressor units, will delay the project ...

Even the trickle of Soviet gas shipments to France this month may be a sham. Western energy specialists believe that the gas is travelling through a previously existing network of Soviet pipes rather than the new line from Siberia. Some Western businessmen in Moscow doubt that the pipeline will be completed before the end of 1985.

* * * * *

In Paris, white synthetic fir trees shook their tiny Christmas lights on the Champs Elysées, the Moulin Rouge was a blaze of neon ads, and in the neighbouring streets and alleys Palestinians dressed as Santa Claus enticed passers-by into nightclubs and brothels.

Siegfried Shertz sat in a noisy bistro on Montmartre, now and again raising his eyes to stare blindly through the glass of the verandah window at the street swept by a damp wind before lowering them to his tiny table. On it was a cup of coffee and the letter over which he had agonized for days:

To: USSR, Urengoi, Yamai-Nenets District CID
                    Directorate Investigator Anna Kovina

Dear Anna,
In the hustle and bustle of the last few days I was in Urengoi, I did not manage, or more exactly could not pluck up the courage, to thank you for saving my life! Forgive me — and thank you! I do not think I shall be visiting the USSR again, after all I went through during our short acquaintance. I was particularly struck by my last conversation with Mr Chebrikov when, because of a number of circumstances you can probably guess at, I was obliged to take a vow of silence concerning everything that had taken place in Urengoi before my eyes and yours. Naturally I shall have to keep my promise and hold to my word as a businessman. But the memory is not subject to blackmail and the orders of generals — even KGB generals. I remember you, I remember your friend Benokan, and even Ani-Opoi.

299

Anna! If ever you find yourself in the West on business or on a tourist trip, I beg you to call me collect from any place in the Western world. My secretary will find me wherever I may be, and within hours I can be anywhere you name ...'

* * * * *

That letter had no chance of reaching its addressee, even if by some miracle it got through the inspection of foreign correspondence at the USSR Ministry of Communications. The simple fact was that on the day Shertz dropped his letter into a Paris letterbox, Anna Kovina was no longer in Urengoi. She was travelling south by train across the whole of Siberia, towards Voronezh. In her case was a brief notice of posting, on a CID directorate form:

'For resourcefulness and effective action displayed during the rescue of the American citizen S. Shertz, CID investigator Lieutenant Anna Kovina is posted to training at the Voronezh advanced police academy ...'

Kovina lay on the upper berth, gazing through the window at the snow-laden Siberian forests, but — like Shertz in Paris — saw nothing. She was going to the Voronezh academy joyless and with an empty heart. It seemed to her that the snowstorm outside still smelt of burning ...

* * * * *

And up there on the Yamal, where the usual blizzard was in fact bearing the burning ash of the Urengoi compressor station out over the tundra along with the smoke of the gas flares, there in the polar night, in a swaying reindeer choom, at that moment a two-year-old was crawling out from under the hides which made a bed for him, his sisters and his father. He tottered on his little bare feet to the entrance flap, stepping over the sleeping dogs, and went outside. The storm rocked the little boy and the needle-sharp wind drove frozen snow into his face, but he stood his ground and did not turn away. Holding his *khote* in one little hand, he began to pee in the dark, fierce face of the blizzard.

'Hudya!' shouted Melkune from the choom. 'Close the flap, it's draughty, cold!'

'Not cold, however,' said the little boy, youngest child of Ani-Opoi.

THE GLITTER DOME

Joseph Wambaugh

'BRILLIANT AND TERRIBLE.
Wambaugh is a historian of the American underworld like no other that ever dipped pen in blood. A stunning read.'
The Spectator

A compelling blend of wild humour and powerful drama, this is the story of the cops who work the Hollywood Division, a grim world of vice, drugs, child abuse and bizarre murder. For these men, a visit to the Glitter Dome – a bar of kaleidoscope lights and plentiful groupies – is the only way to recover from the fear and violence of their day. And when two veteran detectives are assigned to the murder of a studio president, they too discover how much they have been seduced by Hollywood.

'An addictive blend of human and flinty realism. Wambaugh is a master artist.' *Publishers Weekly*

'Superb. Mr Wambaugh is a writer of genuine power, style, wit and originality.'
Evan Hunter, New York Times

Futura Publications
Fiction
0 7088 2161 8

DANCE FOR DIPLOMATS

Palma Harcourt

'Palma Harcourt's novels are splendid'
Desmond Bagley

Catherine Rayle, history don at Oxford, becomes
Britain's first-ever woman permanent
representative to NATO in Brussels. But her initial
instinct to refuse the position was a good one, for
Catherine gets drawn into a cloak-and-dagger world
involving a defecting Russian ballet dancer;
suddenly all are dancing, to a tune they have not
called.

'The story unfolds with pace and excitement'
Evening News

Futura Publications
Fiction/Thriller
0 7088 2573 7

All Futura Books are available at your bookshop or
newsagent, or can be ordered from the following address:
Futura Books, Cash Sales Department,
P.O. Box 11, Falmouth, Cornwall TR10 9EN.

Please send cheque or postal order (no currency), and
allow 60p for postage and packing for the first book
plus 25p for the second book and 15p for each additional
book ordered up to a maximum charge of £1.90 in U.K.

B.F.P.O. customers please allow 60p for
the first book, 25p for the second book plus 15p per
copy for the next 7 books, thereafter 9p per book.

Overseas customers, including Eire, please allow £1.25
for postage and packing for the first book, 75p for the
second book and 28p for each subsequent title ordered.